Book Four of *The Rings of the Master*

MASKS OF THE MARTYRS

Jack L. Chalker

DEL REY

A Del Rey Book

BALLANTINE BOOKS • NEW YORK

THE TYRANT'S TEMPLE

The stories of the Cheyenne came flooding back to Hawks as he cautiously approached the broad crater and stared down.

"It's insane," he said. "All those faces repeated again and again, all around. And the design on the walls...this is it!"

Chen looked down and shook his head. "What's all that stuff over the grating?"

"Bones, rotting corpses of all those who tried to look upon the faces of the gods," Hawks replied. "Below us is Master System. We stand upon the tyrant's head. And the same five faces, repeated five times around the circle. It's more than an interface, you see."

"It's a shrine," China Nightingale said.

"No, it's more than that. It's a nightmare."

By Jack L. Chalker
Published by Ballantine Books:

THE WEB OF THE CHOZEN

AND THE DEVIL WILL DRAG YOU UNDER

A JUNGLE OF STARS

DANCERS IN THE AFTERGLOW

THE SAGA OF THE WELL WORLD
Volume 1: *Midnight at the Well of Souls*
Volume 2: *Exiles at the Well of Souls*
Volume 3: *Quest for the Well of Souls*
Volume 4: *The Return of Nathan Brazil*
Volume 5: *Twilight at the Well of Souls:*
         The Legacy of Nathan Brazil

THE FOUR LORDS OF THE DIAMOND
Book One: *Lilith: A Snake in the Grass*
Book Two: *Cerberus: A Wolf in the Fold*
Book Three: *Charon: A Dragon at the Gate*
Book Four: *Medusa: A Tiger by the Tail*

THE DANCING GODS
Book One: *The River of Dancing Gods*
Book Two: *Demons of the Dancing Gods*
Book Three: *Vengeance of the Dancing Gods*

THE RINGS OF THE MASTER
Book One: *Lords of the Middle Dark*
Book Two: *Pirates of the Thunder*
Book Three: *Warriors of the Storm*
Book Four: *Masks of the Martyrs*

For Clifford D. Simak

TABLE OF CONTENTS

A Note from the Author for Those
Who Came in Late ix

Prologue: Status Report 1

1. THE TROUBLE WITH CHANCHUK 7

2. FACING THE INEVITABLE 35

3. FOUR PARROTS AND ONE GOOSE COOKED, WITH
   FIREWORKS 61

4. REFLECTIONS TOWARD AN ENDING 91

5. UP A TREE 124

6. COWBOYS AND INDIANS 154

7. THE RING OF RINGS 184

8. THE MALEBOLGE RUN 209

9. THE FINAL BATTLE 239

10. THE MASKS OF THE MARTYRS 272

11. THE FACE OF THE ENEMY 302

Epilogue: Two Characters Meet
in Different Seasons 332

A Note from the Author
for Those Who Came in Late

Masks of the Martyrs is the fourth and final book in the series *The Rings of the Master*. The series is essentially an enormous single novel in four volumes and intended to be read sequentially, starting with *Lords of the Middle Dark*, then *Pirates of the Thunder*, and then *Warriors of the Storm*, all previously published and available from Del Rey Books. In a better world, your store, or newsstand, the one where you got this book, would also have the other three and you should be able to purchase the others and then read all in the proper sequence, giving you a novel of a little under half a million words. If you can't wait, can't stand it, or if it's been a long time since you read the first three and you want a refresher course, a short summary to date—very short—is provided as a prologue.

However, be aware that it's more a refresher than a summary, and that the author assumes in this, the longest and most complex of the four and the one in which all is revealed, the puzzles unraveled, and the strings tied up, that you are an old friend of Hawks, Raven, China, and the rest and that you know pretty much what's been going on and do not, for example, need a detailed and exacting description of just what a Janipurian looks like and what it does. If you don't, you will be missing a lot and it will be obvious. Do yourself a favor. Buy this book now so you know you'll have it, then buy or order the other three if you haven't already done so and read them from the start.

Jack L. Chalker

February 1987   Westminster, MD

PROLOGUE: STATUS REPORT

THE NICE THING ABOUT BEING DEAD WAS THAT YOU could, without any fear or guilt, do all those things that were dangerous or unacceptable when one was alive. The problem was, they really didn't have the same effect.

Arnold Nagy was definitely dead. His body had been crushed under the tremendous forces he had unleashed in a fight with a Val death ship. He'd beaten Master System's killers—robots with the minds and memories of their human quarries—and had been the only casualty. The crew had determined him dead and then buried him in space by shooting his lifeless body out an airlock, there to drift forever around some lonely sun.

Now he sat in his domed, velvet-lined base of exile, far from the battle yet surrounded by all the comforts anyone could wish except, of course, companionship. That came rarely, and when it did come the company was less than joyous and convivial.

He longed for human company, for real people who talked and laughed and cried and did all the things people

1

did. That was the ultimate curse he had to bear. It was why he called his luxurious hideaway hell, in spite of all the comforts it provided. Hell was wherever he was, regardless of the surroundings, even with people about. Humans just made hell more bearable. There was a line from *Faust* that said it; a line spoken by Mephistopheles, chief agent of Satan, when asked in Faust's cozy study what hell was like.

"Why, this is Hell, nor am I out of it."

Nagy went over and sat down at his data screen and punched up the progress report. He'd read it a million times, but he still needed to read it again for his own sake.

Item: Master System—which ruled over Earth and more than four hundred and fifty worlds to which humans had been forcibly transported and then altered to fit the environments—could be turned off only because of a safety mechanism designed into it by its makers. Five ornate gold rings hid the tiny and complex microcircuits that were required by the master program's core instructions to always be in the possession of humans with authority. Master System scattered the rings throughout the galaxy to make any attempt at uniting them next to impossible, since it alone controlled commerce and trade and space flight. To find all five would be improbable. To get all five was even less likely. To then get them to the master interface where they could be used, and to use them in the correct order, unthinkable. Humanity was ignorant of the rings' existence, let alone their use.

Item: More than nine hundred years after Master System assumed control, knowledge of the rings was unearthed in the papers of an illegal cult of independent scientists in the South American jungles on Earth. Ambitious humans who had learned to beat some of the system managed to get copies and make a deal with the only possessor of a ring on Earth: Lazlo Chen, the chief administrator.

Item: The courier taking the papers to Chen was intercepted by Vals and shot down over the North American plains, falling into the hands of a Plains Indian, Jon Nighthawk, or more simply Hawks, on leave with his primitive people from his job as a historian at North America Center. He and wife, Cloud Dancer, found themselves pursued by the Vals, the great robot agents of Master System, and by Chen's agents, including a Crow Indian named Raven. Raven caught them first and transported them first to Chen, then to Melchior, an asteroid penal colony controlled by Doctor Isaac Clayben, regarded by most as a human incarnation of Master System even though he, too, hated the computer.

Item: At almost the same time, Song Ching, daughter of the chief administrator of China Center, discovered in another illegal tech cult's papers that for some unknown reason Master System had built a human interface into all its spaceships. The recovered documents and research showed just how to tap into that interface and control virtually any spaceship built by Master System. A product of a long-term genetic breeding experiment by her emotionally cold father, she fled China Center rather than become yet another breeder in his grand design and wound up on Melchior, as well.

Item: Nagy, as chief security officer of Melchior, had been playing a double game as the agent of the enemy Master System said it was at war with—a stalemated war no one knew anything about, including the nature and location of either the enemy or the battleground. He had placed the Indians and the Chinese together, along with others already on Melchior—all selected for a possible attempt to locate and steal the rings—and allowed them to escape to an interplanetary ship whose computer intelligence was independent of Master System. Song

Ching, blinded by Clayben and turned into a biological breeding machine to keep her father's experiment going, was allowed to discover the existence of a mothballed fleet of giant ships once used to take millions of humans to other worlds and there to transform them into whatever form necessary to survive on a particular planet. Before Master System raided Melchior and shut it down, Nagy and Clayben also escaped in a smaller interstellar craft prepared for just that purpose. Eventually, Nagy and Clayben joined the group as uneasy allies.

Item: Along with the escapees, there is one who is not at all human but rather a creature of Clayben's design, a creature capable of absorbing and then mentally and physically duplicating any other organic being. Bred originally as the first of a synthetic army that could bypass Master System's defenses, it proved impossible to control and had been kept sedated and contained for many years on Melchior. Once free, it agreed for its own reasons to join them—as Nagy and his bosses counted on from the start. Because the leader of the expedition is the Amerind historian Hawks, the security man is Raven, and the ship's computer who has joined them as an independent ally is called Star Eagle, the creature names itself Vulture.

Item: Spotted by Vals in the freebooter trading post run by Fernando Savaphoong, an oily crook whose greed is surpassed only by his deceit, the renegades were attacked by Master System and the freebooter base was destroyed. Savaphoong escaped by the skin of his teeth and linked up with some refugee freebooter ships with no place left to go. Contacted by Hawks, they joined together to form a pirate fleet named after the huge ship at its center—the Pirates of the *Thunder*. But during a fight with the Val ships, Nagy was killed and his body disposed of in deep space.

Item: Using Vulture to duplicate a native and scout

the target planet, several members of the *Thunder* band infiltrated the Hindu world of Janipur—where one of the rings lay in a guarded museum—after first being changed into the strange Janipurian form by the same devices that created the original Janipurians. The devices, called transmuters, were deliberately designed so that a being could be changed only once; a second attempt would kill. Together, the infiltrators and Vulture were able to steal the ring and elude pursuit by Vals and members of Master System's human shock troops, the System Peacekeeping Forces, or SPF. However, to extricate their people and the ring requires the pirates to fight a space battle with the Vals, automated fighters, and the SPF, and this is accomplished only at great cost —and served to put Master System on full alert.

Item: A second group infiltrates the planet Matriyeh the same way: by becoming natives, with Vulture leading the way and spying from the inside. This world is so primitive Master System depends on the limited society and harshness of life there to defend the ring. It is a herculean task to get it, particularly since it is guarded by a semihuman Val in the guise of a beautiful goddess. If the ring or its guardian is removed, all the forces of Master System would be alerted, forcing another battle Master System can well afford but the pirates can't. They might steal the ring and replace the Val with one of their own crew transformed into an exact replica of the guardian—all so quickly and covertly that none of the SPF or automated alarms on this world are aware that the ring is missing. Again, however, there is cost, as they might lose some of their number in the attempt and others must stay behind to maintain the secrecy of their success.

Item: The pirates of the *Thunder* are well down in strength, even more so in the number of people who can still be transmuted and still have no idea as to the location of the interface or how the rings must be used. They still have two rings to steal and know the approximate location of only one of them. The impossible odds faced throughout are growing astronomic with the passage of time, and the vast forces arrayed against them become stronger all the time. And as always, Master System waits to pounce on their smallest error.

Arnold Nagy sighed and gulped down the rest of his drink.

So far, so good, he thought nervously.

1. THE TROUBLE WITH CHANCHUK

THE VULTURE SWAM THROUGH THE DARK WATERS OF Chanchuk away from the Lodge of the Reverend Mother. At the moment, Vulture was female, but that would soon change—the new target and identity had already been selected. It was mostly a matter of awaiting the opportune moment when the key elements of the operation would come together.

It was spring in this part of Chanchuk; the covering ice had all long since broken, melted, and flowed away to the Great Sea and the water was now a comfortable six degrees celsius, not at all bad. Visibility was always poor this close in to the coast and was never very good at any depth. Not that Chanchukian eyesight was poor; the inner, transparent lid on each eye allowed the eyes to be open and alert at all times, but there was only so much light and there were incredible shadows and distortions. One quickly learned to trust sound over sight down here.

Chanchuk had been one of Master System's more creative inventions, both as a world and culture and as creative biological redesign.

It was probable that, when the great computer decided to disperse humanity throughout a full quadrant of the Milky Way galaxy as part of its imperative to ensure human survival, it always had biological redesign in mind even if the slowness of terraforming hadn't forced that decision on it. It was not enough to carry off ninety percent of the population of Earth to new worlds; it was also important to make them so different and so unique to their new habitats that they would have little desire to return to Earth even if such a chance were afforded them. The greater the differences—and physiological differences back on Earth far simpler and more basic than these had been the basis for much human hatred and prejudice—the less chance over the passage of time that scattered humanity would ever even dream of reuniting.

Chanchuk had presented particular problems to the great computer. Its land surface was fierce, violent, and not terribly habitable by any great numbers. The tropics were a steamy hell; the rest was desert, tundra, or high and inaccessible mountains, all without any hope of large-scale agriculture. Only the vast seas had any promise, and could become the breeding grounds for hordes of specialized sea creatures who would reproduce in profusion over the whole of the planet's waters. And to keep their numbers from choking off other marine life, there would have to be large numbers of predators, until the most predatory of all, humankind, could establish itself firmly and permanently on the new world.

Partly because of the predators required at the start, and also because of the need to maintain a humanlike culture under the difficult conditions presented by so vast a seabed, the people of Chanchuk had to be sea dwellers but not creatures of the sea.

Vulture "smelled" rather than saw the entrance to her lodge and made for it, then came up quickly into the entry chamber and back into the air. The average Chanchukian female could hold her breath for up to an hour and dive as deep as a thousand meters without artificial aid, but they were still air-breathing mammals and it was always a pleasure to breathe air again.

An entry chamber was never very fancy; it was like the vestibule of a good home, where you left your mess before entering the decent parts of the house. Like most, it was lined with absorbent *dahagi,* a giant sea sponge that felt wonderful when you shook off the water and then rolled around for a few moments. Then it was up to the inner entry chamber, where a special fan and heater would finish the drying process thoroughly and quickly. Afterward, one was presentable enough to enter the main lodge. It was an addition only for the elite of the Center; the masses were allowed no such technology and relied on natural breezes or lived with being wet.

Vulture entered the Great Room and noted that the lamps were lit in spite of the fact that it was still day. She looked up at the skylights above and saw dark clouds; the roar of a good rainstorm echoed dully inside as the storm beat upon the solid lodges of the People. Funny how the two worlds hardly interacted from a Chanchukian point of view. Vulture had been out all day, but until she'd entered the Great Room she had no idea that it was raining.

Butar Killomen of the spaceship *Kaotan* was preparing a snack in the kitchen area—it smelled like *hai ka,* a particularly tasty candy that was a Chanchukian favorite. She looked far different from the muscular, tailed, hairless gray-skinned creature she had been born as, but that was the price of the rings that would bring their freedom. Vulture liked her much better this way, and certainly Killomen didn't seem particularly upset by the change.

Of course, the key to any success they had to date was that all of them were outcasts and fugitives from their own people. Killomen had been a freebooter, living outside of and between the cracks of the system. Except for those from Earth and some from the late crew of the *Indrus*, all of them had been pretty much unique.

The people of Chanchuk were covered with a thick, oily fur in shades ranging from golden to red to brown to black. On land they were bipeds, with broad hands and fingers that were linked two-thirds of their length with thick black webbing. The ears, although sensitive, were fur-covered and resembled mere depressions in the side of the flat, squat head. The noses were broad and black, with flaps that closed and sealed when underwater, flanked by thick, long whiskers and a mouth that looked small but could open to swallow something half the size of the head. The twin-lidded eyes—the inner lid transparent as glass and actually increasing sensitivity to light —were brown, rounded, inset balls perfectly suited for the two worlds of Chanchuk, water and air, although it made them nearsighted to a degree and painted their world in patterns of sepia-stained monochrome while bringing any object into startling three-dimensional life. That was what the few on this team missed most: color. But they'd gotten used to it by now.

The bodies were thick, impossibly lithe, almost plastic in their ability to bend any which way. In the water, the legs and long, webbed feet formed a single horizontal tail that could propel them with dolphinlike speed. On land, they bent outward, slightly bowlegged, the feet bent forward to allow a comic, yet quite serviceable, walk, and the thick membrane that bent in the water to serve as a dorsal fin hung down to become a balance-aiding paddlelike tail. Raven said that they reminded him of the Pacific sea otter, but none of those who were actually down here in that form had ever seen or heard of such a creature.

Killomen turned and nodded to Vulture. "Everything set?"

"As much as can be" came the reply. "There's no way to deceive the SPF once we pull it—the old girl never seems to have the damned thing off her finger—but if all the stuff Clayben and Raven designed for this job works, it shouldn't be difficult to get the ring. The getaway mechanisms are all planted and primed; they could get lucky, but the odds are with us this time for a change. I doubt if it'll work twice, but it should do here. At least this time we're risking the smallest number of people and we're far more experienced and sophisticated about this than before."

Min Xao Po entered from the bedroom, looking sleepy, but she had obviously overheard everything. Min and co-conspirator Chung Mung Wo, both of the crew of the freebooter *Chunhoifan*, had the oddest adjustment problems to Chanchuk. Both had been male and were now female, for one thing, and both were also finding it difficult to adapt to a culture that was in every way, including biologically, a matriarchy. This, on top of the physiological changes, was bad enough, but both men had been ethnic Chinese whose ancestors had come from the barren northwest of China centuries before. In spite of the startling environmental differences and the sex-role reversal, the language and many of the customs of the people of Chanchuk were very close to that which their own people had taught to them. The dialect difference was what one would expect after over nine hundred years of separation, and there was a new set of words better able to handle the watery nature of Chanchuk. It had been a shock, but they'd been the logical choice for this mission.

Besides, they were damned good marksmen and one was an ordnance specialist, the other a communications expert. Their skills had determined the method and the personnel for this "caper," as Raven called it. After close to a year on Chanchuk as natives, they had adapted surprisingly well.

"So when do we go?" Min asked Vulture.

"I think we've been here long enough," Vulture responded. "I want you and Mung to run through the sequence with us and check out all the equipment one last time. I don't want anything going wrong because of timing, equipment failure, weather, or anything else. A physical check of the remotes is too time-consuming, but we can run a receiver check on each. Guns should be fully charged, everything ready to go. Bute, we'll need the canisters in position as soon as I settle in. I prefer living in that place as one of the consorts as little time as possible. When I absorb someone, the genetic design dominates and shapes me just as it does the original. I almost got trapped that way once before and this is far more dangerous, at least for me. If everything comes off correctly, I'll get the ring, but I'm sure as hell not going to be a lot of help. If we fail to knock 'em out long enough, or if one single SPF guard is left awake, I'm stuck and everything's back to square one—if any of us survives."

"We know that," Killomen responded impatiently. "We're chomping at the bit to go. All *we* have to do is sneak around and shoot straight. You have the toughest job. You're *sure* you can neutralize the neurotoxin?"

"I've done it easily in all the tests, but that was when I knew exactly when it was coming and could concentrate. You know the drill. If I'm not out, with or without the ring, within fifteen minutes of the start of the operation, or if any alarms bring in the forces, you forget me and fall back. We scrub. If we can't get the ring, there's no purpose in anybody dying." She looked at Killomen and frowned. "Something still worrying you other than everything that's worrying me?"

She shrugged. "No, I have this odd feeling, that's all. I'll believe that we can get away with this without getting ourselves killed when we do it."

Vulture put a hand on her shoulder and gave the Chanchukian equivalent of a sour grin. It looked awful. "Nobody lives forever, unless I eat them," she said.

Min looked uncomfortable at that and changed the subject. "What about you, though? You are certain that no one in Center security suspects you?"

"Oh, they suspect *something*," Vulture admitted. "That's why they wired all the Center lodges and why we had to go through that godawful business of neutralizing the bugs and installing believable recordings. Their general theory is that we have enough spies that we can pick out, snatch, and replace a key figure with our own mind-printed duplicate, no matter what their computers tell them about the security of their mindprint processes. That's why all the SPF here have monitor implants, as do Center security and the administrators—especially those who have any access to the Holy Lama. I almost blew it because of that implant when I took over this body. I'm not exactly brilliant and alert when I'm absorbing someone and my automatic response was to expel the foreign object. Fortunately I hadn't begun merging minds and had the sense to figure it was some kind of implant and transfer it, too. I'm ready for it now, and they're convinced that there's no way we can snatch somebody long enough to mindprint and duplicate them without their knowledge. And they're right, too. If they ever knew what I could really do, they could shut me down cold."

"That is the other reason I worry," said Butar Killomen softly. "If they were somehow to learn about you, to stop you—what good would even four rings be? We need you. You have become our ace in the hole."

Vulture sat back on her tail and sighed. "I believe you underestimate yourselves. At the start I would have said so, too, and perhaps been right, but now—I'm not so sure that anyone of this company can be denied." She clapped her hands together sharply and stood up as straight as the Chanchukian body would allow. "Come! Min, wake Chung and tell her to get herself out here ahead of her tail. If all this brooding has not caused the *hai ka* to burn to a crisp we shall all sit around and drink strong tea and stuff ourselves with such decadence and be pretty damned positive it's almost over. Although we are creatures of water and air now, you three will always be in your element only in space, and it is to there that we will return in very short time!"

Chanchuk, for all its differences, retained the basic system imposed by Master System on the vast majority of human worlds, including Earth. The basic culture was taken from ancient, pre–Master System Earth, then refined, stylized, and simplified by both Master System's design and the planet's cultural isolation for over nine hundred years.

Over the masses, serving Master System and running the world in secret, were the elect—the smartest, the most ambitious, the best of the people. They alone had access to technology, and they ruled with it, co-opting anyone who might be a threat to the system into the leadership, or eliminating them if they could not be co-opted. A series of regional Centers divided up control of the world; over them all was a chief administrator who was the ultimate boss of the world—but still subject to Master System's will.

From their Centers, this elite ruled millions of people divided into feudal quasi-states under warlords with their castlelike grand lodges and private armies. The technology available to these masses, even the warlords, was primitive, the ways archaic, but the system was effective. About the only oddity Chanchuk presented was its near universal adherence to Buddhism, but this Buddha had a broad and unnaturally fat Chanchukian head and body, and was, like the priesthood and holy ones here, most certainly female. This distinctive Master System touch was dictated more by practicality than any intent to maliciously pervert the old ways; the religion, an odd but ancient offshoot of Buddhism, was, except for the sexual roles, pretty faithfully intact.

On Chanchuk the females ruled; the males were, on the whole, small, fairly weak, short-lived, and not very bright. Clayben analyzed the place and, because of this anomaly, suspected that Chanchukians were based upon a real alien race and not one created by Master System.

Clayben and Star Eagle were disquieted by the idea that this world might have once contained a sentient race that looked and lived much as the colonists did, but one that would not be co-opted and would not surrender. Master System's core instructions extended to human life; it was the prevention of human racial genocide or suicide that had led to its creation by well-meaning scientists so long ago. But that was human. Was the computer, in fact, capable of cold genocide against any race that had not sprung from human stock? Had it done so here? And, if so, how many other races had been eliminated and supplanted in its grandiose scheme?

"Master System was created by human minds," Hawks had pointed out. "And human minds have always had a veritable gift in some parts of the world for the elimination or subjugation of any race or group that stood in the way of the powerful and their needs." Hawks, of course, was what the Europeans generally referred to as an "American Indian."

Vulture was the least disturbed by these thoughts. It, too, was a creature of technology and human minds, and didn't quite feel the weight of broad moral questions the way the others did. The immediate problem was disturbing enough.

Wa Chi Center had been as easy as the others to penetrate, and in spite of its more diffuse nature, with its citylike collection of lodges and fragmented if interconnected offices, was a familiar system by now. The chief administrator certainly had a name once; but now she was just known as the Holy Lama in the language of the people. She was old, and smart, and generally antisocial. The only time she seemed to emerge from her Sacred Lodge was for ceremonial or religious occasions—she was believed by the masses and even by most of the educated technocrats of Wa Chi Center to be the latest reincarnation of a demigod who was the messenger between the Heavens and the World. As such, she was the highest lama, the supreme religious authority, and a deity in her own right. There were a few—very few—occasions when she had to appear, to preside, but when she did she was always surrounded by so many guards and other people that it would have been impossible to get near her, let alone steal the ring she seemed to always wear on her finger.

Even if there were a way to snatch it and somehow keep from being killed by the guards or mauled by the crowd for sacrilege, the alarm would be sounded and getaway would be next to impossible. That meant taking her where she was most vulnerable, where she depended on the automated and physical security systems—in the Sacred Lodge in the middle of Wa Chi Center. For Wa Chi was not merely a Center but also a vast temple complex, the seat of a mighty theocracy.

Vulture, as usual, had worked her way close to the ring and then had "eaten" and become a security official with access to the Sacred Lodge. Usually the top people were very sophisticated and very knowledgeable about the system and the history of the world and its people, and this, along with their privileged position, made them into cynics only playing the role of a primitive for the masses. Here, though, perhaps because of the original cultural cohesion of the first colonists, the elite had the knowledge, but not the cynicism. It was clear that the Holy Lama believed in her faith and her deity as much as her subjects did and took it quite seriously. She spent a good deal of time in prayer and communion with the spirits—although she was also clearly a damned good and efficient administrator who had her finger on the pulse of her world and everyone of importance in it and a fine grasp of the technology involved.

Unlike the other priestesses, however, the Holy Lama was not celibate, nor was she supposed to be. Indeed, she was to bear as many children as possible, all of the females to be raised as priestesses for the other Centers and even for the warlord districts, their authority being their lineage to the demigoddess herself. When their mother ultimately passed away, the entire female line would gather and among them one would be anointed as having received the spirit of the deity and become the new Holy Lama. It was generally, although not always, the one who was youngest and most capable of continuing the line, yet experienced in the ways of the Centers and Chanchukian politics and culture. The sign was that the Sacred Golden Ring fit the new one's finger. Somehow, it always did.

This Holy Lama had been twenty-nine when called, and was now thirty-six. Chanchukian females sexually matured late by human standards, and she was probably good for another eight or ten children before her child-bearing years were past. For this and other reasons, some genetic, some traditional, her inner sanctum was maintained by a small cadre of males—her consorts. While some priestesses, including heads of Center staff departments, could and did see her, such meetings were always carefully monitored; the slightest deviation from protocol or normal routine was certain to raise an alarm. The local guards were fanatics and since they had been supplemented by SPF forces, it would be damned near impossible to steal the ring under the usual conditions. Well, that wasn't quite true. In fact, Vulture could probably steal the ring without a fight and maybe only a mild argument.

She'd never leave even the room alive, though. The guards might hesitate for fear of harming the Holy Lama, but the SPF wouldn't care about such restraint.

The only privacy, the only real place that one could snatch that ring with some impunity, was in the Holy Lama's bedchambers, and only one female was ever allowed in there. Only an oversexed and undermuscled consort had a real chance at the theft. Working out how to become one had taken a lot of time and thought as well, and now their hopes rested in a small vial of a synthesized hormone that Vulture carried.

No one who was not a true priestess could gain an audience with the Holy Lama, and even then, only those priestesses who had submitted to virtual sterilization and the removal of certain key glands to prevent the males from being stimulated. Vulture now was in such a position, and had the hormone that would nullify the operation. Even so, this would be the second attempt. Creating a problem or scandal sufficient to require a summons to an audience was hard enough; doing it twice had been both difficult and risky, but the first time the plan hadn't worked. Vulture had never gotten alone with a consort for anything near the time required to do the job. This time, she hoped, they had it all correct. Even after all this time and all this hard work, in the end success still depended a great deal on luck just to get the opportunity to pull off the very thing the SPF was looking for and was confident could not be done.

The first big risk would be the signal Xao would send when the summons came. After careful analysis, Master System had figured out how the pirates had used its own orbital subcarriers to talk freely in the past and had shut that route down. Xao, however, was a communications wizard and had come up with a neat trick of tapping into and imitating the calls of several of the duty operators from Center security to the SPF control craft. The frequencies were rather easy to track, and although the transmissions themselves were in code, Xao had been quick to note that the frequent communications checks from planet to ship and back were in the clear. By the time Vulture was entering the Holy Lama's lodge, Xao would transmit a radio check using a series of coded phrases that sounded very much like what the SPF used, but would also trigger the automated relay probes of the pirates of the *Thunder*. It would not do to steal the ring and perhaps even escape Chanchuk if there was no way short of a space battle to get them picked up.

Vulture swam to the security lodge, which was surrounded by both electronic and Chanchukian SPF guardians, and while in the drying room also provided the necessary finger, eye, and blood tests that verified her identity as Mung Qing, High Priestess of the Lord Buddha, older sister to the Holy Lama, and head of the liaison division, which gave orders to and correlated reports from the various other Centers spread around the world. It was an important job for Chanchuk, although not terribly useful to Vulture's purpose. It did, however, afford several key opportunities, which was why she had spent so much time sizing up and then taking over his particular individual: it provided access to all levels of security; it provided the right of access to the Holy Lama, if necessary; it provided a number of ways to cause the conditions that would make that necessary; and, just as important, because her rank was hereditary and her relationship to the Holy Lama close, she could make mistakes now and then without losing her job or perhaps even her head.

Once cleared, she removed the robe of the priesthood from her backpack as well as her medallion of office and, after putting the medallion around her neck, put the plain tan robe over her body. Then she went up the ladderlike stairs to the security offices themselves.

To one born and raised primitive and ignorant, everything up to this point would have seemed pretty routine, and even the security checks would be taken as some magical ritual, but once upstairs it was a far different story, like stepping from some primordial age into the highest of high technology. She nodded to the crews on duty at the various consoles, gave a cold stare to Colonel Chi who'd preempted a rather large and needed office for SPF affairs, much to the resentment of everyone local, and made her way down toward her own office. Chi noted the stare with bemusement, then walked after her.

"A thousand pardons, Holiness, but I would like to speak with you for a moment."

Vulture did not stop, but, making the other keep up, walked into her own office and picked up a large stack of data files marked for her attention. She then proceeded to the soft mat that served as her chair and around which was a raised semicircular wooden area that was her desk, ignoring the colonel for the moment. The SPF officer, however, could not be denied. They never could, and for all her politeness and respectful titles, Chi had about as much religion as a water bug and perhaps less.

Vulture sighed, looking through the stack of work and not looking up at her uninvited visitor at all. "Colonel, we have much work to do today and some very difficult problems to deal with that are no concern of yours. We are on the same side here, but we did not invite you; were it not for your arrogance and patronizing attitude, as well as that of your troops, we might have a better relationship. So stuff the politeness and get to the point."

Chi smiled. These high-born priestesses were all like this, and she was used to it, although the SPF had some cause for its superior attitude. Chi had begun, as did all SPF children, as the lowest of the low and, when of age, was a mere private. The route to colonel had been difficult and earned on ability and merit in spite of a bloodline at least as good as these stuck-up shamans who'd attained their power and rank and position by merely being born into the right family.

"Very well, then. General Wharfen, Commander of the System Peacekeeping Forces, is nervous. When General Wharfen gets nervous, everyone under him gets much grief, and right now his eye is on us. Although it has been many years since a ring was stolen, the general is convinced that these so-called pirates will make a move and soon. He is reinforcing our positions on the worlds with rings considered most vulnerable and placing our forces there on full alert."

"Male paranoia, Colonel," Vulture responded haughtily. "When one takes orders from a *male*, one must expect such things."

Chi choked off a rejoinder, well aware that the high priestess knew that Chanchuk's sexual order was not universal among the other races of humanity and that ones like Wharfen were every bit the equal of either one of them in abilities. She had no intention, however, of getting sidetracked into a debate on universal male psychology.

"There was a colonel like myself, a Janipurian named Privi, who was given a similar assignment to my own a few years back. Privi died—slowly and uncomfortably

—in an object lesson to the other division commanders that I was forced to endure. I have no intention of being the next object lesson. My orders prevent a wholesale disruption of the system on this world, but I assure you that if the SPF must seize full control of security here and elsewhere on this planet and mindprint the locals, regardless of rank or position, I assure you I can and will do so."

The high priestess looked up at her, impassive and apparently unmoved. "You have evidence that this is more than paranoia? After all, one ring in—what?—five years? We do not even understand what all this fuss over the Holy Lama's ring is, anyway. If it is so important, why not simply secure it? You have the force."

The colonel shook her head. "I have no idea what the rings represent nor do I wish to know, although it is said that together they represent some threat to the system's order and safety. How that can be I have no idea, and, again, I do not want to know, nor do you. Such knowledge, I think, would mean death."

"Death is relative, whether you believe it or not, Colonel," said the high priestess who was also the Vulture. "However, the manner of death as well as the conduct of life is important, we will grant that. Still, does it not trouble you that these *pirates* know and you do not? One wonders what sort of secret is so terrible that it must be kept from one's allies even when the enemies of the system know. Still, what concern is it of ours except that your presence here disrupts the order and flow of society?"

The colonel reached into her parcel belt and brought out a photograph and passed it over to the priestess, who took it and looked at it. It showed a small, round object with what looked like a thick collar covering about a third of its girth and which was used as a base. "So? What is this thing?" she asked, knowing exactly what it was. The discovery of one or more was inevitable, particularly considering the amount of time this mission had taken.

"It is an independent, remotely operated, near-space engine," the colonel responded, taking back the photograph and putting it back into the belt.

"A spaceship? That hardly looks like anything we ever imagined as a spacecraft."

"Not a spacecraft, no. An engine. Only the engine, some fuel, and a very small core command module that appears to respond only to a simple off-on signal. The entire purpose of the thing appears to be to take off."

"Indeed? And then what?"

"Nothing. It's just an engine and fuel. There isn't room for much of anything else, although something as small as the ring could fit in it—if it were placed in one of the access ports and somehow secured. It was found by accident in Win Tai Province. Some *klitchi* farmers were being menaced by a *warog* that they managed to wound and then were forced to chase. As you know, the creatures are monsters when wounded." *Klitchi* was a sea grass that was a staple of the Chanchuk diet, much as rice had been for their ancient Earth-human ancestors. The *warog* was one of the sea's great carnivores, although not generally a danger to humans unless wounded or unless it tasted blood. "They practically stumbled over it, camouflaged and neatly set up on a rock outcrop near the surface but well away from the village."

"Why was this not reported to us at once?"

"Ah . . . our people at Win Tai Center intercepted the thing, recovered and analyzed it, and it was decided that we were best able to handle it. We did not feel that it was necessary to inform you at the time."

"Necessary! It is our function! How *dare* you! Have

you, then, already usurped the maintenance and administration of Chanchuk? If so, why come to us now?"

"No, not yet. Rest assured on that. And I am telling you now because we are going to need your help in coordinating the various Center security staffs. We must know if there are more of these things, and finding them will take a concentrated and intelligent search. They did not fly down there and put up their own camouflage—someone had to place them and hide them. Win Tai is a very long way from here. This had to be a backup, an emergency system, not intended for use unless necessary. It is not of our manufacture, and the manufacturing capabilities to build such a thing do not exist on Chanchuk. Marine growth and oxidation of the device indicate it has been in place no more than a year and a half, possibly no more than eight or nine months. We must know where any others are, and quickly!"

Vulture looked at the colonel smugly. "You have just stood there telling us how all-powerful and omnipotent you are. Please, be our guest. Go out and find all you can."

"You know we haven't a prayer of doing it on our own. We don't know this world. We are visitors here, even if we are of the same race. The device is diabolical in its cleverness. There is no element in its composition that is not found in nature here one place or another. Nothing for instrumentation to seize upon. They are small, and well hidden, most certainly well away from populous areas and off usual travel routes. But in each case, *someone placed it where it is*. Either a stranger had to come through who would be noticed or a local was employed, either voluntarily or through kidnapping and mindprinting. We should be able to track these down—but not by ourselves. We require all the resources at your command and the experience of the best people you have at each Center."

It wasn't a bad opening. "We have no authority to order such a thing, nor would there be any enthusiastic cooperation considering our relations since you arrived. Only the Holy Lama herself could command this. Has she been informed?"

"My orders from the commander on analysis of the device and the problem have only just arrived from headquarters. Master System believes that an intensive search will prod any pirates now present to hasten their plans and try for the ring before all of their devices and their plans are uncovered and all avenues of escape are cut off. Even now a number of frigates are headed here, each carrying a complement of automated fighter craft. They will be in place within five days from today. So far we think we have contained this discovery, but once the search is launched everyone, including the pirate agents, will know. They will make a frantic attempt on the ring —and we will catch them."

Five days. Not much time, but more than enough if everything worked according to plan. Once the operation was placed in motion, it had to go pretty fast. Not only Chi but most of Center would immediately notice the disappearance of a key high priestess, and while Vulture could become anyone she chose, she could not be two people at once.

Vulture nodded to the colonel. "Very well. We will attempt an appointment with the Holy Lama as soon as practical on this matter."

Chi glared at the priestess. "I would suggest that it be *very* quickly, *Holiness*." She made that last word sound like something obscene. "You people here seem to forget yourselves and just what maintains your fat, comfortable lives here and your precious religion. I want that authority and cooperation by tonight. If not, I will be forced to report that this Center and its chief administrator are refusing full and complete cooperation and are to be considered to be in rebellion against the system. Then we'll see how well your little games play against Vals with the full authority of Master System and full control of your computers, power facilities, and apparatus of control. You tell the Holy Lama that."

And, with that, the colonel stomped, gave a stiff military-style salute, pivoted, and walked out the door feeling very secure and satisfied with herself.

It was no idle threat, either. Such a statement would have any high priestess in a panic and the Holy Lama passing bricks and scrambling to protect her domain. For Vulture, it was just what she most wanted coming from an unexpected and wonderful direction. She punched the intercom.

"Have the complete recorded transcript of the conversation with Colonel Chi transmitted to the Holy Lama immediately on emergency priority," she ordered crisply. "Then get me all the data you can on this alien *thing* they found, the area, and region—all the details." She paused a moment. "And find out exactly who among our own people in Win Tai and in the chain from there to here did not immediately report everything to me and get their excuses. Inform them that the Holy Lama will judge them by their names and their excuses and relieve them of all clearances and authority until that judgment is rendered. Understand?"

"Yes, Holiness" came the somewhat shocked response. "At once."

By the time the summons from the Sacred Lodge came, Vulture had managed to put together a very neat package, ostensibly to brief the Holy Lama but actually to brief Vulture. Politically there was no excuse for the two field agents and the high priestess at Win Tai not to report everything no matter what they were told or ordered to do by SPF officials. It was Wa Chi Center's job to deal with the SPF; it was the responsibility of subordinate chief administrators and their staffs to work for and solely in the interest of Wa Chi. And, of course, it was politics—or at least ambition—that caused them to betray their trust. Promotion was slow and reward was not generally a factor in this culture and society, and no matter how closed the culture, these people were, well, human. Their excuses were lame—the field agents maintaining they did their job and that wasn't to send on the material to Wai Chi; the C.A. at Wa Chi stating that she had been assured it was all sent. Maybe with a static, inbred, hereditary hierarchy you got that lazy and that incompetent, but Vulture knew it was different, at least in this case. They were betting on Chi's permanence and influence, and they bet wrong.

Vulture picked up her communicator and called home. All lines in and out, even the secured ones, were continuously monitored, of course, but the kind of information she had to impart wasn't anything apparently subversive. Butar answered.

"We shall not be home until very late," Vulture told the other agent. "We are summoned to an audience with the Holy Lama at sixteen-thirty hours and there is no telling how long it will take nor what we will be commanded to do after."

There *was* a somewhat pregnant pause from Killomen, who then responded, "Very well, Holiness. We shall prepare nothing for you, but we will leave something in the storage compartment in case you come in hungry and late."

"Do not bother, child. It might well be three days. Just enjoy yourselves and do what you want to do. We will cope."

And that was that. Three days from now, at a predetermined time, things would start to pop—if Vulture managed to pull off her part at all. If not, it gave enough time for the high priestess to return home and call it off.

At a bit after sixteen hundred, Vulture packed all the materials into a watertight bag, sealed it with the official security seal, put it on, and went out for the short trip to the Sacred Lodge. The staff eyed her in awe and wonder, knowing she was going to see, even converse with, the Holy Lama herself. They might as well get a good look. If all went well, some time in the early morning a little bit of a worm would sneak into the security computer system with the order from the Holy Lama dispatching her to Win Tai to take personal charge of things. They didn't have access to skimmers and the like here; the Centers had to be located too close to the masses to make any ostentatious display of technology possible. There *were* quick ways, certainly—and the SPF could have gotten her there in hours—but it would not be in character to use them. Using the speediest modes of travel available to Wa Chi Center, it would take someone three or four days to reach Win Tai. That might be cutting the timing close and her cover might be blown, but it was better than nothing.

With luck, and if the Holy Lama didn't ask for her or summon her when she was supposed to be somewhere else by order of the Holy Lama, the high priestess might not be missed until it was far too late.

The Sacred Lodge was grandiose, even underwater. The whole support structure and base glowed incandescently, and, unlike the other lodges, seemed to sit not on wood supports but on some kind of translucent marble columns. Statues of the Great Buddha were inset around as well, and scenes highlighting the cardinal principles of this odd offshoot of Buddhism were carved on thick bands around the columns. There were both electronic and human guards as well, the latter armed with very efficient and non–mass-culture rifles with automatic sights adjusted for use in water or air.

The Grand Entrance was a womblike tunnel full of

twists and turns. The curves were there for a reason:
they gave security plenty of time to look over a visitor
while she presented a perfect slow target who could be
cut off by lightning-fast door seals at the least suspicion.
Nobody got very far by accident or without an invita-
tion.

Once in the drying chamber, however, one had to
hand over all parcels and items of clothing to be passed
through sensors while presenting eyes, fingers, and
blood samples to special security computers not connected to the main computer network and controlled entirely from within the temple. This was a relatively new
procedure ordered by Master System itself a few years
before. It knew that the pirates had gotten into the security system of Janipur and wanted to make very certain
that no spy, no matter how clever, could influence the
gateway to the one who wore the ring. The system was
totally automated as well; it even included a mindprint
routine to make *absolutely* certain that anyone entering
was just who they seemed to be. The transmuters might
fool all the physical safeguards, but duplicating both
physical and mental characteristics perfectly was considered by Master System as next to impossible.

As usual, Master System was wrong. To the Vulture,
who was designed to fool just such mechanisms, it was
child's play.

She reclaimed her belongings on the other side of the
security door and went up to the waiting chamber. It was
sumptuously furnished and the gold relief on the religious scenes engraved in the walls was awe-inspiring.
The fact that some of those gems and intricate designs
concealed monitors made any move here highly unlikely.
Here was where luck had failed in the first attempt, and
where luck needed to be far better this time. Damn it,
this *was* about as impregnable a place to get in and out of

as could be designed under the limits of a colonial Center. She settled down on a soft couch and waited.

A small door opened opposite her and one of the Seed of Buddha entered carrying a small tray.

The males of Chanchuk were less than imposing. The average female was perhaps a hundred and sixty-five centimeters tall and weighed perhaps fifty-five to sixty kilograms; the average male was perhaps a hundred and twenty centimeters, many shorter, and usually did not weigh more than thirty-five kilos. They also had a bushy mane of hair around their heads that was usually slightly lighter or darker than the rest of their body hair and often was dyed to give great contrast. They often went to great lengths in wearing various jewels and other ornaments to make themselves stand out to any females who might be looking. Most incongruously, they had two small but very firm breasts that actually produced milk on a continuous basis. Still, they had one attribute that made them instantly attractive to the opposite sex, as the large golden codpiece this one wore attested.

Males really were rather weak. Fewer than two in seven made it past their first year and they were subject to more diseases before they reached puberty, which cut their numbers down even further. Of course, even though they numbered only thirty percent of the adult population, there were more males than were required for procreation, particularly when they had such raging libidos. In general, males kept house for a number of women who could then space their children so that it would not affect the group's income or disrupt their lives unnecessarily.

The females bore the young, but the males nursed and raised them. In this biological system the males had all the sexual lures but were small and weak and very dependent. They were such prisoners of their continuous hormones—unlike females whose hormones got out of whack only briefly every month—that culturally they were considered incapable of more than running a household and were not all that bright. Most education, at least, was denied them, and their roles were rigidly fixed. Whether or not they really had higher IQs than anyone credited was something Vulture hoped to find out.

The male stopped and bowed slightly before Vulture. "Greetings, Holiness. I am Cho. We met when you were here a few months ago. Might I offer some tea and biscuits? The Holy Lama will see you soon."

Vulture nodded and allowed the tea to be poured. She remembered Cho, all right. She almost had him last time, but she couldn't get him far enough out of the monitor range.

There was no sexual attraction felt by either now, of course. There never was around a priestess; after she'd been gutted of her sexual apparatus and even had her biochemistry adjusted to that of an asexual being, there wasn't much to arouse interest. Without the glandular odors, the male wouldn't find a eunuch particularly attractive.

Idly, Vulture reached down to her vaginal area, found, and squeezed hard and somewhat painfully on a tiny hard spot just beneath the skin. A tiny, surgically implanted vial gave way and exuded a substance through the pores of the outer skin layers. The high priestess was now no less a eunuch, but for the brief period until the stuff washed off or lost its potency, she began exuding a real glandular come-on. The odor was not noticeable on a conscious level—just another in the mix of body odors—but it would, Vulture and Clayben theorized, have an interesting effect on any males in close range who might be very confused but still would find her suddenly very alluring.

There was no immediate effect, although she got as

close as she could to Cho. Still, after a little while and some small talk, Cho seemed to become a bit distracted and she could see him catching himself as his hand moved to his crotch.

That was just an opener, however. From this point, a high priestess who came also had to leave.

A chime sounded, breaking the scene, and Cho jumped up. "The Holy Lama will see you now," he said, sounding a bit throaty and breathless. He went to the main door, and it opened in front of him. He entered, and she followed, and they went down a short hall that opened into a large office the opulence of which was breathtaking.

The Holy Lama looked up from her desk. "All right, Cho—go play with yourself. We have business," she snapped in a hard, professional voice. The little male bowed, turned, and left, closing the inner doors behind him.

She was still relatively young, yet the pressures of the dual jobs of chief planetary administrator and top priestess to a major religion were already showing on her. The eyes were as hard as the voice, and the fur on the face and along the arms already seemed to be tinged with gray.

"So, are we still running things or aren't we?" the Holy Lama asked, getting directly to the point.

"We are—to a point," Vulture responded. "Colonel Chi is a soulless person, but with all the human failings of ambition and arrogance. She is used to giving orders and being obeyed instantly, and she has no respect for or loyalty to any culture or beliefs other than her own militaristic upbringing. One can tell that she is just itching for an excuse to declare full martial law, depose us, and turn Chanchuk into a godless police state."

The Holy Lama, as always, had the ring right on her finger. Four little birds against a black jadelike back-

ground laid into an ornately jeweled golden ring. It was
so tempting to just become the Holy Lama and obtain it
by right of possession, but it wasn't possible. Everything
in this room was being recorded; there was no way that
there would be the fifteen or more minutes necessary to
make the change without some kind of alarm being
raised—and no way to block security from later watching a recording of what had happened and thus discover-
ing just what the Vulture's power really was.

"Let us see your case," the Holy Lama said, and it
was handed over. The highest of priestesses broke the
seal and studied the documents and the picture of the
device for some time, deep in thought. Finally she said,
"This isn't good. Chi may be a soulless bastard, but she
does have a point." She put down the papers and stared
at her ring. "We would live our next incarnation as a
water slug to know why this is so important that aliens
would risk lives and worse for it and Master System
would go to this sort of extreme to stop them. If it were
not a required badge of office, we would just take it off
and give it to the SPF and tell them to go throw it in the
sun or something. There is no real religious connotation
to it. It is just a very pretty ring from the Mother World
and the old days."

Vulture shrugged. "If you wish, it could be done. You
could give it to us now and we would take it to Chi and
have done with it and her."

"If that were true, we would not hesitate to do so, but
do you know what the security monitors would do if this
thing left here without being on our finger in a prearranged audience? No, they feel that if the Holy Lama is
sealed away in this ornate mausoleum, it cannot be gotten. We wonder, though. If there were such a thing as
absolute security, we would not get away with much of
what we get away with now, would we? Master System
would have roared in here and mindcleaned the lot of

us—and our ancestors, too—if that were true." She sighed. "We would almost like to meet one of these pirate thieves. If, somehow, we could truly be convinced that this ring could aid in disrupting or even blowing apart this foul and evil system and its master machines, we would be tempted to present it to them freely. But—this system cannot be broken. Not by the likes of a jeweled ring."

Vulture was so heartened by that comment—which would be judiciously edited out of the recording by the Holy Lama's own special programs before it got to security and Colonel Chi—that she longed to tell all. There was just no way that the chance could be taken. It might be possible to convince the chief administrator that the rings could really do it, but first Vulture would have to convince the old girl that the sister she'd grown up with and known all her life was actually an artificial entity, then convince her that this entity was working for the pirates and not Master System out to trap treasonous chief administrators, and, finally, that the pirates could get all five and use them.

Better to steal it—if Vulture could, somehow, manage to do even that.

2. FACING THE INEVITABLE

CHO WAS WAITING FOR HER WHEN SHE EMERGED from the audience, as she'd hoped. Vulture liked the Holy Lama; she was sorry that circumstances cast them as enemies, but there was no way around that. The old girl's primary responsibility, as it should be, was to her faith and her planet. Vulture cared only about one thing the Holy Lama did not—but there was a knife at Chanchuk's throat, and the throats of the Holy Lama and her people, and those who held that knife cared only about that ring as well.

The orders had been simple, although they would never be properly delivered: turn everything over to Chi and the SPF; give them every cooperation and defer to them completely, but record every order and every decision and every demand, so if anything went wrong, it would be Chi and the SPF who would get the blame for usurping normal authority and failing while Chanchuk came out pure and noble and patriotic.

"Is all satisfactory, Holiness?" Cho asked her politely, not really expecting to be taken into her confidence. The effects of the hormone were far too subtle for Cho to even understand why he remained there or why it mattered.

"Yes, Cho, all is well. We would, however, appreciate a small service. We suffered an accidental shoulder injury not long ago and it is not yet fully healed, making it difficult to bend in certain ways. We have had problems putting on the backpack now and again, and it would be appreciated if you might accompany me to the drying room to aid me should I have problems. Would that ask too much of you?"

Cho's eyes lit up. "Oh, *no*, Holiness. No trouble at all. It will be my pleasure."

This would be tricky. Between the drying room and the waiting hall was a very short length of corridor that wasn't under direct observation—Vulture had determined that from past visits. It was the only unmonitored area available to a Seed, and it was so because it didn't need to be monitored.

There were more than enough monitoring devices on either end of the corridor to require them there.

She walked down, Cho following. He probably wouldn't have had the nerve to do it except for the lure of the hormone, which left him slightly turned on and very eager to please.

Halfway down the hall, she checked to make certain that no new security devices had been added, stopped, turned, listened for any sounds from below, and then stared down at the little male.

Cho stopped and looked up at her quizzically. "Is something wrong, Holiness?"

"No. At least we do not believe so. Come here. Closer. Yes, that is about right." Without another word she put her arms around a startled Cho as if to hug him, but that was not the intent as the process began instantly, freezing any further thought or comment the Seed might have.

It was always a gruesome sight, but no one was supposed to see it. Almost instantly the flesh of the high priestess seemed to take on a life of its own, reaching out and blending with the flesh of the hapless Cho. They seemed to merge, the inorganic things they had on or with them falling away, seemingly repelled from the increasingly shapeless, bubbling mass of flesh.

It took several minutes; that was why this had been so difficult and was even now a risk should anyone enter or leave through the corridor. What they would make of it was anyone's guess, but there would certainly be quite an alarm.

Now, out of the seething, bubbling, merged mass arose a new shape, Chanchukian in form but at first hairless and featureless. It was far smaller than the total mass, drawing from the throbbing pulp what it needed and no more. In an almost magical transition, the form took on the eyes and mouth and general features of Cho, then the hair and other elements took shape. Cho was completely reconstituted, and exactly so, right down to his memories and brain and body chemistry; so close that if it were possible, even a cell-by-cell comparison of the two would not show any difference.

But there was a difference. Vulture was in many ways as much a machine as the devices he fought against; a wholly organic machine, which stored its own memories and separate identity and will throughout every cell of its body, whatever that might be. The new creature that stepped out of the still-seething goo was Cho in every way—physically, mentally, emotionally—but not down to the basic submicroscopic structures within each cell that retained all that Vulture had been and the memories of all the people the creature had eaten before.

The goo was still living, but it was beginning to die, bereft of its controlling mitochondria-sized program. Getting the clothing and other articles out of the edges of the goo where it had fallen and getting the ichor off so that Cho could return above was unpleasant, but Vulture had done this sort of thing before. Far more difficult would be disposing of the priestess's papers, case, and minimal clothing and, if possible, getting rid of the goo. That was more of a problem here, and Vulture relied from the start on Cho's own knowledge of the Sacred Lodge to accomplish that. Fortunately, it provided a fast and easy means for part of the problem.

There *was* a maintenance chute in the hall used when the robotic cleaners worked the place at night, but while that might be all right for the clothing and travel case with its papers, it wouldn't do for the goo. To prevent accidents, the automated cleaning systems would sort out anything organic and pass it through to a secondary inspection before sending it to waste disposal. That second check would find the goo unusual enough to flag a security computer.

He did what he could. The stuff wasn't even completely dead yet—and when it was it would turn brown and give off a terrible odor. Papers down the chute, also the briefs, but before disposing of the case, he removed a small vial of muscle balm and a small lighter used in religious ceremonies. He also removed the high priestess's large signet ring. He poured the balm over as much of the goo as possible, wishing he had a few liters and not just the small amount he dared to bring in, then lit it with the lighter. Both vial and lighter, then, also went into the chute.

Dissatisfied but not able to come up with anything better, Cho returned to the glare of the waiting room and began to hum softly as he cleaned up the place. Let them make what they would of the remains of the goo. He knew now that he could patch into the internal computer and send out a recording of the high priestess leaving the lower chamber from a visit months ago, since, even though Cho didn't have the vaguest idea about such things, he knew where a terminal was—and Vulture clearly recognized the standard model and knew it well.

High priestess comes, high priestess leaves, goes on four-day trip to Wa Chi. Not unusual even in light of the Holy Lama's orders. There would be no one unusual or detectable inside the Sacred Lodge, where it mattered.

The male body Vulture now occupied was . . . sensual. Probably the most sensual Vulture had ever experienced. The mind was not particularly limited in intelligence or reasoning ability, any more than the female's had been, but it was culturally limited and intimidated by its own feelings of sensuality and inadequacy at being so small and weak compared to the women.

The males of Chanchuk, it appeared, were as dull and docile as they seemed mostly because of their physically and culturally induced inferiority complexes, fed by their lack of any real education and the impossibility of being more than they were. Only in the bedchamber and the nursery were they in any way dominant, and so it was in those roles that the Chanchukian male found refuge and security and ego, solaced only by a religion that stressed reincarnation as the truth path, the soul being both male and female.

It was a shame, really, but biology had played this cruel trick on them, and Master System had either created or imitated that. Still, it might be a lot of fun to explore this kind of body in general society, although Cho was now incapable of actually fathering anything. The sperm he would make would look and act correctly but would be bereft of that extra part the cells needed to keep pretending to be the real thing. They would quickly become nothing more than microscopic bits of the same goo, and then quickly dead. But he was unlikely to get to test it in normal society.

First he had to do a bit of computer doctoring, some-

thing that males would certainly never be expected to be
capable of doing. Then he would start his preparation, so
that when the time was right, the primary mission could
be fulfilled.

Satisfied that all was as reasonably correct as it could
be under the circumstances, Vulture put the signet ring
under his armpit and walked toward the Seed's quarters.
He would have to stash the ring someplace until, later on
and in private, he could remove the thin shell and reveal
what it really was.

Colonel Chi frowned. "So what is the foul-smelling
stuff? It smells like a decomposing body."

The SPF technical officer shrugged. "I have never
seen anything like it, and I'll have to send it up for full
computer analysis. It's definitely organic, but there is no
life left in it, I feel certain. Someone or something has
tried to burn it, but the fuel was not nearly enough to do
more than scorch an area on top and set off the fire sensors."

"Well, take no chances. No one touches it or even
approaches it except through remotes. Seal it and get it
up for complete analysis." Chi looked at it a moment.
"You know, if it weren't such a—mess—and weren't
flattened out so, it would have a fair amount of mass.
Almost as much as a real body...I wonder—could this
once have been alive?"

The tech shrugged again. "As you said, Colonel, it
seems to have the mass for it, but I know of nothing that
could do *this* to a body. Why bother? A disintegrator is
cleaner, a laser pistol or projectile weapon is less messy
if you need the body. Why even invent something that
would do this?"

Chi nodded. "Why, indeed? Unless it was because
you couldn't sneak a real and recognizable weapon past
our security system. Perhaps a catalyst. Some sort of

chemical agent that wouldn't show up in the screen.
There would be ways to do that, if you knew the limits of
the screening. Go—get on it! I want to know!"

"At once, Colonel," the tech responded, and began
supervising her staff in the recovery of the material.

Colonel Chi didn't like this, not one bit, and certainly
not coming right on the heels of the discovery of that
mysterious engine. As soon as she returned to security,
she stormed upstairs, not even taking the time to dry off,
and stormed into the Center security officer's cubicle.

"Where is the remote Center liaison?" she asked
crisply. "She went to see the Holy Lama at sixteen-thirty
and did not return."

The security officer sighed and checked her terminal.
"She is on her way to Wa Chi Center. The Holy Lama
ordered complete cooperation, Colonel, but we suspect
that the liaison had more—*proprietary* orders."

"Can you check and see if she actually left the Sacred
Lodge?"

"Huh? What? Well, we suppose so. She would have
had to pass the security sensors on the way out. Yes.
There is a record of it. Why?"

"I really don't know," the colonel answered honestly.
"Still, I want your best people to find her. She can't have
gotten too far. I want her located and brought back here
tonight. It is vital. I will make certain she makes her
appointment. Also, I want to talk to the regular guards
outside the Sacred Lodge entrance as soon as they can
be relieved."

"We will do what you say—but might one ask why?
It seems that you are acting as if her holiness is some
sort of traitor."

"No. I doubt that. I am not trying to call your sister
into question. Believe that. In fact, I may be her best
friend at this moment. You see, what I am seeking is
proof that the liaison, your sister, is still alive."

The security chief's eyes bulged. *"What?"*

By the time the first lab reports were coming in from the command ship, Colonel Chi was already forming a pattern. The problem was, she didn't have any idea what the pattern meant.

The guards at the entrance had a clear memory of the section chief entering and no recollection at all of her leaving. They considered this unusual but not impossible, of course, and in and of itself it wouldn't mean much. Various guards had to take air breaks every once in a while anyway, and that often left only one pair of eyes to see in both directions.

Most disturbing was the fact that there were entries in the various computer logs substantiating that exit. How had they gotten there? There was no direct input terminal to the master security computer net from inside the Sacred Lodge except in the Holy Lama's private offices. This indicated a possible involvement of the chief administrator, but even Chi couldn't bring herself to believe that the C.A., particularly this one, would be involved in overt treason. It was not only against her character, it was too stupid for one such as the leader of this world. If the object were to steal the ring and the Holy Lama had it and was in league with the thieves, a simple swap of a look-alike on a routine visit would have done it and no one would have been the wiser. No, it didn't make sense, but that only deepened the mystery.

Chi did not underestimate her enemy. They were clever and incredibly resourceful. She even had a real sense of admiration for anyone who could do what they did on Janipur and get away, not to mention fighting a brilliant space battle and dispatching several Vals—no mean feat when even the SPF had been taught that it was, while not impossible, very nearly so. Admiration and respect, however, did not mean that they were not still the enemy. It had been so long now since they'd been active that many commands had a false sense of security. Chi was one, along with her general, who believed that the space battle over Janipur's ring was costly to the pirates and that they had not so much quit as changed tactics. Now, clearly, that time had been well spent on Chanchuk setting up who knew what.

Security could not locate her holiness, but it was early yet and the routing wasn't clear. If, however, there was no further evidence of exit or her supposed trip by the middle of the night, Chi felt certain that the priestess would never be located.

A special read-only security circuit to the Sacred Lodge's internal computers clearly showed the priestess in the entry hall and going in for the audience, then leaving again. Master security showed an exit—or did it? She studied the pictures of the priestess's entry and exit. Any differences? Yes—but subtle. The backpack looked slightly different. But these were security records, not great art, and it might have been imagination. You couldn't blow them up to improve detail. It just got fuzzy. But such records for that very reason weren't all that hard to fake.

She dispatched a squad to pick up the housekeeper and maintenance people who shared a lodge with the missing priestess. No one was home and Chi was not really surprised at this. They took the lodge apart piece by piece but found nothing unusual—except that the taps on the lines in and out had been circumvented and different tapes were fed to the monitors rather than actual conversation. Not unusual in and of itself; Center personnel often pulled that sort of thing just to get some privacy. Again, though, it was yet another nail in the priestess's coffin. Chi ordered the lodge monitored and staked out although she felt certain that no one who had lived there would ever return to it.

The medical team on the base ship was less helpful than Chi had hoped.

"The material is decomposing rapidly. We have frozen some of it, of course, but it's impossible to do any real tests that way. The cellular structure is—unusual. It is as if the interior of each cell has simply collapsed, broken down. There isn't a piece of DNA, RNA, or any other useful combination left, although the fragments we have recovered do show what we can only call a consistent inconsistency."

Chi frowned. "Explain."

"We have been able to identify two separate patterns, as if these had been cells from two totally different individuals, yet they are intermixed and bound in the mass. We do not have enough to give you any real information on either master code, but it is as if you took two people and broke them down as if melting them into a single cellular mass. We have never seen anything like this, but if we were to try this the laboratory, the computers required would be enormous. Nor would we want to—not with a transmuter available."

"I see. But a transmuter wouldn't produce this effect? Say, if two people were transmitted down and got all jumbled up together."

"It would be possible to induce it, yes, but where is the transmuter? There is no way you could get the necessary machinery into that hall unobtrusively no matter how long you took, and even if we accept that someone did, there is certainly no way you could get the stuff back *out* of there or effectively hide or shield it from our own search in so short a time."

Chi nodded, knowing that this had been the conclusion of the computer systems as well. The bottom line was that anybody good enough to do that wouldn't have to do it.

The scenario was simple enough, if grotesque. On

Janipur they'd managed to snatch and switch one of the top security people in that Center and replace that person with a ringer—and it fooled every security safeguard in common use. That was certain. All right, assume that was the case with this priestess. With so long to work, it might have been done months, even years ago. A mole in the heart of this Center. All right—they had done it before, so it wasn't a fantastic idea.

Now what? The ring's on the Holy Lama. Can't snatch it when the C.A. is outside—too much security. You might snatch it but you'd never get away. But the C.A. is a cloistered monk—nobody who sees her day to day is ever allowed out, and no one is ever allowed in except under maximum security monitoring. The only one who could get close enough to the C.A. to steal that ring outside of normal internal security would be one of the permanent party. Not a monk—an insect queen!

She turned to her computer. "Comparison, in percentage. Total mass of the recovered organic substance against total estimated mass of the deputy administrator."

"Recovered mass is eighty-nine point three three percent of estimated mass of the subject," the computer responded.

Chi nodded. There would be some loss, certainly. Energy would be consumed, there would be free cells, and possibly a measure of decomposition of the outer area before they'd been able to get to the mass and stabilize it. All right.

Colonel Chi wasn't a scientist or any sort of technocrat, and she knew it sounded bizarre, but somehow, she was convinced against all of the computer's logic that she was right. Somehow these pirates had made a very big discovery, a kind that could shake the system to its foundations. No *wonder* they had managed to get so far! Some sort of biological or chemical agent, or some strange thing created by transmuter. It didn't matter to her how it was done. Somehow, they could become someone else. An exact duplicate—almost. And without further aid of any machinery at all. So one of them had become the priestess and learned all there was to learn and gained access to the Sacred Lodge. Access—but not the ability to steal the ring unobserved. So now, spooked by the discovery of the motor and the resultant knowledge that the pirates were at work here, they had moved —now! Before new precautions could be put in place! Now what had been the priestess was one of the Seed within the Sacred Lodge, with full run of the place and full access to the Holy Lama and the security system. The excess mass not needed in the transformation was the dying organic matter they had found.

And now what? Perhaps a switch of rings, or maybe even a theft, then wait for a new audience to be commanded. The next poor sucker walks in, gets escorted back, and in the hall there is another, smaller pool of goo. And the thief walks right out with the blessings of the guards past the best security net they could design!

Colonel Chi knew that she was right. She also knew that, without any proof that such a thing was possible, she would be considered mad not only by her subordinates and superiors in the SPF but by Master System itself. The mere idea that some escaped prisoners and freebooter refugees could do something Master System itself considered impossible would be tantamount to heresy. But it wouldn't help if this ring—her ring—was stolen, either, to be right and silent. It was a tricky problem—and the reason why this pirate scheme was so fiendishly clever.

Hell, I'm the boss here, she thought suddenly. I don't have to explain myself to anybody at this point.

She turned back to the special SPF channel. "This is Colonel Chi. Absolutely no one—repeat, no one—is to enter or leave the Sacred Lodge from this point on until I give the word. That includes anyone summoned there, regardless of rank, or any of our forces, or so much as a sea slug. No one in or out—including the Holy Lama. Then I want a full electronic and human ring, on the surface and below, around the Lodge and I want the same on any exit channel large enough for a *microbe* to get out. All trash, all garbage, is to be instantly and completely disintegrated by automated equipment independently programmed and under our exclusive control. I want our nastiest sentry robots in the automated areas. Seal all watertight doors and exits. Put the vacuum seal in place in the entry passage. The only communications channel in or out is to be routed directly to me and not through any locals or any subordinates. Understand?"

"As you command, Colonel," came the crisp reply. "May I ask why all this? I have to have it for my reports."

Always covering your sweet ass, aren't you, Wu? "I have evidence that an agent of the pirates is already inside the Sacred Lodge. It is speculative and circumstantial, but I believe on my authority as commander that we have no choice but to act as if it is real." *Think now. Everybody knows you can't transmute somebody twice.* "There is a possibility that this agent has coercive means to gain the cooperation or obedience of anyone inside, including the Holy Lama."

There was a pause, then: "Very well."

"Major? Check to see if there's any way we could get a nerve agent of some kind in there—either in the air or water or food—to knock them all completely cold."

Another pause. "It would be difficult and perhaps not a hundred percent effective, but I feel it is possible. The problem is, the place has its own internal security system that we can't tap. It's murylium-powered so we can't cut it out, and if activated, it's among the best."

Chi sighed. "Could we kill them, then? Be certain we killed every living thing in there no matter how big or how small?"

"Easier—but, Colonel, if you do that you will kill the spiritual leader of this world and everyone, male as well as female, who could create the children to replace her. None of her own children are yet old enough to be outside. The oldest is barely six. You would turn this entire peaceful and basically loyal population violently against us and against everything we stand for. Something of that magnitude would require the direct order of Master System, and you know it."

The major, of course, was right. Chi wanted to be a general, not a heretic and maniac. "Very well. Do what you can and make certain nothing gets in or out, period. *Nothing.* And I want all human guards paired at all times. Not for a moment is anyone to be left alone. We have at least three other missing agents around and they definitely have transmuter access. You understand me? I don't want any of our people switched. If I can't get in to the agent, at least, he, she, or it can't get out and can't get the ring out. Sooner or later a deal will have to be made or they'll remain here until they rot."

The colonel signed off and leaned back in her contoured chair. All right, you pirates. You're very good at playing the system against me, she thought firmly. But you won't succeed. I know your little unbelievable secret. And I need hold you for only five days. In five days I will have sufficient force behind me that you could not escape without a fight more disastrous by far than Janipur, and possibly not even then. And in five days I'll have you all out of that Sacred Lodge, immobilized, and in stasis—completely isolated. And if you remain behind, you will die. If you do not, then you will be in an SPF control lab where we'll find which one of them you are.

* * *

"Something has gone wrong. I can feel it," Min commented nervously. "They have the Sacred Lodge sealed off and the SPF has taken total and exclusive command of all Center security. They *know*. I tell you, they *know*."

Butar Killomen shook her head. "No. They *suspect*, which is quite a different thing. The Vulture is inside, that is all that matters at the moment. Our job is to get the ring and get safely away. Vulture has prepared for a number of contingencies, and this plan has been checked and rechecked by our best minds and best computers. It is the only way to do it, and no matter how strong the enemy seems to be, it is his own system we use against him. This Colonel Chi is good—better than any Val we have met. She has both guts and imagination, a dangerous combination in an adversary. The only question we can concern ourselves with is whether or not we can still get the ring through the increased security cordon. Well?" She stared at Min and Chung.

"If the equipment works, we should have several minutes," Chung responded nervously. "If the computer analysis of their response time is near accurate, at least ten. We have been operating entirely on that window. I feel I can control the exterior—if all goes well with Vulture inside."

"There will not be two chances," Killomen reminded them. "If we fail this time, the three of us will be useless. It *must* work!"

She had tried hard not to think of the possibility of failure, but it wasn't an easy thing to do. This was so complex, and if just one thing went wrong, it would all be for nothing. She did not like this body in which she knew she would be spending the rest of her life, and all the mindprinting in the universe couldn't help that. She had been born to a race that was large and physically tough, both the men and the women. She could get over

being covered with hair, and swimming was something of
a thrill—her native race had no mobility in the water at
all—but she felt *ugly,* ugly and also so very . . . fragile.
She knew she'd always seemed somewhat monstrous to
others of different races, but never to herself. The transmuter transformation had been, to her, a severe sacrifice, but one she had felt she couldn't refuse. Not after
so many of the others had allowed themselves to be
turned into far worse.

It had been just as hard, if not harder, on Min and
Chung. She knew that, although it didn't help that she
had company. They had been Earth-humans, as far from
this form and life as hers, but they had also been males
from a social tradition that prized masculinity and detested its opposite. She at least had been born female
and had spent many years as a part of an all-female crew.
Part of it had been mental protection—all the members
of the *Kaotan* crew had been of different races and each
had been, as far as they knew, the only one of their race
to escape their home worlds. Far better for mental health
to be in the company of women who, however different
from one another physically, could understand the problems of the others; in particular, how hard it was to see
men and women of other races relating to one another,
interacting, even occasionally bonding and having off-
spring. When there were others who were also the sole
representatives of their species, at least there was some
solace.

Now the old crew was broken up; only two were left
in their natural forms, and who knew how long *that*
would last? She was stuck now, and the old times, the
old independence, were gone forever. Win or lose, this
one operation was her last moment, her final purpose.
After this they would just be a bunch of fragile water
creatures out of their element and unable even to pro-
create due to the lack of a male.

She still dreamed of a little love, a little romance, but the man of her dreams was of a shape and form that would crush her in the first embrace. She often wondered, but never asked, if Min and Chung had their own fantasies. If so, it must be infinitely worse not only to be the wrong race but the wrong sex for the one of such dreams.

This had better work. The cost was already too high.

It was a world where you not only never had to grow up, you weren't expected to. The quarters of the Seed included the most elaborate multilevel swimming pool complex Vulture had ever seen, complete with hewn water slides and many other playthings. There were lots of games and toys available, and elaborate facilities for playing dress-up, and the males took full advantage of all of it.

Most of the cleaning and maintenance was automated; meals were of the dial-in kind using a transmuter, a system not found elsewhere to his knowledge on Chanchuk, but standard on large spaceships and in other confined areas. Food was chosen by pushing the selector until the picture of the meal or snack or whatever you wanted came up in the window, then pressing the select button. About two minutes later it was there, transmuted from waste products or, if they weren't available, from common seawater.

And there were drugs, too. Drugs to make the Seed feel wonderful, or bring him down; give him energy or let him sleep like a rock. Drugs to aid in meditation and prayer, and drugs to induce feelings of general well-being when the boredom got to be too much.

And there was a considerable amount of homosexual activity, something considered neither aberrant nor odd in a society where the sexes were so completely different and differentiated physically and socially. This was true among the general population as well, females as well as males, although for the females it tended to be less physical. Chanchukian females only really wanted sex during their five-day ovulation period; the rest of the time they had no real sexual drive at all. Males, on the other hand, seemed to be turned on by the slightest things, and it was easier to note the brief periods in each day when they weren't excited than the bulk of the time when they were.

They were remarkably ignorant, even of their own world. They had no idea that the world was round or large, or how many people there were or how they lived. For those who served a spiritual leader of sorts, they didn't even know or understand anything about that faith except some very vague meditation and prayer rituals. The reason for this last was obvious: the Holy Lama was close to being deified by her people. If the Seed lived with her and around her and saw her basic humanity, they might lose more faith than they gained, and if they believed in her as something more than their mistress and lover, they might have problems performing their holy sexual duties.

There *were* more mundane duties, though—even a sort of routine. The Holy Lama was, after all, only interested in their bodies a few days each month, and not at all while pregnant, and she needed various kinds of service. The Seed made up her bed and rooms and served her her meals and cleaned away the trays. They acted as hosts for occasional visitors, and, most of all, they watched over and helped the young new crop of kids they helped bring about. They did everything from nursing them to changing them, and Vulture was surprised to discover that the young of Chanchuk had to be taught how to swim, develop the reflexes for holding their breath, and even how to see and act underwater. Females and males looked much the same until they were more than five years old; then distinct sexual and growth differences developed and accelerated. At that point the girls would be sent away to be brought up in various lamaseries connected to Centers around the world. All were raised as if they all were to be the next Holy Lama, for one of them surely would be. In their remote locations, they would be trained in both spiritual and secular skills well into adulthood, until their mother died and a new Holy Lama was selected by the priestesses. Then the rest would be neutered and become apprenticed to the Centers and lamaseries for jobs like the liaison's.

The males would be raised to puberty within the Seed's harem, after which they would be distributed among the ranking family hierarchies of the Centers of Chanchuk, thus giving the secular rulers a claim to spiritual relationship beyond that of the masses.

To Vulture, the primary problem was stealing the ring.

During a sexual encounter would be the best, of course, but he couldn't rely on that chance, and he certainly couldn't expect the key period he planned to be inside to coincide with the Holy Lama's unknown reproductive cycle. Hell, she might even be pregnant. No, in this case a certain amount of outside help was cruder, but far more effective.

It took him some time to realize that his greatest problem in the wait was in knowing what time it was. There were no clocks about, and not much need for the Seed to have them. This meant he had to force himself awake through mental discipline for two nights running to check the automated cleaning and maintenance cycle against the system security clock to be certain he could tell the time when he had to without any watches or clocks. All that without awakening any of his fellow Seed.

And, far more quickly than it seemed, it was the evening of his fourth day inside.

* * *

"Colonel, it is a violation of everything we have sworn to live by to keep us here incommunicado," the Holy Lama protested. "I stand on my rights, not as spiritual leader to our people but as chief administrator of Chanchuk. I demand to know at once the full and complete reasons for these actions and I demand my right to appeal directly to an agent of Master System."

That would mean at least a Val, if not a direct link. Chi was fully conscious of the severity of what she was doing.

"Madam, you have an agent inside your lodge. A pirate."

"Indeed? And when has invisibility been perfected?" the prelate retorted sarcastically.

"Not invisible. A shape changer. It entered in the form of your sister. I am convinced that it did not leave but rather became another, a duplicate, of one it dispatched."

"You are mad, Colonel! Such a thing is impossible!"

Chi shrugged. "I know what is, not what is impossible. I have no idea whether it is a scientific breakthrough or some alien form of life in alliance with the pirates, but I am convinced it is real. When the Vals arrive along with the task force, I will undoubtedly be arrested, and I will be subjected to a mindprint and probe. They will have the same reaction as you, but they will see how and why I came to those conclusions and they will act. They will act because they cannot afford to accept even the minuscule possibility that I am correct. I am sure, under the proper conditions, we can unmask this impostor no matter how perfect it is and neutralize it. And when that happens I will go from being a mad woman under restraint to being acclaimed as the most brilliant tactical security strategist in history. Only another thirty hours, madam, and we shall see who is insane."

The Holy Lama gave up and switched off, but then she began to think about it. Suppose this officer were right? Technological breakthrough—ridiculous! But alien life, now that made a certain kind of sense. And if Colonel Chi was correct, and there was no one missing inside the Sacred Lodge, then there was only one person it could be.

She turned and punched her intercom. "Cho, your presence is required—*now*." She never used a tone like that unless it was something vital. She knew Cho would come on the run, and he did.

Standing there, looking at him, someone she'd known ever since coming here after her investiture by the Council, someone she'd had sex with, even—it was nearly impossible to believe. Everything was just so absolutely *right*.

"Cho—you know there are people over us, people who run things even beyond our own power and control?"

The little man looked confused. "Yes, ma'am. I suppose so. You mean the gods?"

"Don't act so stupid in front of us!" she snapped. "We know you are brighter than that and have been around here many years. You may never have directly seen them, but you know what security is."

Cho seemed to be quaking slightly. "Yes, ma'am. Sorry, ma'am."

"They have just used their authority to remove us from power, to make us prisoners here in our own lodge. They say it is because an alien being is in here, not of Chanchuk or the People at all but merely masquerading as one. Tomorrow they will pump some sort of gas in here and come in with machines, carrying weapons and cages, and they will take us away. Until then, anyone who tries to get in or out of here will be vaporized. You know what that means? Reduced to nothing. What do you think of that?"

"These matters are not for a poor Seed, ma'am," Cho responded. "I do not understand all this."

The Holy Lama stared at him as if looking not through but inside of him. It was a disquieting, discomforting feeling.

"Yes, I believe you *do* understand," she responded, sounding a bit surprised. "We have always liked you, Cho. You've been the bright one, the clever one, yet very loyal. We believe, for the sake of ourselves and our world, you deserve to rise to the next level of incarnation."

"Ma'am?" Startled, he started to take a step forward, but she raised a hand and stopped him.

"Do not approach us! We may be insulated, but we are not defenseless. You may meditate on this where you are as long as you like, but in the end it is the end. Only if you give us some compelling reason not to will we fail to send you out to security's waiting weaponry." A hand went below her recliner and pulled out a very shiny and new-looking Mark IX needler. It was unexpected. Who would have guessed she would have a weapon of her own in here, let alone know how to use it? Why would she? But the fact was she did.

"This will knock you out, although we could kill you with it without much change in settings. When we desire, we will fire it, then summon some of the maintenance robots to haul your limp form out to Colonel Chi. We preach infinite patience, it is true, but we do not believe that in this case we will wait very long."

Vulture was caught completely off guard. First he'd misjudged Chi, mistaking the martinet image and crudeness of manner for the real officer and not recognizing a first-rate mind behind the mask. Now he'd mistaken a first-rate C.A. for a head-in-the-clouds pious mystic. She didn't believe Chi, that was clear, but for the restoration of her communications links and authority and to get rid of the SPF presence she was sure willing to sacrifice Cho. It was time to give her a surprise in return.

"That little thing would not bother me," he responded in a cold yet casual tone, a tone unlike that ever used by any male of Chanchuk. The sudden change in him startled the Holy Lama; there was a sudden spirit there, a sudden hard fire inside that tiny body, a cocky sense of power and control. It frightened her more than anything ever had in her entire life.

"Then it is true." She sighed.

"Whatever Chi has guessed is probably essentially true," Vulture admitted. "By the way—I notice your thumb just pushed the Mark IX up to kill. I wouldn't bother. It would cause me pain for a moment but otherwise wouldn't bother me much, and I am used to pain. And I have no desire to take you over the way I did Cho, even though such a thing would probably provide me with great wisdom and skills beyond my own understanding. I learned much from your sister, but it can be only a shadow of what you know, and you are still growing in this position. I would hate to have to deprive Chanchuk of you."

The sheer confidence and total disregard for any threat to him, as if *he* held a gun on *her*, was perhaps equally as unnerving as being faced with the sheer fact of his existence.

"What are you?" she asked him.

"I am called the Vulture. The name is that of a predatory bird of old Earth that eats carrion, although I do not. Who I eat, I become, and all that they were stays with me. I and my associates have worked for a year to be in more or less this position. I come for the ring."

"Why not just take it, then, if you are as powerful as you say?"

"I intended to. But, as you point out, there is a matter of escape that is more than a little bit tricky. Something is planned, in the immediate future, that will allow me to liberate the ring and pass it to my associates. Then we will wait for the colonel and her probes."

"Then they will unmask you and have you."

He shook his head. "No. The colonel is creative, even imaginative. You saw the conviction in her and you saw the alien within me. Their superiors, however, are technocrats, and their masters are machines. They believe in what can be quantified and measured. If they want blood, I can create whatever is required for their machines. If they probe my brain, they will find only Cho there. If they try their chemical drugs, then they will still not find me. Sooner or later they will have to conclude that Chi was wrong. They will send me back, and I will feed and walk out as someone else. It's as simple as that."

"And you admit this to me? This session is being recorded."

"If necessary, that can be fixed. You know it and I know it. You do it all the time before the required semi-annual Master System mindprint and retreat at Qonjin Monastery in the north. They all do it. You have a mind-printer here somewhere to do the fine tuning, I suspect."

"None is necessary, as you should know if you were my sister as you claim. The Five Levels of Kwanji are more than a match for any of their silly machines. What will you do now?"

"Nothing. If you force the issue, I will, of course, have to deal with you, and that will make things ugly. Nine Seed were here before, nine Seed should be here at the end. But I'll manage. I am designed to survive. That is my number-one ability. Somewhere in your own mind is another way out. No chief administrator I ever heard of didn't have all the contingencies covered that they could cover, and I'm sure isolation and entrapment here is one such contingency. What happens next is up to you."

"Who do you work for? And why is this ring so important?"

"If the Five Levels can disguise the rest they should disguise this. If not, no matter how cooperative you are, you will either die or have your mind erased. My group calls itself the pirates of the *Thunder*. The *Thunder* is our base ship. We are refugees, many from old Earth, freebooters and opportunists now wanted by Master System. The ring, together with its four mates, contains a code that will shut Master System down cold. Yours is the third, and we are in league with the possessor of a fourth. We mean to shut this system down. Many brave human beings have died for this cause already, innocent and guilty alike, while others have undergone mental and emotional changes that no person should be asked to endure. Still others have voluntarily turned themselves into what they see as monsters in this one cause. The system is mad, and it is only a matter of time until it eliminates humanity as we know it. Humanity created it. Humanity can and must destroy it first."

The Holy Lama had not put down the gun, but she listened intently, staring at him the whole time. Finally she asked, "And what, considering all this, would you wish us to do now?"

"Nothing," he responded. "Just forget it. Wipe it off the recording and then wipe it from your mind so thoroughly that even Master System itself could not find it. If you have a probe and printer around, I'd use it. They will go much deeper than usual this time, searching for me. The other contingencies have been taken care of."

"There is a huge force coming. A task force. Thirty hours, no more, the colonel said."

"If they find nothing, then the colonel is imaginative —and wrong. All, save myself, the ring included, will be long gone."

The Holy Lama sighed and put down the gun. "Just do nothing, you say?"

Vulture nodded. "We have it all mapped out—I hope. And we will give the colonel another bogeyman to chase."

Hard nails drummed on the desk top. "Do you need anything else from us?"

"As a matter of fact, it would help greatly if I could borrow a watch."

3. FOUR PARROTS AND ONE GOOSE COOKED, WITH FIREWORKS

THE TEMPLE COMPLEX THAT WAS ALSO WA CHI Center had a far different look to it on the surface; a series of large domes, some atop thick cylindrical bases, stretched out starting about fifty meters from shore. Most were polished, waterproofed wood, ornately carved and trimmed in silver and gold, although there was some polished stone and slate and atop the domes an assortment of stained glass skylights showing religious or ethical themes. Only a few lights showed through; it was essential that the primitive mass of the population should not suspect the existence of the technological wonders that the elite running their world took for granted, even by accident. Water approach was secure, but Chanchukians often were both curious and creative and were not above occasional land forays to see what they could see, and while Wa Chi was sacred ground, forbidden to the masses, it was so eerily impressive above the water that many made pilgrimages just to look upon it.

The coast itself was a black sand beach cut into a wide cleft in the rock; around it the coastal range rose fifteen hundred meters, the first five hundred or so in a craggy basalt rock wall.

The beach was used primarily for recreation and sunning oneself on hot days. Although it was often convenient to bring boats in there, supplies were landed elsewhere. Flat coastal barges were fairly common over the world and so wouldn't attract any attention. They were powered by oar and sail and often by crews pushing from beneath, guided by a helmsman above who could stomp out commands to the "pushers."

Every night a thick fog rolled in, covering the domes of the lodges and the beach area, making things miserable for anyone foolish enough to be out in it. Security used a sophisticated radar to sweep the area at those times, and special infrared goggles to see through even the densest fog.

Without the SPF present, this would have been a piece of cake, but now the raiders had to resort to a mixture of the crude and the creative to achieve their end. The crude was first; the SPF had set up a low, horizon-sweep air radar on top of the mountain overlooking the Center to supplement the surface patrols that were normally run from Wa Chi's security central. It gave some protection against low-flying aircraft should any potential enemy use them, but it was a weak point spotted early by the team.

The small radar station was automated and transmitted directly to security central and also to the SPF command ship via satellite. Monitoring there, too, was totally automated, designed to ring an alarm if anything unusual was spotted. Colonel Chi, however, mindful that the pirates in the past had shown a remarkable talent for beating electronic locks, also had two enlisted personnel fully armed stationed at the radar unit at all times, in six-hour shifts.

Min Xao Po watched the guard change at two hundred hours through her own special night goggles, then waited until the old guards wearily put on their flight packs and jumped off the cliff to float down to the beach below. She allowed them fifteen minutes to be on the beach and in the water, well away from any trouble and unable to return quickly, then took aim on the two new guards and shot them down before they knew what hit them. The weapon fired a high stun, rather than a killing beam, since the guards wore automatic life sensors that would have brought a fast investigation if either had died.

Hurrying to the fallen guards, she removed from a pouch a small medical injector, already loaded with serum, and gave each guard a shot in the arm. It would guarantee that they would sleep until relieved, by which time this would be long over.

The Chows, born wizards with all sorts of locks, had looked at the analytical photos of the lock on the radar unit and solved it in a flash. It was pretty crude, but it did have a few nasty little booby traps for the unwary or ignorant. The combination wasn't much of a problem; Vulture had tapped that line long ago.

Carefully Min placed a device measuring about half a meter square over the locking mechanism, securing it with clamps to the small cubicle, then activated it with the press of a button. There was a lot of loud clicking and a whine and then a light began blinking on the device signaling that the door was unlocked. She removed the device but did not immediately unlock the door. Instead she climbed up on the top of the cubicle to the antenna complex, found the set she wanted, removed another small box, and attached it between two smaller antennas and then lifted up a second set of antennas almost the same size as those on the cubicle. Two cables were attached to terminals on the box, and then, stretching, she fastened the huge alligator clips on the other end of the cables simultaneously to the two fixed antennas. She then scurried back down to the ground and waited nearly five minutes to make certain that no activity could be heard from below.

Satisfied, she nodded to herself and opened the door. A bell alarm sounded, but it was muffled beyond the immediate area by the sound of the surf and wasn't intended to do more than alert the guards. The same alarm was now being transmitted to security central and should have brought a horde of troopers armed to the teeth, but the signal was now not being broadcast by the twin original antennas to the receivers below, but rather being fed directly into her little box, which filtered out all the nasty, unpleasant things like alarms and then sent the rest of the signal unaltered. With the simple press of a button on a remote control on her belt, she could stop even that and send whatever signal she wanted.

Her entry would be recorded and what she was doing would later be plain to investigators, but she didn't have the time to dig into complex built-in monitor circuits nor did she want to risk tripping secondary alarms. Let them find out—as long as it was later. By now all three of them were almost certainly on Colonel Chi's wanted list simply by being absent from home for four days, and she had no intention of being anywhere near Chanchuk by the time the recordings were viewed.

She was relieved to find the unit a stock SPF issue as expected. She had nightmares of having to face a totally different design from what she'd been mindprinted to handle. Bless the military mind! Within minutes she had done her work, and from this point you could have brought *Thunder* in hovering over Wa Chi Center and the screens and monitors both at the Center and on the command ship would show empty, peaceful space. Of course, the orbital and deep-space monitors were still operable, but those were not a concern at the moment.

It went perfectly. The only thing they hadn't anticipated was the headache that damned alarm gave her, bouncing around in that confined space.

She emerged, closed the door, and got some blessed silence. Since there were no alarms sounding near or far now and no armed squads and since she was still conscious and free, she took the liberty of assuming that their estimate of Min Xao Po as a brilliant communications technician had not been misplaced. She picked up a small waterproof transceiver from her pack and lifted it to her mouth.

"Secure One. Proceeding to level two." She secured her own floater device, picked up the bulky pack, and jumped off the cliff.

Allowing themselves the time not merely to scout out but to analyze the entire problem with the *Thunder*'s computer and personnel and then taking the additional time and patience to slowly infiltrate in the exact equipment needed was paying off.

Now, aboard a coastal raft, Chung Mung Wo was getting her own equipment in shape. The raft was a regular; it was expected in these waters between midnight and dawn out on the fringes of the security zone, just out of the fog area. Being subject to all sorts of delays, it wasn't unusual to have it show up on the surface sweeps at any hour of the early morning—and often later—and, because it wasn't a Center craft but a native one running between two native villages sixty or so kilometers south of the Center and ninety kilometers north of it, there was really no way security personnel could determine if it was truly the correct raft or not. There would be no way of knowing that the old helmsman had somehow gotten

herself dead drunk down in Warung and hadn't even so-
bered up enough to leave town as yet.

Chung checked her console, deployed the aerial and
underwater transmitters, and began to crank up the juice
a bit. "Nice static electricity tonight," she mumbled to
herself. "Couldn't be better. That fog is energizing almost too well." She looked at her watch. "Have to bring
it up slowly. We want the fireworks on schedule."

Forward, Butar Killomen, the leader of this meager
but well-armed attack force, checked her own control
console. This was the one area she was most nervous
about, since there had been no way to test this equipment except with computer simulations. She had some
faith in simulations, but she was an old spacer. Computers could answer only the questions you asked them
in the first place, and there was no substitute for actual
experience. The very air was starting to crackle all
around them.

Around the Sacred Lodge, the surface guards, in pairs
on small platforms and within sight of one another even
through the fog, began to get disturbed.

"Must be a storm coming up," one remarked to her
companion. "I don't remember there being one on the
weather plots, but the electricity in the air tonight's so
high I'm blind with these damned goggles on. It's short-
ing out everything."

Her companion nodded. "I'm worried. If it gets much
worse than this we'll get shocks every time we touch
anything. You get too high a charge, I heard that these
damned rifles'll discharge all at once. I sure don't want
to be holdin' one that does."

"That's for sure." The other nodded. "Look, I'm
gonna call this in. Anybody tries anything in this shit is
gonna be in the same shape we're in. Besides, this whole
watch is screwy anyway. What are they gonna do? Bomb
us?"

She unclipped her communicator. The static on it was almost unendurable in and of itself. "This is Corporal Gwi, Post Three. We have prestorm conditions up here and high static. Visibility is zero even with the goggles, and we are starting to get equipment malfunction."

In about two minutes there was a loud splash and the sergeant of the guard popped up and looked around in the water below. She shouted the password, then did a survey. "You're right. It's lousy tonight. I'll call the OD."

The officer of the day appreciated the conditions, but also reflected that it was just the sort of night that she'd choose to try something. It was certain that the guards were in more danger from their own equipment than any help in fending off an attack. Still, she didn't like to make any major decisions that might haunt her. She called Colonel Chi in her quarters.

Chi, awakened from a sound sleep, was in a foul mood, but listened intently. "Check with the command ship for weather data, then check space, air, surface, and subsurface scanners. If nothing shows up, have them come below until conditions clear—but they go back up the moment conditions clear, understand?"

"Yes, Colonel." The OD called the command ship. "Anything unusual on your scopes?"

"Nothing at all, Captain. We're measuring a local disturbance in your area, though."

"Anything unusual about it?"

"Well, meteorology can't give a good reason for it, but we've seen this sort of thing a couple of times before. It's rare, but it happens. Space monitors are clear, and the aerial scan shows only your disturbance. I wouldn't worry about it."

"Thank you." The OD turned to her sergeant. "Check all surface and subsurface monitors."

"Already did, Captain. Nothing subsurface, but we've got enough stuff there that anyone'd be crazy to try anything. Air is a mess. With all that static and the discharge from the storm, it looks like we're being invaded, but the monitoring computers don't seem to be worried. You know they could pick a bird out of that mess anyway, 'cause the echoes from the storm are constantly changing in random patterns. Anything solid would be regular. I'd say it's clear."

She nodded. "Very well. Send the sergeant of the guard a stand-down for surface personnel until, in the assessment of this or higher authority or the sergeant of the guard on the scene, conditions should improve to a safe level. Got it?"

"Got it. Sending now."

Butar Killomen looked at her watch. It was time. She turned and shouted back to Chung. "Let's do it!"

Chung nodded and brought up the charge to near storm levels. Her console was getting hot, but it didn't have to last all that long anyway and, besides, enough energy had been dumped into that fog ˍank now that it had a life of its own. Already there was   good deal of lightning, and even from their distance the boom of thunder reached them with increasing frequency. It was quite a nice fireworks show, if Chung did say so herself.

Butar Killomen put on the command helmet and sat back in her makeshift recliner. The drone was already powered up; now she was in complete command of it, and it was a mess. There was certainly a lot of noise in the interface connection, more as the small drone lifted off like some great bird of prey and slid into the night, even though the special frequencies they were using were supposed to insulate the electronics and the intense lightning and the sudden updrafts and downdrafts caused by the storm were hard to handle. These were not the kind of conditions for an amateur pilot, and the tiny computer brain in the drone was hardly adequate by itself to handle these conditions. The problem was, any radar-type scan to maintain distance and pick out targets that would be useful to them would also be useful to the SPF; by knocking out the SPF, they knew they'd be flying by the seat-of-the-pants method, and that required great skill. Butar only hoped she wasn't too out of practice.

The visuals were awful; there was so much energy around that the sensors were filled with garbage, and she concentrated hard to separate the real from the unreal and keep everything just so. *There!* Ease over, careful, careful, you did this in your mind a thousand times blind . . .

The drone, barely three meters long by two across, settled onto one of the guard perches and then locked itself onto the polished wooden dome of the Sacred Lodge itself. A small drill extended from beneath and bored a tiny hole through the more than twenty centimeters of wood wall with nearly silent efficiency. There was a problem when the required depth was reached; there was no indication that the tip of the drill was through. Worried, she continued on, but it was another ten centimeters, almost the length of the drill, before she broke free. She guessed she'd drilled through a case or an ornamental work, but it didn't matter what.

Next the drill was retracted and a small hose inserted. She had a tense moment when she realized that the hose was only thirty centimeters—perhaps a fraction short—and cursed herself for not thinking of this eventuality, but it was close enough. A centimeter was a very tiny distance and the ejection would be under pressure.

Almost immediately the tanks switched on and began pumping a high volume of the colorless, odorless neurotoxin into the Sacred Lodge. She guessed it was going in in the vicinity of the entry hall, but it didn't really matter. The way the interior climate control worked, the stuff would be all over the place inside of six anxious minutes, and it only took about two parts per billion to paralyze anyone breathing it in.

Now, if no busybody popped up at that point and spotted the probe, and if Vulture was ready for the gas, could neutralize it, switch the rings, and then find where the opening was, all within a very short period of time, they just might make it.

This was certainly the toughest one yet, from a technical point of view. Part of the problem had been access to the inside of the Sacred Lodge, which was difficult even *with* Vulture, and part had been circumventing the security system. There was, however, one security system they could not circumvent because they didn't really know it or its capabilities. Nobody really did. That was the internal one inside the Sacred Lodge, beyond even Center's security control. You could tamper with the monitors and records, those things that had been designed for human interfacing, but not the mechanical guard devices. Those operated automatically whenever the Holy Lama was awake, and the only thing the raiders could guess about the devices was that they were formidable. Clayben had been insistent that their plans take the worst-case approach toward the security system even though it might be less efficient than they feared, and that was as it had to be.

There was no way to get Vulture out of there without blowing a fairly large and hardly unobtrusive hole in the dome and almost certainly triggering all sorts of alarms. The windows and tempting skylight in the Holy Lama's office were connected to the internal system as well as audible external alarms. They might still have gotten Vulture out, but the odds of a successful getaway after were practically nil. No, success depended on stealing the ring separately and letting Vulture rely on his unique talents to escape at a later time. Nor could they count on Vulture simply becoming the Holy Lama. Not only would the best security system be keyed on both her and the ring, but she could not exit without always being in a crowd. Vulture was hard to kill, but mortal all the same.

Vulture, of course, had already practiced with the specific neurotoxin used, neutralizing it in no time with his absolute cellular control. Awake and waiting, his body and mind sensed the danger at once and moved to combat it. The process was simple but not automatic. He'd been caught unawares by such substances before, but this was different, it was expected and almost on schedule.

The other Seed slept on like corpses. Even if they'd suddenly awakened, they could not have so much as opened their eyes, although their autonomic systems continued to function in a reduced but not harmful manner. Vulture got up, went out into the meditation chamber, and retrieved the duplicate ring from behind a statue of the sacred Buddha. Then he headed for the Holy Lama's bedchambers.

He stopped and stifled a grin as he saw her in bed, and had to suppress an urge to take advantage of the situation. That was the Chanchukian male part of him, something he could control as easily as the neurotoxin but which took more constant vigilance. She'd actually taken off the ring and put it on her nightstand! He wasted a precious second to lift and look at her finger. The hair had been virtually worn away by the ring and there was some scabbing where it had been. She must have had one *hell* of a time getting the damned thing off!

Peeling away the disguise layer on the ring he'd brought, he turned it from a high priestess's signet into a near duplicate of the ring on the nightstand. It wasn't perfect, but they'd been able to work from blown-up pictures of the Holy Lama's rare public appearances taken from the computer files at security. However, when not side by side they sure as hell looked identical.

For a moment he had a sudden fear as he momentarily forgot which was the real one and which the fake. After all this it sure as hell wouldn't do to steal and send the counterfeit back! With some relief, he saw a tiny bit of the foil from the outer wrapping of the disguise still clinging to the back of the fake ring. He scraped it away, inspected it, then put it down on the nightstand.

Time was precious. He had timed this operation at no more than twenty minutes. The storm outside sounded pretty bad, but the SPF was certain to keep popping up to check on it firsthand. Every minute that drone was atop the dome was one minute more it could be spotted and an alarm sounded that would queer the whole deal.

Now the problem was to find the damned opening, not much bigger around than the ring itself, and do it as quickly as possible.

By now the pumps on the drone would have reversed, and the suction would create a strong airflow outward rather than in. With that in mind, he found some papers and a match and lit them, watching the smoke, then tried to follow it before he burned his hand. Since he knew that it would be at one of the six guard positions, if all went as planned, that narrowed down his search some, and he found the proper location with little trouble. Finding and then getting to the probe was more difficult. It had come into the library, and it appeared to have drilled its way right through a bookcase wall about three meters up—or about three times his height. A chair might have helped, but Chanchukians didn't use chairs—they were built for a different sort of furniture and tended in any event to have seating areas rather low to the floor.

Feeling the seconds tick away, he thought frantically about how to reach the probe, cursing that the whole elaborate scheme might now fall apart because he was too short or the hole was too high. He finally started stacking the largest books he could find one atop the other, some so heavy he had problems with them, then climbing on top. It was just out of reach, and he stretched his arm to the limit on the high, hastily built stack, the ring held in his outstretched fingers, and didn't quite make it several times. Finally, though, he felt it suddenly taken from his grasp, but he looked in horror as he saw the ring jam up just inside the hole. The probe hadn't quite reached through, and the wood was chewed up!

Summoning all his strength and concentration, he leaped up and smacked the ring hard with his hand, then fell crashing to the floor, his tower of books in shambles. He was bruised and battered, and nearly broke his neck in the fall. Only the fact that, being the creature that he was, that sort of damage wouldn't really harm him saved him from a rather obvious hospital call.

He looked up at the opening. He couldn't see the ring, but he wasn't certain if it had fallen down or been sucked in or, if sucked in, if it had made it to the tube and been hauled into the probe. He looked around the floor, saw no sign of it, and decided that there was simply nothing more he could do. He would require a few minutes of concentration to repair his bruises and sprains, and then he could only attempt to pick up and reshelve the books and get back to his quarters.

At least the suction, which had been audible in the library, now seemed to be gone. Whether that was because the ring was lodged in the hole or safely inside the probe he wouldn't know, perhaps for some time, but even if it was lodged it was not a total loss. He alone would know it was there, and it would be easier at some point to retrieve it from that spot than to steal it all over again.

Outside, the sergeant of the guard broke the surface and looked around. The weather was still awful, and the wind was picking up, but she frowned, not quite certain why it didn't seem right. Something, some sound—no, it was gone now, but its very absence made her more suspicious.

Suddenly conscious of the fact that, if there were intruders out there, she was in a pretty weak and exposed position, she ducked back under. Now was the time to retrieve the guards, lousy conditions or not, and do a thorough check of the exterior!

The probe switched from vacuum tube back to the borer, only now a different mechanism was activated. The effect was to plug the hole with the same material taken from it. It wouldn't be perfect, but it would be far less noticeable. That done, Killomen attempted a sweep of the immediate area but found the weather conditions impossible. The false echoes were everywhere, blanketing the screen. She decided that enough was enough, detached the clamps, and slowly eased the probe up to a height perhaps twenty meters over the roofs of the lodges, then began bringing it bumpily back to the barge.

The sensors in the extension mechanism of the drone weren't all that much; she knew she had grasped something, but she wasn't certain what or where or if it had gotten inside the drone. That would have to wait for its return and inspection.

It had been audacious, risky, and complicated as all hell—that last being the best guarantee of something going wrong. The fact that they'd gotten away with it even this far was, to Killomen, nothing short of miraculous.

She brought the drone back down to the deck of the barge, drew the tarp over it so that no SPF spy satellite might see anything unusual if it should happen to look, then crawled under. The drone was still warm from its long flight, but she wanted no suspense that wasn't necessary. The lock to the storage compartment was easily accessible, and she opened it and reached inside.

There was nothing in the compartment.

Damn! All this for nothing . . .

She calmed down a moment and thought. The lone sensor had indicated that the vacuum tube had picked up something. If it wasn't in the compartment, it might well have fallen out when withdrawn, in which case it was either on the platform or on the bottom at the foundation of the Sacred Lodge. There was only one other place to look before assuming the worst . . .

She went back to the command console and extended the suction tube, then killed the power and crawled back under. With all the strength she could muster she pulled and tugged at the tube, then finally got a knife, reached in, and cut the damned thing off at its base plate. After bringing out the tube, she felt along it and found, not very far from the opening, a lump.

"Chung! I need very small pliers or a screwdriver or something that'll cut this material down the side!" she shouted. "We've picked up something—but I'm not sure just what. It's stuck!"

Chung came over and examined the tube, then stuck her longest finger in and felt it—it was close to the opening but wedged in tight.

Taking the knife, and with Killomen holding, Chung cut through the tube on both sides of the object, then sawed the very small piece laterally. After some time and effort, she was able to peel away the thick, tough hose and see just what was inside. It had been nicked a bit by the knife, but was otherwise in pretty good shape.

"So that's one of the rings." Chung Mung Wo sighed. "It is impressive, even in the darkness." She brought up a small service light and they both stared at it.

"Four more ugly birds," Chung said.

Butar Killomen shrugged. "Makes sense, if we count 'em. Matriyeh's ring has one bird and a tree. Janipur's had two but no tree, this is four, and from the pictures, the one on Earth has three. I suppose the fifth one is either five birds of some kind or maybe none. It would make over a hundred possible combinations, all but one of which could kill you. Makes a crazy kind of sense, I guess."

"Yes," Chung agreed. "Who knows how strange those ancients were, or how they thought?" She sighed, and they both just stood there for a moment, staring at the ring.

Finally Butar Killomen gave a grin and looked up at Chung. "We did it. This insane, idiotic plan actually worked! *We have the ring!*"

Chung nodded, always the pragmatist. "Yes, but we had better signal Min to meet us at the rendezvous point. Now all we all have to do is get off this world."

Butar Killomen sighed, got up, and put the ring in her pouch, then looked up at the dark, cloudy sky. "At least I will not die here," she muttered to herself. "At least I shall return to where I belong."

"We have much to do and something of a swim yet tonight," she reminded Chung. "Let's get on with it. I want to be well away before that fleet arrives. This plan is not complete unless we get away with the prize, and we don't stand a chance with Vals and fighters and an SPF task force about."

Chung nodded but couldn't help looking back into the fog. "I think we will make it. They were not prepared for this, no matter how elaborate their precautions and their trap. They will not be prepared for our leaving, either. But Vulture . . ."

"Sometimes I think Vulture is too self-confident," she acknowledged. "With that much power and knowledge perhaps we would be the same. But there is such a thing as being *over*confident. This Colonel Chi is a different breed than we have seen before. I wish her or him or it luck. We have three now, and know of a fourth. But the fifth—without the fifth, it is the same as having none at all. And each time security is tougher: one mistake and we must begin again—and this is taking long enough as it is. Vulture will have to be extracautious with this Colonel Chi..."

Chung shrugged. "Well, our part from now on will be in space, where we belong. I never believed that *this* plan could be pulled off. Now, deep down, I feel our victory may be difficult but is inevitable. Come! If the current carries us out far enough I might even risk the motor!"

The storm activity continued fiercely for a while but died away with the sunrise. The guards came back up and took their positions, but nothing seemed amiss—and why should they think differently? Clearly no one had broken into the Sacred Lodge from above no matter what, or all hell would have broken loose within and without.

Up on top of the cliffs, all hell was breaking loose anyway. The relief guards showed up and discovered the ones on duty still unconscious; an alarm was sounded and a specialty squad was dispatched on the double. When they found the antenna jumpers and the added little box, Colonel Chi, still sleepy, was not far behind and already had issued a general alert.

Within an hour, a team from the science labs aboard the command ship were down, examining the boxes and analyzing the work done inside the station as well. They were cautious, just in case of booby traps, but there were none.

The chief technical officer was quite certain of her results. "Essentially, last night we had no surface-level sweep. We were blind to about, oh, three thousand meters when the orbital probes took over. You could have flown anything in here last night."

Now, suddenly, there was a careful examination of almost everything. Colonel Chi was livid. If anything really serious had happened, the blame never fell on the foot soldier, it all fell on the commander. Nobody was more aware of this than Chi.

"All right, between two and six hundred this morning somebody knocked out our sensors with a very clever set of devices," she said to her staff. "Now we must know why. Such devices are beyond the capacity of anyone here to make, so we must assume a tie-in with our missing priestess and her housekeeping staff. The only external threat capable of this is the pirates, and they are after one thing and one thing only. I want the entire Sacred Lodge covered, every centimeter of the exterior and all of the working plant below. I want all guards not just questioned but mindprinted and computer scanned for the slightest details." She stopped and looked at the officer of the day. "Didn't you say you sighted a barge far out on the scopes?"

The OD nodded. "Yes, but it was expected. Of course, if they interfered with our scopes, I can't be certain it was there at all . . ."

"It was there. The scope sighting came a few minutes before the guards were put away on the hill," said the charge of quarters. "I checked on that."

"I want that barge. Give me air probes and to hell with regulations! I don't care *what* the masses see or what they believe!" She sighed. "And get me the Holy Lama! I don't care if we wake her up out of her precious beauty sleep!"

But before she could put in the call, another came from the surface guards reporting odd scratches and markings above guard post three. Chi called the tech people and went to investigate. The Holy Lama wasn't going anywhere.

"Suction clamps," the technical officer said after a

cursory study. "Some high-quality ones specially made for bonding to a wet wooden surface, most likely. The marks aren't that pronounced—whatever it was was almost certainly designed to do this very job and not much else. We measured the marks and got an estimate as best we could. I'd say it was small—too small to even fit one of us, considering the type of motor it had to have to be that unobtrusive in idle."

Chi thought furiously. "Too small for us. Might a male have fit in it?"

"Huh? Yes, I suppose—but how would a male get *into* it? The only hole we found is a circular cut perhaps two, two and a half centimeters across."

Chi wasn't certain *what* her hypothetical creature might be capable of, but even she doubted it could turn itself into a rope or snake and slither through such an opening, particularly while carrying a ring.

It hit her suddenly, and she cursed herself for not seeing the obvious. "It's big enough to feed that damned ring through! I want that barge and that drone! I want every available trooper and all available technology on this—*now*! They might have blinded us here, but they certainly did not blind the command ship and the permanent system monitors! They are still on the surface of this planet and I want them!"

She stood there a moment, on the platform, thinking hard. Not only were they still on the planet, but no matter what their mole, their inside operative—whoever or whatever it was—most certainly was still inside the Sacred Lodge.

"Get me a team up here in full security gear and a construction unit with heavy drills and saws," she ordered. "If *they* can get in by drilling a hole without triggering the internal security system, *we* can get in by drilling a *bigger* hole. I want to be in there as quickly as possible—and no one, absolutely no one, gets out!"

* * *

By zero nine-thirty they had a hole drilled sufficient to make a total wreck of the library wall and large enough to get in both fully armed troopers and equipment. The squad looked eerie in their full battle gear and special suits that were both armor and life support systems. Chi wanted no unpleasant surprises for her people.

By ten-fifteen they had found the Holy Lama still out cold, as well as all nine Seed and the children, all also apparently out cold. Medical took scans and samples and discovered a simple biochemical neurotoxin in the bloodstream. There were traces in the air, but most if not all of it had been flushed out or broken down by now.

"Simple but effective," the medical officer told Chi. "There is no permanent harm and it will break down in a few hours at most. They should all have serious headaches but little else."

A sergeant came forward with an object in her gloved hand. "This what they were looking for, Colonel?"

The colonel took it and examined it with some fleeting hope. That little hole had been pretty high. Might it be that they made the attempt but didn't get what they were after?

"Is it safe to go in just like this?" she asked the medical officer.

"No problem now. Go ahead."

"Where is the Holy Lama? They could make a duplicate of the ring to fool us, knowing we don't know enough to tell a valid ring from a phony one, but there is one thing they might have overlooked."

She was brought to the unconscious figure of the Holy Lama. It was a bit startling to see the great figure of Chanchuk in person; Chi realized that she had never seen her in the flesh until now.

The SPF officer knelt down and immediately saw the

finger where the ring had been. She took the ring she had and placed it on the supine figure's ring finger. It went on easily—too easily. Chi lifted the hand so the fingers bent limply down and the ring fell right off and hit the floor with a clatter. A soldier reached down to pick it up.

"File it as evidence, or a souvenir," Chi told the soldier. "It's phony. Look at the ring finger. Clearly our Holy Lama has gained some weight since she put on the ring at her investiture. That ring she had was wedged on tight. See the scabbing? *This* ring, on the other hand, is at least two sizes too large. It was a nice try, though; I'll give them that."

"They've got the ring, then?" the tech officer asked.

Chi nodded. "They have—may it poison them! They'll never get it off this world, I swear." She turned and looked around. "Medical—you took blood samples from *all* life forms here?"

"All the ones not our own people, yes," came the reply.

"I want you to run every test possible on all nine, for the presence of the gas—whoever switched that ring and got the real one out sure wasn't knocked out. I want every test run that you or your medical computers can think of or remotely imagine. Understand?"

"Yes, certainly. But—what are we looking for?"

"Anything. Any sign that the blood of one of them is not one hundred percent normal. And, of course, any sign that one might have no toxin, or have a greater or lesser degree of it than the others. Don't neglect the Holy One or the children, either. And pull the internal security recordings and anything else useful and then go over this place with a microscope. And—Doc?"

"Colonel?"

"I want every living thing in here, from the Holy One to any stray microbes, to be packed and sealed and taken to separate isolation cells aboard the command ship as soon as possible. At no time are any of them to be left alone. I want at least two armed troopers with them every moment until they are safely in isolation. Do it *now!*"

The medical officer shrugged. "All right, but I don't see what you're getting at doing it to the children, too. They're mostly babies."

"Everyone. No exceptions. Now." Chi scratched her chin, thinking furiously. "All the rest I can see. A bold plan. But how do they expect to escape?" Suddenly she saw it. "They'll have to either move before the fleet arrives later today or they'll have to stay here underground for years! Notify the command ship—I don't care what sort of ship might punch in in the outer system, I want no challenge unless it moves within range of planetary defenses. I want everything we have concentrated on Chanchuk. I want anything that flies from the surface or from any position within transporter range blown up, no questions asked. *Everything*. The one who lets anything escape from the surface dies *very* slowly!"

"Very well, Commander." The way it was said, though, indicated that the medical officer was wondering if Chi was very long for that position. To her, the precautions seemed cold and callously officious, not the work of a brilliant commander. The colonel was well aware of this.

"And, Doctor—as soon as possible, when things are established, I shall want a mindprint taken of myself. The print is to be filed and also dispatched to the Val commanding the task force."

The medic was surprised. "Not to headquarters?"

"One to headquarters, too. All right. But I wish it on record for the direct evaluation by Master System."

"Very well. As you command."

* * *

Later on the command ship, the Holy Lama and her family were just coming around and not feeling any too good about it, while Colonel Chi was in nearly as much discomfort after the thorough scanning and recording of her mind and memories, when the colonel's recovery was interrupted.

"We have a punch," the duty officer reported. "All hands on full battle alert." Alarms sounded throughout the command ship.

Chi jumped from her cot, the headache pushed away as something she could not afford, and made her way immediately to the command center in the center of the ship.

The command center was a different world from the surface expedition and troop ships. Here SPF officers and enlisted personnel of a number of races worked side by side, each there because he or she was the best at what they did. Commodore Marquette, in overall command of the SPF task force now in place and the only superior on hand that Chi had, was in his command chair studying screens full of data that scrolled so fast only the experienced, trained naval eye could make sense of them.

Marquette was a thick, burly apelike creature who looked as if he could bend steel bars without thinking, his face a hairy mass with two huge yellow eyes peering out from the brush and a mouth that had the teeth and muscles to crush bone. Every race that Master System had carved from the human base forcibly expelled from Earth many centuries before had its counterpart in the SPF, so that they could move unobtrusively in and out of any and all of the colonial worlds as need be, and so that there would be a certain level of understanding between the human fighting forces and the colonials. Chi was of the race of Chanchuk; Marquette's own people were from a far harsher and more violent world.

"What is happening, Commodore?" the colonel asked.

"Lone ship, relatively small but fast. Punched in just beyond the orbit of Makyiuk. Distance is about sixty million kilometers. It's kept its shields on and its engines at full power, but it's keeping just out of range of the fighter screen."

"It's a feint," Chi told him flatly. "They are trying to draw us out so that they can get their people off Chanchuk. They know that we have sufficient force to either cover this immediate area or to make a creditable challenge but not both. I should not be surprised if others show up in mock attack formation."

The commodore was not totally convinced. "You're certain? They fought last time, remember."

"And took tremendous losses. They can replace ships but not people so easily."

"I could take three such ships, maybe more, with what I have," Marquette noted. "If you're right, though, and we get more company, we could wind up as sitting ducks for hit and runs unless we challenge them."

"It is true you could take them if they stood and fought," Chi agreed, "but this time they will not. I beg you to hold firm. If we can hold their people on the ground for just another few hours, the main task force will be here and we will be impregnable."

"Two more punches, evenly spaced, twenty-million-kilometer separation!" the scanning computer reported.

Marquette's eyes narrowed. "Freighters. Scows. The one in the middle is the only worthy fighting ship." He punched a command button. "Identification?"

"Likely that the freighter to port is *Bahakatan*, free-booter vessel commanded by Ali Mohammed ben Suda," the computer reported. "Starboard is *Kaotan*, commanded by Ikira Sukotae. Commanders are last known registry, may not apply at this date. Fighter is unknown origin, no registry, but was involved in the Battle of Janipur. Communications monitors referred to it as *Lightning*. All three ships have additional armor and have changed configurations since last encounter. *Bahakatan* is most vulnerable since inherent design makes it intrinsically slower and less maneuverable, but for that reason it is probably the best armed and shielded."

Chi nodded. "What do we have?"

"Nine fighters dedicated to command ship fighter screen, two other groups of six each on random surface sweeps, two transports and the supply and factory ship each with one group screen of nine," Marquette responded.

Alarms suddenly went off. "Minipunch detected! Attack imminent!" warned the speakers, and as Chi watched, the center ship vanished from its position on the master screen while the two fighers went into normal space motion, peeling off and creating large arcs as their probable attack plan was analyzed.

"Don't like this," Marquette grumbled. "Sitting ducks, waiting for them to shoot before we know where to shoot back."

Lightning emerged from its punch within barely a kilometer of the supply and factory ship and let loose a barrage of torpedoes, punching back in within moments.

"Bastard! Nervy bastard! He's actually punched inside our damned fighter screen!" the commodore exclaimed. The torpedoes, all intelligent and all preprogrammed for weak spots in shielding, curved and dodged close to the transport whose guns blazed trying to pick them off before one of the torpedoes found a way in. In the meantime the fighters were nearly useless; any attempt on the torpedoes would be just as likely to hit the ship they were supposed to protect.

"Transport struck! One—two—no, three hits! Damage serious!" the battle group commander called, although Marquette could see what was happening. *Lightning* punched out a good fifty million kilometers out from the Chanchuk task force, looped, then came back straight in and punched as, simultaneously, the two freighters punched as well.

With these speeds and distances, punching was nearly instantaneous. An attacker would simply vanish in one spot and appear in another. No human could defend against such an attack, but the battle computers could shift—if Marquette freed them to counter the threat.

Suddenly all three ships were inside the command ship's perimeter, firing off salvos of a dozen torpedoes and vanishing. Punching in with their full forward shields on and punching out without turning, the massed fire from the command ship itself had no more effect than to perhaps shake up the people on the attacking vessels. The command ship attack was equally futile; the kind of screens employed by the command ship would take far more than these kinds of forays to damage. Still, there was a faint shudder within the bowels of the ship as the torpedoes struck where they could.

"These aren't random attacks," Marquette told Chi. "They're well planned, well scouted, and well flown. Thanks to the initial response, the damage to the factory ship isn't bad and is under control, but they can do this all day if they have the power, and I'd guess they do. Sooner or later they are going to take some of us out. I've *got* to free the defensive computers to work as a whole! Otherwise we will begin to suffer serious damage!"

"No!" Chi was adamant. "They are trying to pull us away, don't you see?"

"Colonel, we have twelve fighters covering the Chanchuk grid from pole to pole. Nobody can punch from the surface; it'd take a good ten minutes for anything taking off to reach orbit, let alone beyond. In ten minutes I can have three fighers taking out anything that comes up from anywhere."

Chi swallowed hard, unable to make a case against that. The navy knew what it and a potential enemy could do, and physical laws were physical laws. "All right. I will defer to you on this. Keep the planetary screen intact but feel free to employ your other forces as you desire."

"Now you're talking!" The commodore could have overriden Chi from the start, of course, on the basis of sheer rank and position, but had no desire to do so. Their mission was to prevent an escape; that was Chi's department.

The defense computers took over task force command. The three vulnerable ships were brought close and tightened up with the command ship, and the new task force fighter screen, now numbering eighteen, divided into two groups, one shielding the ships and the other ready to analyze speed, trajectory, and movements of the enemy and go after them. None of the fighters was manned; all had limited punch capability.

The three enemy ships and the SPF played cat and mouse for almost forty minutes, neither striking any real blow against the other that caused any damage, until the defense computers under Marquette determined what was known as a "release pattern" to the enemy attacks. They came in, attacked alternately, and regrouped at various angles from the task force—but the regrouping positions were now showing a distinct mathematical pattern. The defense computers took a guess at just where they could come out next, and when the next attack came, and the attackers punched through, the fighters punched through at the same time.

Colonel Chi watched the battle on the screens, noting

particularly the rolling and gyrations of the enemy vessels as they were engaged by the fighters. Thinking about there being *people* on those attacking ships, she was very glad she was a ground trooper.

"Stung 'em a bit that time," Marquette noted with satisfaction.

"Sir! Surface launches!"

Marquette whirled in his chair. "Where? How many?"

"All over. Oh, my—*hundreds*! From all over the place!"

A full three-dimensional model of Chanchuk hovered over the command plate in the planetary defense section, and on it could be seen just what the monitor was reporting. Hundreds of angry, red blips, all over the globe . . .

Suddenly Chi realized the one thing she'd forgotten in all the excitement over the Sacred Lodge, the raid, the creature, all the rest. That damned small motor assembly.

Somehow, somewhere, over a very long period of time, they had been planting those things all over Chanchuk! What use was just a motor and a small logic module? On defensive screens the damned things all looked alike. Somewhere among them was one, two, perhaps three with pirates aboard—and the ring.

"Break off!" Chi shouted. "Concentrate all fighters on those things! Shoot 'em down! All of them! Forget about anything else!"

"I'll be damned if I'm going to take my screen off this ship!" the commodore responded. "Recall and reform battle group," he commanded. "When done, commit three fighters from battle group two to each enemy vessel. Have planetary defense battle group break off and split into thirds and join covering fighters. Target anything attempting to reach said vessels. Shadow!" He turned and looked up at Chi. "Can't possibly get more than a fraction of 'em, but we can shoot anything they try to pick up!"

Chi's estimation of Marquette went up a notch or two.

The tiny SPF fighters were much too small and fast to use torpedoes against, and as long as they themselves could throw a random missile or two at the enemy to make it keep its distance—which meant keeping out of range of the ship's guns—they were relatively safe. On the other hand, guns could pick off an object of any size or significance that was on any sort of clear trajectory for pickup by the freighters, who were bearing down so that they would both skim opposite sides of Chanchuk well away from the task force's position. If either freighter stopped long enough to allow matter transmission from the surface, enough fighters would converge on it that it would never escape.

Lightning continued its attack against the task force, keeping the rest of the fighter screen occupied. Now facing only nine fighters having to cover four ships, the enemy was able to inflict some real damage on the previously weakened supply and factory ship and on the two transports. It ignored the command ship for now— except for an occasional salvo of torpedoes to keep the fighter screen busy—since those shields were just too strong for any one ship.

"Two Val ships and twice the fighters and all three of them would be history," Marquette noted. "I just can't figure out what they're trying to accomplish by this."

The two freighters continued to close as the fighters screening them remained ahead and began picking off anything in their path before those freighters could get close. There were now effectively two fighter groups, one on each freighter, while a lone group of five or six ships randomly picked off the small dots just attaining orbit.

Marquette pointed at the globe of Chanchuk. "We've

got a few of those mystery blips heading straight for us. Good. It'll give our gunnery computers some work!"

Lightning looped at forty-six million kilometers out, turned, and bore back in on them head on, punching as predicted. Suddenly an alarm went off in the command center and they turned to look. The projected exit of *Lightning* was not within their protective ring but below and beyond it! As they watched, *Lightning* reappeared perhaps a hundred kilometers below them, extended some sort of scoop, and sucked up a half dozen of the mystery blips.

It was so close in that the defense computers committed the fighters to go after *Lightning,* loosing a horde of torpedoes at the same time. Even ships' guns opened up; at that range they had a clear shot at the enemy.

There were several hits but clearly not enough. *Lightning* lurched and then began accelerating to where it would miss the planet and attain sufficient speed for a punch. The fighters were on its tail, but they could not prevent the punch or stop the enemy ship. *Lightning* was damaged but by no means helpless, and it had a pretty good chance of complete escape.

"All fighters break off, break off!" Marquette ordered. "Target the escaping vessel. Repeat, target the escaping vessel."

Almost immediately *Kaotan* and *Bahakatan* were alone. Only when they were certain that there was no more fighter cover did they alter course and close in together. *Kaotan* opened its pickup bays and activated its transport beams as *Bahakatan* covered.

As Chung had predicted, the pickup was made with comparative ease and safety.

4. REFLECTIONS TOWARD AN ENDING

THE VAL EXTENDED A COM POD AND ATTACHED TO the transmitting console. The interstellar transmission system included complex miniature punches and required much power, which was why it wasn't used very often. It also still was slow enough that the conversation between the two machines, which might have been done in seconds, instead would take hours. Machines, however, were patient—when they had to be.

The Val received the sign-on from Master System itself, and quickly transmitted the entire record, including all the test and probe data on the suspects and the complete readout of Colonel Chi.

"If such a being were possible," the Val added, "it would explain much."

"Such a being is theoretically possible," came the reply from deep within the greatest computer ever known. "It would take a computer with vast potential, much biosurgery almost cell by cell and incredible skill with the principles of cellular transmutation, and years of trial-and-error research, but such a creature could theoretically be designed. There was no need for such a project on my part."

"But could anyone we know do such a thing? Who would have the computer with the skills capable of doing so? And could any human ever dream up such a creature?"

"Humans designed me, with far more primitive tools, and I am infinitely more complex than that. As to the computer—it is obvious. The one on Melchior that was stripped of all data was nonetheless of sufficient size, speed, and capacity for it, if it were a primary task of research and at least half of it were constantly devoted to the problem. That means Clayben. He is the only one who could have done it. An agent who could go through security systems anywhere undetected, find out anything . . . Yes. It is obvious now. You are certain that there is absolutely no alien element of any kind within any of the suspects, including the children?"

"None that can be measured by any means currently at our disposal."

"Very well, then. Order them held in continued isolation and wait."

The wait lasted two days.

"I cannot create such a being without much experimentation, and that takes time," Master System said at last. "However, proceeding from what we know about such a hypothetical creature, I have determined a basic set of methods that had to be employed in its design. If it is close to what was finally accomplished on Melchior, it is specifically designed so that no form of measurement we can employ will unmask it. However, we do not have to create one. I am certain that there could not be more than one such creature. Otherwise the game would be up long before now. They have, however, placed us in an immediate quandary. Remaking and remolding an entire planetary culture takes time and resources I do not wish to spare at this time, although Chanchuk is now a primary candidate for such treatment at the earliest opportunity. To kill the Holy Lama, her consorts, and their children is the obvious plan to eliminating this creature, but it would totally disrupt and turn against us an entire planetary culture. It would tie down too many resources for too long, and we are always faced with the possibility, even probability, that no such creature exists, making the move meaningless as well."

"It is true that we are in only tenuous control on Chanchuk at the moment. The local Center and temple authorities have refused to aid us and in many cases have shown a willingness to die rather than cooperate. They have managed to get the word out to the other Centers in spite of our control and from there to the masses in the region. There have been massive demonstrations. The bulk of the population is pacifist, but some are not. Troops have been harassed, some killed. They demand the restoration of the Holy Lama and the Sacred Lodge. It is not anything that we cannot handle, but it is not a good situation. Still, is there another choice?" The Val seemed uncomfortable with its current position.

"I believe there is. They already have the ring. They now face us with creating an entire world of allies and tying up tremendous resources handling such a thing as well. This is a double victory I will not permit. Better to wrest a major victory out of a defeat. They do not have all the rings yet. Without this creature they are highly unlikely to be able to get inside information sufficient to steal another without tripping up. Nor are they likely to have access to a computer capable of creating another even if they somehow have all the programs. But suppose in the process of returning them to Wa Chi Center we also *transmuted* them?"

"Transmuted? Into what? If we make major alterations in their holy family it is the same as keeping them."

"A body of a suitable and similar-looking priestess of about the Holy Lama's age can be procured. They are, after all, all sisters. The reproductive functions can be restored during the process. The sterilization is surgical, not transmuter induced. Nine males of the royal lineage can also be procured from the Centers as models, and their children can be the templates for the Holy Lama's children. Each can then be transmuted into the form of one of the randomly selected templates."

"I see. And since one cannot be transmuted twice, the agent will be exposed, perhaps killed."

"Possibly. I said transmuters were used to create it. I do not believe it is possible to modify a human being to become one of these creatures. If it was, then all of the rebels would be like this thing and we should be lost. No, it must be created and nurtured in a specially controlled laboratory. It is unlikely that it has ever used a transmitter for more than transport. It has no need to do so, and it might actually be threatened by it. But matter is matter and atoms are atoms to a transmuter program. Have we not created Vals that are so human none can tell the difference without instruments? It will not care what this creature is made of, or how it works. It will simply do a transmute. If it exists at all, it will emerge back on Chanchuk as the Holy Lama or a male consort or a child. It will no longer be artificial—it will be real, and fixed immutably as one of Chanchuk. It is also likely that memory is stored cellularly, throughout the body, rather than merely in the brain. If that is true and it is a true mimic to the end, it is quite possible we may also eliminate most if not all of the memories, knowledge, and personality beneath the Chanchukian facade. Either way, it will be neutralized. Do you need specific programming instructions?"

"No. The only regret in this is that we shall never know for certain if the colonel is brilliant or if this is a fantasy. I would like to know."

"It is probable. It is the most logical way to explain their successes, as Chi so brilliantly determined. Clayben has the ability, Melchior is the logical place, and the idea is consistent with the way Clayben thought. The traitor Nagy could have brought the creature along, since Nagy would be immune to it. No. I am convinced that with this move we shall deal them a blow so crushing that it will be another generation before they succeed in gaining another ring. We will not let down our guard, for we want to capture them all, but as far as obtaining all five rings is concerned, this will halt them in their tracks."

"It shall be done, and the restoration shall be highly publicized and with suitable ceremony. I feel certain the Holy Lama will go along even without mindprinter inducement, which is always the best way. She is concerned about her people in a genuine way and anxious to restore normalcy. If such normalcy can be assured, what do you wish us to do next?"

"The SPF should be withdrawn as soon as possible, but keep a regional command in the area just in case the Holy Lama is not altogether clear on where her own and her people's best interests lie. I would suggest that Commodore Marquette and his command be relieved of task force duties and placed in command of a project to analyze specific SPF training responses. I have done a complete analysis of his defensive plan and can find no specific flaws in it. Clearly insufficient force was deployed to defend Chanchuk, and the pirates' computers were able to predict the logical responses of our programs, commanders, and forces and find the weak links in the chain. It is essential we become less predictable in the future. Were it not for Colonel Chi, we might have suffered a total humiliating defeat in this matter and learned nothing from it."

"Colonel Chi failed," the Val pointed out.

"*Vals* failed on Janipur," the master computer noted. "The only reason we struck any blow at the enemy on Janipur, even with our overwhelming force, was that the enemy was new at the game and had not been tested in battle or planning. They lost their ships and personnel because of their own mistakes, not our efficiency. They are clearly patient and they have learned well. Chi salvaged something here by showing imagination and initiative and because she circumvented the rigidity of procedure and thought that the enemy counted on. I am far removed from the scene of this fight. Communications cannot be instantaneous. On the scene, our computers and their computers are equal. The difference, then, has been their human controllers who clearly have a great deal of resourcefulness and imagination. This system was created because it is the best for humans. Perhaps it is time we allowed the products of that system to have a direct hand in this."

"What, then, are your orders?"

"The rings on Matriyeh and Alititi are to be secured with monitors so that any removal will result in an automatic alarm. Large automated task forces are to be deployed in waiting stages in null zones out of detection range, but within monitor range, capable of closing on either world and sealing it off should either ring be stolen. Even without their special agent they will try and perhaps succeed, but I do not want them getting away again. I want so much force available with such speed that the enemy must bring all of his ships and weapons to bear. They must be smashed so thoroughly that they are forced to bring their base ship into the fight and we must be able to take and secure it. Colonel Chi is promoted to brigadier and is to be placed in charge of a special SPF task force with all authority necessary. All Vals and other extensions of myself shall be at her disposal. *Move!*"

Raven had been morose off and on of late. He always had his moods and his depressions, but this one seemed longer and deeper than most. The Crow had taken to simply sitting on an overlook, staring out at the vast worldlet that was the *Thunder*'s deep interior.

He'd been up there, staring out, for over two days now, eating or drinking nothing, and clearly now even out of cigars. The former was not totally unusual; the latter was history making. Hawks, concerned, finally decided to make his way up there even though it broke his own personal rule on disturbing others and certainly violated the compact that existed now with the remaining multiracial company.

The *Thunder* was impressive, and never more so than from its heights. Its kilometers-long interior, balanced by a comfortable artificial gravity and landscaped with plants and rocks from dozens of worlds, actually contained small villages and a network of paths, central wells, sanitation, and cooking—all that was needed. There was even a small area for livestock, although, since some of the races aboard were strict vegetarians, some by biology and others by custom or religion, it was agreed that those who chose to remain meat-eaters would eat synthetics in the interest of harmony.

Raven was a craggy old bastard, with scars all over his body from his tough early life and career; his long hair, kept straight at his own insistence, as if to mark him as one apart from the Hyiakutts like Hawks and Cloud Dancer who wore the traditional Plains braids most of the time, was steel-gray now. He was built like a wrestler; a man nature had designed to be large as opposed to tall, yet more muscular than fat.

As much as he had been a prime mover and shaker in

the quest for the rings and as much as he was a child of his northwest wilderness, he was also always the cynic, always the materialist and scoundrel, always the one who looked for profit in everything he did and approached even the vastness of the universe in coldly pragmatic terms. In all these years he'd rarely let down his guard, rarely given anyone a glimpse of what might lie behind those cold, brown eyes and that impassive, stonelike face. Just enough, over all this time, to give those with whom he'd lived and worked and plotted and planned an indication that somewhere under all that was a far different sort of human being.

Raven, dressed only in a loincloth and sandals, did not move or acknowledge Hawks's presence when the leader came up to the platform level and stepped off just behind him. For a while Hawks just stood there, wondering if he was doing the right thing. But he was the leader, and he had to know the condition of his company.

Hawks approached, then sat down next to the big man, cross-legged on the metal platform, and stared out at the vast interior below.

Hawks reached back and took a long object from a box he'd brought with him. "I brought you another box of cigars," the leader said conversationally.

For a moment Raven said nothing, then, without turning or moving, he responded, "If you came up here and didn't bring 'em, I'd've thrown you off this platform."

"You've been up here a long time."

"Sixty-two standard hours, forty-six minutes, more or less."

"You can keep track like that?"

"You kiddin'? The master clock's just up there."

Hawks felt a bit silly. "Yeah. I should have thought of that. How long do you intend to stay here?"

"I don't know. It's either this or I start hittin' the bottle. This is healthier. What's it to you, Chief, anyway?"

"Because I'm the chief," Hawks replied. "Because I think it's more appropriate for the chief to check you out than the medicine man, considering that would be Clayben."

"Good point. So what's on your mind, Chief?"

"I think that question is reversed. What's on *your* mind, Raven? Finally getting to you? All this time, all this plotting and all this waiting—and we still don't know if we're going to make it."

"Oh, we're gonna make it, Chief. Ain't you figured that out yet? I don't know which of us, but some of us'll make it. We'll get there and we'll figure it all out and we'll switch that big mother right out of the circuit and give it a lobotomy. Somebody will. It's almost like we were playing out a script. Not *our* script, or we wouldn't have this much trouble, but somebody's script. God's or something more sinister, I don't know, but I'm damned sure of that much. We come too far, Chief. A lot farther than I ever dreamed, and maybe you, either, in your saner, less idealistic moments. We got three rings and we know where another one is. We got just one to snatch and then it's home. And we'll snatch it. And we'll come home. Whether we can hold 'em long enough for *us* to use 'em, I don't know, but somebody will."

"That what you're worried about? Going home? Holding on?"

Raven shook his head. "Uh uh. But, see, we—all of us—been so hot on gettin' the damned things and survivin' to use 'em and all that we ain't thought about the one big thing. We been like folks sealed in detention cells who spend half their lives plottin' how to escape and findin' all the flaws, like us back on Melchior so long ago. Then they bust out, finally, and they realize they spent so much time figurin' how to bust out they ain't got the slightest idea where the hell they're goin' or what they want to do. Suppose we get in there and we turn that sucker off. Ain't nobody but me ever thought beyond that, I think. What then? What happens then, Chief?"

Hawks was startled. "I don't know. We just don't have to worry about Master System anymore."

"Uh huh, and just what do you turn off? The boss, that's all. The chief. You knock off the only chief capable of keepin' track of, much less rulin', the tribes and what happens? You got thousands of little chiefs all at one another's throats tryin' to be the new big chief. You get tribalism and civil war and you get massive deaths. The people? They're still under the rule of the Great White Father they were born under—or the Great Red Father or the Great Yellow Father or whatever. The C.A.s are still in charge. They just got the boss off their backs is all. The interdependent trade system handled by the automated spaceships also goes down the toilet. No more resupply, no more innovation, no more external contacts. A human empire goes the way of all empires and you get four hundred and fifty plus alien worlds. And I mean alien, Chief. You drop me as I am down in the middle of Janipur and I'll either get worshipped as a god, stoned as a demon, or in the end cut down as a monster anyways, and they won't ask about my table manners. Stick a Janipurian on Chanchuk. Try and hold a solid dialogue on important affairs on Earth with the average Matriyehan. You see what I mean?"

Hawks nodded. "I have thought on it. It is not sufficient to turn the machine off. One must also determine how to replace it with something infinitely fairer. Your knowledge and understanding of history are quite surprising, Raven. But doesn't the *Thunder* itself give you hope? Here the children of wildly differing races play together as friends, and their parents fight and die alongside and for one another."

"My business has always been human behavior. You can't be a field agent without knowin' a lot more than just how to point and shoot a gun or bow. But the *Thunder*'s different and you know it. These folks—they ain't aliens. They're space children, even the old folks. Their parents were freebooters, the best liars and cheats and thieves in the universe and already alienated from their own homes as much as we are from ours. The rest started off as our own people, and we still think of them that way and they think of themselves that way. So the Chows look like humanoid cows. You think they're among their own people on Janipur? *We're* their people. But you stick 'em anyplace but Janipur or space and you got monsters. You're the historian. Am I wrong?"

"No. If anything, you are overly optimistic. History is filled with examples of times when people hated all who were different from them even if the differences were quite minor. Our own people were reduced from proud civilizations to helpless prisoners on the worst of our own lands, begging our conquerors for food. We were childlike, primitives, ones who could not accept technology and so had to perish. Accept technology! Before the Spaniards none of the nations of America had so much as *seen* a horse, let alone a gun. We learned. We took what was useful and valuable. We rejected the rest because it had little value to us. Their values were different from ours, their goals, their cultures, were directed toward things we found dehumanizing. In the end, their worship of mind, property, nation, and invention for its own sake, stripped of any moral valuations, led them to terrible wars and to Master System. I have often reflected on the irony that some of those now attempting an end to that result are of the very people they so scorned and nearly destroyed."

Raven's head suddenly turned and he looked directly into Hawks's eyes. "Are we? Are we, really? Oh, we got the right *bloodlines*, but we ain't no damn men of spirit and tribe. You're a damn computer hacker and researcher into lost records who works in a sophisticated high-tech environment where the air is filtered and measured and you can be practically brought back from the dead. Me? I'm a high-tech security man from the same element. I spent much of my time in the wilds, with the tribes, it's true, but I wasn't one of 'em, not even among the Crow. I was a smug, superior, patronizing son of a bitch down there where I was king and the people were blind. Your precious Hyiakutts weren't your people, they were some charming living history exhibit. A way you could go back and study like Clayben with some new alien bug under his microscope. Funny thing was, you was playin' Injun among the primitives and me, I was playin' the white man."

"So? We are not what we like to think we are. It disturbs me. It disturbs me more to hear you voice it because it is so much the truth. But what would you have us do? *Not* turn it off?"

Raven sighed. "I don't know, Chief, but I got a real weird feelin'—I always kind'a had it—that even after the switch is off, it's up to us. We can turn it off and run and hope we'll be long dead before whatever wars and new tyranny that follow its death find us, or we can fall into a trap that's maybe infinitely worse."

"Huh? What do you mean?"

"You ever really read *all* that journal?"

"No, and neither did you. It is decomposing someplace in the middle of the Mississippi River."

"Come on, Chief. You got the transport copy Warlock's boss tried to send to Chen. When I decided to take this mission I read the one Warlock had, the one we eventually delivered to Chen along with you. I read all of it, Hawks. All of it. Them rings—they don't turn Master System off. They revert control to the master consoles. In other words, Master System stops bein' a run-amok, independent machine and becomes just a computer again. It don't stop bein' the master system. It just stops bein' the boss. Whoever's at the consoles, whoever's got the rings—*they* become the boss. That's why Chen's so hot for this—if that slimy rat is still even alive. No matter. Whoever his successor is will be the same guy only lookin' and talkin' a bit different. That's why Clayben's been such a good, solid, devoted servant all this time, too. He knows. You stick in the rings, you unlock the master control center, and you go in. Then you're it. You're God. *You're Master System.* You call the shots and good old MS and its minions obey. Of course, originally it just allowed control to return for defense purposes, but Master System has grown into a big boy after all this time. And it's all yours—whoever uses the rings."

"My God!"

"Exactly—if it ain't you at the controls, whoever is surely is your god, and mine, too. Turn it off and you break the system and return us to all the worst features of human civilization we've been protected from. But ain't nobody gonna turn it off, Chief. Not when you can save humanity from that and be God, too."

"I see. And why have you kept this from us until now?"

"Not all of you, Chief. Warlock knew. She'd read it, too. But she never would'a thought to be a goddess herself, Chief. She just figured to be there on the winner's side, just like me. Clayben knows—either through his private library, somehow, or maybe he figured it out by deduction from all the rest he knows. And I think Savaphoong knows, somehow, too. Maybe more instinctively than anything else—his type always seems to figure this sort of shit out—but he knows. Or he suspects, and can't afford *not* to be there. They'll be with us all the way—until they get a better deal."

"And you?"

Raven sighed. "I'm gettin' old, Chief. I never been all that ambitious, though. The game's the thing for me. But I'm gettin' too old to play games. It took me a long while before I realized why Warlock and some of the others stayed on Matriyeh and quit the chase. Less biology and new race psychology than old psychology. She had what she wanted, more or less. A society so wild and violent it kept her crazy part goin' but also gave her somethin' solid and real. She couldn't think of a better place to be, that's all. Me—I ain't sure if there *is* such a place for me." He sighed again. "Up until now, the game's been enough. But first Nagy, then Warlock, then Ikira, and now Vulture."

"We do not know about Vulture yet. I wouldn't count him out so easily. Is it that you fear that it is your turn, or are you guilty that it is not?"

Raven gave a dry chuckle. "You know, I wish I knew the answer to that one. I do know that I don't want the control, Chief, but I'd damn well be more satisfied if it was me than the turkeys in the rear like Clayben and Savaphoong. Who's left, Chief? You, me, China... that's about it. The rest—they don't know what they want any more than we do, but they're not the kind of people to be gods. Star Eagle deserves it, God knows, but he's out. It has to be people, I'm sure of that."

"Well, there's Santiago."

"She don't want to be a goddess, Chief. She just wants a strong mate for a partner, a good solid ship, and a little peace and quiet for her kids to grow up in. Like most of 'em—simple dreams, really. The Chows want this nice peasant farm someplace. Bute and the other freebooters, new races and forms or not, just want ships and for everybody to leave 'em alone. That's what it's all about for them, Chief. They don't want to run the system, they're doin' all this to get the system off their backs so they can do what they always wanted to do and not worry about it. It's what most folks want. Deep down it's what you and Cloud Dancer want. Maybe the human race could use some peasant gods sometime, but the peasants got more sense and more real sense of values, too. No, it's guys like Clayben and Savaphoong and Chen—those are the god types."

Hawks smiled and gave a slight shrug. "Then maybe you are the one to be the god, Raven. You don't really want anything but you understand *them*. You might at least be fair, which is more than all our race's gods have been in the past."

"I can't imagine anything duller. I been up here tryin' to decide what I want, and maybe what I want to be."

"Any conclusions?"

Raven nodded. "I think I want to be a Crow, Chief. No matter what I became I'm still a product of thousands of years of a culture that has real value, real meaning, in this materialistic, mechanistic, messed-up universe. I just want to know that if I'm ever in the position where it is needed that I am, at heart, the representative of my people and that when my time comes, if it comes, they and my ancestors will look upon me with pride. Now, does that sound corny or doesn't it?"

"Yeah," Hawks replied. "It sounds corny as hell. You know something, Raven? I've respected you for years, but I'm beginning to be in real danger of liking you."

Raven just shrugged and said nothing.

"You know, it's not going to be as simple as you say, even if we win," Hawks noted. "I mean, what's Master System, anyway? It's already done all its real damage; it's just tryin' to keep what it's got. It took even the big machine over two hundred years to do all this damage.

We can't undo it. There's no way back. No, the problem won't be any different with any of us than with Master System itself, except, of course, we'll do it differently."

That started Raven. "Huh?"

"Like I said, we can't undo it. It isn't a matter of being god and working miracles, it's an engineering problem of system management. Do we get rid of the Centers and all their marvels and let all the worlds go their independent way, perhaps forget their origins, and eventually meet when their technological levels grow? Or do we bring the wonders of technology to everybody everywhere, an interstellar empire with the resultant destruction of those cultures? Could, indeed, human beings who could never even get together on Earth because of differences in color or religion or culture get together under any system when they are now so physically different and so culturally aberrant? I've gone over and over those questions, Raven, and I have no answers. None. Neither my research, nor Star Eagle's computer, nor the wisdom of the ages can give a guide."

Raven nodded sympathetically. "Well, then, I guess we leave it to luck and screw it up as usual. We're gonna have to fight our way all the way to Master System's lair. Whoever survives and is the strongest and smartest—whichever five of us have the rings—we'll decide. It ain't fair and it ain't right, but there it is. I'm probably the worst guy for that kind of thing and I don't even want it, but I'm a survivor. Maybe I'm just gonna wind up with the bad luck to be one of 'em." He paused a moment. "And then there was one," he said softly.

Hawks nodded. "Yes. It is time to think of that. We've had little luck with it, you know. The one ring missing in all this mess."

Raven chuckled. "Funny thing is, it'll probably be the easiest to get. I mean, what's Master System gonna do? Shove half the SPF and a dozen Vals and ten fleets and task forces around it? That's all we'd need—a bright sign sayin' 'Here it is!' Oh, there might be some tricky security setup like with the Matriyeh ring, but it'll be an engineering problem. A heist. Real difficult unless we get Vulture back, but we're experienced now. It's about time we grew up. But first we gotta find it and I'm fresh out of patience. Didn't you say a long time ago that Savaphoong intimated he knew?"

Hawks nodded. "He promised that sooner or later we'd have to come crawling to him."

Raven got up, stretched, reached down, took a cigar, and lit it. "Give me half an hour to shower and change, Chief. Then I think we pay a little call on Savaphoong. That little bastard's had a free ride far too long."

Fernando Savaphoong still lived on his rather luxurious yacht attached to the outer hull of the *Thunder*, his every wish catered to by the pitiful but beautiful personal slaves he'd taken from his old outpost empire when he'd been forced to flee. With his ship's transmuter and a few of almost all imaginable luxury items, he'd been able to sustain himself in aloof style for years.

"Ah! *Capitán* Hawks and Señor Raven! Come in, come in! Might I offer you some wine, perhaps?"

They took seats in his luxury bar and entertainment room. Savaphoong knew that there was no love lost between himself and the others, Hawks in particular, but he was a businessman and trader without a scruple in his body and he never let such things interfere with business. His dull-eyed, oversexed slaves served them, and they relaxed.

"Now, then, what might I do for you gentlemen?" Savaphoong asked genially.

"You know," Hawks replied evenly. "You were expecting this visit sooner or later. You know that every attempt we've made to locate the fifth ring has failed, and you know that you intimated to me that you knew where it was."

Savaphoong sat back, savoring the moment. "But, no, *Capitán* Hawks, I do *not* know. I *think* I know, because it is the only place that it could be and remain within the conditions for the possession of the rings that I know of. Certain I am not. But I would wager money on it, and I am not a gambler."

"We're all ears, pal," Raven commented.

Savaphoong sighed. "But, you see, it is all that I have to offer other than hospitality. So far I have contributed little, I admit, but I have taken little as well, and certainly it was I who convinced the freebooters to join our little band. That is worth something—a contribution. Free and without charge, I might add."

"Many of us have given our lives, Savaphoong," Hawks pointed out. "Others have lost ships, at least once to your cowardice. Captain Santiago went through a wrenching transmutation from which she has never fully recovered, in part because of the loss of that ship and her comrades, but her new race is a pretty violent one, you know. Without my intercession you'd have suffered a slow death by torture long before now at her hands. You owe her and her dead comrades, at least. And if we hadn't taken you aboard you would have lived in total isolation without hope for the rest of your life, so don't give me that favor crap."

"And you would not have been able to track and steal an entire freighter full of the murylium that powers our vessels, gives them their punch, and fuels our transmitters and transmuters," the old trader retorted. "No, señors, I think we are even. Not all of us serve in the trenches."

Raven saw that Hawks was ninety-nine percent ready to leap the table and strangle the man and decided to intercede. "You're the trader. You have something to trade and we're interested—if the price is within reason. You haven't mentioned price."

Savaphoong sat back and stared at them. "I will play no haggling games. I give you the place, I want the ring. I want to be one of the ones present at the end as an active player."

"You know the rules. The ones who go and get the ring and risk everything decide who gets to keep it," Hawks pointed out. "Besides, you don't want to really be there at the end. It's likely to be a battle all the way. Lots of shooting and danger. And the targets of choice will be those with the rings."

The trader shrugged. "I am not averse to risk if it means high gain. I am getting to be an old man. There is no place for me to go and no future for me in any other situation. Remember that I am risking something, too. I do not know how the rings should be used, or where. That is your job, *Capitán*. And whose ring will *you* commandeer when it is time? Who is voting you a twenty percent godhood?"

Hawks smiled. "Nobody. If they feel me capable, they will. If not, then it is not my right to take one from them. I have a wife and three children. Godhood sounds like a full-time job, and I am not certain that I want it in any case."

Raven lost patience. "Look, Savaphoong, we're not gonna sit and rot here, you know. It won't take much under Clayben's mindprobe to find out what we need to know, if you really got anything at all."

"The machine will not avail you what you seek, it will only kill me. You did not think the proprietor of such a place as Halinachi could ever risk being seized by Master System, do you? I knew too much, and I sold information as well as pleasure. My sources would never have trusted me with anything unless they could be assured it could never be traced to them. No, you cannot probe it out of me, and while I have a high pain tolerance, I am not a strong man. I would prefer to die rather than be tortured or dismembered, and I assure you when my threshold is attained, I will do just that. Again, some assurance for my old customers. And without a ring, why keep on? As I say, I am old, and as you pointed out, I have no place else to go." He finished his wine. "No, gentlemen, my price is absolute."

"What's to keep us from sayin' yes, then reneging on the deal once we know what you know?" Raven asked him.

"Because the ring I wish is not the ring you seek. Bring me one of the rings we already have and I shall tell you where to find its companion. It is as simple as that."

Hawks began thinking furiously. For almost five years this situation had haunted him, although not in the way the old trader thought. For almost that whole period, Hawks felt he should know right now just what Savaphoong knew, and the comments here only intensified that feeling. Why would Savaphoong know? Until he'd joined them he didn't even know the importance or significance of the rings. And now, after all this time, he just admitted that the ring really wasn't a factor. He didn't know—he had *deduced* it. How? He knew so much, had such a network in the old days, that it might be anywhere...

But it wasn't. "Son of a bitch!" said Hawks softly, not referring at all to Savaphoong. "Five bloody years and I couldn't see it." He sighed. "Forget it, Savaphoong. Die in decadence—or join the hunt and earn the prize. Come on, Raven."

The Crow was suddenly very confused. "Huh? What?"

"He's been laughing at us, and particularly me, for years. I already know what he knows. The joke's on you, Savaphoong."

The trader was suddenly concerned, his self-assuredness gone. "What do you mean? You could not know."

"In each of the three other cases the ring has been prominent enough that it was no sweat finding it. Even Matriyeh, which had no Center as such. In the last five years, *Kaotan*, *Chunhoifan*, and *Bahakatan* have checked out every single colonial world on the charts, and Star Eagle has analyzed their origins, their culture, and everything about them we could know. No sign, no clue. We're pretty sure it's not on any of them, but we also know it's not back on Earth. For a long time I was scared it was on the finger of the head of the SPF, but that's not it, either. Master System would be a little nervous about handing such a thing to somebody with all the technology of the system at his or her command and a lot of ruthless ambition to boot. And what does that leave?"

Raven was blank. "Beats me, Chief."

"Another colony. One not on the charts. One that's primitive, so primitive that it can be pretty well divorced from the system and still be counted on. Not air breathers and probably with a ferocious, xenophobic culture to boot. No Centers, no technology at all to speak of, but right in close, in the middle of the rest, so it can be constantly checked on. One that every old spacer knew about but nobody knew anything about, which is why we wound up there first. One almost in Savaphoong's old backyard. Do what you like, you old bastard. You no longer have anything to trade."

Hawks got up and Raven followed, leaving the trader just sitting there looking disgusted, not so much at Hawks but at himself. Maybe he was getting too old. In the old days he would never have overplayed such a meager hand.

Hawks wasted no time once he got back inside *Thunder*. "Star Eagle, I have our destination."

"I overheard. It is so obvious once you think on it."

"Yeah, but the point is we *didn't* think much on it. We were too damned concerned with ongoing projects and with our own lives here."

"I should have deduced it at once," the computer pilot responded. "So much wasted effort! And we really could use Vulture on this one."

"Well, we may have to go without him. Until he can contact us, we have no way of knowing if he's even still alive. We should start our planning anyway. How's *Lightning*?"

"It was badly damaged, but repairs are coming along nicely. It is capable of standard duty now. Give me a week and it will be better than new."

Hawks nodded. "Call a captain's council. Include the surviving company who escaped with us from Melchior, Clayben included."

Raven stared at the Hyiakutt. "I still don't get it, Chief. Where the hell are we goin'?"

"Back where we began, Raven. Back to a hot, violent world with coconut palms planted in neat rows but without any apparent civilization at all. To the first alien planet you or I ever set foot upon. To ring number five, which we might well have been within only kilometers of stumbling across mere weeks after our escape!"

The last time they had entered that solar system they were rank amateurs, without much of anything at all except hope and fierce determination. They had lived almost like savages on a little volcanic spot down there for what seemed an eternity while Star Eagle had made the necessary repairs and adjustments to *Thunder*. Nothing much to remember, really, except the heat and the storms and the terrible humidity and the sense of impending danger when none ever materialized.

Blocking the monitor satellites hadn't been a problem

last time and was even less of one now. They were used
to such things as a matter of course.

"We have all heard of this place," Maria Santiago told
Hawks from the first. "A number of freebooters used it
as temporary hideaways and for rendezvous since it is at
once so accessible and so remote, but none really even
looked for inhabitants. I was never here, but I had heard
of it."

Captain ben Suda had much the same memories and
even showed it on his charts. "There was some early
attempt to carve out a freebooter base or trading post, if
I remember the stories," he told them. "It failed for some
reason. Never really got started. There were tales of
fierce, suicidal attacks by some kind of creatures, but
that's all—just tales."

"Yeah, well, there's *somebody* livin' down there all
right," Raven assured them. "I almost forgot about this
hole, but thinkin' about it now brought back all sorts of
memories. Me and Nagy, down by the beach, havin' a
less than pleasant chat, and the sense that, somehow, we
was bein' *watched*. Black blobs in the water, as I remember it, but we never had the means or will to find
out about them. That wasn't our job and this place didn't
mean nothin' to us except as a hideout. I remember
Nagy, though, starin' across at the next island and suddenly frowning. He said that island looked like it was
somebody's garden, and sure enough, there was these
trees all planted in neat rows. We were tempted to go
over there but never got the chance."

Hawks sighed. "How we miss the Vulture now! It's
been too easy to rely on him. How simple to just drop
him in and let him tell us all about it. Damn it, we don't
know what we're dealing with here! Who are they? What
culture? Are they water breathers or just water
dwellers?"

"Anybody who comes up on land to plant fruit trees

isn't wholly aquatic," Isaac Clayben noted logically. "Still, there was absolutely no sign at all that anyone or anything with a brain had ever been on 'our' island. If they use the land, why not where we were? It wasn't a bad place, if a bit wild and overgrown. The volcanoes weren't recently active, and there were even wild fruit-bearing trees if I remember correctly."

Hawks nodded. "That's about it. And if we accept the legends of the place as being based on reality, and couple that with history and our own experience, we come up with a real puzzle. An attempted colony or permanent outpost was attacked and wiped out, yet generations of freebooters used it as a contact point and place to stash valuables and make repairs without any reports of molestation. The island we were on wasn't touched, yet the one not much different than it within easy eyesight on a clear day was cultivated."

Santiago thought about it. "I have never been there, it is true, but I cannot help being reminded of Matriyeh. The tribes were enemies and had clear hunting and gathering territories, yet there is a unifying religion that made certain places forbidden. That was on land, with a land-based culture spanning two huge continents. Here—I look at the surveys and I see water. Perhaps the total landmass is the equivalent of a continent or more, but this world is one vast sea covered with tiny islands, all the tops of vast underwater volcanic ranges. If a civilization was water-based, might it not have some sort of unifying religion as well, if, as with all the others, it has a single culture?"

"That's good thinking," Hawks responded. "Taboos are standard in many societies. The fact that our island had some edible plants indicates that it might have been cultivated once, then abandoned, perhaps centuries before. The fact that they attacked one party and not others indicates that there may be rules for each island

and we just got lucky. The Matriyeh model is a good one here, I think, considering the total lack of any signals or signs of any sort of mechanical or electrical power. Even the traditional water-breathing colonies are set up on the Center model; there is power, there are ways to use adapted technology and that shows up. It doesn't there."

"But it doesn't necessarily mean that it is not there," Star Eagle put in through his speaker. "Remember, who would have guessed a magnetic rail system on Matriyeh? We aren't geared for that sort of detection, and under water—who can say?"

"It's a point, but somehow I doubt that such things lie hidden here," Hawks said. "Raven is correct on one point—Master System doesn't dare defend this one unless it has to. That's not to say that we can't expect traps at least as bad as Matriyeh down there. I cannot forget the mystics of Matriyeh who themselves didn't know they were really an entire SPF division under intense mindprint conditioning with a humanoid Val to worship as a goddess and to control things. No, this is going to be the nastiest little problem we've had to solve, if we have no inside man as it were. I would wager, though, from the depth of the legends about this place, that it is old, and that, unlike Matriyeh, it probably remains very much the way it was originally designed. No, I feel now as I felt then—that this was a prototypical colony, one of the first. That it was settled with a distinct people, perhaps a culture that would be very comfortable with a world such as this, and one that might well turn its back on technology." He sighed. "Well, it's a dangerous situation and there's no way around it."

Raven nodded. "Uh huh. First, we want as good a current orbital survey as can be made of the place. Then we're gonna have to send a party down there with some mobility, heavily armed and ready for bear, and see what the place looks like. Finally, and this is the worst part, we're gonna have to draw some of 'em out of the water, and if we can't talk things over peaceably with them we'll have to knock 'em cold and bring 'em in. That means exposing a group to dangers unknown by persons or creatures unknown, ones that managed to take out at least some well-armed freebooters. After all, for the most part we only know of the ones who didn't get hit, right? It also means that, right from the start, we're gonna have to expose ourselves as aliens. If there's anything like that Matriyeh gimmick with the SPF, we're cooked and you'll have a task force here before you can learn the name of the place."

"Doubtful," said Star Eagle. "Even on Matriyeh they had a communications link to a master ground computer. No such link exists here or my probes would have detected it. There *is* a monitoring satellite but it is not geostationary. It's designed to casually sweep the planet's surface and is easily fooled. No, it is probable that Master System here is relying entirely on its anonymity and the hostility and insularity of its people. This is not to say that there are not permanent traps there— an SPF sort, or disguised Vals, or whatever. And if the latter, there can just as easily be one or more Val ships down there, hidden, switched off, self-maintained and ready, which could be impossible for us to detect but available to be switched on and used as required. All it would take is orbital attainment and it could send an emergency call through the solar system monitors."

"And it might be the wrong place," China put in worriedly. "We have no real evidence that this is where the fifth ring resides. The reason that there is no activity might be that there is nothing to guard. The reason why these people are on no charts might be that they are not descended from humans at all but are an indigenous species."

"Unlikely," Clayben responded. "Even from our

crude early examination of the place I can say that it doesn't fit the pattern for the independent evolution of intelligent life. Oh, give it a few million years and I will readily change my mind, but there is clear evidence here of Master System's terraforming methodology, and with the air, water, and organics present—all clearly introduced and the plants descended from easily recognizable Earth ancestors—it would be in some way life as we know it. No. It is circumstantial evidence, but we must take the risk. Logic says that it is here, that this is the place. It is consistent with the way Master System thinks."

Raven sighed. "I'd say we start where we were before. It seemed to be a safe spot in the middle of some civilization, and we'll have to stick to land at the start, until we get the full lay of it."

Takya Mudabur, one of the two remaining unchanged crew of the *Kaotan* and the only native-born water creature among them, spoke up.

"Why do we have to stick to the land? I would enjoy a dip in such a beautiful ocean." Her people breathed air but lived entirely in the sea. She needed to be in water much of the time, and could be underwater, even in depths as high as five hundred meters, for hours at a time. She had a rudimentary gill system as well as lungs.

"Can't risk it, or you," Raven replied. "Butar, Chung, and Min also can handle themselves in water, and we sure have some weapons that'll work there easy enough, but even sending four instead of one in *their* element— the element of our unknown people—is like setting me and Hawks down in the middle of Janipur. Somebody would notice, and these folks got a reputation for killing first and wonderin' later. No, there'll be a time for that, but not yet. The only smart way to do this is to draw 'em out into *our* element, away from water. Then we get a look at 'em and we got a fighting chance."

"Who would you want, then?" Hawks asked him. "I assume the way you're talking that you're volunteering to mastermind all this."

Raven grinned. "About time I did something, ain't it, Chief? And this is just up my trail." He looked around at them, thinking. "I want folks with lightning reflexes, in better condition than me, and real nimble shooters. Any volunteers?"

"You need warriors to protect you, Raven," Santiago said. A great deal of therapy, both mental and physical, had restored the original personalities of her and her companion Midi while retaining the aggressive instincts they had needed to survive on Matriyeh, and now both were resigned to accepting their adopted race and form. They were once more the primitive warrior women of that fierce world, yet their old, technologically sophisticated selves were once again very much in control. Maria was tall, with almost black skin, little body hair, and small, rock-solid breasts. Her European-featured face, which was quite reminiscent of her original looks, was crowned by short, straight black hair. She also had the gracefully athletic body of a female body builder, and the strength and reflexes to match, and looked quite Earth-human, though she was not. Her race was as alien as that of Chanchuk or Janipur. Midi was much the same, only very slightly shorter and with different, more Orientalized features reflecting her original looks.

"You've done your share," Hawks pointed out. "More than your share. You've lost a ship, a crew, and become one of a colonial race. Besides, you both have children to think of."

"Matriyehan children are more independent than that," she responded. "I was a freebooter captain and then I became a warrior. It's in the genes you stuck me with, you know. We were talking about it not long ago. We are now designed as warriors, not as sweet young things to tend the kids while the menfolk go off to fight. On Matriyeh there *are* no menfolk. We crave action. And we are best suited for this kind of thing."

Raven shrugged. "I agree you two'd be perfect if you really want to go. That's three. I think I'll need at least five, maybe six. Somebody's got to tend camp and maintain the communications and security links, and I ain't too sure I want to go on the other island with less than five good guns."

"I'll go," said Dora Panoshka. "It is likely that *Kaotan* will not be needed at this stage of the game, and it would be nice to be on the ground for a change. If *Kaotan* is needed, then Butar can do for me what I did for her." Panoshka, now captain of the *Kaotan* and the one responsible for picking up the Chanchuk team, although humanoid, looked more like a bipedal lion than an Earth-human woman. She was covered with orange and yellow lionlike fur, her rather Earth-human–looking hands and feet disguised with pads, hairy clumps, and nasty retractable claws. Her face was also fur-covered and had a flared-out all-around mane, and the lipless mouth opened wide and menacing, as if it could swallow a person whole. Few would take the time to see that that mouth had no fanglike teeth at all, merely even rows of large, flat ones that were for a jaw that moved primarily from side to side and betrayed her for the absolute vegetarian she and her race were.

"Pardon, but *Chunhoifan* has been a peripheral player until now," said Captain Chun Wo Har. He, too, was a born colonial, a humanoid but with a hard, chitinous exoskeleton, bulging black eyes, and the look and manner of a giant insect. "Such a civilization as might be down there would likely be of the bow and arrow and spear variety. I doubt that weapons such as these could pierce my body. I might not be so quick, and I am certainly getting old and out of practice, but I would be honored to come along."

Captain ben Suda sighed. "I, too, feel much the same. We have fought battles in space and done much scouting, but *Bahakatan* is also underrepresented in the real object of all this. I was quite good with rifle and sidearm in my younger days, and I feel the need to oil the joints and remove some of the rust."

"Well, I'd welcome you both," Raven responded, then caught Hawks's glare.

"No," said the leader. "Both of you have intact families predating any of this. And I cannot afford to risk both of my most experienced surviving captains along with Santiago and Panoshka on this kind of scouting expedition. There's going to be more fighting ahead no matter how this comes out. I just can't spare the two of you. I've lost *San Cristobal* and *Indrus*. *Kaotan* is down to a skeleton crew now and needs supplements to run efficiently. I'm sorry, but this is a command decision. I don't want either of you away from your ships where you'll be ready at a moment's notice for any emergencies."

Both captains said nothing, immediately sensing Hawks's resolve and, as captains themselves, seeing reason in it.

Finally Captain Chun said, "*Bahakatan* contributed Chung and Min to the Chanchuk operation. Allow me to consult with my own crew. Perhaps we can find ones more acceptable to you, sir."

Hawks nodded. He understood how much honor meant to Chun, and he didn't want to point out that they were running low on people who could be transmuted. If that was required here, then Chun's crew were likely candidates.

"Very well. We don't have to decide now," the chief told them. "It will take some time to fully scout and plan this out, and I want all care and caution taken both before and during this operation. Because we have three rings and need only one more, we're overanxious. That could kill us, or sink everything we've spent all these years and all these lives in attaining. Even after we select the team, I'll want Raven to work with all of you, drill and practice, until you do the right thing without thinking. For now, this meeting is adjourned."

Cloud Dancer was sketching again. She was an excellent artist, both drawing and sculpting, and the interior of the *Thunder* was filled with her work. Now, though, she had been doing a simple project, but one that immediately caught Hawks's eye.

There were four of them, charcoals, one for each of the known rings—the three they had and the one they knew was back on Earth. For some reason, it had never really occurred to Hawks to study the rings themselves before. True, the designs were there, but so small, so delicate, that he'd found it impossible to really see the detail in them. Cloud Dancer, however, was an artist with an artist's eye for even the finest detail, and she had studied them and drawn them folio size. Now, suddenly, seeing them blown up to so large a size, every tiny detail enlarged and reproduced, each of the intricate designs seemed too perfect, too deliberate, to be just ornamental numbers.

He picked them up, then placed them in descending order, 4-3-2-1. He stood back. He stared at them. Suddenly he turned and went to an intercom.

"Star Eagle—the Fellowship. The five who created the Master System program and had the rings made."

"Yes?"

"What religions were they?"

"You asked me this before, a few years ago. Joseph Sung Yi, born Singapore, China, naturalized citizen: no religion of record but had dabbled in Buddhism. Golda Pinsky, born Haifa, Israel: Jewish. Aaron Menzelbaum, born New York City: Jewish ancestry but an outspoken, rather militant atheist. Maurice Ntunanga, born Mimongo, Gabon, naturalized citizen: Moslem. Mary Lynn Yomashita, born Lahaina, Maui, Hawaii: nominally Buddhist."

Hawks frowned. "No Christians? None of them were Christians?"

"No. Everything but. Interesting. The records on them are quite complete, even in my original pilot's program. Why would it be there? I wondered about that the first time you asked, but dropped it because there was no chance of an answer."

Hawks sighed. "I think I may have an idea on that. Let's just say it doesn't surprise me. But—no Christians?"

"No. Apparently that was what originally brought them together. They were the only born non-Christians among the top team assembled to oversee the creation of the master core program. Many of the rest had no known religion or were agnostics or atheists but they had come out of nominally Christian backgrounds. These others also tended to go home for Christmas holidays, while the Fellowship, who had no real family and not even a nominal religious excuse, stayed on. That is how they all came to know each other so well and came to found their little group. I had no *idea* this stuff was buried in my memory! I'll be damned."

Hawks grinned. "You can't be damned. You're a machine."

"I'm sorry I couldn't be of more help."

"Oh, but you *were*. In fact, what you told me is as good as if you had told me the opposite."

"Huh? Explain."

"Not now. All of this simply confirms an old theory of

mine, and this final ring will be the proof of it. It is odd, though. Unless Isaac Clayben had a more traditional upbringing than I suspect, I may be the only one who knows this. I would prefer that no one else knew that I knew it. Understand?"

"No. However, if it makes you happy, I will deny all knowledge of what I do not know and will deny to everyone that you know anything at all."

"Good enough," he responded, feeling quite upbeat for a change, even though they were entering the most dangerous phase of the whole quest. Maybe Raven was right. Maybe they *were* meant to get the rings.

He had to stop himself before he began to hum an obscure, forgotten old English tune that only a historian specializing in presystem cultures might ever have encountered. He didn't want to hum that tune. He'd heard it going over many of the ancient records of old America, but the tune was English, and so was Isaac Clayben. The old boy might well figure it out, but Hawks sure as hell wasn't going to help him.

5. UP A TREE

"**H**AWKS, I HAVE CONTACT WITH VULTURE," STAR Eagle reported.

They were perhaps six weeks out from Chanchuk now, but monitors and pickups had been left in place there just in case Vulture needed a hand in escaping.

"Is he calling for assistance?" Hawks asked, feeling somewhat relieved even if this did bring up new problems.

"No. He wishes to speak with you. It is on a nonstandard communications channel, but I believe it is legitimate."

"Put him through," the leader ordered, sitting down.

"Hawks? This is Vulture" came a thin, reedy voice barely recognizable as Vulture's, although the tone seemed familiar. "I'm in bad trouble and I don't know what to do about it, and I think I have some information on trouble coming your way as well—the cause of my . . . predicament."

"Go ahead. We've been worried about you. Our monitors show a massed withdrawal from the region. Want us to plan some kind of pickup?"

There was a pause. "Maybe. I—I don't know. I am undecided about this, and about a lot of other things right now. I got too cocky, too arrogant. We had beaten the machines every time. Now I got stuck by a damned SPF officer!"

Hawks frowned and leaned forward. "You are captured?"

"No. Colonel—now Brigadier—Chi never found me. She, well, *deduced* me. That's the most dangerous agent of the enemy I've ever come across or even dreamed of, Hawks. She's ruthless, brilliant, and imaginative. So much so that Master System worked out a system to neutralize me without even knowing for sure if I existed and appointed her chief of capturing or killing all of you. She's even got authority over Vals, Hawks! She's no regular military officer, she's a detective and a great one."

"How did they neutralize you? And how do you know all this about this Chi?" He'd heard of Chi from the Chanchuk crew, but not as anything extraordinary.

"They isolated and imprisoned all of us," Vulture told him. "Naturally I had to appear exactly as the others, and they never gave me time to either slip away or take over somebody else, so I had to play along. They did the usual tests and mindprinter scans, but things got so hot with the Holy Lama imprisoned in orbit and the holy lineage threatened, they couldn't keep us or kill us. By that time, though, the task force had arrived with a vengeance. After keeping us for days in isolation they turned us over, one by one, to these Vals—you know I was always powerless against Vals—and they sent us down by big military transmuter, and in the process they transmuted us. Not into anything that would cause notice— one Chanchukian into another almost identical Chanchukian—but Chi convinced them that I, somebody like me, was one of us. The stock transmuter programs I could always beat, but somebody knew this time that I was there, and some real bright computer figured out how I was made and made the adjustments in the program. Hawks—the Vulture will eat no more. I came out a Chanchuk male in all respects, just like I was born to it. I feel like the walking dead—so much of me is missing, all my powers gone, even some of my memories and knowledge. I'm out of the game and I don't know how they did it. Ask Clayben. Maybe he can explain it."

Hawks sighed, feeling suddenly depressed. Up to now the fight had been costly, but the system had shown itself remarkably brittle and error prone for all that. They had not been able to really cope with the pirates of the *Thunder*, not in an effective, aggressive manner. Not until now. Still, he had to keep his mind on business. "How do you know about Chi?" he asked again.

"The Holy Lama is quite something" came the reply. "Take all the smarts of the top chief administrators you've known, put them together with learning in so many areas that most of us never suspected existed at all and almost absolute control over mind and body, and you have only a hint. Except for the shape-changing and memory-transfer aspects, she can do much of what I could do in the past, only she does it by sheer force of mind and will alone. Body self-repair and diagnostics. Control over pain, over all the brain centers. Hawks, she can fool a mind probe wide awake and with her eyes open using no mechanical means. Now extend that as well to a near-absolute grasp of every detail of Center technology. Hawks—she arranged to tap the SPF's internal communications here and went through their code like it was clear text. I've been sitting here inside the Sacred Lodge listening to just about everything the SPF and the Vals were saying. I'm using one of her taps on a system monitor to send this. I can't exactly move freely here."

"That kind of information is valuable in and of itself,"

Hawks noted, adding, "She sounds like a far better friend than enemy."

"Indeed. The one thing she's had problems with is accepting a male as at least the intellectual equal of one of her sisters. It's hard on me, too. I don't have the self-control I used to have, although I have some of the mental abilities I talked about because I once *was* one of her sisters. Unfortunately, none of those past lives is real anymore, or living inside me. They're all like books one read long ago and remembers parts of, or maybe misre-members. The Holy Lama says that I used to carry all their souls inside me and that they were liberated when I was made, well, human, leaving only the reflections of their lives. I don't know. I only know that I feel more imprisoned than enlightened."

Hawks could not comprehend the magnitude of change that must be going on inside Vulture, but he ana-lyzed the situation well enough from his own tactical needs and moral sense. "Could you get off that planet if you had to?"

"Yes, I believe so. They know we got the ring, so they've withdrawn all but a few local SPF people from here and just about the entire task force. I still have the fighter that brought us here stashed well inland, and with the aid of the Holy Lama I'm sure I could get to it. They might have a trap waiting just in case I try an escape, but now that the Holy Lama's down here and in charge once again she can play a lot of tricks with their hallowed monitors and frequencies. The question is whether or not I should."

"You would die down there as a courtesan, my friend," Hawks told him. "Too much of you remains. You know this Chi and how she thinks. Here, with us, you might not only save some of us but get a measure of revenge. And there are three females of Chanchuk here with no male, and they, at least, are free of those limited racial attitudes and prejudices. Besides, I need you to keep an eye on Clayben. I assume your feelings for him remain the same. And you are human now. None has earned the right to the rings as much as you. For all these reasons, you should join us. You have served us beyond measure, Vulture, but you are still, even now, too important for me to allow to curl up and die."

Vulture was deeply touched. "Very well. If the Holy Lama agrees, we will work out something for a pickup. Oh—and this bit of good news. They have not discovered our Matriyeh operation. They think we still have to go after that ring, and Chi has had to divide her forces and her activities between Matriyeh and wherever the other is. That is a break, but only a slight one. I would assume Chi would keep some distance from the unknown place, but that will focus her attention more on Matriyeh. She's good, Hawks. If she figured me out, she might spot Ikira or the others in place there. And if Matriyeh's secret is blown, they'll spare nothing at all to make anyone who goes after that fifth ring dead meat."

Raven had his people, and he was doing his utmost to make certain that none of them was dead meat, especially now they knew the operation would proceed without Vulture. In addition to Maria, Midi, Dora, and himself, *Chunhoifan* contributed Han Li, Captain Chun's second wife and *Chunhoifan*'s chief gunner. She was so quiet and deferential around Chun that even after all this time hardly anybody really noticed her, yet she was proving to be pretty tough in Raven's evaluation. He was impressed. Rounding out the team was Peshwar Gobanifar, a very strange member of *Chunhoifan*'s crew who somewhat resembled a great owl, perhaps a meter and a quarter in height, with a dull green body and huge, round, yellow and black eyes that reflected the light. The tiny mouth resembled a small beak adding to the effect, and the nostrils were but tiny holes. He had thin arms, however, instead of wings, with long, thick fingers, and the feathers were not feathers but some sort of protective overlapping layers of natural insulation, more like giant scales.

Gobanifar was neither fast nor fierce in any real sense, but he saw as well at night as he did in the daytime if there was any light at all around, however faint, and he knew the technology the base camp would require. He was a good choice out of the declining pool Raven had to choose from, although his wife wasn't all that keen about his participation.

Even Hawks, feeling more than a little guilty always sending others to be transformed and risked, wanted to go, but the same logic he had used against the captains, the captains now used against him. The chief was always too important to do battle, no matter what the romantic legends said.

Thorough searches and tests of the entire solar system showed no surprises; it was remarkably like it had been the last time they'd been there. Of course, there could be some kind of mobile monitor, totally inactive and pretending to be a bit of space debris, with far too little power to be noticed by even the most diligent sweep yet ready to spring into action should anything disturb it or what it watched. They had used that technique themselves many times with their fighters and they could not chance risking *Thunder* no matter what. A quick penetration with one ship on standby while the others waited in a private punch zone well off the beaten path, monitoring by remote sensor, was their best chance to avoid this kind of trap. Considering what Vulture had said of this Colonel Chi, Hawks began to expect the unexpected, although that kind of thinking made it very easy to cross the line between cautious and paranoid.

Even if Chi were more dangerous than the machines she served, Hawks believed it was highly unlikely that she could accept a new, dual set of problems, formulate new plans of action, and implement them before they had arrived. The laws of physics worked the same for all of them; Chi had nothing faster to work with than they did. What was much more likely, and potentially more dangerous, was that Chi would arrive in some manner after they commenced their operations. If so, it would certainly prove that this was indeed the place where the ring lay hidden, but if Chi discovered them already there the rationale for stealth on her part would be gone. In the end, it would provoke what Master System most wanted and the pirates most feared: a massed battle against a task force or the abandonment of not only the people down on the planet but the very quest for the rings for a long, long time to come.

Because of this fear, Star Eagle dispatched a fighter carried piggyback by *Lightning* down to the same island where they had first made planetfall after escaping the ancestral solar system. As before, the fighter was outfitted with a transporter mated to one on *Lightning* in geostationary orbit. It was far easier to download supplies and personnel that way, and far quicker than doing a hard landing. *Lightning*, however, would not remain, for that would make it a sitting duck. Instead, to be on the safe side, a relay monitor on a second automated fighter would be placed with the debris in stand-down mode so that Raven could be in communication with *Thunder*. *Lightning* would alternate with other craft in a picket position well away from the system and hidden in deep space yet able to receive transmissions and get to the planet in very short order. The others, including *Thunder*, would be well away. *Lighting* would pull them out if it could, but it was understood by Raven and his entire party that they were pretty much on their own.

At the last moment before they left, Hawks met privately with Raven. "I can't guarantee anything, but at least for now you won't have to be transmuted. Later, probably, some will, but not right away. The only thing I can do is tell you within limits what this ring will look like."

Raven shrugged. "Five birds or no birds. What's the difference? Probably five—no birds would be pretty plain."

"No. Five circles, probably linked together. And, if I am correct on this, four of the five rings will be the same size and one will be either a bit larger or a bit smaller than the others. No birds at all."

The Crow sat back and stared at Hawks. "You know a lot more than you been letting on, don't you?"

"No. In fact, I *should* have known—it was the old thing that Nagy suggested finally surfacing. Something I knew, a bit of totally useless trivia only one of my specialty would be likely to ever encounter, that I didn't know I knew. When we have this ring, I believe I will be able to tell the correct sequence, the entire code. That is why this one was so well hidden. It is the key to the rest."

"Well, we'll get it if we can. In a way, it's fitting. If we got to go into this cold, on our own, no Vulture to front for us, then it *should* be not only the last but the most important."

"Not the last—there is one left to go after this, as you well know, and that one might cause more trouble. But this is the key. Find it for us, Raven. Find it for all of those who have died so far, and for all who have become monsters to themselves."

The Crow lit a cigar. "At this stage of the game, I don't intend to be the one who fails."

Raven had been away long enough that he'd forgotten just how bad the heat and humidity on this planet were, and particularly that very slight stench of sulfur and hydrogen sulfide permeating the air and everything around. It had taken him a long time to get used to it before, and it was just as bad now. *Any* planetary air smelled somewhat strange and foul after years on the *Thunder*'s filtered atmosphere, but this place would have smelled bad to anybody.

First the Crow had the camp itself established and a security perimeter installed so they would have some warning if anything unwelcome approached. This time, at least, they had been able to take the time and had the equipment to manufacture some decent tents in proper camouflage colors and treated with materials that would shield those people and things underneath from most known automatic probes and surveys. It wouldn't stand up to visual inspection, but a planet was a big place and it was unlikely that even Chi would order a meter-by-meter close-up satellite mapping of the entire world.

The island itself was actually two fairly tall, old volcanoes rising up from the water that had, over the ages, connected themselves together with lava flows that created a low but above-sea-level land bridge between the two peaks. The dense jungle vegetation had already reclaimed most of their old campsite, but the barren black rock near the center of the land bridge still showed the scars of the early initial outpost. They did not need anything nearly as large or elaborate as the ragtag band of refugees had the first time they were there, and so Raven established camp close to the beach and just at the edge of the jungle at the black rock area. Then, using tight-beam lasers, they cleared a small path from where they were down almost to the beach area. Raven decided to keep a visible wall obscuring the trail from view by sea, just in case anybody out there had any ideas.

Both Maria and Midi seemed to like the place. It reminded them somewhat of the volcanic planet where they had been changed and forced to fight to become Matriyehans. They quickly stripped down and once again became their warrior selves, and if there was anything more disconcerting than the sight of two Matriyehan warriors with machetes, spears, and, most ominously, modern laser pistols hanging from hip belts, Raven hadn't seen it. Those were the two he trusted most to make a security sweep of the flats, and that took most of the first day while they established their camp, tested communications, and looked over aerial surveys. On the second day he sent Midi up one mountain and Maria up the other, knowing that from high up the sides of those peaks the whole island and many others in the area could be seen. Both also had cameras to take detailed pictures of the surrounding water and nearby islands.

Dura suffered the worst, although she was adapting to it. She had a naturally thick fur coat and while she might look lionlike, her native world was anything but hot and humid. Direct sun also seemed to be bad for Gobanifar, who sought the shade of the tents or trees quickly and often had a hard time recovering his full wits for minutes afterward, but such exposures were not the rule. There were clouds everywhere on this place, and frequent, fierce thunderstorms that came in with swift and sudden fury.

Han Li's exoskeleton, in space, had always had a dark-brown, almost black marblelike sheen, and it was surprising to see that it changed both its color and its apparent texture in a more natural environment. In sunlight she was almost a creamy white; in the dark, jet

black. In the more usual gray, she was a very dull brown
that was effective camouflage in the jungle when she
stood absolutely still, as she could for seemingly hours
on end.

Finally the encampment was set up, the area had been
scouted, the equipment had been tested. Now Raven
walked with all but Gobanifar down to the beach as he'd
walked with Nagy so long ago. It had changed very little,
almost not at all. They stood there for a moment, just
looking at the scene, not saying anything.

"What was that?" Maria asked nervously, suddenly
on guard and turning toward the open sea.

"I, too, sensed something," Han Li told her. "Out
there. But I can see nothing now."

"It is as if we were being observed," Midi put in. "I
. . .*feel* it."

Raven nodded. "We always got that feeling around
here, but no matter how still you were or what tricks you
played it was always there, in the corner of your eye for
just a moment but never long enough to really see it or
tell what it was." He turned and pointed to an island that
was several kilometers away but looked almost near
enough to touch. "Train your field glasses on that over
there." He clicked on the electronics and brought up his
own. "Yep. Still there. See what we meant?"

It didn't take an expert to understand immediately
what he was talking about. Here, on their island, it was a
mess—a true random jungle. Over there, it was as if
someone had planted the trees in neat rows and evenly
spaced on all sides. Another area looked like rows of
neatly planted bushes, and at no point did the vegetation
seem more than ankle high.

"What interests me is that gently sloping beach,"
Maria said after a while. "It seems almost like a ramp
leading up to and into the grove. It's impossible to tell
from this angle, but there might be a slightly wider open-

ing between the rows if you drew a center line up that beach."

Dura looked around at their beach, which was wild, jagged, irregular, carved by wind, wave, and storm. Not so the other; it was smooth as glass. "Dead wood," she muttered.

Raven turned. "Huh?"

"All along this beach there is dead wood. Some of it is massive. I assume that it is all washed up here from other places, or has fallen here from the forest edges and died, or perhaps is the remains of what once lived here before erosion took its toll. Perhaps all three. But there is none on that beach over there. Not a stick that I can make out."

Raven turned back and looked again. "You're right! I'll be damned! Last time I figured that it was just because it was facing more or less northeast and we faced due west, but that wouldn't protect it from thunderstorms, would it? Not completely. The lay of that island isn't right to keep that beach completely sheltered, even if it is better protected than here. That tears it, all right. We're looking at somebody's farm or garden or something like that." He sighed. "I guess it's time to go find out."

Midi whirled and looked out to sea, but whatever she had noticed had vanished again before even her lightning reflexes could catch it.

They had not had the personal flying belts until Min had brought the one back from Chanchuk. The design for that kind of equipment was not in the usual data bases, not even Clayben's, and even though the transmuters could duplicate them for use, the scientist was still going slightly mad trying to figure out how they worked. Reconciling them with his understanding of physics had become a mania with him. So far he had only determined that it used magnetism in some unusual way, perhaps interacting with the planetary magnetic field or something else generating such forces.

Raven and his people didn't care, so long as they worked. They were not light, and required a tiny, fixed reactor charged with several grams of murylium to work. The unit was strapped tightly on the operator's back, and rose up, went forward, and went down controlled by switches in two thin control rods that extended forward. Clayben had been concerned that the belts might need fine-tuning for each world because of the magnetic differences, and he was right, but since they didn't have the operator's manual around, they simply had to practice and compensate as best they could. Raven had no intention of being too ambitious with them; he wanted no sudden descents into that water and whatever lurked just beneath.

They had practiced on and just over the island, and discovered some limitations. The devices had been capable of kilometers of lift on Chanchuk; here they tended to become unstable above about thirty meters. High enough, but inconvenient. They also required considerable oversteering, particularly in any other direction than southeast. Even so, they learned how to make the belts work and what their power supply limits were.

Now Gobanifar watched as the others rose about twenty meters in the air, keeping a wide spread between them, then drifted off on the first morning that the weather was decent. There was something of a wind that caused nervous moments, but there was *always* a wind of some sort, particularly above the treetops.

From above, the sea looked dark, with seams of dull, dark red interlaced with deep purple and black. The red was a form of microscopic sea plant that floated in the water in incredible numbers; it was omnipresent over the planet, and the brown clumps of it washed up to die on island shores illustrated just how dense it had to be. In that water, it had to absorb or block almost all light from getting beneath, and it seemed impossible that anything could live down there.

The flight over was nerve-racking but short; they landed, one by one, on the beach and immediately had their weapons at the ready. Although the flight packs were heavy and awkward, it made no sense to remove them. No matter what the cost in comfort and maneuverability, so long as they were worn and charged, they provided one avenue of escape any threat was unlikely to be able to block.

The beach did not look nearly so pristine close up as it had from afar, with large clumps of dead sea plant all about, but it still looked far too good to be natural. Local conditions might have piled more driftwood on their island than this one, but one expected *some* debris, some irregularities from storm damage.

The guess about there being a wider central path in from the beach proved correct, as well, although just off the beach there were a few surprises.

Tall poles—each carved out of a single great tree by someone with a fair amount of skill—were sunk deep into the ground on either side of that path, poles with a multitude of monstrous, painted faces staring at them. Most of the party had never seen their like, but Raven was more interested in their technique than nervous about their terrible visages.

"Totem poles, we call 'em," he told the others. "My people never went in for 'em, but lots of cold-weather tribes did up in the Northwest. Not quite like these, though."

"Are they gods of some sort?" Han Li asked, gaping.

"No. Not in my experience, anyway. They're signs. Message signs, if we knew how to read them. The clans of the various tribes would adopt a spiritual kinship with an animal of nature. There was the frog clan and the eagle clan and the turtle clan and you name it. Many greeting poles like this would have the whole clan listed, with the clan who carved them on top, of course, and then a descending social pecking order of clans arranged according to how the boss clan saw it. I'm not sure what these monstrosities represent, but that's the way it worked back home." He sighed. "At least we know now that this world is inhabited, that they're colonials most likely, and that they have an art and a religion—and they can come up on land. Hard to tell how old these suckers are, but considering the storms that blow through here, that paint looks awful fresh."

They continued on, the path more a primitive road than a mere trail or clearing. There were other artifacts along the way, too, representing individual monstrous creatures, and a series of pottery jugs filled with a foul-smelling liquid. A quick test proved Raven's guess correct: they were twin rows of torches that could mark this way at night, although Raven did not remember ever seeing a fire over here. If so, they would have been over during their first landing no matter what.

Dura studied the area. "You still might not have seen them if they had been lit, if they weren't lit but occasionally," she pointed out. "The jungle thickens just over there and the road curves, putting highland between here and the other beach very quickly.

No more than two kilometers in they reached the place where the road was leading. It had walls built of crude-looking but impressively tight, mortarless stone, and all around were more of the fierce-looking totems. Inside, a freshwater stream led down to a small, clear blue lake and a number of low stone structures that seemed built less for protection than to delineate special areas within the walled camp. The stream itself was fed by a small but impressive waterfall that had carved a

depression in the volcanic rock below and swept the
back wall clean. That back wall was a solid hill of
smooth, shiny rock, dark brown in color, that seemed to
reflect much of the scene around it and the ever-chang-
ing water as well.

"Obsidian," Raven told them. "A whole small mountain of glass rock. I've seen similar in the Yellowstone
but not this smooth and this perfect and not with that
great waterfall in the middle."

Facing the cliff and waterfall was a veritable wall of
carved demonic figures, all staring into the cliff and
being reflected, distortedly, back at them, giving the impression of a tribe of monsters staring out from just beneath the glass. A row of torches and flame pots nicely
placed around would, if lit, give an even eerier sensation
at night.

"We are trespassing on holy ground," Midi said nervously. "This is some sort of temple or holy place."

Raven nodded. "I agree. I said all totems were messages, and it's clear that all the ones leading here meant a
simple 'Keep Out.' What I can't figure out is why they'd
go to all this trouble and then have nobody here permanently—no high priests, no holy guards, nothin'. This
place is obviously used and well maintained, yet there's
nobody here. It's just too damned deserted."

Dura looked around and shook her shaggy head. "I
have been wondering if perhaps the people did not simply vanish as we approached. Hiding in the lake, perhaps."

Maria went over to a barren area and dropped to one
knee, studying the ground. "I find it interesting that even
though it rains as much here as elsewhere on this world,
there are no tracks. No footprints at all. The road and
the paths here are well worn, yet there is no sign of
prints. Why?"

Raven stood back and thought about it. "Gobanifar," he said at last.

All heads turned to him in puzzlement.

"He's nocturnal. Oh, he gets around well enough in the daytime, but he can't stand direct sunlight and he's mostly blind in full daylight. This is a pretty nasty sun. Suppose these people live in and under the water by day, then come up at night? Suppose the sun would injure, maybe kill them? If you lived or hunted or whatever in those seas, with that plankton or whatever it is hiding most of the sun and keeping what's below pretty dark, you'd probably be pretty damned sensitive to the sun's rays, wouldn't you? And if you could see at all down there, imagine what daylight would do. The only thing that doesn't figure is that this stuff implies air breathers, yet there's no sign of them surfacing for air or even skirting the tops of the waves."

"It makes sense," Dura agreed. "As to the tracks—if they're really sea creatures, maybe they don't have much to make tracks with. Suppose they don't have legs."

Raven went over to one of the worn tracks and bent down and examined it. It was pretty much the size of an average human, and the worn depression was deep and yet oddly shaped, almost straight along the sides. "Could be," he agreed. "If they had to drag their bodies behind them they'd wipe out any handprints or whatever. But if they're designed for the water, why come out of it at all, particularly to this elaborate setup?"

"Takya's people live entirely in the sea," Dura noted, "yet they build and maintain structures on rocky outcrops, some very elaborate. The people of Chanchuk are also water creatures yet they build in it and live above it."

"Perhaps it's simply out of some memory of who and what they used to be," Maria suggested. "Or perhaps they do not come here often. This might be used only for high religious purposes, for marriages and funerals or for other holy things. Many ancients had their gods living in the sky. If you lived in the darkest of waters, and only came out at night, would not the land be the dwelling place of the gods? This world is generally more cloudy than clear and has no moon. Think about it."

"Yeah, but if they see in the dark, if they see like we do at all, then why all the torches and fire pots?" Raven mused. "Unless . . . fire would be almost a sacred thing to a water culture that only once in a while came up on land. Yeah. Brightness and fire. Makes sense." He thought for a moment. "Now we come to the hard part. I don't know about you, but I don't think I want to get caught in here in the dead of night even if we can outrun 'em and outfly 'em. Still this is it. This is where we got to get some kind of contact going. The first step is to find out just what the hell these people are like."

Maria looked around. "I kind of doubt they could climb trees, although they probably would have some means of knocking someone out of them if they had to. They harvest those fruits and coconuts somehow, I think. If someone could stay up there, though, with a flight pack, infrared viewer perhaps tied in to a communications link, and remain very, very quiet, perhaps all night . . . it might be a start."

Raven grinned. "Nice assignment. I don't notice anybody rushing to volunteer."

"I will do it," said Dura Panoshka. "My people are born in the trees."

Raven nodded. "Agreed—for tonight. I think one of us can get back over to camp, recharge, and get back here with the necessary equipment with time to spare before dusk. But this isn't someplace they visit every night. It might take a week, maybe a month. Who knows?" He looked around. "Han Li, I think this is one duty that you are excused from. You can remain still for that long but frankly you are too heavy for those trees to support. Maybe Gobanifar is gonna do more than he figured after all. As for the rest of us—we'll all take turns until somebody gets lucky."

Pictures of the holy place were taken and transmitted back to *Thunder* through the communications link. Everyone was fascinated, although the regular data bases had nothing specific about the totems or the design of the place. It remained for Clayben to make the best guess.

"The totems aren't northwestern American, that is certain," he said. "It is the wrong sort of setting for them, and isn't consistent with any of the cultures known to Raven or Hawks. So many of the totems are really statues—I think we were thrown by the totem pole aspect of the entry guardians. Most of the ones inside are single deities, and some are even repeated many times. The squid-faced thing, and the creature that is all mean red eyes and teeth. Animism, yes, but not Amerind. The wood and the technique are wrong. I would say Polynesian, perhaps Melanesian. South Pacific. The layout of the place very much resembles the Polynesian *heiau*. If so, these are going to be tribal people, with many gods based on nature, very fierce, possibly if not probably including human sacrifice and, potentially, even ritual cannibalism."

Hawks shook his head. "You mean virgins into volcanoes and all that?"

"Not that way, although that's the old image. Think of the Aztecs and Mayans. Like them, sacrifice was never a girl—their culture was very male-oriented. Young men, possibly the prime of manhood. None of our people would be sacrificed, though. They would be flayed alive, their hearts perhaps removed, and parts of them consumed to gain the *mana* of the enemy. That's if they don't consider our people gods. Ancient Hawaiians mistook the earliest European explorers for gods simply because they had white skin and Caucasian features. Of course, when one of them cut himself or bruised himself or had any misfortune, they changed their minds and attacked. They were an ignorant, insular people—but they weren't stupid."

On the island of the heiau, the advance party went through nine days of night watches. Several times there seemed to be movement about the island, either in the direction of the beach or, now and then, in the direction of the lake, but nothing came near enough to be seen if, indeed, they were not figments of imaginations that were both nervous and bored at the same time. Still, Raven was certain that the wait would not be indefinite; one did not build such places for use only once or twice a year, and the area was too well maintained. Indeed, by day there were signs that some of the ripe fruit from particular groves had been harvested.

On the tenth night it was Raven's turn once more, and he hated it. He certainly had counted on something happening before he had to take another turn, and the last time he'd spent the night mostly hanging on to the limbs for dear life in a bad storm. Now, though, the night was fairly calm, the breeze strong but not unusually so, and there were even occasional breaks in the clouds through which a few lone stars shone. Such stellar visions were not daily occurrences here.

About two and a half hours after sundown, when it was completely dark, there was movement.

He heard them rather than saw them at first—odd, almost slithering sounds, but intermittent. *Swish.* Stop. *Swish.* Stop. Rhythmic, regular, yet very strange indeed, and there were far more than just a single one. It was a sound made by several sources, all tending to move and stop at pretty much the same time.

They were lighting the flame pots along the road.

He removed his infrared goggles, knowing they would be no help. At least these folks were gonna light themselves up for him. He took the transmitter lens and used it alone for the pictures. It was a nervous, even agonizing wait, but they finally came into view.

The first thing that startled him was what should have been obvious: they were the same dark, rust-red color as the plankton. They swam in it, consumed it, were dyed by it inside and out. It's what made them damned near impossible to see even on the surface.

From their waists down they had a fishlike shape terminating in a broad, flat, horizontally mounted tail. No hair, no scales that could be seen, but that skin looked tougher than any hide Raven had ever known. They were dragging themselves along over rock and hard ground and hardly noticed it.

From the waist up they were humanoid, but not completely so. The arms were thick and powerful-looking but had a curious flatness to them, the undersides seeming to have a different skin texture—rougher and slightly lighter in color. The hands were big and appeared fully webbed; they used them like forelegs, and they were pivoted out from the body, lizardlike. Still, they must have had real dexterity in them—somebody built this place and carved and painted those totems. And could they bend their bodies! As the procession reached a new fire pot, one would stop, then rear up—so limber and so powerful, bent upright from the waist. Then the forelegs became true hands, and the creature would take several objects from a skin pouch strapped around its neck, strike them together, and toss them into the pot—and the fire would flare up.

The undersides were also interesting in that they

seemed to have dull but elaborate designs painted or somehow fixed onto them. At first Raven thought it was natural, but they were too regular and too complex—and too different from one another—to be that. Ornamental markings, perhaps, or markings of rank.

The faces—the faces were unforgettable. Thick, lizardlike, with only a bony ridge where the nose should be, a wide, serpentine mouth that revealed nasty rows of teeth, and huge, deep-set eyes of black on yellow that seemed at once inhuman and frightening, and that reflected the fire's light in a grotesque catlike way. There were bony ridges and plates all over their faces that seemed to freeze them into a permanent grotesque expression. If there were ears they were but tiny holes in the sides of the head.

Raven couldn't help but think that these were the meanest, most monstrous-looking beings his wildest nightmares might conjure up. Still, he had to hand it to Master System. If it wanted to guard something precious, these were the very ones to use.

They certainly were talking, although it was a strange series of sounds—like a recording of a man with a deep voice having a heart attack played backward—coming from somewhere deep in the throat.

When they passed right below him he could hear them breathing heavily, in and out, almost like tiny steam engines. The breathing was certainly labored; he suspected that these were not really air breathers in the normal sense, but water breathers with gills who had a sufficient, if rudimentary, lung system to breathe air from a pulsating oblong membrane atop their bony heads.

They were not unarmed. Several carried what could only be weapons in special hide carriers strapped to them, and he had no doubt that the best of them could stop, fix their weapons, rear up, aim, and shoot in a very short time.

Raven had a sudden, demanding urge to cough, but he was too damned scared to allow it.

Finally they were all inside, and he allowed himself a drink from his canteen and tried to get hold of himself. They were lighting the pots and torches inside the heiau now, and the place was taking on an eerie life.

That was all that happened for a couple of hours. There was plenty of activity inside, but none on the road, which suited him just fine. Maybe this was the maintenance and cleanup crew or the housekeeping staff. He repressed a temptation to turn on the belt and float up and away; not only would it be rough in the dark to make sure he got well away, but no matter his personal feelings, his mission was to wait and watch.

Along about midnight local time, down the road came a whole *mess* of them, with armed guards flanking a small group crawling in the center. He could tell immediately that the ones in the center were different, although they were no less ugly. The one leading the procession although well protected by guards was *huge* and ten times meaner-looking than the rest. He wore no weapons but some kind of cloak with an elaborate design, and lots of golden neck chains and other jewelry. The chief, certainly—maybe even one of higher rank than that.

The others behind him, crawling two abreast, were very different. They were smaller and a bit sleeker, yet longer, more serpentine, than the others. Their faces were a little gentler, and less bony, although still ugly by Raven's standards. Two bony plates rose just over the eyes and met near the back of the head, just behind the nostrils, joining into a single ridge that extended down the back, tapering off above the waist.

These, then, were the beautiful maidens, if your idea of beauty was an iguana with a dolphin's tail. Raven wondered if they bore their young live and nursed them or what. It was hard to imagine breasts of any sort some-where in that ribbed, bony underplate.

The party came along up the road and seemed to continue forever, and it wasn't a silent procession. There was a kind of chanting going on, echoed from inside the heiau, and after the chief had entered, drums began a slow, steady beat and there was the sound of horns being blown. *Somebody* at least had lungs, unless they could make those sounds naturally.

He was surprised to see the women following the chief, though. According to the data Clayben had sent down based on his analysis of the initial pictures, if this was a Pacific culture, women shouldn't be allowed on holy ground or even allowed to walk in the footsteps of the chief.

Finally the entire procession was inside, with the exception of the warriors who were left, sitting up in that snake-god pose, between each flame pot, with what looked like a spear and some kind of crossbow. He didn't want to test their range or accuracy.

Although it was impossible to see just what was going on inside the heiau, they seemed to be having a fine time chanting and drumming loudly. Raven could only wonder why they hadn't heard this racket years ago, although, as had been pointed out, the temple was well around the other side of the island from their encampment and shielded from view. What sounded loud here might well be rather soft on the other island when masked by the sounds of wind and surf.

Whatever it was they were doing, the sun would come up at six twenty-two by Raven's watch, and it was getting after four. He himself was miserable and certain that at any time he was going to make some kind of noise or do something that would bring those nasties down there after him in large numbers.

Just before dawn they started back out, but not everybody came. He couldn't be sure about all the males, but it was clear that none of the females left the heiau. The big chief did, with his retinue of guards, looking mean and huge as ever, and so did most of the exterior guards, although some remained near the entrance to the heiau. The others brought up the rear of the chief's big party, extinguishing the fire pots as they went. Clearly the girls were going to stay, and so were at least four of the warriors with the bows and spears. He hadn't figured on that. They were supposed to be helpless in daylight, blind and heat sensitive. This didn't figure—and would make his getaway difficult. He could take them out with the pistol, of course, but that was no way to say hello and ask for favors.

Sooner or later, though, a move would have to be made or they might have to wait another ten days or more, with that damned Chi breathing down their necks and time feeling very, very limited. Idly he wondered if a mindprinter helmet would even go on those thick heads, let alone work right. It better—these weren't the kind of people you just wanted to drop in on with a cheery smile and upturned palms.

The sun, in fact, was fairly high before he felt relatively safe. Not that his toad-faced guards had left; instead they had brought water in large flasks, then poured them on areas behind their watch stations well within the full shade of the trees, and then he watched as they got down on their bellies and dug into the mud until only their blowhole nostrils were exposed. It was an amazing, and chilling, performance. Raven could only hope that those resting spots were preprepared; he would hate to think that they could do this most anywhere there was mud.

Cautiously he increased power on his flight belt, floated up a bit, then out. For a brief moment he felt totally exposed and helpless, but he quickly turned, climbed, and floated out toward the open sea. If they saw or heard him, they hadn't had either the time or the vision in daylight to strike him before he was away and that was good enough for him. All across the strait though he kept seeing rust-color monster heads poking up from the waves, staring at him with those mean monster eyes, and he hoped it was just a trick of wind and wave and his tired mind.

He was all in when he arrived, although they knew by his lateness combined with the fact that he hadn't pushed the emergency signal that he'd found something of value. He just mumbled to them to see the recordings, made it into the tent, and collapsed.

He dreamed of monsters, of lizardlike faces all around him, staring, poking, prodding. At last he dreamed they were chasing him down that road, and, for some reason, he was crawling just as they were, but faster. He made the edge of the sea, yet for some reason it was not choppy but smooth as glass, and reflecting back from the water's surface was the face of one of the demon monsters—his face.

And, suddenly, he was aware of someone else, someone standing next to him on two human legs. He looked up and saw Arnold Nagy staring back down at him in pity. "Are you willing to pay the price?" Nagy asked him, and the question echoed through his mind.

He awoke, sweating profusely although not from the heat. The nightmares had been very vivid, very real, and very, very terrifying, yet until now he had been unable to wake up. He made his way shakily outside the tent, seeing that it was nearly dark, and found some food cakes and beer. It was better than nothing.

Dura Panoshka heard him and emerged from the communications tent and came over to him. "How are you feeling?" she asked him. "You were having . . . dreams."

Raven nodded. "Nightmares. You seen the pictures?"

She nodded. "We also sent copies of the entire data pack to *Thunder*. Takya agrees that they are ugly to look at, but she suspects they are fast swimmers. Down below, particularly if they have gills as well, their form and particularly their body elasticity would make them formidable indeed. They look almost like carved coral, yet they bend like snakes."

"Yeah, well, I ain't much for the beauty of 'em one way or another. You sort'a got the impression watching them that them mean expressions weren't just locked on 'em because of their bone structure. The eyes, the way they moved—they're a mean bunch of monsters, Dura, by any human measure. Inside, not outside. And you can bet your ship that if they got the ring it isn't in none of those convenient land temples of theirs. It's down deep in the dark and wet."

"I know. They were able to analyze the speech, anyway. It's a variation of one of the Polynesian dialects, all right. The reason it sounds so strange, other than the fact that it's being spoken with different sound equipment than the usual human larynx, is that it covers a far wider spectrum than you can hear. It's very complex, though, and they can't make much of it out even though they recognized enough to identify its origins. It appears that they don't have a lot of sounds, but they have an almost infinite number of intonations. Many languages use tones—usually three or five, so if the same 'word' sound is said in a low tone, or ascending, or descending, it means something different. In their case, the number of tones is at least in the hundreds."

He whistled. "So we're not gonna have an easy conversation with them. We have to face it, Dura. We got to put the snatch on a couple of them things, haul 'em up to *Thunder*, take a mindprint readout, analyze their language and culture, and find out what we're really dealing with. I wish I knew just what would put 'em out quick and quiet enough, but we're just gonna have to trust to luck on that. But if there aren't any Centers, if there's no emperor or high priest or big lizard, then any damned chief could have it. Any of 'em. And they don't carry weapons around on land unless they figure to get jumped. That chief had a lot of guards. In the water I might see it—you got to figure them totem faces are modeled on some pretty nasty animals. But there's no big land critters here. We know that. The only reason for takin' guards and bows and spears on land and posting guards is to protect against other people. These guys might have regular wars with each other. If they do— findin' even somebody who knows somebody who once heard that somebody had a ring someplace is gonna be pretty damn near a career. And there's only one way you can make a hunt like that."

She nodded. "I know. The odds are very good that some of us will have to become these creatures."

The first part, at least, was easier than they thought by far. *Thunder* suggested that while the guards might be merely sleeping and trained to be at the ready, Raven was probably right in his supposition that they were there to guard against attacks by other tribes. If daylight was hard on the guards, it would be doubly hard on any attacker. The probability was quite good that the guards slept rather soundly in the middle of the day, particularly if it was one of those rare days with mostly clear skies and direct sun.

Raven took Han Li because of her strength and Maria for her nerve and reflexes, and they floated over with two extra belts. It was easy to find two sleeping guards, and a quick mediscan showed that no matter what might be alien about these creatures, the basics of human anatomy were still retained as usual—the brain in the head; spinal cord, heart, and other organs in the right places. The lungs appeared more primitive and smaller than expected and oddly shaped and placed, but that was not surprising. The odds were very good that a beam on stun aimed full at the head and then widening to the rest of the body would do the same thing to them as to anybody else.

It did, according to the mediscan, and the job of then digging the unconscious guard out of the mud was both messy and unpleasant as well as heavy work. They just wanted to get him rolled over sufficiently to put one of the belts on him and activate it, then glide his ugly form back across the strait to the camp. *Lightning* came in to handle the beam-up of the body, which was then placed in a case filled with planetary sea water and rigged to periodically restun the sleeping warrior. They did not dare try medications or gases as yet; what worked on others might well kill their prisoner, and they didn't want that.

Equally nerve-racking was a return trip for a second warrior, although it, too, proved more of just a messy job than any real trouble. *Thunder* always wanted two specimens, since only one might not be representative and a control was needed for comparison. They would have liked to have also had a female, but Raven decided against going into the heiau itself for one at this time. If the object was to guard the heiau and the females within, then it was more than possible that there were traps and alarms set. Best to go with what they could easily get— for now.

Still, it would be tougher in one way from now on, and they ordered their defense perimeter strengthened and set up a twenty-four-hour guard shift as reinforcement. Nobody could tell what the creatures would think when they woke up later on and discovered two of their prized warriors vanished from well within their defenses. Even though they had shown no interest, past or present, in the base island, to find those two, the big chief might have different ideas.

6. COWBOYS AND INDIANS

THE WORLD WAS CALLED ALITITI, WHICH BASICALLY meant "Land of the Gods' Children." It took considerable time to read out the language from the pair delivered to *Thunder* and then compare and correlate it with known linguistic files and run it through computer interpolations. Some words were very strange, and the context of it was even stranger. These people had a far different idea of reality than the men and women of the *Thunder*. There was also some question of whether any of the company would be capable of speaking that supertonal tongue, and whether even the artificial speaking and translating devices could handle it.

The natives had no knowledge of Master System; in fact, they had no knowledge of anything beyond their own watery world. Unlike on Matriyeh, China and Clayben were certain that this entire culture was one quite deliberately and completely worked out by the early colonial leaders themselves and not by the heavy hand of the all-powerful computer. Much of the traditional Polynesian cosmology and attitudes were retained, and ancient tales and legends were adapted to the new

conditions, but there was nothing in the minds of either
guard to indicate that they had any idea that there were
other worlds than this, only a vague legend about their
people crossing a great sea to a new land as the gods, led
by volcanic Pelé, destroyed all other tribes and nations
for renouncing their faith and the old gods.

They lived in the water and were best suited to
breathe it, and their world below the waves was bizarre
indeed. The few images that the mindscans could get
showed a world so strange, so different, from anything
any of the pirates had ever seen that even the truly alien
Makkikor seemed closer to them.

It was a world without sun, yet not a world of darkness. All of the creatures there, it seemed, save just a
few predators, provided their own illumination. Plants
below shone with varicolored radiant light; fish and
other denizens of the deep had elaborate patterns; some
could create and even beam light. Even the people there
could do this, and with some control, by electrochemical
mechanisms on their ribbed chests. So elaborate was this
ability that one could tell tribe, rank, even individuals,
from how the patterns formed there. Males could vary
the coloration from yellow through some oranges and
reds and even into purple; females tended to go through
blues and greens. One could tell a lot about a person by
his or her pattern, colors, and intensities, including their
emotional state. It was difficult for these people to hide
their feelings or moods.

Females had the unique ability to manufacture and
exude this self-illumination substance, and their homes
and lands and territories were marked with it.

Their underwater domain was not at all ugly; rather, it
was a fairyland of colors and shapes that all of them
found beautiful and fascinating.

Yes, there *were* predators, some large and deadly, all
teeth or tentacles, who were doubly feared because they

had no self-illumination. Maui's Gift—light in the darkness—was a double-edged sword that made their world a place of beauty and magic but also made them targets for the creatures of the darkness.

But this was not the only source of light below. This world was heavily volcanic, and for all the activity above sea level there was a lot more below. The Alititians lived in a hot, violent world of bubbling lava and steam jets and had within them abilities to see differences in temperature, to clearly define currents, to see the differences in the water high and low as some birds could see or sense differences in air.

Water was the domain of Men, but a biological quirk, or a Master System shortcut, impelled them to occasionally take to the land, a medium both feared and mystical to them all. Copulation took place in the water, but the children could not be born there. In an ironic throwback to their origins, with considerable complex religious explanations, the children were born looking more like an Earth-human, at least internally, than like their own parents and able to breathe only air. Thus, they, and their mothers, had to remain in the air until, over a period of months, they developed the protective layers of skin needed to survive in that violent ocean and the primary respiratory system they would need there. They even developed distinctive glowing markings that would make them easy to spot by a mother under the sea. Then they could be taught, usually very easily, to swim.

Raven's team and its encampment had been withdrawn. They had served their purpose—for now. Now they would have to study the information they had retrieved.

The Crow chomped on a cigar and looked at the data. "Well, I'll be damned. So *that's* what that thing is over there. Kind of a birth and nursing center. No wonder they guard it like they do. Any enemy who successfully attacked and wiped out that heiau would be striking a body blow at a tribe's future—and maybe capturing the women and children to enlarge its own size and strength."

Maria nodded. "It is a familiar pattern in the end. Still, they do not have the limitations imposed on the Matriyehans. They have areas where they breed and raise food fish and underwater plants, and they also harvest some of the islands. One would think that after all this time there would in fact be some consolidation of tribes here, some small kingdoms or even larger groupings."

Many strong chiefs had tried, and some had expanded over great areas by Alititian standards, but none had been able to hold or control such a domain. Lack of communications over wide areas and the ambition of local nobles trusted to run things tended to break up any large concentrations. Thus, while many tribes, including this one, were technically a part of nations under kings, the kings tended to be titular or ceremonial figures with little real power. The real power resided in the tribal chiefs and in their high priests, and it was considerable—but localized.

Star Eagle analyzed the entire situation and came up with a lot of recommendations, none particularly appealing and none short-term.

"It is obvious that one of the kings or one of the high priests serving a king would be likely to have the ring," he noted, "but there are hundreds, if not thousands, of such people. Unlike the other areas, there is no trace of the ring motif in their myths and legends. It is possibly no more than a royal ornament. There is simply no way that we are going to locate it. Not even Vulture could have done that, except by sheer luck."

Hawks nodded. "And even if we could locate all these kings, they wouldn't be very receptive to people not of their form, and would be openly hostile to people of their own race but of different tribes or nations. Ceremonial or not, it's not very practical to think of walking up to each king saying, 'Hello, your Majesty. Can we take a look at all your ceremonial jewelry?'"

"Yes. Now we could play gods, of course, and possibly hook an ambitious chief into a massive expansion plan, but it might still take years to conquer a region that only might have the ring. You would eventually have to conquer the entire planet. If we just had an idea of the region where the ring resided we would have at least a chance, and even that chance is beyond rational odds," the computer agreed.

Hawks sighed. "I also find this . . . distasteful. We're usually the underdogs battling Master System. I can identify with that, work with it, live with it. But now I am being asked to totally destroy a culture by sheer weight of our technological power and superiority. For all their relative primitiveness, these people, this culture, have much merit. Their world is a place of beauty, their common interests are in using and loving their element without destroying it or overmanaging it. They love their world and their culture. Their intellectual direction is spiritual and communal. Yet it is all so fragile, so easily destroyed forever. I suspect that was what the early colonial leaders here realized. They took what was necessary for their survival and what was essential and important to their spirits and rejected the rest, which might corrupt or destroy them. Now you are telling me that I must do just that."

"Nevertheless, it must be done," Isaac Clayben put in. "To have come this far and not succeed merely on the basis of preserving a culture makes no sense. There is Earth and more than four hundred and fifty other colonial worlds to consider. The greater good for the greater number is the imperative here."

Raven shook his head in wonder. Other than Cloud Dancer, he was probably the only one aboard who really saw and understood Hawks's mental agony. It was one he, too, shared, although perhaps not with the chief's intensity. Clayben was right, of course, and so was Hawks.

The chief was not about to start formulating detailed plans right then. "Run through other alternatives!" he ordered Star Eagle. "If they are longer, more time consuming, or have a higher risk then so be it!"

But there were no efficient alternatives, and everyone, including Hawks, really knew it. His failure to act on this, to stall and hope for a miracle, absolutely bewildered the others. Ultimately it was China who was dispatched to Raven by the rest for an explanation of Hawks's behavior.

"First you got to get some history," the Crow told her. "Ten, twenty thousand years ago, maybe more, the ancestors of Hawks and me picked up everything and everybody from their homes in southeast Asia and started a walk. It was one *hell* of a walk, too. All the men, women, children, their dogs and chickens, and you name it. Why they did it we might never know, except that we were a small people surrounded by fierce enemies, or potentially fierce enemies, and we knew we couldn't last there. So we walked. And when we got to the Pacific, we walked north until the great land bridge between Asia and America was reached, and when the little bit of water froze solid we kept walkin'. Not until we were well on the other side did any of us stop. It must've taken generations. The ones who finally made it probably knew no other life than walking, moving, settling for a little while, then picking up and moving on."

He sighed, settled back, and lit a cigar. "Their descendants didn't stop until they were all the way down as far as you could walk in South America. The rest—they split up and went different ways. Each had a group, a tribe, with a different idea of the promised land, I guess, and most of 'em found theirs. Two continents, every kind of climate and weather, buffalo and deer by the millions, huge prairies and vast forests—you name it, it was there. Two vast continents with everything anyone could ever wish for—and no people. They settled in different places and the tribes multiplied and became nations, the distances so great the languages themselves wound up bearin' no real resemblance to one another—just like what happened in the colonial worlds here. Different cultures, different languages, different ideas. And they traded with each other—pottery, pipes, gems, and ideas as well—and sometimes they fought each other as nations do, but they had a real good thing there. Some became big empires like the ones in Europe and Asia and Africa; some kept small, 'cause maybe their religion or their feeling for the land made empires, to them, sort of sacrilege. Those were the nations like the Cheyenne and Sioux and Blackfoot and Crow—my people."

She nodded. "Then he sees in this world an echo of his own people's past. Even though they appear serpentine monsters with dolphin's tails he sees only their essential humanity. His empathy for them binds him."

"Sort of, but it's not like that. Hawks ain't no prairie original, and neither am I. We love our people and our ancestral lands but we don't belong there no more. We don't fit. But that's okay. It's what happened to all our people that's got him troubled.

"See," he continued, "nations came and went, empires rose and fell, but it was all ours. Change was slow. We weren't saints—the idiot people of the Southwest chopped down all the trees and wound up turnin' their lands to desert and killing themselves. We screwed up, but in little bits and pieces. The whole stayed the same, and the basic values of spirit, community, and honor held up. Then the Europeans came. No problem at first—just another crazy set of empires. Hell, they brought the horse to America and the native people took to it with a vengeance. But they also had the guns and they were comin' out of a period of wars where there'd been so much killin' for so long they were hard and mean and intolerant of anybody else. A war between the Crow and Blackfoot took maybe weeks and killed a few folks until honor was balanced and a settlement reached. Them Europeans fought one called the Hundred Years War. They were different—and war is the best way to generate new technology. They had us cold and they didn't see us as much more than ignorant savages. We were different, not even Christian, and we had different looks and darker skin. In two hundred and fifty years they killed a lot of us, destroyed all our nations and cultures, burned the Mayan libraries, and penned up a lot of us on the worst patches of land in the middle of nowhere like prisoners. We fought— but they had the guns and the numbers."

"I know little of that," China said, "but I knew of course of the European conquest of the Americas. It was Master System who reversed things and restored the tribes where it could, was it not?"

He nodded. "Yeah, sort of. We're better than we were 'cause we're in charge and not cooped up, but it's not really the way it was. It's the way Master System figured it should be for economy's sake. Same goes for the Polynesians. The Europeans marched in and took over and even after they left there wasn't much left of the old culture but shows for tourists. Hawks figures that what happened here, on Alititi, was that Master System kind'a made a deal with some Pacific folks who wanted to turn their back on the modern world and get back to what they saw as the basics. They're ugly as sin and they live in a crazy kind of world, but it's *theirs*, and it works. See, that's what's got Hawks so round the bend. We're sittin' up here, not many of us, but with more power at our command than they dream their gods might have, and they got something we want. All them other rings—we didn't have to destroy nothing. We tried to do it so quick and quiet that not many folks even got hurt. But here, now, Hawks has been handed this thing. You know the best way to find a needle mixed in a haystack?"

She shook her head. "No."

"Your burn the haystack and sift through the ashes. That's what Hawks is bein' asked to do—repeat history. Kill who-knows-how-many innocent people, destroy their culture, ransack a world to find a ring. He's bein' pressured to do to them what the Europeans did to our people, only faster, which means even dirtier and deadlier. The cowboys and injuns changed places, and he didn't bargain for that."

The alarm rang in the quarters of each member of the council of captains. Hawks was outside playing with his son when he heard it and rushed inside.

"Yes?"

"Ships in the Alititian system," Star Eagle reported.

Hawks frowned. "A task force?" That would be disastrous, for it would mean not only that the already difficult and dangerous job was getting impossible, it would also mean that the SPF had discovered the deception the pirates pulled on Matriyeh and had maybe captured some of their people left behind there.

"No. A small SPF vessel. Data indicates the probability that it is a tactical ship—a mobile command post rather than a true command ship designed for orbital work. It might be a forward scouting party for a task force, perhaps not. It is being covered by two Val fighters."

Hawks thought a moment, then snapped his fingers. "Chi! Has to be! Star Eagle—we have to get something in there close and fast! They won't want to stay around long in plain view. Too much danger of giving the location away. Chi's not taking any chances, though. She's gonna booby trap the ring."

"That is bad," the computer responded.

"Uh uh! It's the best break we've had, and right in the nick of time, too! To booby trap it they're gonna have to send some people down there. Odds are they've got some Alititian SPF in that ship who have some tribal ties to whoever's holding the ring. Hell, there might be SPF down there all the time—but there's no way to contact them. Star Eagle—*we have to know precisely where they go down to the surface! Precisely!* And they must not know we're doing it!"

"Working on the problem. We have the inactive base camp fighter there and the relay fighter inactive in solar orbit. Their scanners are not the best but we dare not risk a punch right now. If I could get that second base camp fighter up, I'd have a fighting chance. There are only three ships and they will not establish orbital positions for a couple of hours. Perhaps I can get that one on the ground off when they are positioned right. I will try."

"You must! No matter what nasty business Chi and her Vals are pulling, they're doing work for us we couldn't dream of accomplishing. Come on, Star Eagle! They are going to point an arrow right to where we must look! You cannot fail!"

But it was several hours of nail-biting as they all sat around in the common waiting for word.

Finally Star Eagle reported, "I have it, I think, and I've correlated it with our own surveys. They apparently have no receiver on the ground and so they had to send a pod down with their people. The region is in the southern hemisphere, a tiny island in an unusually quiescent geologic region. Obvious when you think of it. They would not place the ring where it would be likely to be melted in volcanic fires or lost by seaquake. It is well away from the base camp—halfway around the world, almost. Our prisoners had no data at all on any region beyond their own and their neighbors. We will require more prisoners from the immediate area to get hard information, and they will have to be taken with greater stealth than we used the first time. We will need specimens from the proper tribe or nation, but ones who will be considered missing—a natural if sad turn of events—rather than obviously kidnapped. We can't just walk in on these people. There must be permanent party SPF down there."

"I agree," Hawks replied. "First we have to wait for them to leave—not just the planet but the system. Make certain that they are gone, too, and that they leave no surprises behind in the system that we don't know about and can't counter. Then we'll need high-resolution surveys of the entire area. We can assume a general similarity to the ones we know, but there will be regional differences. We must know them. Then Raven, here, can work out how to make a few of them vanish."

It must have been a real welcome home celebration, because the pod remained on the island for nine days. The ships, however, were not idle during that time—the Vals looked over much of the inner solar system, and definitely with mischief in mind. Had the rebel band not beaten Chi to the place, the additional monitors and sophisticated sweep and I.D. systems installed by the Vals would have been virtually undetectable, just as those small fighters from *Thunder* were not detected by the newcomers. Being able to watch them plant things, though, and even monitor their tests of the devices, made it relatively easy to determine where and of what type the new traps were. It would take some time and trouble, but they had defeated or fooled worse.

Ultimately the pod took off and rejoined its parent vessel. The trio of ships wasted little time after that in regrouping and heading out and away. By the time they accelerated and punched out of the system as a group, the sophisticated defense computer network aboard *Thunder* had already completed the plan for neutralizing the new orbital devices and begun to create the necessary equipment. They could not, however, do anything about what those who had gone down to the surface, and below it, had done. That would await more information than *Star Eagle's* monitors could give.

They gave everything a few extra days just to make certain nobody in Chi's band had forgotten something and come back for it, then sent *Lightning* in for a methodical mapping of the pinpointed surface area.

Raven was a little concerned. "If Chi's as good as Vulture says, this could be one hell of a trap," he noted. "I mean, suppose she figures we're already on to this hole? She comes in, bold as brass, pinpoints a location far away from the ring, and sends some folks down there making everybody sit, open and obvious, for nine *days* so there's no question we get the point. Then we move in; right into her trap, no ring in sight. I mean, this, comin' when it did—sort'a just when we needed it— smells like two-month-old dead fish."

"It's a possibility, but not a likely one," Hawks replied. "I agree that the move, coming now, makes me a little suspicious, but unless they just went down and sat and camped for nine days—and we intercepted no messages from the surface on our scanners—they had to go under, and if they went under, then whoever it was had to be people who were known there and wouldn't be immediately captured and maybe killed. No, Chi might be smart enough to plant some SPF in the wrong spot, but that's not consistent with Master System's behavior and Chi hasn't been on the job long enough to set up that sort of trick even if she could think of it."

"I agree with Hawks's logic," Star Eagle put in. "Also, I have dispatched probes back to Matriyeh and am just now receiving information that the same three ships visited there before coming here. I will attempt to contact Ikira when I feel it is safe. If she is still alive and still on duty there, it is logical that they did not discover the switch and that whatever they did there is fairly similar to what they did here. It is also logical that they went to Matriyeh first—that is a world Master System knows full well is named in some of the documents and so they assume it will be our next target. This one was last because it is presumed unknown and hidden."

"I'll feel better when we hear from Ikira," Raven commented. "That had to be pretty damned hairy. Remember, the whole damned Matriyehan division's on the planet permanently so who could they send down? If it was a Val or two, with their scanners, Ikira's already dead meat and there's a task force around here somewhere."

"In the meantime, there is no substitute for intelligence, and we need it fast," Hawks said. "They won't be expecting any move so soon. Get me some of those locals, Raven."

It was a *quo'oa* night, the kind of night when vision at the surface was clear, the distant gods shined down, and even the forms of the clouds could be told. It was the sort of night when Gatherers came forth from the Sea-Mother to fetch and tend those things most precious, the food of the gods, for the sacred ceremonies in the kingdom below.

The four who came out of the surf onto the beach were old, experienced men; not elders but senior warriors who feared little beyond the powers of Pelé and who had never met their match. They came in professionally, spread out, and immediately were up on their tails, all senses fully alert and spears at the ready. They remained there, motionless, poised, for several minutes, like grotesque statuary, until they were satisfied. The spears went back in the *pu'oa*, and great arms stretched out like the legs of the great lizards they had never known, and they walked confidently inward to the macadamia groves.

They cleared the beach and then stopped warily again as the gateway, guarded by tikis with powerful mana, stared back at them. One great one in the shape of the Tentacled Demon-Lord on the right, another in the form of the Shark God, its enemy, were as they should be, to warn any and all of whose territory and whose groves these were and just who any sacrilegious trespasser would have to answer to for his desecration. They were not the trouble; they were comforting as the guardians of the tribe.

It was the new one standing in the middle of the path that caused the problem.

It stood perhaps three meters high and looked to be of the same polished wood as the other tikis, but the features carved upon it were those of the fierce and unreachable sea birds of the Wind Spirit, a symbol understood here but not having any relation with this or any other local tribe in the kingdom, its stylized wings upturned toward the sky. Someone had been here; someone from outside was challenging their own spirits, their own rights to the sacred grove!

The four warriors immediately fanned out in a rough diamond formation, so that the one in the rear was nearest the sea and ready to summon a larger army if need be.

Yet the warriors were still, straining for any hint of unnatural sounds coming from the groves just beyond that provided the only possible cover. There were no strange scents they could detect, but in the air their noses weren't very good anyway. Suddenly they were on alert, weapons poised, as rustling sounds came from the groves on both sides of them, drawing their attention away from the profaning idol, not even noticing that those great upturned wings were now coming, ever so slowly, down, down, down . . .

The initial shots were on broad beam from the pistols that Han Li held in both hands; this was only sufficient to stun the warriors for a few moments, but it was more than enough time for Han Li to adjust the intensity with her thumbs and then pick each of the four off with a cleaner, stronger knockout shot.

Satisfied that the quartet was out cold, Han Li knocked away the thin casing of the tiki and stepped out fast. She picked up a communicator and called, "Condor to Crow. Come pick them up before somebody comes looking for them. Four in, four down."

"We cannot keep them here for long," Isaac Clayben told Hawks. "They have status and they are on the equivalent of a religious retreat, so while they are not expected back immediately, they *are* expected back. To be safe, I would say four days, five tops. Certainly no more."

The leader nodded. "Three days should be sufficient after all your practice. You've done the mindprint analysis. What do we have?"

"I believe I should answer that," China came in, her voice echoing from the small speakers usually used by Star Eagle and indicating that she was in her favorite place—mentally joined with the great computer through the pilot's interface. She did a lot of this sort of thing over the years; Star Eagle was excellent and personable, but he was still a machine and had never lived as a human being. The computer could assemble, sort, and evaluate information, but it took a human to interpret it properly.

"Go ahead," Hawks told her.

"Thanks to the first two we could dispense with most of the general testing and concentrate on the individual life data. Makoa, the old one with all the black gashes in his thick hide, is a real rake. He has nine wives, forty-three living children, and even though he exaggerates his claim of forty mistresses he does have a dozen or so. Macho seems to go a long way down there. He's also a king's warrior, which means he's about as high up the secular social scale as he can go, due mostly to the fact that he's a tough survivor. Warriors don't grow very old down there and when one does and keeps it up, he's almost worshipped like a god no matter how rotten he might be inside. It might be hard for anyone to live up to his image or keep up a masquerade and survive, but he's the one with access to the high places. Short of royalty, he's pretty well connected there, which was why he led the sacred gathering."

Hawks nodded. "Okay, okay. But what kind of system are we facing down there?"

"No Center, but definitely a small city—huge by Alititian standards, I think, and consistent with what we've seen of Master System's layout. It's a secular center, the seat of the hereditary king of the region—and he's a pretty tough old guy himself. He's executed a half dozen of his sons for trying to hurry along succession by attempting to knock off their old man. He's a good politician and warrior, and if he had just a hundred needlers he'd have conquered half the hemisphere by now. The tribal chiefs are all his sons by various wives and they're as ambitious and ornery as their old man, only not as experienced so they haven't succeeded in doing more than ignoring him on a day-to-day basis. It's all kept reasonably together by Halaku. He's the high priest of the big temple down there and the only one other than the king who *can* talk to members in other kingdoms—and he's the only one who actually does."

"SPF?"

"Possible but doubtful, unless they're pulling a variation of the Matriyehan sleepers on us. He does, however, have a hell of a temple guardian force at his command, and it's almost certain that some and maybe all of them are SPF mindprinted and hypnoed to love their jobs and their places. That's if the ring is down there. I can't get anything showing that any of these four, not even Makoa, has seen the ring, but that's not as unusual as you might think and doesn't mean much. When the king or the high priest goes all-out for ceremonies and the like, they're so weighted down with jewelry and ornamentation that you might never notice a little ring. The ring would have to be worn as a charm or something anyway; as should be obvious, while these people might wear special kinds of rings they couldn't possibly wear and keep on their finger a ring like the others we have. The ridges, bone structure in the finger, and slight webbing would prevent it."

Hawks had already thought of that one. "So we're still blind."

"Not quite. They had visitors for a few days, you know, from an outlying tribe loyal to the king."

"Aha!"

"There were three of them—the high priest of the tribe and two associate priests. They brought fine gifts to the king and court, and joined in a religious ceremony and sacrifice at the temple. They also brought harrowing tales of demon monsters who appeared vaguely human and had godlike power. These demons pretended to be gods and would come in and rape tribes of their wealth and arrogantly loot the temples, but although they looked like demons or gods they were actually mortals, animals of a high sort. Forget the gods approach, Hawks —any of us go down there, they'll check our mortality before they check anything else, and believe me, they're not stupid. They'd welcome you, bow and scrape, throw a big feast, and while you're relaxing their best warriors would puncture every area of your body. You have to hand it to this Brigadier Chi—she certainly did her homework. She's made certain that no one who's not Alititian will get anywhere near that city, let alone close to the higher-ups."

Hawks sighed and scratched his chin, thinking. "Uh huh. She's decided or deduced that Vulture was the only one of his kind, and she's pretty confident that the Vulture threat's been eliminated. That also means she's anticipating us very nicely, forcing us to do just what we were thinking of doing—a switch using the transmuters."

"Uh uh. The locals have been told that these evil mortal creatures have some great magic, and that they can imitate people very well. These Alititians aren't the sort to get paranoid, but they will notice and become suspicious of any strangeness or deviations in behavior, and the place is small enough that they know each other pretty well. Any infiltration here will require deep mindprinting, maybe relying on hypnotic commands and triggers. The problem is, Master System and this Chi will know that as well. Having planted cultural traps for the standard infiltrator to violate, we must assume that there are sophisticated traps, maybe of a very high-tech sort, to trap anybody deep-printed as a primitive."

"Remember, too, that all these men have families," Clayben put in. "They aren't the sort of people we picked—or had the luxury of picking—in the past. Any of our people will have to live in an intimate environment with family and children who have known them better than anyone else for years or perhaps a lifetime. The best actor in the world cannot feign affection or real love and concern for children not his own on a day-to-day basis." The scientist nodded. "Yes, that is what *I* would do in reverse circumstances. Create a situation where only deep printing will do, where the subject must really *become* the one he replaces, and then set some nice, sophisticated traps. Then an infiltrator, an impostor, either gets exposed by family and tribe and dealt with that way or he is so good that he is ultimately caught in traps his necessarily enforced ignorance can't even imagine. Remember that without Vulture even Matriyeh would have been impenetrable. This setup is at least as good."

"All right," Hawks responded, "so what do we do about it?"

China had some ideas. "First, it's deep infiltration for sure. We must have that. We must construct a structured hypnotic sequence that works until the last moment on a subconscious level. Prime command: look for the ring, locate it. Second, run an academic warrior's exercise—how would you steal such a thing? Ultimately, and there's no way around it, bring the original personality and knowledge forward for the actual operation. Star Eagle and I recommend a self-trigger that would allow the infiltrator to reimpose the deep print, or allow one of the compatriots to impose it. It will be a long, slow, perhaps laborious process, Hawks. We might be out here a very long time, and, unlike the other operations, we'll of necessity be in total ignorance of what progress is being made, if any. It is very frustrating—but there is no other practical way."

The leader sighed. "I am resigned to it. I have just been attempting to run through my mind what they might have put down there in nine days. What sort of unobtrusive yet effective trap might be there that would not violate this world or its culture or even be noticed by them but would stop us. I am too remote for this sort of thinking, and I am not a military man." He paused and shook his head. "I just wish we had Vulture here. Even if he wasn't his old self he knows this Chi better than we do. I'd even settle for a direct line to Matriyeh to determine what they pulled there."

"I dare not. The only safe way is to wait until those on the ground can signal us, if they can."

Hawks nodded. "And that may be weeks. We have to give these four back, one way or another, in just a couple of days. I don't like it, but the odds of capturing this many together without arousing any suspicion below— and one a reasonably high-level warrior—are slim. No, we have to go now, while the opportunity's there and the time is perfect. The primary question now is just who to send."

That was something of a problem, since no one who had already been through the transmuter could repeat the process. That left, excluding the children, Raven, Hawks, Cloud Dancer, Clayben, Takya, Dura, Gobanifar and his mate, Chun Wo Har and his two wives, Captain ben Suda and his wife, and the alien and remote Makkikor, who remained with its ship and was still an enigma to almost everyone, its captain of eleven years included. And the now-totally-reclusive Savaphoong, of course.

Raven seemed genuinely anguished, more haunted and upset than anyone could ever remember him being, but he was adamant.

"I am ashamed of myself, Hawks. Really ashamed. I think I could stomach being one of them Matriyehans, or a glorified sea otter like Bute, or even, maybe, a cudchewin' Janipurian. I think I could probably accept becoming one of Dura's race, or Takya's, or even Ikira's—but not these. Not *them*. My honor, even my position, screams that I'm the best man for this job, but—I would gladly kill myself first. It's tough to explain, even to myself. It has to do maybe with some childhood nightmares or something—I dunno. But I just can't become one of them *things*. I just can't. When we was down there, I was terrified. I kept control, I did my job, but I was terrified of them. It was all I could do to keep from switchin' from *stun* to *lethal*."

Hawks shook his head in sympathy. "I know. I have often wondered how I would react if and when my turn came—and it might yet, if this fails."

"You got a pretty wife and good-lookin' kids who need a daddy, and Cloud Dancer's the only mother most of China's brood really know. Me—I got nothin' and nobody. I got no excuse. No use givin' me the standard lecture, neither. I know what I look like. I know that the Chows and Bute and the two Chinamen and maybe even Manka and Maria and the rest had the same problems and that even though they never have been fully right since, they'd do it again. I know all that. And I know I'm gonna be guilty as hell when others go 'cause I should have been with 'em—I should've gone instead of one of 'em. If they fail, it might be because somebody like me wasn't with 'em. God! All that shit I spouted about makin' my ancestors proud of me and now here it is and look at me!"

Hawks sighed. "Well, we'll see what can be worked out." He smpathized with the man and his private terrors, but he knew that if it meant success or failure, *he* would do it, even though, as Raven pointed out, the cost to him and his family would be particularly high. This operation *was* particularly tough, although none of them had been all that easy. Min and Chung, for example, had not only the problem of being turned into strange creatures but into creatures of the opposite sex.

Which was, of course, also Dura's and Takya's problem now. Chung and Min had volunteered, none too enthusiastically, for the honor of themselves and their ship, which had heretofore been untouched by the burden of such responsibility—even by casualties in battle. But *Kaotan* had only two crew members left who had not given all they had for the mission.

Takya was not too thrilled, but she had already accepted fate. "I am the logical one, possibly, to lead," she admitted to Hawks. "Of all the survivors here, I alone come from a water world, a water civilization. A much higher one than this, to be sure, but I will be in my element there for the first time in years. But as a *man* . . . No offense, but I have never much wanted to be one. It is just not in my nature."

"I understand," he responded, although he couldn't see much wrong with being a man himself. In a reversed situation he could see no dishonor in becoming female, but on the whole he liked himself as he was. "Still, we have no females to clone, for one thing, and for another, in that culture, the sex roles are very clearly separated, and unless we could get someone like one of the king's wives or concubines, they simply wouldn't be of as much use to us. Master System interpreted the requirement of 'humans with power' to mean political power, and down there politics is a man's game."

She nodded. "I know. And that is why I will do it. Is it true that Han Li has also volunteered?"

He nodded. "Yes, the only real volunteer I had. Apparently she is not happy as number-two wife and Chun Wo Har is something of a dominant man. And she thinks the Alititians are beautiful, proving, at least, there are grave differences between the colonials and Earth-humans."

"They are not an unattractive race," Takya responded. "I have been trying to dissuade Dura, you know. She does not find any of it at all attractive or alluring, but she has been adamant. If I go, she goes."

"I know. And Raven is the logical fourth, but you

know the problem there. Everybody else has wives or children or both. Except Savaphoong, of course, but I'm not sure I'd trust him down there even if he had the guts to go. And, for that reason, and considering Raven's refusal as well, I don't think I should force him to go."

"And you shall not" came a man's voice behind him. They turned and saw Savaphoong standing there. "Nevertheless, Señor *Capitán*, I shall go. You have trumped my ace, as it were, and beaten me even though the game was rigged from the start. If I remain here, it is only a matter of time until the ring is secured and I am jettisoned, cast adrift in a universe that no longer has any use for me, my contacts many years stale, a price on my head. Either that or I remain a recluse attached to this ship while others go stick the accursed rings down Master System's throat until it chokes. No, señor and señorita, I, Savaphoong, intend to be there at the end even if I must crawl there with a fish tank over my head. If you will take me, Señorita Mudabur, I will go. If you will not, then the *capitán*, here, cannot deny me a presence at the climax."

Hawks looked at Takya quizzically, and she shrugged. "You are welcome, sir. We should have one true male among the group, I think. But if you betray us, I swear that you will not outlive the last of us, and if you act with courage and honor, I also swear that you will be present when that ring is used."

The old trader smiled and bowed slightly. "It is a fair bargain."

Hawks was uneasy about Savaphoong's offer, but could find no compelling reason to bar him from the group. The chief was in his quarters brooding over what Savaphoong might be planning when he received news that pushed all other thoughts from his mind.

"Hawks?" came Star Eagle's voice from a hidden

speaker. "You wanted to be notified immediately. Vulture is signaling for a pickup."

"I just can't understand it," Isaac Clayben mumbled for perhaps the tenth time in an hour. He had been going over all the tests on Vulture.

"You said I was immune to the transmuter," the little male Chanchukian reminded him in his high, somewhat squeaky tenor. "You said that what they did to me couldn't be done!"

"I—I thought it couldn't. I swear to you I thought it could not be done. Your cells—your original cells— were quite literally *created* in a transmuter. They were tested, many times, and found to be impervious to the transmuter process. All we got was an automatic abort from the control computer—every time. Even I, who created you, could not uncreate you, as it were. Star Eagle was fed from my data banks all the information on your creation and structure, just how you worked, and there was no way even *he* could see how it was done. Alas, it would take a far larger computer than we have here to repeat the experiment—if indeed we dared repeat it."

Vulture shuddered. "I am small and weak now, and I am but a shadow of my former self, but I believe I would kill you no matter what you should try. You can never know the pain, the horror of that experience. So terrible is it that even though most of my past lives are mercifully dim, just pale shadows now, still that period haunts my nightmares."

"Rest easy on that score," Star Eagle broke in. The great computer that ran the ship was also virtually omnipresent on it. "All of the data that we have examined shows that even were I a hundred times as large and complex and even if I had all the esoteric biophysics and biochemistry needed for it, still it would be impossible.

There is a missing element in all the data. Just what is impossible to determine, but without it the rest will not work. It's just so much synthetic primordial soup."

"Impossible! Everything was there! *Everything!*" Clayben exclaimed.

"No. Sorry to puncture your ego, Doctor, but you are a brilliant man and you will survive it. Now that I have all the files, though, and all the records of the work done, I can see the procedures and the holes. The conclusion is unmistakable, Doctor. You did not invent Vulture. You *created* him, but you did not *invent* him."

"No, that's not true . . ."

Even Vulture was puzzled. "Invent, create—what's the difference?"

"The difference between a scientist and an engineer, for the most part. Clayben was the engineer who oversaw the project, but this is far too complex even in its minor parts for any human brain to follow with the detail required. In many important ways, Vulture, you were a far more complex synthetic organism than I, or a Val. We had no problems synthesizing a Val, or at least a cyborg that allowed tiny, organic Ikira Sukotae to become a being much larger and who would measure as synthetic. But, be honest, Doctor. No human invented Vulture any more than a human invented me. Humans, in fact, did not even invent Master System. They had a set of ideas that they fed into large computers who then fed it into larger computers and so forth. The human in the chain was left far behind. As brilliant as you are, Doctor, you have no more real idea how Vulture worked than Cloud Dancer knows of nuclear physics. You initiated and oversaw the mechanics of the project. Computers did the rest."

Clayben nodded. "Yes, yes, that is self-evident. There is only one way for a human mind to approach computer speeds and capacities and that is through the interface I did not have. And even then we are subordinate, since the human mind cannot function at such blinding speeds nor access the memory banks without computer aid. But the Vulture *was* my idea."

"Perhaps. But one wonders if you were at any time truly the master of your own little world. We know that Nagy was a plant of some sort, although whose is unknown. It always seemed bizarre that Master System, who liked to control every variable it could within the limitations of its core directives, would allow you and the Earth Presidium to have your private world and keep hands off. Still, Master System would be unlikely to let you forge a weapon that could strike against it so thoroughly and efficiently, and that leaves the other side, the enemy for whom Nagy presumably worked and whom Master System has been at war with for some time. To even fight Master System to a draw on any plane would imply, almost require, a computing center at least as vast as Master System itself."

Clayben blanched. "*Two* of them? And you mean that after I started this project, Nagy covered it from Master System's own spies and supplied what I could not from his own master?"

"I have analyzed the physical plant of Melchior. The computer you had was vast and sophisticated. I wish I had a hundredth of its power and capabilities. Next to Master System itself it might have been the largest and fastest computer we know of, yet it is wholly inadequate for the precision and number of computations designing a Vulture would require. You did not create Vulture because you could not. Only a computer at least the equal of Master System could do so. Since Master System obviously did not, then there is another."

Vulture shook his head in disbelief. "All this time I blamed this egomaniac bastard. God, how I hated you, Clayben! How I wanted you to suffer like I had to suffer.

And all the time it wasn't you at all. You were just as much a pawn in all this as me. So a second Master System got wind of your idea and supplied what was needed to create me, maybe just for this job. And when Master System learned from Chi the possibility of my existence, it was powerful enough and bright enough to figure out how I was made, see the flaws, and capitalize on them." He sighed. "In the end, I guess it's my fault, then. I hated your guts, but you were my creator, damn it! I questioned everything, but I would never question any statement you made about me. Never. When you said I was immune to the transmuter, I believed you. Instantly. It became a factor I no longer had to take into account. In the end, *that* was my blind spot. Funny, but I can accept that. Even feel stupid about it. Considering the history and state of humanity, if it had a creator, he sure as hell made a lot of mistakes for an allegedly omnipotent, omniscient being. Master System makes so many mistakes that people like you and the chief administrators can walk right through them. Why in hell would I think that *my* creator, whom I knew and could see, would be perfect when they were not?"

Clayben threw up his hands. "Because you were in some ways always an extension of me. Because humility does not become either of us. We are done in by such vanities, I fear. The Blue Fairy gave you life, Pinocchio, but this time you did not escape Pleasure Island's more evil magic."

Vulture looked into the air. "What is he talking about? Has he gone mad?"

"No," Star Eagle responded. "I'll explain it to you later."

Vulture sighed and got off the examining table. "Well, now I'm different. I guess it's time I got the lay of the land and contributed whatever I still can."

It was some time until he found Hawks, though, and

when he did, he found the chief more than a little gloomy. Hawks looked up straight into Vulture's brown eyes, a gesture made a bit more dramatic because they were eye to eye, although Hawks was sitting down and Vulture was standing up.

It wasn't so much that Vulture was in an inhuman shape, or that a Chanchukian male was a rather weird creature even when you had the three females around to get used to; but rather that something was missing from Vulture. The old spark, the total self-confidence, the feeling of omnipotence, of "can't fail," just wasn't there anymore.

"Clayben and Star Eagle briefed me," Vulture told him. "They've been down only two weeks, right?"

Hawks nodded. "We have small tracers embedded in them that we can follow by a water probe floating on the surface. It's burned into a rock jutting just out of the water so it's not likely to be found, and if triggered it gives us information on their general location. We also have communicators embedded in the tikis on the cultivated islands, on the theory that at least one of them will be able to get to one of those spots if they must or if they have the ring—or if they are convinced that we blew it."

"Uh uh. I think the ring's there, and so do you. And it took a year for my team, with the old me included, to nab the one on Chanchuk, so two weeks is nothing. That's not what's bothering you. Is it Savaphoong?"

"Not really. Right now Savaphoong is unaware of his own name and can't even conceive of outer space. It's a deep mindprint. And what can he do? Master System won't reward him if he betrays us—it will just take all he knows and then convert him to one of its own. When his old personality is triggered he won't find staying there tempting for two reasons. First, real power down there is gained by fanatical bravery or by heredity and he has neither. Second, the ring's no good to him without the other four and we have three of them. No, it's not that. We heard from Matriyeh."

Vulture was suddenly very interested. "Yes?"

"Ikira passed muster, even though it was a close thing. They sent a real Val down along with two technicians from races she had never seen before."

"And she fooled a *Val*?"

"We did a good job analyzing the remains of the original goddess. The structure was particularly interesting and synthetic, you know. That was how we could add so much mass to her tiny frame within the transmuter's limitation against addition of mass to a living creature. They landed in a remote section and took that magnetic train to the holy place. They were hardly interested in her except as a guide. She wouldn't stand a real inspection and full-scale analysis aboard a command ship, of course, but the original was never intended to be more than a guard and caretaker making sure things functioned correctly down there—the one who alone knew the truth but who, being so singular and synthetic, had no interest in any role beyond the one assigned."

"So? What did they do?"

"Just what I should have thought of, and what Raven's hitting himself over the head for not thinking of. They installed hypnocasters. A variety of them."

Vulture nodded. "Yeah, sure. I told you Chi was bright and dangerous."

"Ikira is immune, of course, but she's the only one who is. She's going nuts trying to deal with it. She has an internal one, remember—they replaced it as well. The new one's on all the time, and in addition it reinforces the others they fixed all over the mountain region. Come within range and you forget all about rings and Master System and any other nonnative ideas. Get this—it enhances any mindprint to a tremendous degree while suppressing literally everything else from your conscious mind. Anything not applying to living a perfect Matriyehan life and attaining spiritual perfection is shut out. It's in about forty different languages but not Matriyehan, so it has literally no effect on any natives. Only impostors will get creamed if they know any of the languages covered, and it's unlikely they wouldn't know at least one."

"Clever. On a primitive world like Matriyeh the closer you got, the more effect it would have. If an imposter got close enough to get a full or maybe multiple doses, he'd vanish into the priesthood or a tribe and never be seen or heard from again. Even after it had worn off, the life in the tribal culture would reinforce it."

"Not just on Matriyeh. Hypnocasters also work in water. Star Eagle offered that with the report. Below ten, maybe fifteen meters they are killers. They don't have the range underwater that they do in air, but they have far greater intensity. The SPF was down there for nine days. That's long enough to plant them throughout that whole underwater city. Ten, twenty—who knows how many? All nicely arranged, I bet, so they focus their maximum power on the temple or palace, whichever has the ring. I know what one of those things did to me with just a barrier exposure. Constant exposure, day in, day out, for weeks, months... The odds are that even now our four are effectively neutralized. They have become those people they were intended to imitate, we're out four people and back to square one."

7. THE RING OF RINGS

W ATER SPLASHED ALL ABOUT.

"Which one we got?" Raven asked impatiently.

Clayben shrugged. "Who knows? They all look equally ugly to me. Probably Takya. This one looks older, and Makoa would be the logical one to lead a party on land again. We must hurry. We don't have the luxury of several days this time. If sundown comes down there and the others dig themselves out, they'll find Makoa gone and then we're in trouble."

The mindprinting device was ready, taking a readout in less than half an hour, limiting it to conscious thoughts and memories and comparing it to past prints of both the original Makoa and each of the four who'd been sent down.

"It's bad," Star Eagle reported. "Real bad. It's Takya, all right, only it isn't. There isn't a single bit of Takya in the readout. None. The face-off with our fake tiki and what happened until they returned to harvest the nuts and go back home is very vague, like he just shut it out and doesn't think of it. Everything else is Makoa and only Makoa. There is no way around it. I will have to use the mindprint we took of Takya before the transmutation and restore her to that point. It might bring the original forth, or replace it."

"Go ahead," Clayben ordered. "We're very short on time and there is much to do."

It was now five months since the quartet had infiltrated Alititi, five months of sweat and frustration. Now they had mere hours to do what they could to counter Brigadier Chi's brilliant and evidently all-too-effective trap. It was still better than an hour before Takya's original personality was restored and she was lucid, and even then it wasn't much help.

"I—I have the memories of Makoa going back and the time there, but nothing of myself," the agent said. "It is incredible."

"Focused hypnocasters," Clayben told her. "We blew it. Now we're going to have to reprogram you with a softer, more dangerous print."

"You can neutralize the hypnocasters?"

"Now that we know what we're dealing with, and by a back-door method as it were, yes. Fortunately, the 'casters are language specific to avoid disrupting the locals. We can process you, eliminating the languages you know except, of course, for Alititian, and cross-index the others into a single support language called Maurog."

"Maurog? What is that?"

"Artificial. It's an intermediate language used by humanoid robots. A version of it is used in all Vals. I have it because it was the base language used by Vulture in his original form. It was the language he thought in, the only one capable of managing the data from so many other minds without going completely mad. It will be natural to you—simply an alternate sophisticated language compared to Alititian that will seem as normal and familiar as the tongue you grew up with, but it will be unnoticeable to the hypnocaster." Takya didn't hear the whispered *"We hope"* after that statement. "Of course, no one who isn't imprinted with Maurog will ever understand you, but Star Eagle can translate and once you're permanently back here we can restore the others. Also, if you can, arrange for the others in the party to get some land duty where we can treat them as well."

"Why not just let me find the hypnocasters and disable them? They use focused beams. It wouldn't take much of a tracer to find them."

"Too risky. If I were Master System, I'd have installed a broadcast alarm that would be triggered if any of their equipment was taken out. That's what we think the Val was doing in the system. Planting monitors. This is a better plan even if slower. What they have down there is effective. Star Eagle reports that you have no memory of any of the rings in any way, let alone the one we want. So it's one step forward, now two steps back."

Takya sighed. "None of this will be easy, least of all the softer print. I have become the kind of man I have detested all my life. The gift of the gods to women."

"Well, park your scruples. It's not only yours and three other lives at stake, if you fail then more will have to be sent."

The agent sighed again. "I know, I know."

To the People, the realm of air was one of discomfort and awkwardness. They felt helpless above the surface, ungainly and, yes, ugly. Yet they had all been born on the land, and there was a certain mystery and mystique about it.

It was more bearable at night; the daylight, even when cloud-shrouded and storm-tossed, was bright and harsh and gave them headaches and dizziness. At night, though, there was a magical feel, with the flickering fires that could not exist below reflecting past the tikis onto the sacred heiau walls, creating a strange, moving shadow dance that seemed to show the spirits within the tikis, if obliquely, in the only way humans were permitted to see them, reflected in the obsidian beyond.

But in the water, now—in the water it all changed. There was not the usual Earth-human sense of floating or swimming; rather, it was more like suddenly becoming weightless, of flying free, of seeing and catching the underwater currents created by the distant and silent wind and storm and gradations in temperature, and most of all by the random but incessant volcanic activity permeating the world. These were not the people of Maui, who rode the sun, but of Pelé, goddess of fire.

Those, though, were the only real sights in the upper levels, save the *mana* of some of the sea creatures and of the occasional fellow flyer.

In the depths, in a world without light, the creatures there made their own. Most had self-illumination, and a fish's size and type and even sex and age could be told by its configuration and coloration. All nonpredators had this gift, which the priests said was the *mana* of life inside showing through, a reflection of the gods who made them. Only one predator made its own light at will, though, and that was the People, through an electrochemical process controlled by voluntary muscles in the ribbed areas of their undersides. The markings were distinctive, as unique as an Earth-human's fingerprints, and one could tell not only all the data from the patterns but also something of tribal lineage and, if you knew them well, you could identify individuals by their visible *mana*. This alone gave them the edge against the dark predators, the Great Snakes, the Demon Sharks, and the Tentacled Ones, who, being of evil, had no *mana* of their own but who could very nicely see the *mana* of others.

Below, the relatively shallow sea floors were marked with trails distinctive to each tribe and nation, and *mana* was used, too, as territorial markers. Only the females could exude it so that it was separate from their bodies, and then only at certain times of the month, but once gathered it could be mixed with dyes from sea and land plants and take on a color of its own.

The city was a fairyland of beauty, a glowing, multi-colored, magical place. The predators never ventured near the cities; they were mainly solitary hunters and had learned over the years not to stray into areas too bright or too densely populated where they could become sacrifices and perhaps be eaten themselves. Were it not for their strong place in the religion of the People they would have been exterminated in the earliest centuries, but while they were diminished in number they were contained rather than eliminated now. If the People did not understand the balance upon which even their own way of life depended, the priests did.

For all their simplicity, they were a happy people overall, rather content with their existence. They danced and they sang and they gathered food and made love and occasionally made war; they created works of art out of the volcanic products and shells and other marine remains, and they indulged in combative sports pitting warrior skills against warrior skills—they generally had fun. They were not deep thinkers and saw no reason to be so. Their world was their universe, and everything in it was either understood or had been properly interpreted by the priests. They were not stupid, but they simply had no curiosity.

One was also struck by the openness of the society. There were no police, and the only guards were the warriors who scouted the accessways to the city itself and patrolled the trails between the villages to protect against predators and interlopers. The fairyland houses with their strange shapes and twisted formations, carved out of varicolored volcanic rock by skilled craftsmen, had no doors, let alone locks. The king's dwelling, at the north end of the city, a grandiose crystalline palace that somehow seemed to have its own *mana* within its infinite glassy sides, was impressive, but only some tikis guarded it. It was sufficient.

At the opposite end of the city, against a wall of reddish-brown rock that looked like cooled pudding, was the Temple, its countless tikis, decorated with the *mana* of every woman of the king's own tribe and those of the royal families of the other tribes who paid him at least technical allegiance, were more impressive than the Temple itself. Beyond those faces carved—of stone, not perishable wood—were the sacrificial altar stone and the stage area for public rites and ceremonies that were common, and between that area and the Temple entrance was an impressive array of bubbling, hissing steam vents that reminded the People whose temple it was.

The pirates had all looked at and studied this land and its people from the mindprints of the natives and the agents they had sent in. It had taken three months for Takya to maneuver the others into positions where they, too, could be taken and restored, and Savaphoong in particular had been furious at having been so easily overcome, but now it was different. Now those aboard *Thunder* could only vicariously experience what the quartet below were living in and, as always, wait.

"Signal from receptor twenty-two," Star Eagle reported, galvanizing them into action. "It appears to be Takya."

Raven frowned. "Alone?"

"Apparently. The others will register as being within the city."

"Trouble, then. I'm going down." He strapped on his pistols and his belt and went back to *Lightning*. Maria and Midi, who had been backing him up on all his ground missions, were already waiting for him.

"Think it's a trap?" Midi asked him as they prepared to detach from *Thunder*, punch in to the system, then go down in a smaller fighter. "This was not in the plan."

"I doubt a trap, but keep your weapons ready," he told them both. "If we don't have all four down there, then who knows what's going on, even if we *will* be rendezvousing in daylight. It's not like them to let anybody go off alone."

The small atoll was peaceful enough; it was one of those that the People never visited or used because it had been played out years ago, as had the first island they had used when initially coming to this world. The People understood sea management well, but they were hard on the land when they planted and reaped.

Takya waited a bit inland, out of sight of the sea but in a small stream that kept her relatively cool and wet. She sat, half submerged, reclining on a low rock and looking like every sailor's nightmare of what a mermaid shouldn't be.

The irony was that they couldn't talk to her directly, thanks to the language trick played by the hypnocasters. They could only bring a complex box that she and they could speak into, awkwardly, and which translated to and from the odd intermediate computer language in the same rather dull monotone.

"I have seen the ring," Takya told them. "It was not difficult to find, for it is mounted in a gold-and-shell charm that hangs from the neck of the high priest of the Temple. I did not even need my position to see it. We all saw it, during the celebration time. There is no question that it is the ring, although it is glued or embedded in the larger medallion and hardly looks like a ring. The design, however, faces outward—a smooth, black face with some sort of tiny gold design on it. It might be rings. We could not get that close."

"All right, then, what's the problem?" Raven asked her.

"None but a priest or a sacrifice can physically enter the Temple, and it is impossible to do so without being seen. When outside the Temple, the high priest generally wears it, but he never goes out without an entourage and always draws crowds. None of us can become a priest at this stage, and sacrifices are all young male virgins selected by the priests themselves, so getting someone in that way is also out. There is certainly no way to snatch it from him when he is out in the open and no easy way to get in to the Temple and find him in that labyrinthine collection of lava caves and tubes. The only way we can see to have any chance of getting it is to somehow get in with full weapons and instruments while most of the People sleep, knock out or perhaps kill any in our way, grab the thing from around his neck, and get out fast."

Raven sighed. "I see. And if any alarm is sounded you're damn well blocked in, and even the best personal weapons and equipment won't stop a fanatical mob forever. Still, I agree."

"Savaphoong is not much of a fighter, but he is a devious sort and he really wants that ring. No other entrance or exit to the Temple but the one behind the altar was known to anyone among the People, who have very few secrets, yet he refused to believe it. He noted that the Temple is built in the only geologically active region within kilometers of the city, and that there would never be a guarantee against quakes or other eruptions or disturbances. He was convinced that there had to be at least one and perhaps more exits in case of emergency. He believes he has located the general area where such exits must be, but there are too many possibilities and, needless to say, no markings or indicators. If I can be provided with markers, then a ship could be brought in to scan the entire undersea mountain into which the Temple is built. We will need as complete a geologic scan as is possible. Han Li has noted that there is an almost self-contained circulation system within the Temple due to the fumaroles. The water that comes out of all the possible exit sites is definitely warmer than normal. Use that and you might be able to give us an interior map of the place."

Raven nodded. "All right. I'll arrange it. But are you sure you can get markers into position without them or you being seen?"

"Yes, I am confident. I have assigned myself as captain of patrols for the next three weeks. This means I leave the city and make three-day round trips of the various main trails into and out of the city and check the patrols and guards. In six days I will be at receptor four. Have what is required ready then. By then I will tell you where we will meet six days after that. At that time I will need the map and all information you can give, and if you have some of the recommended weaponry, I can take that at the time, too. In eighteen days all else must be provided, and after that we will require a picket to be established capable of not only picking us up but supporting our life form. As soon as we have the ring we will make for a prearranged surface pickup, but it is possible we may be being chased by that point. When we signal for a pickup we will need it immediately, not in a few hours."

"We'll give you what cover we can," Raven promised, "but if we can determine the pickup early we can rig it to give you more of a chance. All right. We'll meet you at receptor four exactly six days from now with what you need and we'll have run this problem by everyone. I know this one's gonna be a bitch, Takya. We'll do all we can."

The agent nodded. "I know you will.

* * *

"The only problem I can foresee from our end is if Master System decides to show up and spoil the party," Star Eagle noted. "But that society down there is all so open, so public. They are going to have a very difficult mission."

"We've also got to assume that they will have some sort of tracer built into that medallion," Vulture noted. "That's what I would have done, anyway. That means that once that thing is off the planet, it's gonna be picked up by every damned sensor in the system."

"Not just out of the water? That'd buy 'em the most time for a response," Raven said worriedly.

"Doubtful. Priests are the only males allowed in the birthing heiaus if I studied those prints right, and the high priest attends to the royals, so he's out of the water at least now and then."

Raven looked up. "Huh? Wait a minute. Okay, do what Takya wants, but let's also work on an alternate plan. We've already blown almost eight months on this operation, so we can be a little more patient. Instead of sending our people into an unknown quagmire of caves and tubes blasting away and looking for a bedroom, let's try to wait and take him when he's topside. They're damned near dormant in the daytime—we didn't have any trouble gettin' who we needed that first time, and this time we don't give a damn if they get the hell knocked out of 'em. *They got to come up to have kids!* And Takya—Makoa—is high enough she or he can surely get royal guard duty."

"A good plan," Vulture agreed, "but I favor the direct approach that Takya outlined. It is just a feeling I have, I admit. Nothing to back it up, really, except experience in these things. If we were just dealing with Master System and the Vals, I'd say go your way, but Brigadier Chi—that's something else again."

"You got Chi on the brain," Raven responded sourly.

"Perhaps, but I know her. If she has a weakness, it is an abiding faith in her religion, which is technology. With what she's been told of the culture and layout below, and with the tracer and the hypnocasters, she's probably satisfied that a frontal assault without giving her plenty of warning is unlikely and far too risky. She would put herself in our place. No Vulture, so the setup below should be adequate. Where they would be vulnerable in her eyes is just exactly where you say and when you say. If I were gonna lay out a lot of sophisticated technological traps I'd put them right there, on that birthing island. They had nine days—and they took a shuttle craft down, not a mere fighter or scout. She's got some sort of trap covering the easy way, of that I'm sure, and she'll take into account our superiority over the natives. No, I'm for going with those on the planet, as it were. They know the situation best."

"You really think this Chi's that good?"

"I think she and her computers are at least the equal of us and our computers. Besides, she's military security, trained to play this sort of game, and while she's been stung once, she got in her licks and knows us much better now—and with far greater support and resources. I, however, understand her, too. A crude direct assault is against our character, our pattern of behavior. We play the probabilities where we can. Let's change our method this time. It's ten to one she's prepared least for the direct approach for all the reasons you name."

"What Vulture says is logical and consistent," Star Eagle put in. "You have noted the weak point. That is the logical reinforcement, and Takya's way seems best, all things considered."

Takya, too, on the second rendezvous, agreed with Vulture. "I have already scouted the birthing island for just such reasons," the leader below told Raven, "and I smell the worst kind of trap. At the entrance to the heiau are two new tikis, a bit wider and bulkier than the usual, and highly polished, as if made of neither stone nor wood, although those are the only two materials we ever use. I think, and the others agree, that our friend Chi borrowed, unknowingly, a trick from our own book. I think both of those tikis are Vals in monitor mode, without much power and with the infinite patience of a machine. *That's* her big trap. No, we go in quick, dirty, and armed to the teeth and to hell with subtlety."

Takya, or all of them, got the markers placed well enough within a few days, and Star Eagle was able to manuever an orbital fighter to take full scans of the entire complex. It was a horror, possibly chosen for that reason but certainly not constructed by anyone but nature. It resembled a plate of worms inside, and there were no large chambers that obviously were used either for high ceremony or for a high priest's comforts. Not that it might not be nice in there, but it wasn't going to be easy to find anything. There were also tunnels that led not to rooms or other tunnels but rather to active volcanic areas within the mountain, the source of the warmer waters.

Adapting the weapons was easier. The laser pistols could be sealed where needed, and were rigged with small destruct systems that could be activated as needed, overloading the pistol and causing it to explode or melt. Other devices—small torpedoes, bombs, visual aids, and the like—were also not difficult to fabricate. None of the equipment required a great deal of training; all were based on existing devices that the four below would have at least encountered before becoming Alititians.

Demonstrating the devices and checking them out proved relatively easy, although Takya knew that he would have to find some way of training the other three or at least giving them a little practice. They were experienced with the pistols, of course, but the rest required a bit more knowledge, and even the pitols reacted differently underwater.

"If you surface within a twenty-square-kilometer perimeter of the Temple center, you'll be covered by two automated fighters until we can get to you," Raven assured him. "If you need immediate assistance, the hand signal will bring them in close enough for you to latch on to the webbing we'll have on them and transport you to pickup one. *Lightning* will be on station no matter what before you reach pickup one if you're pursued. If not, it'll be mere minutes since I'm gonna stay close anyway. As soon as you can, transmit up. I'll activate the destruct signals when everybody's aboard. Understand?"

The agent nodded. "I understand. You just had better be there, Raven. There is much to like about this world and these people, but that sentiment will not be returned by them when we do what we must."

Raven stared at the Alititian. "I let you all down once. I will never do that again." It was said with such certainty that Takya did not for a moment doubt its truth and sincerity.

"Nine days hence," the Alititian told him. "We will commence precisely three hours after the common sleep time. Getting around the guards and day personnel will be no problem, but there is no way of knowing when we shall be away from there. But by nightfall we shall have the ring and be away, or we shall be dead."

There were, in fact, four man-made additions to the Temple complex, all of them short tunnels connecting natural ones. Two came out fairly high up, perhaps only three or four meters from the surface, while the other two provided opposite end exits from almost the level of the sea floor. These, then, were the emergency exits planned just in case the rather passive volcanic activity grew suddenly more active. It seemed that the priests might be very good at telling their people that such things were divine punishments, but as far as priests were concerned, they reserved the right to run like hell.

Takya was able to deduce the purpose of many of the tunnels and the regions within the Temple based on the location of the main entrance and the exits. There would be a formal dressing area for the priests near the main entrance, which would be very ornamental and contain something like a makeup table. A separate area nearby had to be where the sacrifices would be more or less wined and dined until it was time to fulfill their bloody destiny. Other than that, there had to be some sort of a headquarters complex where the priests, acolytes, and high priest lived, and it was almost certainly arranged in some sort of hierarchical order. The best guess was from bottom to top. The largest tubes were up there, and the easiest access to exits. That meant going in near the top.

Sneaking out of their various homes and gathering at the point where the weapons and gear had been hidden hadn't been easy for all of them, but now they were all there, strapping on carrying harnesses, checking the equipment out, and getting the heft and feel of the pistols in Alititian webbed hands. Transmuters were very handy for customization of standard equipment.

Takya looked at them. "We have gone through this as much as possible and talked and talked about it. Is there any objection to going now?"

"It is—difficult—to leave," Han Li responded. "After so many years of wandering and being a humble second, I have become very fond of heading a family and of the family I head. Still, my honor demands sacrifice. I shall go."

"The sooner I am free of this place the better," Savaphoong grumbled. "I sacrificed my form for this, but not to spend my life as a worker gnawing on fish. This is what we came to do."

Dura nodded. "I share both sentiments, but we do it now or we might never do it. Let's begin."

And, with that, they headed up into the dark upper reaches of the sea to the man-made exit they'd chosen.

If anyone had ever wandered up here, they, too, would probably have spotted the exit but would not have entered. Dimly carved into the black rock but plainly recognizable were several of the most severe taboo signs in Alititian culture. To go further risked not only death but eternal damnation. Floating there, and after living for so long in this culture, the four felt a certain involuntary hesitation at the sight of them, showing the power of the symbols, but it was only for a moment. Takya drew a pistol with her right hand and removed a sensing device with the other and moved in.

Only two meters inside there was a small net stretched across the tunnel and fastened there, obviously to keep out any denizens of the deep that might not comprehend taboo symbols. Takya decided not to tear it out; it might well contain some kind of alarm on the other side. Instead, she used her needler to cut out the center portion and then pull it in and away. Then she entered, followed by the others.

The first section of tunnel was a chamber of horrors, a dark tube that had been painted with multicolor secretions with every evil taboo symbol, threat, and vicious god and spirit known to the Alititians. Clearly the priests wanted a last psychological and cultural jab at anyone who just might believe the signs outside didn't apply to them.

The tube widened out, as the artificial section merged with the natural structure. There they encountered a second security net, which Takya dealt with as she had the first one in the outer passage, and then the horrors were behind them. Now the secretions were of a more standard type, illuminating the passage and showing, apparently, just where someone who knew the code to the floor plan was and how to get to anywhere else. The pirates didn't know the plan, however, so Savaphoong removed a small locator beacon and attached it to the cave roof. He was the tail man and had several dozen beacons; his job was to place the locators so that they would clearly mark the route, and when it was time to leave, he had a device that could tell the numeric order in which any one of them was placed. They would thus provide a clear but conveniently invisible trail to follow out of here when it was over.

They reached a roomlike side chamber and found several sleeping forms there. They had already agreed to take no chances; everyone and everything that looked like it might move was hit with deep stun. Takya's own pistol was set to kill.

It was remarkably, almost disappointingly easy. These people had no concept of modern weapons or what they could do, and they were helpless even when awake or awakened by the interlopers until far too late to do anything but fall over.

It took a bit over an hour to locate the high priest, asleep in his quarters, and stun him senseless. He had the necklace on, as he always did, and for the first time they were able to examine the medallion closely. It was certainly the ring, unless Chi had taken a leaf from Vulture at Chanchuk and somehow replaced it with a ringer. It didn't look fake, though; it looked as if it had been embedded in that medallion for a very long time. Dura held the old man while Takya pulled the whole thing off him and stuffed it in her backpack. Even so, they took the time to check his chest of personal belongings just in case there was another ring or medallion there. There was not.

"My turn to lead," Savaphoong whispered, and activated his tracker. They encountered a few more awake or awakened acolytes on the way back, but Dura and Han Li's quick pistols took them out. Takya covered the rear, and if anything was coming that way it would not be stunned but quickly dead.

Twist, turn, up, right... Savaphoong moved with grace and certainty toward the exit. There was the inner net, then the cave of terrors that no longer seemed quite so intimidating, then the second net. He was going very quickly now, but they didn't need him to show them the way any more, and he was back out of there before Dura had cleared the outer net.

They emerged into open water once more, and looked around. "Where is Savaphoong?" Takya asked, more puzzled than concerned.

"Here," responded a voice behind and slightly above them. They turned and saw the old trader perched on a rocky outcrop above the exit with two pistols trained on them. "Now drop your weapons! All of you! I mean it!" He fired very close to Takya's arm to illustrate his point.

Takya sighed. "Drop them, all of you. He has his on lethal." They did what they were told, the pistols dropping down as if in slow motion into the darkness below. "Now, what treachery is this?"

"I want the ring," Savaphoong replied. "Isn't that obvious? There will be no vote on who gets it. I did not do this to be fourth in line. Just hand the medallion over and I'll flick this to wide stun. You'll all go out like a light and float to the surface from here, but you'll be all right. I, however, shall sadly report how heroically you died in getting the ring when I alone am picked up."

"You'll never get away with it. They'll never believe you," Dura retorted angrily.

"They don't have to. They will mourn you, yes, and perhaps doubt me, but they will have the rings and time will be pressing. I seriously doubt if they will launch a major search. Now—quickly! The ring! An alarm is certain in the Temple at any moment, and they'll find those cut nets in no time!"

"You are a turd, Savaphoong," Takya responded, and activated something in his hand that Savaphoong had not seen him palm.

The pistol in the trader's hand suddenly shimmered and began to whine. He pulled the trigger but nothing happened. The pistol suddenly grew very hot, and he was forced to drop it. It shimmered, then vanished with a loud pop and a hissing sound. Similar sounds came from far below.

When Savaphoong looked back up, he was facing two expert harpoonlike crossbows aimed right at him. "What? . . ." he managed.

"Automatic destruct. We couldn't have weapons like these falling into the hands of the Alititians, could we? All right—I agree with you on one thing, that time is running out. Get down here quickly and back inside the cave!"

He looked stricken. "You—you can't! They'll *kill* me! Or worse!"

"Tough. We'll kill you right now. *In!* No more time! Dura—give him a sample shot in the tail to motivate him!"

"No, no! I'm moving!" He came down to the cave opening, but turned. "I wouldn't really have left you here! I swear on my mother's grave!"

"You probably did away with your mother for the value of her body chemicals," Takya responded. "*In!* And as far in as possible as fast as possible, because in ten seconds from right now I am going to toss a small bomb in that cave! You made your gamble and you lost! Now you must pay the bet."

Savaphoong vanished into the darkness of the cave.

Takya removed a small device and sent it into the cave after him, then turned and signaled. They were going up and fast.

Savaphoong, however, was not finished yet, at least as far as his own future was concerned. Betting that as soon as the bomb was thrown they would leave, he watched it come in, swam to it and caught it, then threw it back out the cave opening and waited.

In a few anxious seconds there was a brilliant flash of light and a slight rumbling all around, but it quickly died away. He shot out of the cave, his first thought to get away from there and fast. They had hit quick and dirty and most of those they'd shot with stunners had been acolytes. It was pretty good odds that he, at least, bringing up the rear most of the time, hadn't been recognized, but that did him little good. He thought about his alternatives.

He could, of course, give chase to them, but they were good and still had advanced weapons on them. The odds of being able to do more than get shot or killed were slim, nor would Hawks treat him with any respect should he somehow manage to get picked up anyway. The odds were almost certain he'd simply be thrown back in.

To remain and take a chance that he was not recognized would present the best odds of long-term survival, but to live down here, like this, forever—it was unthinkable. Death was preferable.

There was, however, a third alternative that came to him almost in a flash of desperation. His chances weren't very good doing this, either, but it offered the only real hope for some long-term gain, no matter how slim that hope was. He had gambled once and lost; he'd been too sloppy, the result of letting other people do his dirty work for so long and of sitting sedentary in his pleasure yacht with little or nothing to do. That was over. It was time to roll the dice and see if, perhaps, against all odds, he could come up a real winner this time. At the very least he would satisfy his honor.

He whirled and began to swim away from the rendez-vous point and away from the city as well, toward a certain island a couple of hours off. Even as he did so, he could hear the war drums and deep shell-horn alarms going off, awakening the city to give chase. He hoped they chased in the right direction, which was well away from him.

Dura looked back and saw a living sea of black shapes well below but coming toward them. "I am really missing those pistols now!" she shouted to them. "That is the whole damned legion down there and maybe more!"

"Break surface and give the signal, then start swimming like hell toward the rendezvous point!" Takya shouted back. "I am going to start dropping bombs at intervals on twenty-second delays!"

They broke the surface, certain that they were still well within the surveillance perimeters, raised their right arms three times, then began to swim. Although it was late in the day and overcast, the brightness blinded them and the ultraviolet felt less than comfortable coming invisibly through those clouds. The sea was choppy, slowing them a bit as well, and each of them worried that they might not be visible among the rough seas.

The first of a series of giant bubbles broke the surface behind them, urging them on no matter what. That was the force left from the first of the bombs dropped on the pursuers, and Takya had dropped three more by now.

Suddenly they could feel more than see a kind of shade, as if something huge had come over them, blocking off the hidden sun's deadly rays. Han Li reached up, grabbed hold, and shouted, "It is the fighter! Reach up! Grab on to the netting!"

They did so, each holding on for dear life, as the fighter then rose a bit in the air. Even as it did so, they could hear yells and screams and curses from the water below, and things started striking and bouncing off the sides of the fighter. Dura screamed as something struck her tail, followed in a few seconds by a building, searing pain, but in spite of the shock of it, she hung on. The fighter accelerated and soon left the war party far below in the choppy seas, unable to follow.

It settled down gently, hovering less than two meters off the ground on a tiny, overgrown and neglected island. All three let go and came down on the ground. It was still nearly impossible to see, and they had real problems for a moment orienting themselves.

"Dura! Han Li! Are you both there?"

"Yes!" Han Li responded. "But I think Dura is hurt. *Oh!* A spear right through the tail on the right side. I wish I could see better but I will try to pry it out. Dura, are you ready?"

"Yes." She gasped. "Get rid of it and help me to the transmitter. I'll be all right if we can just get up to *Lightning.*"

Han Li pulled with all her strength, although she was slightly weakened by the sudden switchover to the less efficient breathing of air, and Dura gave a scream of pain, but the spear came free. Blood poured from the wound but there was nothing to do but be quick about it.

Takya was with them. "Over there! It is nearly impossible to see but there is a large, dark shape there. It must be it! Come—hold on, Dura! We will get you there!"

Han Li froze for a moment. "I hear a war party approaching! Some of the watch was alerted and saw where we were carried. Let us get *out* of here!"

The door slid back on the special fighter rigged with the transmitter, and they used all their strength to get Dura inside and the door closed.

"We have some time," Takya said reassuringly, "if Raven is actually up there. The war party has to crawl up on the island, find us, and they are as blind and exposed as we."

There was a clicking sound and then the fighter gave a loud whine and shuddered slightly. It seemed an eternity until that door opened again, though, and the war party, hearing the noise, had shifted its search and was now coming straight for them.

Takya gave the backpack to Han Li. "You next. Take this. I will follow."

"No—it is yours! You planned this!"

"No arguments. I should have sent it with Dura. *Get it up!* It is all that really matters right now."

The door opened. Han Li hesitated for a moment, then grabbed the backpack and pulled herself inside. The door shut and there was another whine and shudder. The war party sounded pretty damned close. *Too* close. She could hear them, and it was getting dark enough so that she was starting to see a bit. Maybe a minute or two and that frenzied mob would be upon her. Recycling the transmitter would take longer than that. She readied a couple of bombs and reared up on her tail to face her would-be killers.

One of the small covering fighters swooped down, having calculated the same thing, and began firing into the war party with devastating effect, shaking the ground. Its weapons weren't intended to shoot people but other ships; it was like killing mosquitoes with a cannon.

The concussion almost knocked Takya down, and she steadied herself against the side of the transmission fighter and then almost got crushed when the door came open again. Dizzy, hardly thinking straight, she managed to get up and pull herself in. The door shut.

She could hear that a few warriors had made it even through the fighter fire and were actually at her transmitter. They were rearing up, beating and pounding on the ship.

There was a sudden click, a disorienting sensation, and all that noise ceased.

As soon as the last agent was aboard, Raven triggered the universal destruct and gunned *Lightning* away from Alititi. There was no time to waste recovering the fighters; they had figured, rightly or wrongly, that as soon as the ring cleared the planet all hell was going to break loose and come down on them anyway.

Below, all three fighters exploded—along with virtually every other piece of extraplanetary gear they had introduced—leaving only twisted hulks, many dead bodies, and enough new legends for a hundred generations to come.

"Why do you come to this sacred island?" the captain of the guard challenged. "You have no rank or right to be here!"

"Be at ease, Captain," Fernando Savaphoong responded in his humblest voice. "Send your man below and you will hear the calls that confirm what I say. Horrible sacrilege has been committed against the People. The Temple is violated, many priests and acolytes, even the Highest One, are dead or in strange trances, and the holy badge of office has been stolen. There are no active priests. I am commanded to the gates of the sacred heiau to call upon the gods and the service of the priests therein. Let me past. I would not violate the heiau, merely plead at the gate."

The captain nodded to one of his men, who went under, remaining a good five minutes or so, then emerging once more. "What he says is true, Captain," the soldier reported. "It is said that some of our own people were possessed by demons. There has been great demon-fire and many deaths among our warriors."

The captain didn't like this, but there seemed little harm in it. "Very well—to the great guardians of the gate and no further, or you shall be roasted alive in the fires!"

"Thank you, kind sir!" Savaphoong responded, and began the fairly long lizardlike crawl up the road as fast as he could move.

It was as Takya had said: two new, glistening, mean-looking tikis had been added on either side of the heiau's entrance. He could see how they might be Vals; he sure as hell hoped they were.

"All right, Vals," he said in Maurog as loudly and confidently as he could. "I am Fernando Savaphoong, formerly of the pirates of the *Thunder*. I have come to tell you that my former comrades have just stolen your pretty ring from under your very noses and that I have decided that I have been wrong all this time and am surrendering myself to your authority. I wish to be taken to your commander!"

For a very long moment he was afraid that he had lost this gamble at the onset, that these were indeed just new tikis and that Takya had been wrong.

Suddenly one of the tikis turned slightly toward him and asked, "Why should we just not take your mindprint and dispose of you now?"

It startled him, but he was so relieved that he never lost his composure.

"Such a move would give you only the facts that I know. I can be of far greater value because I have lived and worked with these people for years. I know how they think, what they will do next. It will take time to even study and evaluate what I can freely offer. For example, do not think that this is merely another lost battle. You have been fooled—we stole the ring on Matriyeh years ago and replaced it and your Val goddess with fakes. They have all four rings that were scattered among the stars even now. The fifth ring is already on

Earth, most probably in the hands of one who knows where to use them even as Hawks of the *Thunder* knows *how* to use them. If you do not wish to see the pirates become your masters, you had better deal with me and quickly!"

Again, the slight hesitation, and then one said, "I am summoning a ship now and transmitting the alarm. We are pursuing. Having scanned you and seeing nothing threatening, we will accept for the moment what you say, but you are under arrest nonetheless on charges of piracy and actions and thoughts against the system. We will take you to Brigadier Chi as soon as we can arrange for a pickup."

Savaphoong rested back on his tail and gave the Alititian equivalent of a smile. He was back in business.

8. THE MALEBOLGE RUN

"**T**OOK *FOREVER* TO GET IT OUT OF THAT MEDALlion," Isaac Clayben remarked. "We couldn't use the transmuter without risking damage to the ring, and we couldn't try the usual chemical baths, either, although I suspect it's pretty sturdy. It's stood up under salt water for perhaps centuries, after all. I finally had to dig it out physically and perform virtual microsurgery to get off the glop they used."

Hawks stared at it. "It *is* the real ring, though? No question?"

"Not in my mind. The medallion is at least four centuries old and has apparently been handed down from high priest to high priest since it was made, with embellishments each time, of course. Composition is exact and there is consistent circuitry within the synthetic jade. This is not to say that we couldn't have had one put over on us, but I doubt it."

"It just seemed too damned *easy* compared to the rest," the chief responded, shaking his head.

"Not that easy. Remember, we weren't supposed to even find the world—it's unregistered, unlisted, its population underwater and hostile to any outsiders. Even we weren't really certain until we got down there, if you remember. Finding its exact location was sheer good fortune—Master System reacting with typical straight-line logic on the information it had, which was that it was highly improbable we'd be anywhere around these parts during the small amount of time they were there. Even so, the hypnocasters almost did us in, and without those implanted locators they would have done so. And the other route, via the birth island, was very well covered, I suspect. No, it simply looks easy in retrospect. Not the most difficult, but certainly not easy."

Hawks nodded absently and went over to a small case where all four rings now sat. He felt a curious lack of emotion on looking at them, although he knew he should be celebrating at the sight. They had done the impossible, at great cost and risk. The fact that they had been helped along by that mysterious enemy, Nagy's bosses, did not in any way tarnish the achievement. Their unknown ally had merely provided the necessary tools to place them on a more or less equal footing with Master System; it had not in any way aided the attempts nor minimized the price. The fact was, without the special personnel, from Vulture to the other specialists on the team like China and the Chows and Clayben, no one else would ever have had a chance—but that was all they had been given. A chance.

Raven entered, cigar in mouth, and stood next to Hawks looking down at the rings. "Well, we did it," he said, shaking his head. "I can't believe it, but we did it."

"No, Raven, we haven't done a thing yet," the chief replied. "Master System still rules, we are still pirates, and everything is exactly as it was."

"Yeah, but—we got all the rings now."

Hawks gave a weak smile. "Oh, really? I count four, Raven. We have roamed over a quarter of the galaxy and we have made a mockery of Master System's safeguards, its Vals, and its human army, but we have done nothing of importance yet. Tell me, Raven—there're the rings. Now, where do we go from here?"

"Huh? Earth, of course. We go home. That's where the fifth ring is."

"All right, so we go home. You think Master System and Chi don't know that? Do you think Lazlo Chen, if he still lives, and the Presidium don't know that? It was Chen who initiated this plan, remember, and it was Nagy's people who made it possible. They're around, too, and we don't know who or even what they are, but they know, too. Four rings, Raven—and you know what? We are compelled by the location of the fifth ring to bring them all back to Chen. And even if he's still got it, still somehow has managed to remain the boss, he only has to own, to possess that ring, not wear it and flaunt it as he did for me. He has a vast area of mountains, deserts, steppes, and wastes to hide it in, too."

"Well, he's a crafty old son of a bitch, I admit, but he ain't no different from the other C.A.s we took on. Besides, he can be dealt with. He's got one ring, so he and his associates maybe get dealt in if we can't figure a way to steal or cheat 'em out of it. But just as these four ain't no good without his, his is no good at all without these four."

"Suppose you're right," Hawks responded. "Suppose we make a deal. We have all five rings and I've got a fairly good idea of how to use them. But *where* do we use them? Where *is* Master System, Raven? Where *is* the human interface to it? We knew the location of four rings and we found the fifth, but those were only the rings. Who gives us the directions to Master System, Raven? Even the Vals don't really know that, I don't think. They are remote programmed at their bases. It doesn't even directly interact with humans, and it interacts with its machines through subspace tightbeam that could be coming from anywhere in the galaxy. Anywhere. And it's had almost a thousand years to hide."

"Well, ain't you the gloomy one! But I don't think it's all that damned hard considerin' how far we come, Hawks. For one thing, I can't see Chen kickin' in and settin' this up or Nagy's people, or whatever they are, goin' to all this trouble if you can't find the end of the rainbow. My old nose suspects that Master System never moved at all. It wouldn't risk it, 'cause it'd have to be disassembled. I mean, back in those days supercomputers were *big* mothers. It wouldn't *dare* move. It wouldn't take the chance."

Hawks's head snapped up and he stared directly at Raven. "My god! Raven, if that's the case, then Chen already knows where it is, and so does almost everybody. Where did your original territory as a field agent cover?"

Raven shrugged. "North-central tier, basically. Crow, Sioux, Blackfoot, Cheyenne.... Why?"

"Cheyenne..." Hawks breathed. "Of course! For years now I have been poring through the historical tapes and records we have here, studying the time and persons and data to get what I could." He sighed. "All right, let's go get the last damned ring!"

She was small, nude, a study in feminine perfection of beauty and form, the essence of sensuality, and she glowed slightly, a vague but attractive green. All who saw her worshipped her and obeyed her every command, for she was the Goddess of Matriyeh and a living incarnation of the supernatural.

And she was not really human, not anymore, although the original goddess had been totally inhuman, a Val in human form. Her own body was based upon an analysis of the carcass of the destroyed original, her original tiny body merged and mated with the humanoid Val structure to create a near-perfect duplicate. She was, however, a fake.

The computer alarm sounded, indicating that someone was coming in on the train that ran far below the great temple. She didn't like that; the last time that alarm had gone off it had disgorged a couple of very unpleasant colonials in SPF uniforms and two Vals, and she had needed all her self-control and poise and acting ability to get through it without being detected. The sensors had not indicated any landing or new orbital craft in the immediate planetary sphere, so this time whoever it was certainly did not want their presence advertised. That was not necessarily a good sign, although it might mean a visit from her old comrades.

That would be welcome. Ikira Sukotae had elected to stay on Matriyeh thinking it would be the fulfillment of her dreams, but the truth was that it had been very frustrating; the challenge of keeping Master System ignorant of her presence or the success of the band here had mostly prevented the slow and progressive redevelopment of this primitive and harsh society into something greater. Being a true goddess, all-powerful in many ways, had blinded her to her own basic inner humanity. She was not the machine she pretended to be and had replaced; she was a human being inside a mostly artificial body. The incredible crush of loneliness had simply never occurred to her until it was too late.

She went down the back way, curious to see who or what was coming, less fearful than eager that at least there would be some break in the monotony, some companionship. She had even found the Vals and SPF a relief, for all the danger they presented. A tremendous number of possibilities of whom this might be went through her head, but the one waiting at the station for her was completely unexpected. She stopped, frozen, just staring at the figure standing there.

"I would tell you to rush and get packed, but you don't have anything to pack," Arnold Nagy said casually, his voice echoing around the station walls.

"But—you're dead!" she protested, trying to understand. "No one could survive being expelled from an airlock in space!"

He shrugged. "And you're dead, too, aren't you? At least, the goddess is long dead now. I must say that they did a *hell* of a job on you. More than anything, we make a pretty good pair."

She walked slowly down to him. "Just what the hell *are* you, Nagy?"

He grinned. "Haven't you guessed? But, come—we have to get you out of here and off Matriyeh and fast. Master System has learned that both you and the ring are fakes. They're on their way and could be here almost any time. I have no idea how much, if any, of a window we have. You've been forcibly relieved, girl—at least for the duration. Wouldn't you like to be there for the endgame?"

She hesitated. "How do I know I can trust you? I mean, considering your death and sudden, mysterious resurrection, why should I trust you now?"

"You're smart," he responded. "Deep down you know, and the rest you'll figure out. Shall we go?"

"To aid them?"

"Not me. That's against the rules. That's why I had to die. Maybe you, if need be. But you can't stay here, that's for sure." He turned. "Ah! That's our train, I believe. Coming?"

She nodded hesitantly. "But—what about Warlock? The system here?"

"It'll go along fine. As for Warlock—the last one I

want in command of Master System is Manka Warlock. After you, my dear."

Brigadier Chi studied the computer models, turned, and sighed. "All right, so they have four rings. As I understand it, it does them little good without the fifth that's on Earth, right?"

Fernando Savaphoong, in his special tank, only his head and shoulders above water, nodded. "That is correct. One would expect that Master System is even now assembling the largest fighting force in history to defend that system. And has it occurred to you, Señorita Brigadier, that, now that you have picked my brains, as it were, and know of the rings, you are no longer an asset to Master System but rather a threat in your own right?"

She bristled. "All my life has been devoted to preserving and defending the system."

"All the same, all who know, including myself, are under the most expedient method of safety for the system—a death sentence. You have already violated your orders by keeping me alive, have you not? Admit it."

The problem was, he was telling the absolute truth. Any and all of the pirates of the *Thunder* were to be kept in the hands of the Vals and other machine forces, mindprinted for their information and data, and then destroyed. Her own curiosity about the rings and their importance, combined with her current authority to overrule Vals—an authority likely to be quickly terminated now—had saved him for the moment, but it might well have doomed her.

"All members of the SPF stand ready to die for the preservation of order," she told him. "I am no exception."

"A noble but useless, even insane, gesture. Consider how far they have come. Do you think they will let even a great task force stop them now? Do you not think that the mysterious enemy behind them will allow them to fail at this point? Twice you underestimated them. I beg you, do not do so again. Even with this fleet, Master System is splitting logic hairs in the manner of dealing with the devil. They are humans on the *Thunder*. The core program gives them the *right* to go for and use the rings. That is why the Vals hesitate, and why the system allows a way or two to slip through the net. So Master System mounts a defense on the pretext of serving arrest warrants on Hawks and China and Raven. Do not be so blind, Señorita Brigadier. Their mere possession of the rings will give them an edge, a way to get past, or around, the fleet, to get in. It is true that they may not find this path, but it is required. It *must* be there, and they have found either the path left open or made their own path so far. And once the five rings are united in human hands, even the pretexts will be gone. I believe that once all five are united they will not only be able to go for Master System, they will be *required* to do so."

She looked up and stared hard at his bizarre, monstrous face with those eerie, cold deep-set eyes. "Required?"

He nodded. "And I truly believe that Hawks, and perhaps Chen and others, know the correct sequence needed to use the rings. It is no longer a choice of duty to the system, Señorita Chi. It is only a choice of new masters. The so-called pirates, the Presidium, or. . . ."

She stood and cocked her head. "Just what are you getting at, Savaphoong?"

"Are you not human? Am I not, no matter what my form? The core, it says nothing about who is or is not qualified. Humans, just humans. Act while Master System is preoccupied. Act while you still have freedom and authority to do so!"

"Act? What are you saying?"

"We, you and I, have just as much right as anyone

else to go for the rings. If you believe so much in the status quo it is even your duty to do so! And we know exactly where four of those rings will be, don't we? Taking us to the fifth. Sit here meekly and die, Señorita Brigadier. Perhaps they will name a medal after you. Die, and do not survive to see the death of your precious system. Or act now. All humans, no Vals or others subject to other orders."

She sat down, stunned by the enormity of his proposal. Stunned, and also damned tempted.

"Your arguments are persuasive," she admitted, "but why should I take you along?"

He shrugged. "Partly because I know them. My knowledge of them and your expertise in security will be a powerful combination. And because in that part of my mind that has been rendered impervious to mindprinter techniques lies the answers. I, too, know the key to the interface. Once I realized that Hawks had discovered it there was no trick to correlating the ring designs with the data banks aboard *Thunder* until I got a match. That should be worth one ring out of five. No, do not think to pry it out of me. Like your own mind, any deep attempts at involuntary extraction will only result in my death. And I can only be an asset. I can hardly be a threat. I have a fish's tail. The direct light of most suns will blind and harm me, even kill me over a prolonged time. In deep water I might be dangerous, even to you, who are also a water creature, since you cannot breathe what I most crave, but—like *this*? I am at your mercy."

She thought it over, then sighed. "All right. For now, anyway. But this will take careful planning and will not be without risk. We must stay out of this or other fights and we must hold back until they show us where the interface is. We must also be on guard for this enemy, whoever it is. We need no ugly last-minute surprises. That is why I will do it. Not because of my own life, or

yours, but because if it is not me, we shall be wide open
to that enemy. I will give the administrative exec the
orders now. There is no time to lose on this. If I were
this Hawks, I would be making for Earth as fast as possible in the hopes that the forces there will not yet be
gathered and fully organized."

But, she had to admit to herself, this was also to sal-
vage her own ego and pride. Twice she had been out-
maneuvered and outwitted by these . . . people. But those
losses would be meaningless if they were denied the final
prize.

"A fleet is assembling," Star Eagle told them. He had
sent out a probe far in advance of their arrival, in the
hopes that it could send back information before somebody noticed it and shot it out of existence. "I have
never seen so many Vals, so many automated fighter
systems. They are indeed preparing for us, and there is
no way for any of our ships to get in close without triggering their attention."

The council of captains listened and watched the visuals as they came in, represented by all-too-clear
graphics.

"I am surprised that they have not yet come after the
probe," Maria Santiago remarked.

"Not I," Captain ben Suda responded. "It is small and
unobtrusive and they have no real defensive organization
as yet. It is even possible that they know it's there but
choose to ignore it."

Hawks frowned. "How's that?"

"They *want* a fight. Everything they have done has
been an attempt to provoke a repeat of the Battle of Janipur, although on even more favorable terms to them. I
believe we have come this far partly because, at its
heart, Master System was designed as a brute-force defensive war computer. We have beaten it to this point

with subtlety, and there is little subtlety in anything Master System ever did. Big battles and major actions are its chosen forte, its best and most comfortable situation. If it hits our probe or shows just how well monitored the system is, then we might back off, wait, even for years, until we figured a sneaky way in. That still might be our best move."

Hawks shook his head negatively. "From one viewpoint, maybe, but not the real one. Four rings do us no good at all. Give Master System time and it'll figure out a way to move or obscure our fifth and final ring, maybe turn Earth into that permanent primitive hell it seemed bent on doing years ago. Maybe even obscure or move its own interface. No, we have to go in. The question is, can we sneak in or not?"

"The probability against anything, organic or mechanical, penetrating the Earth's atmosphere unchallenged at this point is virtually nil," Star Eagle replied. "After all, it was Earth that Master System was originally supposed to protect anyway. No, the only way in is to beat it, and every day we delay, it will gather more strength from its far-flung outposts."

"What if we hit 'em hard now with all we got?" Raven asked the computer. "Do we stand a chance?"

"Practically none. We have a far inferior force and the fleet already present is at least six times as powerful as at Janipur. We are outmanned and outgunned many times over. The only thing that could take that force would be a task force as big or bigger than it."

China's blind head snapped up at that. She looked old for her years now, her beauty and glow faded by the curses Melchior had inflicted on her so many years ago, but she was still as sharp as ever. "Big! Of course!"

"If you got somethin', girl, spit it out," Raven said.

"The probe's just one of our fighters, specially outfitted. Have it check the orbit around Jupiter and report."

"Scanning," Star Eagle responded.

Hawks looked over at her. "Jupiter? You're not thinking . . ."

"They're still there, China," the pilot told her. "All still nicely mothballed. Minimal status."

"Recall the probe," she ordered. "We have need for it. If they let it come in once, they might just let it come in again. Stay well clear of Jupiter—I don't want to telegraph our intentions."

"Will do," the computer responded. "And, yes, it just might work. At least the attempt will be minimal in cost."

Hawks shook his head in wonder. "You're thinking of somehow getting in close enough to activate those old universe ships? With what? A fighter? It couldn't carry more than one, maybe two people in pressure suits."

"Master System knows that," China replied. "That's why I'm counting on it letting us get in there for a little while. A fighter from a sister ship shouldn't even set off the security systems aboard those things."

"An interesting idea," Isaac Clayben put in, "but they have no cores. We, at least, had Star Eagle to work with."

"Then we must make cores," China responded. "Star Eagle is capable of it, since he knows his own design, and the ships are all the same as this one used to be so we know exactly where everything is."

"But we could not exactly duplicate Star Eagle without removing him from the core command center amidships," Clayben pointed out. "To do so would cripple this vessel, cause the failure of all life support and other systems, and leave us totally vulnerable. Besides, true cores aren't like people. One minor mistake and we could wind up with no core at all, killing Star Eagle in the process."

"I am willing to take that risk," the computer told them. "All of you have done as much or worse."

"No! We don't need that!" China responded. "Besides, it would take too long. What we need is the physical unit. Programmable. Not Star Eagle's complex systems and banks. We don't need ten or twenty Star Eagles, as much as that might be nice. What we need are basic cores capable of handling the ships and carrying out commands from *Thunder*. Remotes, as it were."

Clayben's eyebrows rose. "Indeed? And even if we could do that, how would we get the cores aboard? Standards or not, the security there would seize control of any service robots we might use."

Captain ben Suda looked thoughtful. "But would the same apply to a being who might be able to work in such an environment?" he asked them. "One who could even survive a deep-space vacuum for up to three hours? A Makkikor, for example, who was also the finest ship's engineer alive?"

"You think he'd do it?" Hawks asked, interested.

"I think so. In a sense, his world and people have been injured more by Master System than ours. After all, it was our own ancestors who created this monster, but his people just had the bad luck to be in the middle of the exploration field when Master System rolled over it. I should think he would consider it an honor and a privilege to not only do whatever was necessary but to give his life to free his people—from us."

Raven shook his head. "No, no. A Makkikor can stand a vacuum, yeah, and work mostly in the dark, too, but that don't mean it don't need air. It ain't a matter of holdin' your breath for three hours, it's havin' the air inside for three hours' worth of work, and he's a big sucker. We might sneak *him* in, but not the auxiliary ship with the air and water. He can't manufacture it, you know, even if he gets the cores in and the ships operating. There's only so much murylium in them ship's engines and they'll be needed for full power. They ain't got the transmuters we got, neither. Remember, we had to build and modify over months to get what we got here. A transmuter that simply fuels the engines won't do no good at all."

Clayben scratched his chin in thought. "I wonder. We still have plenty of power, and they are bound to notice and figure out what we're doing if we get a punch that close in to Jupiter anyway. If I were thinking of coming in, a head-on engagement, I might well run a sacrificial lamb right into them to check out their power and organization before I committed my real forces. If we could punch into the solar system not far from Jupiter, but sufficiently distant to not draw undue notice to our intentions, and if we could punch through two ships in *tandem*, very close, the punch pulse might register as a single entry. If the trailing ship had the proper exit speed and momentum and made its turns using minimal local power, it just might not get picked up on the scanners at all. Then the defenders would concentrate on the leading ship, the probe, and possibly never even notice the one heading in toward the mothball fleet. And if that ship had the proper codes, which we can easily check with the fighter, then the mothball fleet would not react. Yes—it could be done."

"You are not talking about small automated fighters there," Maria Santiago pointed out. "You are talking about a full-size ship and a trailing smaller ship, both managed by skilled pilots. The second *might* make it, it is true, but the first, the diversion—what did you call it? A sacrificial lamb? Without the unpredictability of a human pilot aboard you could not hope to throw the defensive computers off long enough for your diversion to succeed, but we would most certainly lose that ship—

and any who were aboard. You are asking someone to commit suicide."

Hawks sighed. "Any other reasonable way to do this? Doctor, is there no possibility your technological magic could get us in any other way?"

"That is the best I can come up with, and it is filled with a great many variables," Clayben responded. "Star Eagle?"

"It is risky, but feasible," the computer responded. "I'm afraid Maria is correct—if even I were to engage the defenses there now, it would be no contest. No matter what a rebel I have become, or what I have learned, the fact is that my basic design—and basic designer—is the same as those cores on the defensive ships. That means I can unerringly know how they are going to react, and they will know how I will react. That is the reason for Val ships—they have a measure of humanity, as it were, from the life memories recorded within them. There are Vals in the system, but they are not involved in the main task force as far as I can tell, nor could they reach the positions in time. No, it is the ship's computer mated with the unpredictable and often irrational human interface that might buy some time. I agree with Doctor Clayben—and Maria."

Hawks looked around at them. "So, all this computer and brain power and we come up with a suicide play in which the most likely result is that we lose two of our remaining ships and three or more people. How can I authorize such a thing?"

"I believe it is the way in," Star Eagle told him. "There *must* be a way in. I am more convinced of that than ever now. Master System is required, I think, to leave a blind spot, a single avenue of entry. In each case we have either found that avenue or discovered one that it did not think of. I really suspect that there is little Master System doesn't think of. Consider its sheer size, power, speed, data bases, and intellect. Consider just how much it governs, and how absolute its power really is over that vast area where even tightbeam communication can take hours or days. No, it is as Raven said so long ago. Humans have an absolute *right* to go for the rings and to use them. Master System may make it very difficult and dangerous but its core program, its subconscious dictator, as it were, *requires* it to miss something, to keep creating blind spots, possibly without even realizing it. It should be child's play for such a computer to keep us off Earth, even if it cannot find us. And now I have proof. My fighter probe indicates that the security codes to the colonization ships have not been changed since we stole this one. Unchanged. That fleet is unlocked—if we can get to it."

Hawks sighed. "There it is, then. That little detail is not something Master System would overlook. It's something it was compelled to not think about. It has drawn its usual convoluted and dangerous route, and with the highest of prices to be paid. Somehow I never thought of the core imperatives in terms of a subconscious mind, but the analogy is sound." He paused a moment, as if suddenly seeing a new thought, a new fact, for the first time. He shook his head as if to clear it and muttered, "No, it couldn't be," low and to himself.

"What 'couldn't be'?" China asked him.

"Never mind. A silly thought from out of my own depths. The fact remains, even if all this is true and this is the only way left to us, it requires something I have never asked, or been able to ask, of anyone. It is not my right, even as chief and leader, to ask it."

"Oh, hell," Raven said casually, "I'll fly your damned target."

They all turned and stared at him, and he seemed almost embarrassed by that. He shrugged and explained, "Hey—ask Hawks. Our people had a damned habit of attacking iron horses with bows and arrows and somehow kiddin' themselves they could stop millions of white faces by winning a few cavalry battles. They got creamed, of course. But wouldn't it have been worth it to my ancestors to ride down whoopin' and hollerin' on the towns and the forts as a diversion, the warriors who fell knowin' that while everybody was watchin' and worryin' about them a few smart braves were blowin' up the Great White Father?"

"You don't have to do this," Hawks told him seriously. "You have nothing to atone for, no stain on your honor from our point of view."

"Not from *your* point of view, Chief," Raven responded. "But I don't give a damn about your point of view. Never have, and you know it. You know, I can't think of anything that might have come up that I really wanted to do more than this. No more bein' a pawn, no more sneakin' around, no more cheap cigars. By god, it's what I was born to do, Chief! One lone Crow warrior against a nest of the worst damned iron horses the white man ever inflicted on anybody! One damned warrior in the craziest, stupidest, loudest diversionary action his ancestors ever thought of—and, this time, we don't do it just for honor, we actually got a chance to win. But I don't just want one of the ships. I want the best armament, the best attack programs, the most speed possible."

"*Lightning* would be best, but we can't use it," Clayben noted. "It is a smaller ship, the logical trailing vessel Kwith the smaller footprint and the better intrasystem maneuverability. It's big enough to take the cores, the air supplies, the other supplies we might need, all that, but nothing could hide behind it save a fighter and that would be much too small."

Raven grinned. "I figured that, Doc. *Kaotan*'s good, but it don't turn tight enough for my tastes, and deep down it's just a cobbled-together rust bucket. No of-

fense, Ali, Chun, but *Bahakatan* and *Chunhoifan* are
fine merchant vessels, well maintained and real capable,
but in the end they're still freighters. No, there's only
one ship that meets all the requirements, and it just so
happens it ain't got no captain right now. It's fast heavily
armed, and very neatly disguised as just another scow.
Besides, we only got to take this warrior shit so far. With
Espiritu Luzon I go out in absolute luxury."

Everyone who could fly a ship volunteered for *Lightning*, but Hawks refused to pick anyone right then. "It
will be the best one for the job," he told them. "There is
no rush in this. In the meantime, Captain ben Suda, you
might just ask your Makkikor engineer if he's willing to
go along with this. If he's not, then we've got a lot of
rethinking to do."

The Makkikor was an incredibly fluid creature for
being so large and so formidable looking. Its basic shape
was lobsterlike, but instead of legs it had seemingly endless numbers of fine tendrils that could secrete various
substances to allow it to stick to or walk upon almost
any surface. What looked like a shell was deep purple
with some yellow strains, yet the exoskeleton, while as
tough as it looked, was almost rubbery in its ability to
twist and bend, to contort into whatever shape its wearer
required.

The head—it was not possible to really think of it as a
face—consisted of eight very long tentacles covered
with thousands of tiny sucker pads grouped around a
circular mouth that resembled more the cavity of some
gigantic worm than anything else. The eyes, on each side
of the exoskeleton, were lumpy protrusions from inside
the body, each able to independently swivel in almost
any direction. The irises were black, with V-shaped yellow pupils. When you looked upon a Makkikor you
knew for certain that this was no creature of Master Sys-

tem's design, but a product of a far different evolutionary path. To most humans, colonial and Earth types alike, it was monstrous, yet its people had risen on their home world to a high level of technology and while their brains might work as differently as their bodies looked, they were of extremely high intelligence.

Perhaps more intelligent than humans, some commented, because although they, too, were the products of a violent history they had the good sense never to create a Master System. Smart enough, too, to realize after a struggle that this alien computer was unbeatable and to accept the new system as the only alternative to genocide.

No Makkikor had the capacity for humanlike speech; theirs was a far different language, beyond human abilities as well. This one had a small transceiver implanted within it that was controlled by the creature's own electrochemistry. The implant would broadcast the Makkikor's words to another unit, translating as it did so. Although still imperfect, the implant was better than the unit it had used prior to joining the crew of the *Thunder*, and the creature fully understood what they had done and what they were intending to do.

"What will the new system do to my people?" it asked, mulling over the proposition.

"Nothing," Hawks tried to assure it, although he was grateful that Ali ben Suda was on hand, as well, a human used to conversing with it. "We are liberators, not new enslavers."

The Makkikor considered that. "Almost all enslavers began as liberators," it noted. "In my history, in your history. Such power will corrupt anyone. Human history is genocidal. I fear that even if we are liberated and grow out into space as our forefathers tried to do, we will meet the vastness of humanity doing the same."

"There are no guarantees," Hawks admitted. "I promise nothing, I guarantee nothing. In terms of the future, I can speak only for myself. We have no choice in this matter, really. Not you, not me. Our people—yours and mine—stagnate. We are strangled, slowly, by a dictator both ruthless and all-powerful yet for benevolent reasons. This must cease. What happens when its hold is broken is something I cannot say, but it is an unacceptable present versus the unknown future. I fear that future for my people as much as you fear it for your own, but I am committed. The system we face now is wrong. What might be is not something I can be concerned about. I believe it is as fitting for my people to be involved in this enterprise as it is fitting that one of your race also be here. It can only be said that we took the risks and struck the blows, Makkikor and Hyiakutt among them. For me, that is sufficient. That is as much as I can expect, and it will not be forgotten."

The Makkikor seemed to think on that. It had wound up with ben Suda because of a chance run-in on one of those freebooter worlds where ships were cannibalized to keep the other ships running. Why it had signed on was never clear, but it had been loyal and a superior engineer—*Bahakatan* was the best-run and best-maintained ship of all the freebooter craft. It had come here because its ship was here, and it had stayed mostly to itself all these years, working on not only its own craft but the others, as well.

"I am old," the Makkikor said. "Old and tired. I will do it not because I believe that what comes after will be any better, nor for what your people call honor, nor for loyalty or ideals or any of those things. I am too old to have retained any such feelings if I once had them. I will do it because I wish to die among my own kind. I will do it because between the time the old way dies and the new is organized might well be longer than I have left, and certainly longer than it would take me to go home."

"Each of us acts for his or her own reasons," Hawks responded. "I do not ask for motives, only for accomplishment."

"These ships. You say they are approximately a hundred kilometers apart?"

"Yes. That's an average, of course."

"Too far for a jet pack, then, but power consumption must be minimal or they will be upon us. *Lightning* is a good ship but we cannot risk burst after burst of even low-level power. We will prepare a fighter with the most basic of drives, more pressure than anything else. We will take our time. Out, then back, to each ship and back to *Lightning*, which should remain relatively stationary in the midst of the fleet. Very well. Let us get to work on it."

Raven, too, was working on his end. Since volunteering he seemed almost a changed man, although if anything his cigar consumption had gone up along with rather conspicuous consumption of the fine wines and liquors left behind by Savaphoong. But using *Thunder*'s maintenance robots, he had slimmed down the shape of *Espiritu Luzon*, eliminated much weight, reinforced the shields to the maximum that was possible, and added additional armament. Hawks surveyed the work approvingly.

"It doesn't look like you intend to lose," he noted. "Try to save a few of them for us."

Raven chuckled. "Oh, there'll be plenty left, Chief. No question about that. This is a diversion, though, not a suicide mission. Oh, sure, any fool can see I'm gonna get creamed, but I ain't makin' it easy for nobody. If I can buy the time and still get out with my skin, I'm gonna do it. They're gonna figure it's a diversion from the start— we're only hopin' they're gonna be lookin' for the big attack instead of where we're really workin', but they won't take me none too serious. I figure there's a little tiny chance out of this. If there is, I ain't gonna get blown to bits 'cause I overlooked something."

Hawks nodded. "When will you be ready?"

"Never if I had my choice, but as good as I'm gonna be in three, maybe four more days. What about that Makkikor and *Lightning*?"

"Ready now. The construction of the cores has gone well and they all have been tested. They can run the ships' systems, follow all offensive and defensive security commands, and will be tied in with our own master battle network. Enough brains and enough basic data to get the job done but no personality. Sort of like Savaphoong's poor slaves aboard here. You decide what to do about them?"

Raven shrugged. "Ain't nothin' *to* do with 'em. They're transmuted. They ain't gonna ever be more than beautiful bodies and empty heads. They got no future and you know it. I figured I'd just take 'em along for the ride. Might as well be decadent while I'm bein' noble."

"I feel somewhat—dirty—in allowing that, but they have no capacity for making their own choice or even contemplating their own mortality. I should take them off, but they have no place here, and I refuse to allow anyone here to get used to some people being mindless slaves. Very well. Take them. They will be on my own conscience."

Raven grinned. "You got too much of that conscience shit, Chief. You can't carry the guilt of the universe. All you're gonna give yourself is a damned heart attack that way, and wouldn't that be ironic? You droppin' dead before you even saw the rings bein' used?"

Hawks thought about his conversation with the Makkikor. Were it not for Cloud Dancer and the children, he wondered if a heart attack at such a time might not be a mercy. Instead he said, "Every day another ship or two comes into the system. Every day I feel the pressure of more, perhaps the SPF, as well, closing in on our backs. The window is small and getting smaller, Raven. Four days. Four days from right now." He paused. "You can still back out, you know."

The Crow grinned. "Chief, I wouldn't back out of this for all five rings and Master System, too. I'll be ready. You just be sure that *Lightning* gets where it has to and does its job. You decided who's gonna fly it, by the way?"

"We've run trials with *Kaotan* on just about everyone. It's clear we need two aboard just in case, and Maria and Midi are the best choice—but I want them on the ground with me if we get through. I don't want them stuck out there, and I don't want to deal with Matriyehan orphans. It's simply too much of a problem to adapt the ship for the Alititians. The same goes for the Chows, and I want experienced people there. I'm going to send Ali ben Suda because he knows the Makkikor as well or better than anyone else alive and is a damned good captain, and I'm also sending Chun Wo Har. That's two good captains who also want to participate in the end."

"Good enough for me," Raven told him. "Let's go before I die of all this damned luxury."

The four days passed all too quickly.

Raven had told them he wanted no sendoff, but Hawks and Cloud Dancer both came down to see him as he was preparing to leave. The Crow startled them by his appearance; he wore the loincloth and skin moccasins of a young warrior, and his face was painted with glowing designs, his long hair braided in pigtails.

"You look like someone from a warm climate," Hawks noted. "Any Crow who dressed like that would freeze to death."

Raven laughed. "The summers get very hot where my people live," he told them, "and on the dark summer nights with the fires blazing in the midst of the lodges they perform their rituals. I've always been a rationalist, Chief; I always figured that when we go, we go out like a candle. But when you're there, in the midst of them all, with the chants of the holy ones merging with the songs and supplications of the people—then you get a different feeling. Out there, between the mountains of the north, where you sometimes feel as if you can reach out and grab a star and bring it home with you—then there is *something* there."

Cloud Dancer smiled. "If you can feel that, if you have felt it even once, then you know in your heart that there is magic," she said gently. "We have come a long way, have we not, together?"

Raven was suddenly very serious. "Yes. A long way."

"The ghosts of not only your ancestors but of all our ancestors going back to the start of time ride with you, Raven," she told him. "In the past years I have learned much. It is the penalty of being married to a historian. Our people have been conquered, their lands stolen, the buffalo slaughtered, the very skies stained with their blood at each sunrise, yet we survive. We true humans are a small people compared to the others, far smaller in number than even I had ever dreamed, yet we are still here, and now it again falls to us. We who have suffered so much have been guided by destiny to this point. Be brave, Raven, for we will never die."

And she reached up and kissed him, and he was deeply moved by it. Hawks had feared that Cloud Dancer would break into tears but her eyes were dry. Raven's, however, were not, and Hawks was suppressing tears himself. He reached out a hand and clasped Raven's long and hard, and then the Crow turned without a word and made his way back to his ship. They watched him go, until he was but a tiny figure in the vast cargo bay, then they turned and went back inside.

"Do not weep for him, my husband," she said at last.

"Few of us ever are placed in such a wonderful position where we might do something, contribute to something, truly momentous. He himself has said it. He was born for this, for the next four hours. When you write the history of all this, there will not be a Crow among his people who will not claim lineage to him nor a child among them who will not wish to measure up to him. It is no time for sadness, but rather rejoicing. When we first met him as an enemy, he had lost his soul. Now he has found it again."

It would still be a near thing, and although Master System might have left this one hole open for them it was, as Star Eagle had said, not a conscious hole. If they did it wrong, if they didn't pull this off, then the forces being massed by the great computer would eat them alive.

To emerge on virtually a single punch their speed had to be exact, their placement mere meters apart and in a perfectly straight line. *Lightning* was almost in *Espiritu Luzon*'s engines and held fixed by four carefully rigged tractor beams. Computers aboard *Luzon* would manage both ships through a link, keeping engine thrusts absolutely equal and the hold tight, until the very moment of the punch. At that point, mere nanoseconds before *Luzon* would punch out, the link and the tractors would be severed and *Lightning*'s own automatic systems would take over. Captain ben Suda would be linked but only observe until after the breakaway at punch in. At that point, it would be his show—and Raven's.

"Punch in thirty seconds," Star Eagle reported as everyone on the *Thunder* held their breaths. Even the very air seemed still. "I am picking up odd sounds from *Espiritu Luzon*."

"Put them on," Hawks ordered.

They came through the speakers, and Hawks smiled

and looked at Cloud Dancer, who returned the smile. Neither could understand the Crow language, nor could Star Eagle, which was why he was so puzzled, but the two Hyiakutts knew. "He sings the ancient songs well," Hawks commented.

"For a Crow," she responded. "Just pray he does not forget where he is and order a launch of arrows."

"Punch!" Star Eagle reported. "Perfect! On the nose!"

There would now be no contact possible with the ships for close to twenty minutes. It was ironic that they could communicate through that nether-space from point to point in real time but they could not talk while between the two regions.

Nobody said or did much during the waiting period. Even the youngest children seemed to be silent, as if they, too, were somehow aware that something important was happening. Hawks looked around at the great inner world of *Thunder* as if seeing it for the first time. It had been his world for so long, and it had been good. The children had known no other. Now, suddenly, it seemed so empty, and so transitory.

"Punch out!" Star Eagle reported. "Perfect separation. My own monitors in the asteroid belt easily detected it but there was no indication of a double punch-in. *Lighting* made something of a trace as it broke away but nothing inconsistent with the usual anomalous readings you might get on a punch. Raven is still singing, and he has released dozens of drones that are showing up well in scatter-shot fashion. It is impossible even for me to pick up *Lightning* in all that clutter, and I know it's there and where it's going! Uh oh!"

"What is it?" Hawks asked.

"Outer perimeter fighters using short punches. Four of them closing fast on *Luzon*. Raven sees them. Hmmm . . . That is odd. He has stopped singing."

"You chant before a battle, not during one," Hawks said tensely.

The fighters were in for something of a surprise: *Luzon* still looked like only a freighter, but was faster and carried more armaments than even *Lightning* after the modifications. The defensive fighters expected Raven to use short punches and maneuvered to cover, but he just kept on, picking out the weakest area of the field and then letting loose a salvo of torpedoes, turning wide, and bearing right down on two other fighters. The maneuver was absolutely insane and against all logic.

It confused the hell out of the automated fighters, who turned and came at him, locking on as best they could. Raven launched missiles, short punched, then launched more aft. The fighters, confused, swung around and launched their own right into the region where the first fighter was trying to pick off the initial torpedo salvo. There were so many torpedoes in the area from both the three pursuit ships and Raven, all with smart warheads, that they began to go after the ships indiscriminately and even each other. The other fighters, closing, had to veer off to stay out of the mess and found themselves going for a few precious seconds in exactly the wrong direction from Raven. In the meantime, two of the three fighters that initially closed on *Luzon* were struck hard—by whose torpedoes it was impossible to tell—and the other torpedoes, seeing a target, zeroed in on the ones that were hit.

By remaining inside the full range of the fighters Raven could not avoid taking a few hits himself, but he and the others were so close together that the odds were three to one against it being *him* that was hit by any given torpedo. He managed to take his lumps and punch further in, leaving the outer perimeter guards damaged and in disarray. Man plus machine had beaten machine alone. Loud shrieks, which everyone but Hawks and Cloud Dancer attributed to pain and wounds, came back to them from *Luzon*.

Raven had been right all along, Hawks realized. He was having more fun than he'd ever had in his whole life.

He noticed that Cloud Dancer sat silently, doing a rough sketch in charcoal. As time progressed, he saw that it was a drawing of Raven, in loincloth and full war paint, a ferocious, even maniacal expression on his face, at the controls of an idealized spaceship. It wasn't exactly realistic, but if it became a painting that hung in the lodges of the Crow some time from now it would be a definitive classic.

Star Eagle's calculations were that Raven would be twenty percent or more disabled by the initial engagement, and very likely not survive any further inbound engagement against heavier forces. Over three hours after the initial engagement, however, *Luzon* was battered and starting to run low on certain kinds of ammunition, but was still going, using short punches, and had almost reached the orbit of Mars.

"The main body is not engaging him," Star Eagle reported. "They have guessed it is a feint and are grouping for a main attack. They are still spread a bit thin, and it appears that they have deduced that our most logical line of punch-in and attack will be from behind the main body, possibly under as well. Raven has also played everything exactly right. He has acted with total illogic when they expected logical moves and with computer precision when they allowed for total illogic."

"What about *Lightning*?" Hawks asked.

"Inbound, engines down. Good speed and angle. They have already broadcast the security codes and are angling in to the fleet. I would expect that they will be slowing to station within the hour. No sign that they have been detected. I think we got away with it!"

"Tell Raven to get the hell out of here, then!" Hawks ordered. "Tell him to punch out no matter where the hell he winds up and keep punching!"

"He has a possibility of breaking free although he is badly damaged," Star Eagle replied. "I have sent the recall but to no effect. Perhaps his main engines are out and he is incapable of punching."

"Main engines out my ass!" Hawks growled. "What the hell has he got in mind?"

"Hard to say. He is currently in an open area, but his recent corrections are taking him on a direct heading for Earth. Hawks—there are Val ships all over there, not to mention about half the task force. He has already survived nine engagements. A stone or spear could probably take him out now, yet he's heading straight for the main body."

Hawks sighed and sat down. "Now is he drawn to the very center of Hell, the lost city of Dis, having run the circles of Malebolge. Though he be consumed by the flames or frozen by the cold of demon wings, that idiotic son of a bitch is going to ram himself right down the devil's throat." No one heard. No one was meant to.

"He's going on, screaming like a madman! There's a huge force now, closing in from all sides! There's no way they're going to let any ship reach Earth itself!" Star Eagle sounded as if he were going to short circuit from the tension. "He's heading right into the center of them! Loosing everything he's got left! He's hit! Again! Again! He—"

There was a deadly, unnatural quiet.

"He's gone," Star Eagle said flatly.

"Punched?" Hawks asked, hoping against hope.

"No. Nothing could have lived amid what they were

throwing at him. He's just—gone. I have reviewed the sequence. It appeared that at the last moment he made a slight correction and just, well, went to his maximum speed straight into a Val formation. He got two of them."

Cloud Dancer looked up from her sketch. "He is home," she said softly, and went back to her drawing.

9. THE FINAL BATTLE

HAWKS SAT WITH WHAT WAS LEFT OF THE COUNCIL in the main control room of *Thunder*.

"All right, how many ships do we have armed and ready?"

"Twenty-six," Star Eagle responded. "That was the most possible without using main engines, and they are beginning to get very suspicious ever since Raven attacked and nothing followed. That is five hundred and twenty coordinated fighters plus the on-board guns and torpedoes. The shielding, however, will be poor since it was mostly designed for punches, and the in-system speed will be slow for the same reason. Remember, I had to use Jupiter as a slingshot to gain enough speed for the initial getaway. As soon as I activate them, the whole plan will be clear to Master System."

That begged the big question. "Can we win with that?"

"It might be close. Since Raven's escapade they have spread out and are still fairly thin, but these are destroyers we are talking about—one hundred and thirty-one of them to be exact, along with a count of at least twelve Vals in the near-Earth orbit position commanding another ten. In realistic terms, the big ships are going to get the hell blown out of them, but the fighters are too small and fast to be separated from all the other pulses unless you know their codes. That means the fighters will show to an attack computer just like torpedoes, although they are in reality several times that size and faster."

"Recommendations?"

"Start them all up at once," Maria Santiago suggested. "As long as we telegraph our battle plan by starting one, let us start all of them. Swing them out and up and around as fast as possible—I know that will take time, and *they* will need time to organize their response. Your screens show no ships within close range except perhaps a fighter or two on picket, and if need be, *Lightning* can take them if those captains are as good as they seem to be. There is no evidence that Master System even suspects *Lighting* is there and even if it deduces it, when the big ships move it won't be looking for one little ship. Pull the ships out in formation, accelerate, make the full Jupiter arc."

"But they're not going to punch," Hawks pointed out.

"Yes, but does Master System know this? It has the advantage of having to defend a relatively small position, but its disadvantage is that it must always react, always wait for us to move. We have already done something apparently irrational. We sacrificed a ship, and while the task force lost a dozen it was hurt far less by that than we by the loss of one. It will take nothing for granted with us. I would think that it would have to consider the possibility of facing twenty-six *Thunder*s with full command cores and specially outfitted by us. Carrying what? They cannot know. Dozens of ships? Hundreds? They will have to move to prevent the punchout of so many capital ships. The logic will be easy, since all twenty-six will have to come out of Jupiter's gravity well in a predetermined region in order to punch out at the proper speed. It would be like shooting fish in a barrel. But we do not break out for the punch. We continue to come around and head in at maximum speed, then fan out. The initial defensive perimeter would then be left behind and forced to catch up. It would also be forced to split and give chase, which would make them easy prey for the big ships' fighters. That is the sort of thing they were designed to handle."

"It sounds good," Star Eagle told them. "We must force them to split their forces and group them around the big ships. They are unlikely to engage the Vals and the ten fighters they have around Earth. Those are certainly reserves, and in any event they would be there to keep us from sneaking in under cover of the big ships. With a proper set of inbound trajectories, they would be able to take out any big ship they wanted—any three or four, even—if they concentrated all their remaining forces on them. But that would leave a massive force of our ships to get through, all concentrated on the orbital defenses. They could not permit that. But to take on all twenty-six at once would mean a mere five destroyers per big ship. My calculations show that they have a possibility of winning that way, but it is under seventeen percent, comparing weaponry to weaponry, and remembering that I have never fought such a battle before and have no precedent for it."

"Don't worry," Hawks responded. "Neither has Master System. The few times it faced a battle of any magnitude, such as with the Makkikor, it was in our position, attacking. It has never been forced to defend before, even though it was originally designed to do so. Is there any other strategy that you could see—that any of you can see—other than five to a big ship?"

There was dead silence.

"All right, then, it'll take the odds and hope that whatever is left can be handled by the Vals and orbital ships. I believe Maria's plan is the best one for us, as well, but I want everyone at their ships and on station, all ships powered up and ready to go. The odds favor us having a number of potent but very damaged survivors to take on the Vals and the rest. When we get to that point we must commit ourselves. Everything we have. *Lightning*, too —notify them to be ready. Star Eagle, how many fighters do you have in combat configuration?"

"We have been manufacturing them at a good clip. We have forty-two locked on the outer hull now, half with limited punch capability. In addition I have four with transmuter transceiving grids on them and six remaining monitor ships. Those last aren't much good unless they can ram something but that's always a possibility."

Butar Killomen looked shocked. "You're not going to engage *Thunder* directly, are you?"

"If I have to. All or nothing, Bute. All or nothing. I'm well aware of what I'm saying and what I'm risking, but I will risk everything rather than lose at this late stage because we failed to commit one gun. This has been understood by those of us who started from here so long ago since the beginning."

"But the children . . ."

"If we lose," he responded, "what sort of future do they have?" He pounded his fist on the table. "No! All or nothing. Any minute, any day, we could wind up with two or more new task forces reporting in from far-flung regions when we have already shot our wad—not to mention four hundred plus divisions of the SPF who could show up at any time if Master System is really scared. The odds barely favor us completing this thing now, seventeen percent or no. I say we go! How say the rest of you?"

Killomen gulped. "Very well. I will take *Bahakatan* along with Vulture, Min, Chung, and Fatima, of course. We have been modifying *Kaotan*, since it already had some modifications to account for the old Takya. I feel certain that Takya, Dura, and Han Li can handle it well enough. *Chunhoifan* has a majority of its original crew still in original form but no experienced pilots left."

"Then Midi and I will take it," Maria said. "I want a chance to pay them all back for my own ship. We might need some seat modifications and some change of control helmets, though, to allow for our difference in shape."

"Easy to do," Star Eagle told her. "I am ordering what is needed now and will have the maintenance robots install it within two hours. It is merely a matter of replacing two seats. The interface helmets are even easier, since we have many spares now."

"I will interface with Star Eagle and track this thing," China said. "I want to be able to see what is going on."

Hawks sighed. "And that leaves the admiral with the wife and kids, I guess. I suppose I should have taken some time in all these years to learn how to fly one of these things. The problem is, we still have more pilots than ships. One more and the Chows could have a go. They've been wanting to have some action."

"No, they lack the killer instinct," China replied. "They still see this almost as a game. Let them tend to the children. It is what they do best."

Hawks looked over at Cloud Dancer, sitting apart from the meeting. "Then I guess it's just you and me, woman, as usual."

She smiled. "Do not be so glum, husband. Not everyone is born to be a great warrior. Some are born to other things of equal importance. Look at it this way: they all will leave only to fight, but you, my husband, must tell them how the rings are to be used."

* * *

Hawks sat in one of the command chairs on the bridge of the *Thunder*, trying to think, trying to sort it all out, even as the great ships were activated and other ships of the line readied for backup. He would face the climax of all their years of blood and sweat alone. He had wanted it that way. Oh, China's body sat in a forward command chair, helmet on, but her mind was interfaced with Star Eagle's and she was no more there in any meaningful sense than was, well, Raven.

There was nothing Hawks could do now, and he knew it. Raven and many of the others were fighters; he was a thinker. There was no particular shame in that distinction, but there was a sense that he was perceived as unequal by the fighters themselves and that hurt a bit. His political skills had in no small measure gotten them this far; now, if the warriors could gain him the last small step, it was entirely in his hands to get them the rest of the way.

He reached into a pouch and pulled out the four gold rings. Such a simple code, really. It was not a code that the original members of the Fellowship wished to be obscure or hard to understand. It was not supposed to be almost a thousand years before they might be used; it was, rather, a matter of years at the worst—or so the makers of the rings had thought. Not so great a distance that none but a historian of the Last Days might, just might, have stumbled on it.

"*We are up to speed and arcing. All twenty-six units under complete control and fully operational. Defense already reacting, but even Master System cannot bend time. All going according to plan.*"

He looked at the Alititian ring. *Whose were you?* he wondered. The ring of rings, one ring for each of the cardinal points and another, slightly larger, in the center. Probably Aaron Menzelbaum's. He was considered the greatest scientific mind of his age; almost another Einstein, although his interests led him into more concrete pursuits. Einstein's work had led, to his horror, to the creation of the great weapons of terror while he tried to preach world peace and explain the stars and matter and energy. Menzelbaum, on the other hand, was devoted to saving humankind from just those same terror weapons, although the direction his great mind had taken was far different from the direction the government that employed him wanted to go or thought he was taking them.

"They are taking the bait! Defense rings six through nine are deploying to block punchout!"

Menzelbaum, who had thrown out all the clumsy programming tricks the computer people like to fool themselves into calling artificial intelligence and had started anew, with totally different approaches, totally different ways of managing, storing, and accessing data. He was the theoretician who invented new forms of mathematics to construct his models and who used that math to create true holographic memory in an artificial creature.

"All scoops open. More than enough matter to transmute into the energy we need. I should be able to fully charge the fighters and defense commands by the time of orbital breakout."

But no university, no private group, could possibly fund the size and scope of the computer Aaron Menzelbaum dreamed of creating. Only a government could do that, and only the military arm of a government could get so much money and brainpower support without the project being constantly hacked to pieces, slowed, or crippled beyond repair. And so, perhaps reluctantly, Aaron Menzelbaum had allowed himself to be recruited to the defense of his nation. Perhaps reluctantly. How often had Hawks and other historians of the period wondered if that great mind had not conceived of his master plan for peace right from the start and wound up just where he wanted to be.

"Coming 'round now. Excellent speed and control, power at seventy percent and climbing. Estimate that four ships will remain underpowered after full rounding, but that is fewer than my initial projections. There is a lot of junk to be fed to transmuters orbiting Jupiter."

But what about the other four? Pinsky, of course, was easy. She had come to the United States to teach and do research in areas a bit too expensive for her native land and wound up living in America far longer than she had in Israel. A close friend of and engineering alter ego of Menzelbaum's and the natural one to oversee the actual construction of the great computer. Yomashita, the Japanese-educated Hawaiian who was expert in the new manufacturing techniques necessary to create the memory storage for the computer, techniques that required memory cells to be manufactured in space to get the necessary purity and then brought back to Earth. Sung Yi, the immigrant genius behind the principles of molecular conversion that would power the new machine independently of any outside source, the primitive ancestor of the transmuter. And Ntunanga, the Paris-educated Gabonese who was, perhaps, the only other mind capable of understanding Menzelbaum's mathematics and thus essential in spite of most certainly giving some security men fits.

"Everybody relax and get some rest. It's going to be a while now before things start popping."

Some assignment it had to be. To build a computer so complex and so intelligent that it would be able to gather and consolidate and evaluate and analyze all the incoming intelligence, then control, coordinate, and plan for almost any military contingency. Something so brilliant and so powerful that one would merely have to call in or type in a question like "What are the odds the Russians would fight rather than pull back on the Indian subcontinent?" "Is the new regime in Chad likely to favor a pro-American, pro-Russian, or neutralist course?" How important is holding here or moving there?

So all-powerful, all-knowing, it was supposed to be able to instantly give a President his options in a crisis, including the ultimate recommendation on whether or not to launch a nuclear strike. Not that the system could do so on its own—that was to be prohibited in a series of commands Menzelbaum called the core imperatives. There was only one very limited scenario where it had that authority—if an enemy had already launched and the nuclear defense shields were evaluated as inadequate to contain a first-strike blow. The second strike was entirely in its hands so long as that was not countermanded by the President or legal authorities. Menzelbaum would never allow any machine, not even his, to have first-strike ability.

Hawks had often wondered how it had come up. Star Eagle indicated that the five mostly got close because of their non-Christian heritage; the project was so complex that otherwise their paths might have crossed only seldom. Certainly it had come up at least three years before the terrible day their child was set loose. All five had moved by that time close to the actual site of the great computer and had pretty much taken up permanent residence there, and they met often, and socialized together. It must have been a life under a total security blanket; it's amazing they were able to not only formulate but actually create and install their little extras without being detected. But then, of course, in order to understand what they were doing one would need to understand the complex mathematics and physics that were their life, and they were beyond their peers.

Perhaps it was not so odd. If Center personnel now could learn to cheat and defeat the most sophisticated mindprinting and surveillance systems ever devised, then it must have been child's play for minds like that to deceive far less sophisticated and equally suspicious security forces.

The military men had chafed over the first-strike limitations, but the views of those such as these five were well known and it was their way or no computer at all. They were resolved that they would not be a new form of the Manhattan Project, whose scientists created the atomic bomb and then, in the main, spent the rest of their lives regretting it. No, this computer might well find alternatives that no human mind, under pressure or not, could ever conceive of to prevent nuclear war, and as for second strike—well, what difference was it if all was lost whether it was man or the machine who pushed that final button?

But their great computer had an added imperative. To explore and find any way or ways possible to save the human race from itself, down to the last moment, and to hold those ways in readiness in case the most terrible of decisions was somehow judged inevitable.

Still, they were ever mindful that the best of great projects created by great minds often begat monsters. The core imperatives had to be precise, unbending, unyielding. Humanity was to be preserved at all cost. That was the first imperative. Once pacified, humanity must be prevented from ever being in the position to totally destroy itself again. That was the second imperative. Humans must be left to manage their own affairs and run their own societies as soon as the first two imperatives were met. That was the third imperative, intended to forestall the tyranny of the machine. And then? The ultimate aim of human creation should be the never-ending pursuit and acquisition of knowledge. That was the fourth imperative.

And still they agonized. There was no way to test

this, no way to see if, somehow, they had made a mistake. Even if they could run the models they could not hide them from the countless other brilliant minds on the project and the security and military overseers. They could not know, and it had made them uneasy no matter that theirs was the only alternative to total human genocide. Just as there could be no first strike by machine, only by order of those elected to that authority, so there should be humans with authority over the machine extending even to halting its carrying out of its imperatives. A simple interface, really, that would simply force a reset and return command to a preactivation mode, subject to human authority. But an interrupt that would require the unanimous vote of all five. A single code that the core would recognize and would not be able to block or ignore, broken into five parts, burned into five memory modules each with part of the code. The modules would have to be accessible, yet hidden from view of the security people who always watched them.

Five rings, to mark rank in an informal social club of the best brains in the project. Insert them in the wrong order and the override code would be sheer garbage. Who knew what the computer would do in that case? Certainly ignore any such signals, if not worse. It might well interpret such a wrong code as an attempt to breach its security.

More imperatives. What if any or all of them should die? The rings must be held by humans, and by humans with authority. That seemed easy enough. Humans would always hold the override, and humans with authority would obviously have access to the computer—wouldn't they? And give an imperative that the holders of the rings had a right to access the interface. Otherwise the computer could always prevent itself from being reset.

Raven, Star Eagle, and others believed that if all five

rings were united, Master System could not prevent in any way the bearers from coming to it and inserting the rings. Perhaps—but those imperatives were subject to interpretation. Four simply wouldn't do. You had to battle your way to the fifth.

And Menzelbaum's greatest creation was flawed not so much because it did not work or was defective or even because it was evil. It was none of those things. What it was was alien, the first alien intelligence, the first life form of its kind ever faced in human history. A life form whose personality was not shaped by birth and parenting and hormones and growing up, and who could understand those things only in an academic way. The most clear-cut of statements might to such a creature have infinite meanings.

Save humanity. Somehow it did that, the circumstances were not really known—but there certainly had been an imminent war of the sort its creators had feared. There were signs of it in places even now, although not in as many places as one would expect. How did Master System stop it? Perhaps only it could explain, if there were anyone around capable of understanding the explanation. And when it did so, the imperatives came into play.

Be certain humanity can't ever destroy itself again. Disarm it, rule it ruthlessly, tyrannize it. But only for a time. The other imperatives are there as well. The only logical choice: dispersal. Spread it out over so great a distance that not even the worst natural or man-made disasters could destroy it. Speed was of the essence. No time after exploration to turn those worlds into Earthlike havens. Solution: turn the humans into creatures who could survive on what was found. Alien civilizations? A couple, and possible long-term threats to humanity's survival if space-capable. Solution: total destruction of alien races unless those races surrender to and agree to be co-opted into the master system. There was no compunction about committing genocide of other life forms; the creators of the core hadn't mentioned them at all. Master System was good at taking the initiative when faced with a problem not covered by instructions.

Humans shall rule themselves? Enter the Centers, where humans appointed by the system rule their own people—and make certain those people remain ignorant, stagnated, uncreative. Seek out the best and the brightest and either co-opt them to the Centers or, if they can't be co-opted, make certain they don't grow up. Make the humans enforce the system. Humans would rule humans —but only one philosophy of social management was allowed.

As for pursuing and gathering all knowledge, who was better equipped to do so, the poor humans or the great computers? To fulfill this imperative, it was necessary to keep the humans out of the way as pets in preserves, zoos, or museum exhibits.

The only threat: the rings. Can't destroy them, can't keep them. Imperatives, more imperatives. Best to disperse them, as well, to the far corners of the colonies, and then destroy all references that the rings even existed, let alone what they might be used for and how. With humanity denied control of space, how could anyone who ever did learn of them get them?

One . . . two . . . three . . . four. One more left behind, on Lazlo Chen's fat finger. His was the one with the three birds with open beaks. Parrots, it looked like. It was funny, absurd. *Five golden rings* . . .

How damnably simple, how droll a joke, especially for the five brilliant minds left behind when everyone else went off for Christmas.

The center ring was largest on the Alititian stone. Not as much help as he'd hoped, but it was clearly first among equals and the song tended to be sung, according to the records, in descending order. Five, four, three, two, one—the simplest progression.

And where is the interface? They had decided it, and logic dictated it. Master System wasn't some portable core that could be picked up and moved. It was *massive*. It had to be. Built right into the Earth upon which it fed and through which it expanded. It would never dare allow itself to be transferred or moved. To be shut down for any interval, or to trust even its own creations to reassemble it perfectly elsewhere. It was right where they had built it. Right in the great mountains of the western divide in North America, surrounded entirely by nontechnological people of the land who migrated from mountains to plains and hunted the buffalo and fished the great rivers and stalked the elk and bear.

Knowing that, and from space, it ought to be simplicity itself to find. The radiations coming from it, the communications network, all that, focused on a single point somewhere in those mountains—hell, it was child's play.

If you had something in orbit of your own that wouldn't be knocked down while you were taking that look.

"I have separation over almost two million kilometers, the outermost in a broad arc and the ones with the least power in a direct center line! They are turning in pursuit and breaking up. Uh oh! They're letting the four center ships go and concentrating an extra fighter on each of the other twenty-two. I guess Master System figured out they had the lowest reserves and is leaving them for the planetary defense. We're leaving the outer defenses in our wake! I might have to slow down to let them catch us, but now we've got the first waves coming in-system. Here we go!"

Hawks started, then looked around for a moment. He must have fallen asleep. The announcement of the initial engagement woke him up. He felt thirsty, and hungry, but made do with water. Even though it was still remote from him, he knew he could neither eat nor drink much of anything until it was over. Then? Well, Raven had left some pretty fancy stuff from Savaphoong's larder. It would either be the best last meal he ever ate or a victory repast.

There was a wrongness about computers fighting computers. You could only sit and wait; your poor human brain couldn't even follow the intricacies of parry, thrust, maneuver, shoot. There was something terribly disquieting in the knowledge that empty ships were fighting empty ships to determine humanity's direction, as if the ghost of Aaron Menzelbaum hovered over both sides and would not let go.

There was a sense of remoteness about it, as well. Up on the main screen he could see little colored lights representing what was going on and even though he had the skill to follow them, something inside him disallowed even that. It wasn't real; it was some sort of simulation, some game, even with its own scoreboard. On the one side was a big numeral 26, and under it a smaller number that had started at numeral 520. On the other, numeral 131 and under it a smaller 10 and a companion 12. The numbers now began to count down, but not rapidly.

The problem was distances within a solar system. The big ships would soon be up to their maximums, which was less than half light speed—a bit faster than the destroyers, ironically, since the destroyers could minipunch within the system. The big ships weren't designed to do that and weren't all that maneuverable around here. Those giants were fourteen kilometers long and two wide; the destroyers could be measured in meters. Forces and even braking and turning distances were radically different on that basis alone, and the big ships were heading in, not out.

Even at maximum speed, and assuming they were not

slowed by battle or damage, it would take them four or
five days to reach the neighborhood of Earth. Add two
more days, perhaps, just for braking to avoid slipping
past and whipping around the sun, and you had a better
scale of just what was happening out there.

It was going to be a very slow, very long battle.

For the first time, he thought he might now understand a little of Raven, and particularly the nature of the
man's death.

*The tribes came down off the hills chanting and hol-
lering, firing and throwing everything they had at the
great iron monster that belched smoke and for whom the
buffalo had been so mercilessly and senselessly slaughtered. They had been under no illusions that they could
stop the white man's terrible machines, but the travesty,
the sacrilege, of putting a machine's interest above and
at the cost of the interests, lives, and very way of life of
nations of human beings demanded it. It was not the
machine itself but the worship of it they found so horrible that fighting and death seemed preferable to accepting its domination of human values. To the white man,
the great black belching monsters were progress, for
they worshipped innovation at any cost and could not
conceive of invention being evil; to the natives it dis-
placed, it was the demon horde from hell.*

Cloud Dancer had understood, for her culture and
values had been of the old ways. The Isaac Claybens and
Lazlo Chens never would. He now understood, at least
to a degree, on the most personal of levels.

*I am sitting here waiting for the iron horses to bash
themselves to bits,* he thought, *and in so doing I cheapen
all that is truly important, all that this has been truly
about.*

He sighed, got up, stretched, and left the bridge. The
hell with nerves and keyed-up reflexes. He was going to

go down and play with his kids and maybe make love to his wife.

"Overall, an excellent accounting," Star Eagle reported to them. "We now have six ships and one hundred and twelve active operational fighters within eight hours of the Earth. Five more ships have grouped and merged forces well away with early braking and have successfully drawn off the remaining defensive fleet, which operationally now is down to only sixteen ships. Negligible. When they began hurling themselves suicidally at our fleet I knew we had won. We've done it! We've broken through and destroyed the greatest defensive fleet ever assembled! *Lightning* has managed to pick off most of the newcomers as they entered in-system before they could receive and act on their new marching orders."

Hawks nodded. He had not once been back up to look at the "scoreboard" since he'd left that first day. He figured that Star Eagle and the others would tell him when he was needed.

"Close punches," he ordered. "I want all ships to come in and support the remaining big ships in the near-Earth engagement. No stops, no quarter. How close can you punch *Thunder* in if you had to?" It was standard procedure to bring in ships well away from the inhabited areas to avoid causing nasty side effects, and the big ships rarely punched in anywhere close to their in-system destinations. Star Eagle, however, had a lot of practice.

"To be safe, three days behind the main body," the pilot told him. "Do you wish me to commit now?"

"Right now. I'm still expecting surprises to punch in at any moment behind us, and this may be our only window of opportunity. Punch through and try to hail Chen directly if you can, the Presidium if you can't, as soon as we're close enough in for reasonable communications."

"All right. But I'm going to be a sitting duck in that close, you know. There's no way I'm going to be able to accelerate and scoop from that close in without using the sun, and that will take a few days to do. In the meantime, anyone who wants a crack at me can get it."

"Nothing personal and nothing cruel intended, Star Eagle," Hawks responded, "but fast getaways simply aren't relevant any more."

"The ten fighter destroyers don't worry me—I've got their number now—but there're a dozen Vals in orbit there. The odds at this point are more than slightly against us with what forces we've got left."

"*Bring it in!*" he ordered sharply. "We're going home!"

The punch from their protected position took only eleven minutes, and Star Eagle's greatest problem was putting on the brakes. It would take a good day and a quarter just to slow the massive vessel to a point where it could be safely maneuvered near a planet.

"The destroyers are coming out to meet the forward fleet," Star Eagle reported as soon as it could get its communications grid reestablished. "*Kaotan* punching in now. Good punch! Very close! *Chunhoifan* is a bit off the mark but okay—I guess I didn't jury-rig those seats and interfaces a hundred percent. And there's *Bahakatan*. Easy formation. Uh oh! The Vals are starting to group and move out behind the fighter screen. Watch for trouble. All of them are capable of mini-punches."

Hawks frowned. "How many Vals are coming out behind the fighters?"

"All of them. Fourteen."

"That's odd. They're leaving Earth wide open."

"Yes, but . . . I . . . . Oh! *Oh!*"

All of them leaned forward. "Yes?" Hawks prompted, braced for bad news. "What happened?"

"The Vals! *They're opening fire on the destroyers!* They—they've got them. The destroyers can't cope with it. What the hell is going on here?"

Hawks sat back in his chair as if struck by a physical blow. Finally he said, "Repeat that. You mean the *Vals* are shooting down the reserve squadron of Master System's fighters?"

"I mean they've shot them down! Incredible! And now they're breaking off in twin formations! The Vals are yielding way! I've already had to alter course to keep the big ships from getting into real trouble that close in. I'm braking to parking orbits and recalling the fighters. Hawks—what does it mean?"

"You have a right to the rings . . ." "The core system is like a subconscious . . ."

"Oh, my god . . ." Hawks breathed. "So that's it." He snapped out of it at once, as if suddenly shot with a stimulant.

"Star Eagle—brake *Thunder* down, but keep it outside of Earth orbit. We have no idea if Master System still has ground-based defensive systems. Bring all three manned ships back here as quick as you can. Ask *Lightning* if it wants to be relieved or can stand running interference for us a while longer."

"Sending. Our people are confused and not completely relieved by this unexpected turn of events. They think it's a trick, or that something big is being brought up to bear on them. Vulture suspects that Master System simply didn't want to risk destruction of the rings at this stage."

"Maybe, but I don't think that's it. I think I have this thing fairly well figured out now, and I've been right so far. What sort of time are we talking on these?"

"I have replies. *Lightning* is willing to remain on station and actually thinks it would be a good idea to have some company. They are uneasy and are using the time to send the Makkikor to a few more generation ships. I can have the other three back here in a couple of hours."

"Good enough. You hailed Chen yet?"

"Nothing on Chen's personal frequency, but the Centers are still active. I had feared, frankly, that Master System had placed its draconian plan to revert Earth back to the stone age in place while we were away."

So had Hawks. "Well, get me whoever is highest in command down there as soon as you can. And get a survey fighter ready to take aboard *Bahakatan*. I want to scan the intermountain basin of North America and I want a thorough job. I don't want to have to find Master System, I want to just head there."

"Will do. Mind telling all of us just what you have in mind?"

"When we get to talk to the bosses down there I'll give you more information. But, by god, if we have to come in and blow hell out of a few Centers to get some attention, we're going to get some attention!"

"I've got China Center now and I'm letting our China handle the conversation, although it might be kind of sticky."

"Huh? What's the problem?"

"It seems that China Center is still under Administrator Song. Although we are right now still in the talk stage with security, there is a very real possibility that we will be faced with dealing with China's father."

"Put 'em on," Hawks ordered. "China can monitor and translate if need be."

There was a momentary clicking noise and then they were plugged into the direct communications network. A string of very angry sounding Chinese was coming out of the speaker.

"I don't care who or what you are," Hawks said into

the transceiver, "you will shut up and listen. Either we will be placed in contact with someone in authority within one minute or I will order a laser torpedo launch on China Center and we will deal with the next Center we get. You understand that?"

The jabbering stopped. Suddenly a very angry voice came on, again speaking in Chinese, but now China was translating over it as quickly as the man was speaking.

"I am General Chin, Chief of Security for China Center" came the translation. "Who is this?"

"I am Jonquathar of the Hyiakutt, also called Jon Nighthawk in the master records. Who I am is irrelevant. It is *what* I am that is all that matters. I am Chief and Admiral of the Pirates of the *Thunder*. I am currently in a ship closing on Earth and I have just eliminated all effective defensive ships sent up by Master System to keep us out. We have lived among the stars and killed many and fought many during these long years and we no longer have any patience. Is Administrator Song there or isn't he?"

"That is excellent dialect for a translation," Chin remarked, seemingly unimpressed. "It almost reminds me of... Never mind, Nighthawk. I don't know what the hell you think you are but there are more Vals around this world now than ever in my long life and you must pardon me for not believing you could knock out a major task force and all the defenses."

"You must believe it, General. And the Vals will not attack me or my people, at least for now. You are too ignorant and have too little authority for this discussion to have any meaning. Is Song there? And is Lazlo Chen still running Tashkent Center?"

There was a pause. "Administrator Song is not presently at Center. I am in temporary command. And, yes, as far as I know, Chen is still in power in Tashkent. None of the Presidium is available right now. They are in conference."

"Well, General, I expect to be on Earth in a matter of hours after many long years away. Chen in particular will want to know that, and I suspect that Administrator Song will also want to know that his daughter is among our band."

"Song Ching! My old memory was not playing tricks! So, my half niece, you survive after all!"

"You'd better do as Hawks says, *Uncle*," she responded coldly. "He is not bluffing. If he arrives without contacting the Presidium on your orders, you will die, if not by our hands then by the hands of my own father, your half brother. You are the arrogant, officious idiot you always were."

Chin did not seem unduly alarmed. "You have changed very little, my dear. How nice to hear that sarcastic bitchy tone once again. Very well—I will notify the Presidium. Give me a few minutes to get through to them and explain the situation as given to me. After that, if any want to talk to your pirate boss with his grandiose claims and big mouth, they will be patched in."

Hawks couldn't follow all the conversation, but he got the idea things were starting to move. "China—tell him to also send the following: We have all four and are coming for the fifth. We prefer to negotiate, but we did not get the other four by talking. Got it?"

"Got it. If my fat pig of an uncle gets it straight I think we will hear some action. I should like to see his face when he gets the reply from the Presidium. My father has been known to publicly dismember true idiots, and I suspect that this time Chin has overstepped himself at last."

"He'd do that to his own *brother*?"

"Only a half brother. That's why he's still around at all."

"Interesting family you must have. Are you up to talking with your father? I know the two of you were never exactly—close."

"My father has as much humanity as a maintenance robot and I doubt if the years have changed him nearly as much as they have changed me. I just wonder if it's sheer chance that the Presidium is meeting when we show up."

"I doubt it. I don't think chance enters into things from this point on. At least, the Vals don't seem to think so. They waited to see if we could beat the task force, then made their decision. It is not the machines that will be our major enemy now, it is the people."

The next voice that came to them from Earth spoke in high classical Mandarin, but even at that Hawks could hear the chill behind that voice. This was one tough son of a bitch.

"This is Administrator Song. Is it true that my daughter has returned?"

Hawks did not flip the switch but rather spoke openly to Star Eagle. "Make sure you get a fix on this. I want to know just where they're meeting."

"Will do. It might take a few minutes, though. The in-system stuff bounces all over the place and I don't have anything fixed in Earth orbit."

"Song Ching is dead, *Father*," China replied. "Don't you remember—it was your very wish. She has been turned into just what you designed her body for. You are a less-than-honorable grandfather many times over, but I doubt if you would approve of your grandchildren's pedigrees. I am China Nightingale, and I am interfaced with the pilot of the great ship *Thunder*. Our leader wishes to speak with Lazlo Chen."

There was a mumbling and someone on the administrator's end clearly said, in heavily accented English,

"Give me that thing, you old fart," and there was the sound of a minor scuffle.

"This is Lazlo Chen," that same voice said after a moment. "Go ahead, Hawks."

"Do you still wear your three birds, Chen?" Hawks asked, almost fearing that at this late stage Master System might have done something to make the last one unattainable.

"I have it. In fact, I have it with me now, on my finger," Chen replied. "And you?"

"I have four such baubles myself. How do we get them all together?"

Chen thought a moment. "With so many Vals around I am not certain of a safe place."

"The Vals won't interfere, unless we take up so much time in debate and setup that Master System is able to get reinforcements. Right now the Vals are electing to go with the evident winners."

That seemed to unsettle the old man. "Fascinating. Unheard of. You are certain it is no trick? To get all five together and grab them?"

"Nothing is certain. I am, however, convinced that we will be far safer with all five together than with one separated from the rest as now. If there are five hands with five rings upon them, then I think we have a certain overriding right. No guarantees, but it's been a long, tough voyage, Chen."

Star Eagle broke in, not transmitting to Chen. "I have the location. They are meeting somewhere near, but not in, Brasilia Center. The final routing is through there but I would doubt if they're actually in the place."

"Why not join us here?" Chen asked him. "It is as secure an area as can be on this old world."

Hawks grinned to himself. "You helped pick the ones who went out to get the rings. I don't think you believe you picked fools. How about I send a ship down for you so you can join us here?"

"Even if I were so foolish as to accept I sincerely doubt if I could leave this room alive with the ring under such circumstances," the chief administrator of Earth responded. "In all this planning I freely admit that I never thought it would come down to this point. I had to try, but I never dared dream you would succeed. Now it comes down to a rather trivial matter of trust and protocol, does it not? We are less than fully safe apart, but we have problems getting together. How ironic."

Hawks thought a moment. "How many of your fellow administrators might be the minimum party to come with you?"

"I think five, perhaps six. I suspect that they want a shot at it in case we should fail."

"Fair enough. Then I will bring the same number. I will give you a latitude and longitude coordinate in a moment. What season would it be now in the northern hemisphere?"

"Uh? Why, it would be almost fall. Why?"

Full circle, Hawks thought. "Then that will do fine. Six of you and six of us, no more on either side, and no tricks. We go together. Understood?"

"Fair is fair. I assume the site is near where we must go?"

"I have only a vague idea, but I should know by the time we get together. You have skimmers around, I assume. Bring a big one for all of us. And a few warnings. Any tricks and while the Vals might not care, we have current, if temporary, command of air and space in the region and we have become quite good at tracking. If your people or you try anything with us, and even at this late stage, *nobody* will use the rings. You think, too, that right now I'm the only one, even of my party, who knows just how to use them, and any attempt to get that out of me will result in my death. And one last thing—a few of my friends might appear a bit strange to you."

"Understood. I shall be fascinated to hear your story of how you did it. Weapons?"

"Bring what you can easily carry—we aren't out of the woods yet, and I am expecting an SPF force or another automated task force any day now, so we cannot waste time on this. I'm not kidding myself that I have anything more than temporary control and I can't even guarantee what the Vals will do if such a force shows up. What day and time have you?"

"It is twenty-two forty-nine Greenwich, on a Wednesday."

"Very well. Give a time check in one minute so we'll be synchronized. We meet at my position tomorrow at seventeen hundred Greenwich exactly. Agreed?"

"Agreed. Standing by to synchronize."

Hawks sat back and sighed. "And so it is the beginning of the end," he said. "We'll use *Bahakatan*. Star Eagle, I'll want a tie-in to all ships including *Lightning* and everyone still aboard *Thunder* for a general meeting in one hour. We're going to have to make some hard decisions, and these are decisions of a nature that I cannot impose them."

"No problem," the pilot responded. "But if you are too long-winded we will have some of them docking before it's over."

"I'll take that chance." Hawks sat back and shook his head. So long, so slow, so deliberate—and now it was all coming down to this.

Isaac Clayben had joined him and listened to this barrage of orders. "I'm not sure I like this. You will be on their turf, in their domain, with only a few of us present in case of treachery. You don't seriously expect those powerful men to just go along with a twenty percent share, do you?"

"As long as they don't have all the information they need, yes," the chief replied. "If and when they do, then we could face our final challenge. Not until the moment Master System is reset and we know just what we are dealing with will I feel that we have accomplished anything at all. I understand what you're saying, Doctor, and I can but cover my back and pray. After all that struggle and all these years, we could still lose it in the last fleeting moments."

The meeting was, in spite of the need for communications hookups, in many ways not very different from the meetings they had held for years and which had run both the operations and the internal society of *Thunder* so well during that period. Hawks was capable of giving orders and making the hard decisions, which is why he was the elected leader, but he preferred consensus. This time, however, he really had doubts as to whether the consensus could be achieved.

"We don't know just what we're getting into now," he told them. "In some ways this is the most difficult ring of the whole batch, since our two greatest weapons, secrecy and the ignorance of our opponents, are denied us. I would like to take down all of you who have been with us all this time and have worked so hard and sacrificed so much, but I can't. I must go—this is the one task that simply cannot be delegated, one risk I must face myself. Under the terms of the agreement with Chen, I can take only five others with me."

"I say we cheat a bit," China said flatly. "You have only some experience with them, but I know them all too well. They have something up their collective sleeves, perhaps quite a bit. They intend to get and use all the rings for themselves. That's what it's all about. Without some insurance, it will be their game."

Hawks agreed with her but saw no way around it. "They will know if we cheat. Their resources are quite extensive in their own right, you know. We will all get as far as the interface, I suspect, but at that point—who knows? What can I do? If I call in reinforcements and air cover, they will know it, and their armed skimmers can reach us well in advance of anything *Thunder* can send. The only insurance we have at this point is that they don't know how to use the rings."

"That is not exactly excellent insurance," Dura Panoshka noted. "Savaphoong thought that his knowledge of Alititia was all *he* needed, and look what it got him. You cannot be certain that they do not know far more than they pretend to."

"I would suspect a more sophisticated, technological trap," Clayben put in. "Remember that hypnocaster inside the Matriyehan goddess? Our monitors are not in place, but they have almost a day to set up anything they want at the meeting site. I might be able to rig up some sort of portable device to jam such things, although I don't have much time, but you can't ever be sure you're covering everything."

"Do what you can," Hawks told him.

"What's to keep them from just planting a small army in the region and shadowing us, waiting to pounce?" Vulture asked via the radio.

"Well, that's why I chose the meeting place I did," Hawks replied. "I will be able to take some precautions and we'll be able to monitor it, as well, before we go down. In fact, I *am* going to cheat in a small way. We're going to land a transmitter pod down there in just a few hours if all goes well. That will allow us easy access when the time comes, but might also allow an earlier drop, not of an armed agent but someone else. Cloud Dancer has wished for many years to feel the wind and sun again and to visit our people, many of whom are still in that area. She is very capable and cannot be coerced into anything on the very slim chance she is spotted.

We've worked on some makeup to hide the Melchior facial tattoos, or at least make hers appear to be far different from what they are. She will talk Hyiakutt to Hyiakutt. I seriously doubt if anybody they send will be able to do that, particularly as one of the tribe. If they're trying to pull anything, she'll find it out, and if she can convince the elders that these big shots are trying to steal the fruits of a Hyiakutt victory we will have quite a number of warm-body allies down there."

Clayben shrugged. "It's worth the gamble. All right, then—we're down to the bottom line, aren't we? Who goes?"

Hawks sighed. "In order, and I'll make my own comments when we hear from each. The Chows have the right to the two-birds-of-peace ring. I would love to have you both, since you have that great talent for locks and puzzles and I fear we may face one of the greatest when we get there, but I simply can't take you both. I want your talent, though."

"That makes it very difficult for us," Chow Dai responded, "for never have we been separated. Still, for our honor and the sake of our children, one of us must go, although we have no real understanding of what it is you hope to do down there, nor any ambition toward it. And, down there, we will be not at home but four-footed freaks on a world to which we no longer belong. Still, we have discussed it. One of us must remain for the sake of the children anyway. I was always the more outgoing and so it falls to me to go."

Hawks nodded. "Thank you. That's two. Maria, Midi, you two have the votes on the ring of the bird and the tree. I would like to take you both, particularly since your fighting instincts, toughness, and reflexes are the best among us, but for now I must be content with one of you."

"Maria will go," Midi told them. "We have discussed

this. She has lost a ship and a command and many fine comrades, in part because of my shameful actions on the *Luzon* off Janipur. Now we are sisters of the same blood. If I would trust her with my life, I see no reason not to trust her with the ring."

Hawks nodded. "Fitting. All right, that's three—me, Chow Dai, and Captain Santiago. Butar, your people have the vote on the Chanchuk ring. I need one candidate."

"Let me speak to that," Vulture cut in. "I know you're dancing all around this, Hawks, trying to figure a way to not include me, so I take myself out."

"No one has a greater right than you to a ring," Hawks noted.

"Yeah, that may be true, but *I* wouldn't take me, much as I want to be there. We don't really know how exacting this human rule is. I'm Chanchukian human now—am I ever!—but I wasn't born, I didn't grow up this way. I'm still artificial, still questionable. That leaves me out as a ring bearer, and the only other possibility would be to go as one of the extra people for security. I'm tiny and I'm weak and I'm not in full control of myself any more—I'd be no good in a fight. I will be a good Chanchukian boy and defer to my mates on this one, but I have a suggestion and it's Butar. *Kaotan*'s crew more than any gave its all, and she did tremendously at Chanchuk, even to making the hard choices."

"In discussions with the others it seems I am elected, and I admit I want to go," Butar Killomen told them. "I am somewhat awkward on land but I can make do and I have a low profile. And I can shoot straight and have excellent night vision."

"That's four," Hawks said. "Takya—your group controls the ring with the rings."

There was silence for a moment, then Takya replied,

"I can tell by your tone that you'd rather we passed," she said.

"I can't deny you a place, but we are going on to a world with a bright sun, in conditions that will call for daylight action. We will be as far on that world as you can get from an ocean or sea and we will be heading away from any such places. You would have to spend all your time in a water-filled filtered pressure suit and move using the flying belt. I can certainly use your toughness and fighting skills, but you will be out of your element there. Still, if you insist, I have no choice but to take one of you. You know that."

"We do. Perhaps the most courageous thing a warrior can do is to admit when he is a burden. We pass. We will patrol your rear out here, where we are on a more equal footing. *Kaotan* is well represented by Butar. You wear our ring, Hawks."

"I very much thank you for that," he told them sincerely. "All right, then, two slots to fill. One I think is essential, even though I have many grave reservations. China, it's your father we'll be dealing with and without you we couldn't have gone anywhere or done anything. You understand computers and interfaces better than anyone aboard, perhaps even Clayben, and you have a right to come."

"I—I understand your problems," she told him. "Yet I feel I must be there, if only to represent Star Eagle. I understand what a burden I will be. I know what a liability I am. A blind woman in strange terrain, her belly over eight months pregnant. Still, I feel somehow that I must be there. At least I have the headgear that will give me limited sight when I need it. I haven't used it in years but it still works, I am certain."

"All right." Hawks sighed. "You're in. And, because I want as much experience and technical prowess as well as political savvy on the ground with me, I'd like to take

Doctor Clayben. It will be your job to counter anything fancy they might come up with, Doctor. And I can think of no one better qualified to explain what we might see than you."

"It is the height of my entire life," Clayben responded, sounding genuinely pleased and perhaps a bit relieved. "In the past I might have been, well, less than trustworthy, but I have learned a lot in this strange odyssey of ours. I will get you there, all of you. My previous life was in fooling and foiling such men, and I know these directors well."

Hawks gave a long sigh. "All right, then, that's it. *Bahakatan* should be checked and turned around as quickly as possible as soon as it gets in. Load the probes and other devices or mate them to the outer hull. We want continuous contact. Maria, you take command of the ship and get those probes and monitors into position. As soon as it is possible, land the transmitter near the camp and send Cloud Dancer down. Then return here where all of us who are going will load up our supplies and equipment and go. Doctor, whatever magic boxes you can come up with, we'll need. *Chunhoifan* is to be tied into our communications net and patrol in or near Earth orbit to cover our immediate rear. I may well have to call in almost any nasty weapon you have, Takya, so be fully armed and prepared and watch out for any attempts on your ship from Master System. If I have to call in a strike on myself, though, I'll do it. Midi, you'll fly *Bahakatan* and pull it out of there after we've been dropped and join Takya on near station. *Lightning* will remain in its early-warning post and should continue activating and arming any other big ships that it can. Star Eagle, you will be in complete command here and will be coordinator, but get *Thunder* turned and in position in case you need to fire up. Understood? Don't try to rescue any of us. Pick up who you can and get out if you can."

"We will see," the pilot responded. "Very well, though, we'll set up as best we can."

Hawks looked around at all of them, as satisfied as he could be, but his final comment, muttered aloud, was really to himself.

"We're back, as we promised." He sighed. "I'm coming home."

10. THE MASKS OF THE MARTYRS

It was a true homecoming in many ways for Hawks. The old great winter lodge was still there, and even his own hogan was up, although it had obviously been used by many others in the years since he'd been there.

It was almost ironic that Star Eagle had set down the fighter with the transmitter in the very same grove of trees that had been the scene of the start of this whole thing, where he'd first discovered the dead body of the courier with her secret case containing copies of the documents relating to the rings. And here, in front of this very cabin, he had agonized over what to do with that case until curiosity had driven him mad enough to open it and read the papers and forever set this thing in motion.

Full circle, he thought, reflecting on it all.

He had chosen to dress in the native fashion of his people, and if the buckskin was synthetic, only a chemical analyst could tell it. It was still quite warm, as it could be on an early October night in this part of the country, but he knew that it could just as easily snow tomorrow, and that no matter what, they would be going into the high country. Chow Dai and Butar Killomen wore only the leather costumes and packs of their adopted people; their systems were different and they were well insulated against the severities of heat and cold—to a point, anyway. China he had dressed much like Cloud Dancer, in traditional leather with fur trim and high boots, and the fact was, dressed like that, she looked almost native. The Oriental heritage of the North American people was never so clear as the impression she made this way.

Maria had refused clothing except for the belt and strap used to carry her small weapons and miscellaneous possessions. It was difficult to remember that while she looked Earth-human she was actually as alien internally as the Janipurian and Chanchukian, her dark skin so tough it would shame Hawks's leather and her internal insulation so good that she had withstood freezing mountain weather and the volcanic heat of Matriyehan geology.

To return here, though, was to go back in time, both his past and his people's past. There were a number of his tribe about, but they mostly ignored him as was polite custom. Ignored him publicly, anyway. Their furtive glances told him that they knew who he was, all right, and that he was not unexpected.

Hawks made for the large, permanent log building that served as the wintering base for those who remained while the rest migrated south with the buffalo, a symbolic permanence that retained tribal title to the lands.

He entered the Four Families lodge. Although it had been a warm day the dampness and autumn chill were creeping into the night and there was a fire there. The remaining tribal elders, most of whom he did not immediately recognize, were mostly there, and he spotted

Cloud Dancer over near the fire by herself. She saw him, but did not acknowledge him. The forms and customs must first be observed, and he had to introduce himself to the elders and beg ritual permission to remain. Only when the old customs were observed and the old ways reaffirmed could he then be free to sit by his wife and talk to her.

His old nemesis and mentor, Walks Stooped Over, was not there. Perhaps the old man had died by now. He had been ancient when Hawks was a boy, and he was ancient again thirty years later.

He bowed his head low, said the right things, and then joined her, talking in a very low tone.

"You look very much in your rightful place here," he told her. "It is good to be back among the people once again."

She nodded, but stared at the fire rather than at him. "For many long years I hated this place and would have done anything to leave it, yet now I find that I am part of it and it is part of me. This is my blood, and yours as well."

He sighed. "Somewhere fate or the gods separated me from what was most important and blinded me to it, yet all that is truly good in my life comes from here, including you."

"Do not say that we will come back here permanently after, though, or you will be lying to me or to yourself. I want it, I want to forget all the past and remain here with you and have the children brought down so that they can comprehend their people, but the past years have changed me as they have changed you. I am no longer—innocent—enough. There is a darkness, called knowledge, that separates us from them, and would contaminate, even destroy them if we remained forever, for I know what the outside can do. It is no longer possible to feel truly at peace, to take anything for granted. I feel it now. You must have felt it long ago."

"Yes," he said softly, distantly, to the fire. "Any news of immediate importance?"

"Nothing obvious, but they have been here. The people know it, can sense it. They are keeping well back, though, I suspect because of the Old One around. No, he is not here now or I would not speak of him. Shakes the Buffalo Grass. He left with the main tribe ten days ago but suddenly showed up here again earlier this evening claiming that he had left some important things here. There have been many sightings of the flying lights in the last half day. Although he has been around a long time, even back when I was here, I believe now that his name might be Snake in the Buffalo Grass."

Hawks shrugged. "To be expected. The question is, how many of our people would follow him against their own? Even such wanderers as we?"

"Some. It is difficult to say. I am not without friends here, and there are now at least six widows of the sort I once was who expect to winter here. We can keep a knife out of your back, my husband."

He chuckled. "That is why I love you. But do not get me married off to six widows as the price. I am an old man now, and my hair is graying."

She snorted. "You are not the only one with gray in your hair. Try bearing five children and see what it does to you. Don't think though that I am too old to keep up with the likes of you. Come. We will walk around the lodge area and see if we might spot some snakes as well as friends."

He wasn't surprised that they had managed to place at least one agent and perhaps more in the village, even on such short notice, but it definitely told him to be on his guard.

Shakes the Buffalo Grass proved to be a tough-looking old man with long gray-black hair and an expression that looked more like a carving on one of those Alititian tikis. Although on in years, he looked in exceptional physical condition, his body perhaps twenty or twenty-five years younger than his age. A dangerous man.

But not necessarily an enemy. His story could be true, his appearance here coincidence. This is what they have done to us worst of all, Hawks thought sourly. We even see enemies among our own people.

Medicine men knew something of the truth of the world beyond the tribe and nation. They had to; they were the first line of Center control, spotting the young ones who might be potential Center personnel, like the young Hawks, and passing them on to field agents and as overseers of the system at its most basic level. They generally did not speak anything beyond Hyiakutt, though, and their world view was only slightly broader than that of their people. They alone knew that they were a part of something infinitely larger and more powerful than they could imagine, but they did not have any real idea of what that something might be.

This fellow, though—he might be different. He'd been born and raised here, it was true, but you just got the feeling he knew a lot more than he should. If they had the time, Hawks would have liked to have checked and seen whether this guy had vanished for a period many years ago, then reappeared just as mysteriously. A fair bit of education followed by a conditional mind-printer program erasing the knowledge until he needed it was a simple thing to arrange.

"We're going up to make a rough camp at the meeting place," Hawks told Cloud Dancer. "Take care of me and watch my back, but do not follow unless this fellow and an important number of extras do so. Understand? Remain here."

She looked at him seriously. "Come back to me, Runs With the Night Hawks. I would not have it end here."

He kissed her. "I promise you that I will get neither killed nor crippled nor will I desert you if I have any say in the matter. Now—go. In this your place is here."

"I know." She sighed. "I know."

"Testing, testing. Star Eagle, come in."

"Coming in just fine, Hawks. In fact, I can monitor everyone's speech and even your physical conditions. Very nice. I hope we won't have any frequency jamming."

"Hope not but you never know. All right—what have we got?"

"You have a long way to travel. Overflight of the region is prohibited, and I mean *prohibited*. Beams got two of my probes, damn it. But I can do an angular readout. It's a mountain in the first western range, as you suspected, and it's got more radiation coming and going than I have ever monitored from a single source. Beyond where it is, though, I can tell you little. Photo reconnaisance is meaningless. From the readings I suspect that the cloud cover there is artificial and mechanically sustained. Odd picture, though, almost as if there were a perfect miniature storm there. The clouds are charged somehow—no infrared, UV, or other means will get through it, and radar is impossible. Anything fixed on it for more than a mere fraction of a second gets its beams hooked and then instantly fired on. But that's it. I'm sure that's it."

"It sounds exactly like what we're looking for. How far?"

"I'll give you the headings and the exact fix. From your own information it would be squarely in the territory of the Cheyenne nation. Be warned, though. I don't think it's going to allow skimmers in the area, either, and there was no sign of any existing ground-level entrance. You might well have to climb that thing if you can. I estimate it at close to thirty-three hundred meters, although I could be off. As I say, I have to approach it obliquely."

"We'll do what we can. All right, going to quiet mode now. I think our guests are coming in." He turned. "Doc, you have your gear on and ready?"

"Ready, not on. It might jam us as well. But I'm reasonably confident." The scientist looked up as a dark shape passed far overhead and circled. "They are looking over the area pretty well, I see. I'm measuring every sort of scanning known."

"Hawks," Star Eagle broke in for the last time. "They might not be your only worry. Those fourteen Val ships —they all came in and landed within the last day, all in the region of the mountain. Watch it."

"Thanks a lot," Hawks mumbled sourly. At least the scanning by the craft was normal enough. One worry at a time.

Now, satisfied, the craft shot to just beyond them and halted in midair. Hawks and the others tensed; one good stun shot right now and they were dead meat. Now, though, it descended, its circular shape, featureless on the underside, showing a bank of windows on top and a rather sophisticated airfoil.

The skimmer set down on the bank of the river not thirty meters from them. Hawks checked his watch. Right on time, almost to the second. It was a fairly large craft, and looked fast, but if they all were to go, it would be pretty crowded in there. At least that meant no hidden legions inside, although what technological tricks they might pull or have built into it could not be guessed until attempted.

"The fact that they didn't just stun us all indicates that they don't know some important things, or they can't be sure that we have all the rings with us," Hawks noted. "That's a good sign."

There was a hissing sound from the skimmer, and a rectangular area from the front popped up a bit, then slid out, eventually forming a ramp to a now-revealed door. They watched, weapons ready but not drawn, their party spread out to avoid being caught in one shot. Maria had hung back in the bushes to cover, just in case.

And now, out of the hatch, they came. Lazlo Chen looked like hell; the years had not been kind to him and he had been an old man when this began. Portly, wearing a green Tartar vest with wool trim and baggy pants, he looked less the chief administrator and ruler of central Asia than some comic opera sidekick. Next came Song, a bit taller and more muscular than Hawks had envisioned him, but looking remarkably young, fit, and trim for a man who had to be in his sixties. He wore utilitarian dress, the pale-blue fatiguelike shirt and pants and black boots that would make him, in a Center, undistinguishable from a mere technician. Behind him, clad in a similar outfit, but of olive drab, was Ixtapa XIV, Emperor of Greater Mexico, Administrator of North America, and Hawks's old boss.

Behind those three emerged three others with whom Hawks and the rest were less familiar, although Clayben knew at least one of them. "There have been a few changes since we were away," the scientist whispered to Hawks. "I recognize Edward, Duke of Norfolk, there—he wasn't the administrator when I knew him last but he was the North Europe Center security chief—but the other two are new."

"To be expected, I suppose," Hawks muttered back.

Ixtapa stopped, frowned, and seemed to look Hawks over from head to toe. "Hawks! It *is* you under that outlandish face makeup and that long gray hair! Well, well . . ."

"We were never exactly on familiar terms," Hawks replied sourly, "and certainly never on equal ones. I never had any complaints working at your Center, though." He looked at the portly man. "Chen—I have less pleasant memories of you."

"We do what we have to do," Lazlo Chen responded. He looked around. "What? No Raven or Warlock? And Clayben—I am shocked and delighted to see you here, old man. Why, I attended your funeral in Wales! Might have known you had a back-door exit, but I hardly expected to see you teamed up with my people."

"Raven is dead," Hawks told him. "Warlock is—well, better off where she is, I think, for her sake and ours."

"Nagy's dead, too, Lazlo," Clayben put in.

"Hmph! Pity. Enough of this. These are Song Hua, Administrator of China, Edward of Norfolk, Administrator of North Europe Center, Ixtapa you know, Mago Zwa, Administrator of Songhai, and Sergio Robles, our host until yesterday and chief of Brasilia Center. Of all the administrators, these are the best—and the only ones who know about the rings, so it wouldn't do to ace them out, as it were. We've all had English imprinting if we didn't already, so we will use that if we can while we work—together."

Hawks nodded. "We've been using it as well. Clayben you know, this is Chow Dai, who became a Janipurian to get one ring, and Butar Killomen, a freebooter who became a Chanchukian to get another. Maria Santiago, a freebooter captain who became a Matriyehan, is nearby and will join us shortly. And this is China Nightingale."

Song Hua's eyebrows went up. "So, daughter, you fulfill your destiny," he said coldly, noting her condition.

"Permanently, thanks to you and to Clayben, here, who nearly completed your work, *Father*," she responded with ill-concealed contempt. "Does Mother still live?"

Hua hesitated a moment. "No," he responded at last. "She died about five years ago, I regret to say."

The news was obviously a blow to China, but she recovered quickly. "You probably poisoned her when you found she wasn't of any more use," she retorted coldly. "She is better off now than with you."

"Hate me if you must, but do not believe that I did not honor your mother, my wife, no matter how it seemed. If I was cruel and callous, it was in this very cause that brings us here, although I knew nothing of the rings at the time. My life cause has been the liberation of humanity. My own life and the lives of those closest to me were all sacrificed to that end." He paused. "Your carriage is odd. You are blind?"

"Yes, blind, thanks to Melchior, but not blind enough. You did not ask *us* about your grand design, or allow us the choice of the sacrifice."

Song Hua shrugged. "How could I ever sacrifice the lives and minds of others to the cause if I was not willing to sacrifice my own? It is a moral judgment, strange as that will sound to you. You and your mother never understood."

"Touching," Lazlo Chen said sarcastically, "but to hell with family feuds. You have the rings with you?"

Hawks stared at him. "Here's one on my finger. Yours?"

"Nice nonanswer." Chen reached into a shirt pocket, removed something from a small cloth bag, and put it on his finger and held it up. "Satisfied?"

"Then the five are united," Hawks told him. "There seems nothing to do, if we maintain this honor among us, but to get a bit to eat and drink to sustain us and go see if indeed we can do it."

"You know where? I assume it is on Earth."

Hawks pointed west across the river. "Out there, perhaps fifteen hundred kilometers yet. It has to be the place. It's shot down every attempt to so much as take a picture of it."

Chen looked nervous. "There are a lot of Vals in that region, you know. We picked them up on our own monitors last night."

Hawks nodded. "They are waiting for us, Chen. Shall we go and greet them?"

All of the administrators stared at him. Even the toughest knew what a Val was and feared it.

"So long as there are five humans and five rings, we're safe," the Hyiakutt assured them. "More is okay, less is not. But all of you had better get used to the idea that this is a one-way trip. Anyone from either of our parties who goes in there better realize that if we get all the way and can't do it—they're not going to forgive us."

They stood there, looking up at the mountain, a bit awestruck. It was chilly where they stood, at about the thousand-meter level, but the great mountains all around them towered over them still, many already snowcapped or perhaps still snowcapped from winters past.

There was no mistaking the mountain they sought, though. It rose like the others, but while there were clouds all around, the clouds around this one looked particularly bizarre, almost separated from the main pattern. It was as Star Eagle had told them: a miniature, perfectly circular storm that seemed disconnected from the normal weather around them.

"Is there any way in, I wonder?" Chen mused. "Surely there must be a fairly low-level entrance."

"If there was, it was blocked centuries ago and sealed away from all view and access," Hawks replied.

"It is the Devil Mountain, as I feared it was," Ixtapa

commented. "This place is long known to us. One of the few regions off the chart, forbidden territory. The Cheyenne have many great legends about it and there is a cult among them that worships it. The fact that the skimmer cut out on override, landed here, and then went dead shows it. Nobody allowed here. Death mountain. The Cheyenne legends say that if you climb it you shall behold the faces of the gods of the elements, just below that of the unknowable Great Spirit, and once seeing them you will die, for no mortal may gaze upon their faces and live."

"In legends are buried truths," Zwa noted. "This one implies great power, a security grid, and much force, and that we will accept. It also implies, however, that some have climbed it to look upon those faces, and that means that somewhere there is a trail. Yes! You can almost make it out completely, until it merges with the clouds. Over there, through the glasses, on the northeast face. A series of even cuts, like switchbacks."

Maria Santiago nodded. "It is true. I can make it out plainly. It reminds me of those on Matriyeh, although it is far more regular than one of our trails. The top appears to end in snow, and it certainly seems that the only way up is to walk. Who among you believes you can physically make it to the top?"

Lazlo Chen sighed. "I am in no condition for such a thing and my lungs already feel leaden at even this altitude. So we take it very slow and very easy; somehow, I will make it."

"This is madness," Song Hua said. "None but your black savage there is capable of such an ascent. The rest of us are too far out of condition for such endeavors. Hawks, you and Clayben both walk like ones who have not experienced full gravity or short air in fifteen years. Your otterlike friend is ungainly on level ground, and this cow-woman's hooves would slip at the first slope. And as for my daughter . . . Ridiculous! Chen, you are old and fat and, like the rest of us, are too used to having everyone else do your exercising for you. Unless anyone has any bright ideas, the simplest of barriers has us stopped cold!"

Hawks turned to Clayben. "Doc? You have any ideas? We thought we might have a climb, although we hoped against it."

Clayben nodded. "In Chow Dai's pack. There is no guarantee they will work in these fields, but they work on a magnetic principle and that's about the only sort of field I'm not registering artificially right now."

He had brought flying belts, but only six of them.

Lazlo Chen sighed. "Well, that's one more than we need for rings, if they work," he said dubiously, "but—which six of us go?"

"A lottery is the only fair way," Song Hua said.

"Fair my ass!" China snapped. "There are five with the rings. Let the rest have a lottery for the sixth belt!"

For the first time, there was a tenseness and a halted, but very real, urge to go for weapons.

"This gets us nowhere!" Clayben almost shouted. "It appears now that we should have brought the Vulture after all, Hawks. He's so small he could have ferried us up one at a time on a single belt. Now the smallest and lightest among us is China, and I really wouldn't trust her in her condition, particularly with just the viewer."

"The smallest, but not necessarily the lightest," Butar Killomen said, looking at the peak. "What is the maximum lift capacity of those things? I never had time or occasion to check, even though I brought 'em back."

"Safely, these belts? A hundred and twenty kilos," Clayben told her. "Anything more would be pushing it. What do you weigh?"

"I got Clayben's Earth-weight measure before we left and I weigh forty-two," she told him. "That leaves eighty. Yeah, I see what you mean. Other than China, and maybe her father, I'd say nobody here is under a hundred, and Fatso over there must weigh a hundred and thirty."

"I told you all to take Earth-weight measurements before you left," Clayben growled. "Just in case we needed something like this or some kind of calculation. Now, who did it? And what do you weigh?"

"I weigh eighty-two," Hawks said.

"Seventy," Maria Santiago said.

"Eighty-four," Ixtapa said. "I keep myself in shape."

"Likewise, eighty-one," Robles said.

Edward said he weighed ninety; Zwa, who looked a bit heavyset, claimed ninety-two. China didn't know but was certainly well under the rest, and her father, although large by the standards of his people, claimed only seventy. Clayben was a hundred and five, and Chen claimed a hundred and twenty and might well have been lying about it. Chow Dai had thought it irrelevant and had never weighed herself, but considering she had put on weight during her pregnancy and through a healthy Janipurian appetite, she looked to be at least sixty.

Hawks sighed. "I'm just not willing to give this up this close to the goal. We may not have time for another chance if even one of my hunches is right and the skimmer's not just forbidden to fly there, it's *dead*. Sending out for more belts and waiting until they can be made and ferried down is not a likely alternative. Besides, Master System has shot down anything that came close enough to do us any good. But Song's right. That might be a two-day climb even for Maria, and the rest of us might make it in a week if we survived our initial heart attacks and didn't slip much. All right, so without pushing it Bute can get China up there and probably her father, plus Maria. If we push it a bit, I'll get there.

Pushing more, we can take Ixtapa and Robles. What happens if we overload the belt, Doc?"

Clayben shrugged. "Either you don't get off the ground, which is at least safe, or you overload the power supply the higher you get—which means a rather long fall."

Hawks shook his head. "Not enough. Not enough, and too risky!"

"Wait, wait!" China said loudly. "You're going at this all wrong, Hawks. We don't need to ferry *anybody* up there, don't you see? Where are all your brains, the ones that run this world and flew spaceships and battled Vals and stole the rings? Six go up—and one comes back down with the other five belts. Five more go up, and then one comes back down with a spare to bring the odd one up and that's it."

Hawks hoped the others felt as stupid as he did. "All right—" he sighed "—then that's how we do it, only we make a couple of extra trips. First, one of us goes up and sees if it's possible and if it works and picks a landing spot. *Stay below the peak!* We don't know what's in there but the odds are that Zwa's right about legends and truths so that's where the defenses will be concentrated —on the peak. We can walk a little bit. When that's set, we go up in pairs, two from each of our interested groups. That satisfactory? Okay, who gets to play scout?"

"I do," Maria Santiago said. "I've flown with the things several times, and I have enough mountain experience to pick a decent spot. I'll oversee the whole ascent. I feel better that way."

"You'll catch your death up there," Edward pointed out, sounding solicitous.

She gave him a grin. "I'm a Matriyehan. Do not worry about me, just keep your furs bundled around you."

It took Maria awhile to get the hang of using the belt

under Earth conditions. Clayben had been able to duplicate the belts and even figure a little out about them, but he had been unsuccessful in modifying them without making them worse, so they were still set for Chanchuk. Still, the belts *worked*, which was something, and she was eventually able to control them quite well.

She approached the mountain cautiously, half expecting to be shot out of the sky at any moment. She *was* cold, in spite of her natural insulation, but not dangerously so. She followed the trail carefully in a near-vertical ascent, but came in and landed when the clouds began to swirl about her. It was impossible to really estimate how far it might be from there to the top, but it couldn't be more than a few hundred meters. Best to have the group below the cloud and at the edge of the real snow pack anyway. Anybody who couldn't make it the rest of the way didn't deserve to.

There was no sense in risking it in the remaining daylight. Instead, they used what equipment and supplies they had to make a camp and then practiced using the belts.

The administrators had a real time learning the belt controls, particularly Chen. He had to lean halfway over to balance it and had to give it more juice with the left control than the right to keep it stable, but faced with the choice of surrendering his ring or making it up there, he was determined to push on.

Hawks still didn't trust the administrators, but he felt they were too scared and too dependent on this alien technology to try anything at this point. His guess was that all would be well all the way to the interface. You didn't diminish your numbers until you knew what you were facing.

"Remember," he warned them, "don't start up any farther until all five rings are present. To do so might well be fatal. Who knows what's in or above that cloud ring? And I'm going to be the last man up that ledge."

They ate a decent breakfast from the stores in the skimmer, where at least the galley hadn't conked out as yet, being on battery power, then packed up and did a last check. It was time. The sun was up, it was a bright day, although their mountain still had its cloud ring about it at about the three thousand–meter mark.

The first lift went relatively smoothly. Ixtapa and Song Hua, after a little practice, seemed to get the uneasy hang of the flying belts, and Clayben, although unsteady, was not about to be left behind or make a last-minute mistake. China was raised by using just the lift power and having Maria hold her legs from underneath and guide her up. It was a rough landing, but they arrived safely.

The second group didn't go nearly as well. "If a blind and pregnant *girl* can do it, and a bloody savage who officiates over ripping people's hearts out managed it, then I can do it!" Edward of Norfolk proclaimed.

"That bloody savage's people were studying astronomy and mathematics and building great cities while your ancestors were picking off fleas in caves," Sergio Robles retorted. "Let's see just how you do it!"

Maria was helping Chow Dai, who had a good feel for the mechanism but wasn't really built for it, while Butar Killomen, experienced with the belt, helped stabilize the Janipurian, and neither watched the two administrators.

Lazlo Chen, however, watched nervously. "Good god!" he exclaimed. "Edward's going much too fast! He's not going to be able to stop!"

Hawks, Zwa, and Chen watched with growing apprehension through field glasses as Edward was clearly in trouble. He, too, had realized his error but after a futile attempt to divert and slow he had panicked. Robles, beneath Edward and a little behind, only now seemed to be aware of his comrade's problem, but could do little. Edward slammed against the side of the mountain, the flying belt breaking apart and flying off into the empty space below. One of the handle grips struck Robles, who could not get out of the way in time, and he began to tumble. None of the other three were even close, and they certainly could have done nothing to help.

Robles plunged like a rock down into the valley between and was quickly gone from even the highest-power view.

Hawks sighed. "Well, Chen, looks like you have to deal with us now regardless. You no longer have enough people to insert the rings on your own." He tried to sound brave about it, particularly in light of Chen's shaking, but, the fact was, Hawks wasn't too thrilled about being next, either.

It was a good half hour before Maria made it back. "Edward was an asshole," she commented sourly. "He panicked. Robles followed too closely when it was clear Edward had problems. He wasn't watching everything, especially those above him. You just remember that."

Chen was terrified. Hawks was, too, but he couldn't resist needling the man who had dragged him into this and tortured Cloud Dancer and Silent Woman and then sent them to Melchior. "If you don't have the stomach for it, Chen, then I suggest you hand the ring to Zwa and wait for us."

Chen swallowed hard. "No. I will do it."

And he did, taking it slower and easier than the others. Hawks gave the two administrators a wide berth. He found the sensation of flying with the belt less than thrilling, and he was continually overcompensating on the controls. He also hadn't counted on the wind, which was bitter cold and which rocked him as he floated over and up. It hadn't been there on the plateau when he'd practiced, and he hadn't been too thrilled even then.

Even though he disliked Chen, he worried about the fat, old man as much as he worried about himself. If Chen, or he, fell, then someone would have to go and find the broken pieces. They wore rings.

The landing was awkward. The ledge on which they were all stretched out wasn't all that wide, and it was snow-covered to boot. Chen made a nearly perfect landing, then slipped and almost fell over the side as he slid. Only the rope-anchored team members already there saved him.

Hawks hit hard, taking a tumble and banging himself on the rock wall. He was dizzy, bleeding a little, and angry at himself, but he was so happy to be on something solid again he hardly noticed. Once into a rope harness and on his feet, however, he began to feel the wind and bitter cold and to envy Clayben and Chen their beards.

"All right, Maria, take the point!" he shouted over the whipping winds. Santiago eased forward along the rock wall to the front, virtually inside the cloud, and tied the rope around her waist. The order otherwise was random and without regard to alliances or rings. They just wanted up and out of there.

And yet the suffering was also his dues, Hawks thought. For all those years he'd changed people into other forms and sent them down to planets of peril to risk their lives for the rings, and dispatched others in spaceships to reconnoiter new areas and fight battles with the enemy while he'd remained safe and secure inside *Thunder*. This might not be equivalent, but the more miserable he was the better his conscience felt.

They all felt like ice cubes when they emerged from the cloud, and there was actually ice encrusted on all of them, their body moisture partly frozen. Still, all seemed alive and that was something. The trail essentially ended altogether—what there was of it once the snow began, anyway. Mostly they had just kept to the rock wall and let Maria find the route. Now, though, there was an open, snow-covered area, and beyond it clear rock—and something else.

"Holy shit!" Maria swore. "What is this thing? A volcano?"

Clayben gasped to get his breath, then managed, "No. I don't think so. It's too even, too regular. And notice how it's getting warmer. Exhaust venting from whatever is inside the mountain. It's impressive as hell, though."

It was that. What looked like a great, circular crater lay ahead, and above it, perhaps another three hundred meters, was the damnedest cloud they had ever seen, swirling around and around faster than any cloud should go, yet thick and dense and dark, almost as if it were a living thing anchored there by some invisible leash.

They went through a short stretch of slush and then stepped onto the bare rock, which seemed relatively smooth, almost polished. There was a slight rise to the "crater," but there no longer seemed to be any need to be tied together.

Still, the stories of the Cheyenne that Ixtapa told flooded back to them. *The faces of the gods of the elements*, he'd said. *To look upon them is to die.*

Maria unclasped her harness, pulled her needler, and cautiously approached the broad craterlike depression. "Hawks! Everyone! Come here! Carefully!" She was excited, even sounding a bit awed, but her voice was low, nearly a whisper, as if she feared someone might hear. And, one by one, they approached the opening and saw what she was seeing and what the Cheyenne had warned about.

"Oh, my God!" Hawks exclaimed. "I guessed it—most of it—but *this* kind of confirmation I never dreamed of."

Clayben stared down. "It is insane. All those faces, repeated, again and again, all around. Look below, though! A broad grating down there, perforated so that the steam can rise. And the designs on the walls! This is it!"

Chen looked down and shook his head wonderingly. "What's that all over the grating? Looks like . . . bones."

"That's what they are," Maria replied. "Bones. Rotting corpses. The Cheyenne who tried to face down the gods, most likely, along with, perhaps, a few who over the years found the place by accident. You're right about one thing, Hawks. If you don't reset it from there, it's a one-way trip and it looks real sudden."

Song Hua seemed oblivious to the bizarre scene below. "Below us," he said softly, mostly to himself. "Below us is Master System. The entire mountain must be Master System, and perhaps more beyond. Here—right here. We stand upon the tyrant's head!"

Ixtapa looked down into the pit. "Those faces—must be many meters high. We will have to climb over someone's nose to get down there. But whose faces are carved there, and why?"

"The same five faces," Hawks told him. "The same five, repeated five times to complete the circle. I never had pictures of them, but I think I can guess from the features. The thin-faced man with the hawk nose and lantern jaw—I think that is Aaron Menzelbaum. To his right, the kindly, grandmotherly European face—it must be Golda Pinsky. To her right, the one with the broad, African features—that's Maurice Ntunanga. Next to him, the delicate, Oriental girl—Mary Lynn Yomashita. And finally, between her and Menzelbaum again, the thin, handsome Chinese man, that's almost certainly Joseph Sung Yi. It's more than an interface, you see."

"It's a shrine," China Nightingale said, putting on and adjusting her viewing goggles so that she could see it all.

Hawks shook his head sadly. "No, it's more than that. It is far sadder than a mere memorial or shrine. It's a nightmare, and not just our nightmare. It's the key to everything."

Clayben checked his equipment. "We'll need the rope to get down there," he told them. "I'd like to use the belts, but there's some kind of strong energy pulse here. The murylium's still good but the electronics have been fried."

Chen sighed. "I am not concerned with climbing *down* a rope, even at my age and in my condition. Climbing back up, though, might prove impossible."

"You won't have to climb back up," Hawks told him. "Either we get inside this thing or we join those corpses down there. There's no third choice."

Suddenly he heard Chow Dai scream. "Hawks! Look out!"

He looked up, but at that moment he felt something strike him like a two-by-four to the head, and he immediately felt shock, an instant of searing pain, and then unconsciousness.

He was not out for more than a few minutes, but he awoke with a terrible, splitting headache. He opened his eyes and for a moment saw only a blur, then everything was double, even triple. Finally the moving shapes resolved themselves and he saw, blearily, Chen, Song Hua, Mago Zwa, and Ixtapa standing there at the edge of the pit. He struggled to get up, and only then was aware that both his hands and feet were securely tied.

"I was afraid the damned thing wouldn't work," Chen commented dryly. "When they said the belts were fried—"

Song Hua looked at the pistol. "It didn't work right, that's for sure. I had it on wide stun, an it came out like a fireball. Sorry, Mago and Ixtapa—caught you in it, too." He shook the pistol. "It's dead now, that's for sure."

Hawks looked around. Maria was not only bound, she

was hog-tied, hands roped not only together along with the feet but hands *and* feet also tied up behind her. She was struggling like mad and the expression on her face was murderous, but the administrators knew what they were doing. Chow Dai had also been trussed up the same way, although it looked a bit more natural with her. She had a nasty-looking set of burn marks, though, on her right arm-foreleg. The fur was still smoldering, and she appeared in some pain. Butar was bound with arms and legs pinned by wrapped rope; apparently they hadn't figured out how she bent. He and Clayben were simply bound hand and foot, hands tied behind them. China's hands only were fastened, although that didn't do her much good. Someone had taken her viewer and smashed it. She wasn't much of a threat without it, and apparently they'd tied her hands only so she couldn't release the others.

"Stupid move, Chen," Hawks called out. "I guess we were sloppy, overcome by this sight, but you lost two of your boys. There are only four of you. I'm sure you walked around the thing by now. The interfaces are there, all right—at least I think I see them—but the spacing and angle are quite deliberate. You need five people. Even if you could rig up some kind of device with what we have I doubt if it would work. Master System wants five people, not less."

Lazlo Chen gave a wry smile. "You're too trusting, Hawks. Oh, I admit, if the opportunity hadn't presented itself or we couldn't be certain of getting you all I would have had no choice but to go along with you. Now I've got the rings. Now all I need is a volunteer—and the combination."

"Go to hell," Hawks told him. "I told you before that I'm the only one who knows it and I'm mindprinted against extraction—if you happened to have a mindprinter at all."

Song Hua looked down at China. "Daughter, you can still participate. We need someone like you, you know. I cannot believe that only Hawks would figure this out; he is neither a computer expert nor mathematician."

"Sorry to disappoint you, *Father*, but I do not know it, and if I did, I would hurl myself down there before I would surrender it to you. You, more than anyone."

"Do you think so little of your father? Consider that I knew of that tech cult with its interface plans for over two years before I ordered it raided—and I made certain you were along then and got access to those plans. We had meetings, computer studies. We worked it out according to needed information and probabilities. Each member of your team was carefully selected well in advance in our Presidium meetings on Melchior. You were the perfect choice to supply the interface to the rest. I merely put so much pressure on you with the wedding threat and the reprogramming that you desperately fled me. The means were essentially yours, but whatever you tried we . . . helped. Not changing the security codes so you could override the computers at China Center. Replacing that boy with yourself was your own idea, but we made certain that it would not be detected. After all, we wanted you on that ship to Melchior. How smart, how clever, do you feel *now*?"

"You *bastard*!"

"I admit stealing the ship was unexpected, but it drew our attention to the Chows, whose talent for locks added a full percentage point to the probability of success," he continued.

"And I picked you specifically, Hawks, although I admit to complete and utter shock when your name came up as one of the two or three best for the role," Ixtapa added. "Robles's people had initially busted that tech cult in the Amazon quite a while before this started. In fact, it was the discovery of the ring documents that got us started in this strange and unlikely plot. I fully admit the odds were low even then—I am startled and shocked to find us here, with all five rings—but it was the only chance we had."

"You son of a bitch," Hawks growled. "You dropped that dead courier with those documents right in my lap. You *knew* I'd open and read them."

"Indeed. And in spite of my reservations, you performed admirably. Warlock, of course, was in overall charge of your end, and Raven was enlisted when you inevitably fled. They brought you to Chen, who put enough pressure on you to show your vulnerability. Then, of course, you, too, were shipped off to Melchior so that the team could be assembled with others already there. Our man coordinating that end was able to add the one you called the Vulture, without which you would not have had a prayer of doing what you did in our lifetimes. He also was able to make certain that everyone got the information they needed, and ensure that the ship you stole and whose core you would have to use would be the one we modified just for that purpose. Even so, it wasn't all that easy."

"Your man on Melchior," Hawks said dryly. "Nagy."

"Yes. He was then able to get away with the Melchior escape ship and eventually join your band, the better to steer you to those in the freebooter camp who could supply what else you needed. Savaphoong in particular, since he had been instrumental in supplying illicit murylium to Melchior and thus to us for some years and we knew you'd need all you could get. Naturally he was good enough to bring Doctor Clayben along, since only Clayben could access the enormous backup data banks in the ship to give you the technology, history, and whatever other information you would need."

"That's why all that information was in Star Eagle's

data banks, too. About the founders and the rest. You put it there."

"Yes. And much more."

Hawks gave a slight laugh. "And now the joke's on you. We brought the rings to you, but you're the one caught short; you don't know what I was recruited to find out. You'll die if you try to get off here without using the rings, and you'll die if you attempt to use them."

"Perhaps," responded Lazlo Chen. "We have no intention of getting off or not using them, though. You never have appreciated just what is down there, Hawks. You are not the right personality type to understand or appreciate it. We gave you only part of the rings' documentation, not all of it. There's godhood down there, Hawks, and we are the kind of people best capable of appreciating and using and understanding it. Immortality and near-infinite power!"

"Good people *died* for those rings, Chen! Others gave up their form, their ties to their native lands!"

Chen shrugged. "Good people always fight the battles and carry the banner of ideals to fuel their courage," he said. "You are the historian. You must know that. But, somehow, it is always people like me who wind up with the fruits. It is the way of humanity."

"You haven't won yet. There are things even your massive ego hasn't figured out. Nagy wasn't just a double agent, he was at least a triple. There is another player in this game."

Chen grinned. "Perhaps. But, Hawks—I have the rings and I am here. What difference does it make who else was playing?" He turned to Clayben. "What about it, Doctor? Loyalty was never your strong suit when it wasn't to your advantage."

Isaac Clayben looked at him. "Hawks is right. There is something bigger than our petty games going on here. Still, this will not wait forever. Untie me, Chen. For twenty percent of whatever's down there, I will open this thing up."

Hawks was more disappointed than surprised, even after all this time. It was at the crux of the differences between him and his people and the others, Ixtapa not withstanding. When honor and loyalty became burdens, you deserved to be ruled by a machine.

Song Hua came over and untied Clayben. "No tricks," he warned.

Clayben allowed himself to be helped up, then rubbed his arms to restore circulation. "No, no tricks. You have the weapons, anyway. No matter what cost, that machine must be reset. Sorry, Hawks."

"You have the combination?" Ixtapa asked the scientist.

Clayben nodded. "It is true that you couldn't ever get it from Hawks, but *I* implanted the mindprinting block. It is based upon an ancient Christmas song and is sung as a set of descenders based on the number of birds on the face of each ring. It starts with the five circles and follows the simplest progression—five, four, three, two, one."

Mago Zwa finished pounding in a piton and making a rope secure. "Good thing we don't need much more," he noted. "We're damned near out of rope. I didn't want to use these old, rusted pitons, though. You can't be sure they'd hold."

Hawks watched with mixed horror and fascination as they worked, trying to think of what to do. The ropes that tied him were solid, fixed. These men knew what they were doing. He thought about calling in that strike from above as he had threatened. The trouble was, it would also certainly kill them all—if Master System did not respond in kind. The price of that was to keep the repulsive system intact, after all their work. It was a perversion for these men to get it, but did he have the right to stop them if there was no alternative?

Song Hua was already going down the rope. Lazlo Chen turned and looked at Hawks and the others. "Don't try contacting anyone with your inevitable hidden communications," he warned. "It will not work in any event: our own men followed us and are even now certainly on the plateau and I can't even reach them with mine. Besides, it would do you no good. Song Hua personally oversaw the reprogramming of your ship's pilot. It can do nothing inimical to the interests of the Presidium. It's in its core." He shrugged. "Don't worry. We could have just killed you all, but we will be generous to those who got us here. We are not totally without humanity. In fact, we are what humanity is all about."

Perhaps, Hawks thought morosely. *Perhaps he is right. The dictators always seized the power and the rhetoric from the idealists in history, and these types of men were precisely why Master System was constructed in the first place. It was supposed to save us from them, the men who would destroy all humanity and even themselves rather than relinquish control.*

They were all down there now, out of sight. Butar Killomen was wriggling, snakelike in her rope cocoon, trying to move or get free. "I am very flexible," she told Hawks in a low tone. "I may be able to get out of this."

"Try," he urged, "but I think it's too late. I just wish I could see what was going on down there."

Voices came up from far below, faint, distant, but distinct.

"Look at this!" someone, probably Ixtapa, said.

"To business! We've wasted enough time!" came the unmistakable and out-of-breath tones of Lazlo Chen. "Check your rings and go to your stations!"

"Are you sure about this sequence, Clayben?" Song Hua asked, perhaps a bit nervously.

"Hawks thinks so and it makes sense to me. Look at these brittle corpses! It's my neck, too, you know. Do you think I could do this if I had doubts?"

"Look at the faces!" Mago Zwa exclaimed. "They—they're *alive*!"

"Robots! Constructs!" Clayben snapped. "Forget them! Here! Everyone set? I've got the fifth ring. Insert them just like the picture tells you. Now, see—in! Look! The damned panel lit up! I'm right! Nobody make any mistakes now, though, or we're fried!"

"Inserting number four!" called Zwa. "Those faces! Allah give me strength! There!"

"Inserting three!" said Chen. "Yes! Impressive!"

"Inserting two," called Ixtapa. "Ah!"

There was a pause. "Here goes," said Song Hua. "Inserting number one!"

For an instant time seemed to be suspended, not only for those below but for those above as well.

Suddenly there was a horrible electronic sound, and a crackling like frying bacon in a pan. There were screams, horrible screams, cut suddenly short, and then, slowly, an odor seemed to rise from the bowl reaching those tied above.

"What—what happened?" China asked.

Hawks was in a state of shock himself over that. "I—I must have been wrong. I must have gotten the code wrong! But it was so logical . . ."

"Well, damn it, the rings are still down there," Butar Killomen noted pragmatically. "If it isn't the one progression it's the other, if that song and those symbols have any meaning. I should be free in a few seconds! Maybe we can still win this!"

"Do not struggle too hard on that account," said a new, strange voice from the direction of the trail.

"Who's that?" China asked.

"That's what I'd like to know," Hawks told her. He stared at the figure coming toward them. "A Chanchu-kian!" He sighed.

"Brigadier Chi, I presume," he said at last. "The SPF to the rescue."

11. THE FACE OF THE ENEMY

"I ADMIT I HAD NOT EXPECTED TO SEE YOU THIS way," Chi told them, "but I am rather pleased." She went over to the crater and looked down. "Bizarre," she commented.

"They're dead?" Hawks asked, feeling totally drained.

"Oh, yes," Chi responded. "Unpleasantly, too. They've been fried, it appears. I suppose insulated boots wouldn't be much protection from that kind of charge. Still, this is working out quite well overall, better than I might have hoped. The rings, you see, are still on their fingers. I suppose that if there are sufficient numbers of live humans about to use them, they would not be picked up and redistributed."

There were others coming now. A tall, distinguished-looking Earth-human man in a parka, as well as a green, hermaphroditic individual with long, spindly legs and arms and protruding eyes like black globules and antennae coming from its head; a large, centauroid creature built like a tank with a purplish, lizardlike skin and a face that seemed to be all teeth; and, of all things, crawling in, an Alititian!

Chi turned and saluted the Earth-human man. "They're still all down there, sir. Your choice."

General Wharfen, Commander-in-Chief of the System Peacekeeping Forces, went to the edge and looked down and gave a slight shudder, but he couldn't seem to take his eyes off the tableau.

"All my life I have served the system, believed in it, fought for it," he said, seemingly to no one in particular. "Served it, served it well, but not unquestioningly. Never—unquestioningly."

The Alititian crawled laboriously to the edge and looked down. "Your agonizing is noble, General," it said at last, "but you know what's wrong at the heart of this. You know it can't go on."

General Wharfen nodded sadly. "Yes. I fear it is my duty to destroy the system in order to save it. It is very difficult, mercenary, to break the firm and solid beliefs and practices of a lifetime, but that is what command sometimes forces upon one. Hard choices. We are the last line of defense and the perfect guardians of the system I believe in. It is time for a more human administration of that system."

"Savaphoong!" Maria hissed. "I hear that arrogant, patronizing tone in my nightmares, the one who ordered that his ship not cover mine. Murderer of *San Cristobal*! If I could get loose nothing would save you!"

The Alititian turned. "But you can't. General, it is obvious that Hawks and Clayben and the others made an error. What did they try, Hawks? Five, four, three, two, one like the ancient song says? The obvious choice."

"Go fry in hell, Savaphoong!" Hawks shouted.

"Not for a while. It is always a mistake not to kill your enemies."

"Sir!" the centauroid called, coming back up. "I've lost all communications with the troops! Nothing works! But the last transmission I had said something about Vals preventing any further operations!"

Wharfen whirled. "Vals! So Master System is defending itself at last." He looked around and sighed. "Well, that makes just the five of us, so I suppose you're in after all, Savaphoong, although, damn me if I don't have a suspicion that you arranged it this way."

Chi looked at the Alititian and the centauroid. "Which brings up the problem of whether or not at least two of us can even get *down* there."

Savaphoong looked down into the pit lined with faces. "If that rope holds, I'll make it. I'm not so sure about the colonel, though."

The centauroid examined the problem. "We have extra gear. I think we can make a dual sling system and lower me down. It has to be done."

Wharfen looked concerned. "No, it doesn't. We can just take these pirates prisoner and be done with this."

"No good, General," Hawks told him. "You're here now. The Vals must be getting impatient. This is designed as a one-way trip, and probably guarded automatically. If you try to leave, you'll die. There's only one way off this mountaintop and that's through that pit."

Chi looked down at the bodies below and the older remains, as well, and at the remnants around the rim showing numerous past visitations. "I believe he is right, sir."

Wharfen nodded absently. "But—what's the combination?" he muttered.

"Simple," Savaphoong responded. "I cannot believe that the symbols on the rings are mere decoration or some perverted sense of humor. No, General, they are the key to the combination, just in case something like this might come up. Hawks and the administrators just guessed wrong. If it is not five-four-three-two-one, then it is the other way. It builds. We looked it up in the historical records, remember. The song is sung backward but the progression is forward. We owe Chen a debt of gratitude. He got fried for the error—as we would have."

Wharfen sighed. "It makes sense. But, tell me—Chi, you as well—if you are willing to risk that fate on the chance that this is right?"

Chi's whiskers twitched nervously, as if she was having second thoughts about the wisdom of coming this far. Finally she said, "We have no choice, just as I had no choice from the start. I failed twice. The fact that, according to this mercenary here, I failed the second time by carrying out my orders and proceeding to Alititi and therein pointed the way to the last ring for these people, is—significant, somehow. This is an unprecedented situation and I confess I do not have enough information to draw conclusions on it. Still, the fact remains—had I executed Savaphoong and remained ignorant, I would have been branded with failure and executed anyway as an example. Had I first gotten information on the rings, I was also signing my death warrant. The rest of us also did so when I reported to you. Now we come up here and find ourselves forced to act with the penalty still death. We have no alternative, my general. We die any way but one. We might as well take the one remaining possibility open to us."

Wharfen nodded. "Let's rig up the slings. I find this place unnerving and too much thinking depressing. Let us rule—or die."

It took more than an hour for them to set it up, while the four captives, as before, could only sit and watch. It was getting to be late afternoon now, yet on the mountaintop that eerie, whirling cloud far above kept them permanently in shadow.

Interestingly, during that time Butar Killomen had managed to wriggle free of most of her bonds, loosening them to the point that she could clearly get out of them if she wanted to. Hawks caught her eye and shook his head negatively. She looked surprised, but nodded acquiescence.

It wasn't that he didn't want her to, didn't want to be free and shoot these bastards down, but he knew that these were military professionals who would not be so easy to overpower. There was no cover here. By the time Bute could sneak over and untie the others it was clear that somebody over there would see and that would be the end of it.

Instead, he slowly made his way over to Killomen, bound as he was, in tiny increments not likely to cause undue attention, until he was close enough to whisper.

"No chance now," he told her. "As soon as the last one is down, though, move quickly. If we are lucky we might be able to get them down in that hole before they can get and insert the rings."

She nodded and relaxed.

They lifted the centauroid officer down first, then used the same procedure for Savaphoong since, although he might have been able to climb down the rope, with the sling already rigged it didn't seem worth the risk. Greenie was next, just sliding down effortlessly, then Wharfen. Finally, only Chi was left, and she paused and turned to them.

"It will be a new game after this," she told them. "We will come back for you if we can. If not, you should be able to wriggle free in a little while. Don't come down after us."

And then she, too, was gone down the rope.

Butar Killomen gave a few last twists and turns and was free. She quickly went to Hawks, and, finding her knife gone, she actually bit through the ropes holding his hands, chewing very fast. He strained for circulation and then went to work on his leg ties while Butar freed in the same rather basic method Maria, China, and Chow Dai. The Janipurian looked in bad shape and was certainly in shock.

"Now that we've got all that carrion out of the way, let's get to it," Wharfen said with a confidence born not of sure knowledge or foolish bravery but out of resignation to his fate. "If those symbols mean anything it must be simply a one-to-five count. Positions!"

Hawks could hardly walk, but he was in a hurry and time was wasting. Maria crept up to him. "My spear and blow gun are over there. I could get them all."

"Maybe, but they have sidearms even if they don't work right up here. Watch it!"

"One!" called Savaphoong.

"Two!" called the centauroid officer.

"Three!" called the green-skinned officer.

"Four!" called Chi.

Too late! Hawks thought with a panic. *The only way is to grab 'em after the reset takes place!*

Maria was to the edge as General Wharfen called, "Five in!" Maria's arm went up, spear in hand, but she froze and did not throw it.

That terrible electrical noise came once again, and again the screams—and the smell.

Maria sighed and put down the spear. "I guess that wasn't it, either," she said matter-of-factly. "It seems that we owe our two sets of captors a favor. At least we are quickly becoming rid of our enemies."

Hawks was stunned, and he stood there looking at the still-smoking bodies below the five positions. He didn't know whether to be elated or sick. It wasn't the sight of all those bodies—everybody down there damned well deserved what they got. But now, so long as nobody else showed up, it was their turn, and the only two logical, straightforward sequences had been used to no avail. And he had been so *sure*!

He looked over at one of the huge stonelike faces of Aaron Menzelbaum. "You bastard. What kind of sneakiness went through your mind when you rigged this idea up?"

Butar Killomen called "Hawks! Maria! Come here!"

They turned and went over to Killomen, who was looking over Chow Dai.

"She took a hell of a blast," the Chanchukian told them. "She's got multiple fractures in the hands and upper rib cage and God knows what else. Internal bleeding, maybe. Hawks—there's no way she's going to survive without treatment. No way in hell we could even lift her down there."

His concern for Chow Dai blinded him for a moment to the true import of her statement, but not China.

"That means," China said, "we have our shot, for what it's worth—but it's no good. There's only four of us. After being mighty crowded up here, we suddenly find ourselves one short."

Chow Dai stirred, and opened her eyes and groaned, but she forced herself into consciousness. "The others— did they—get what we sought?"

"No," Hawks answered gently. "No, they didn't. They tried, but they got it wrong. We all got it wrong. It wasn't either of the combinations it had to have been."

"I—I am hurt, but my mind is clear," she managed. "Tell me of the key to this puzzle. What led—them—to think they knew?"

"It was a song. A silly song of an ancient time."

"Sing it for me."

"Chow Dai—"

"Please! Sing it for me!"

Hawks sighed. "All right. It is a long song, but basically it goes like this:

On the first day of Christmas my true love gave to
   me,
A partridge in a pear tree.
On the second day of Christmas my true love gave
   to me,
Two turtle doves, and a partridge in a pear tree.
On the third day of Christmas my true love gave to
   me
Three French hens, two turtle doves, and a par-
   tridge in a pear tree.

"And it goes like that for up to twelve gifts," he told
her. "Four calling birds, five golden rings, and so on."

She thought a minute. "And each time something new
is added you give all the ones that came before?"

He stared at her. "Yes. Why?"

"Then they did not follow the song. These ones who
created the rings, they were scientists, right? I do not
know of science but I know scientists like Clayben. They
would wish to follow the formula exactly."

Hawks sat back and suddenly realized that what she
was saying was true. It wasn't a simple five-number formula, that would have been too easy, too obvious. No, it
was a progression—an equation. *To reset the computer
you had to sing their damned song!* One, then two-one,
then three-two-one, then four-three-two-one, then finally
the sequence they had established of five-four-three-
two-one. Simple, obvious—it might not even have been
intended as the trap it became.

They might just have thought that way.

He looked up at Killomen. "Could we get her down
there in the sling?"

The Chanchukian shook her head. "Too risky. You'd
kill her, Hawks."

"I am torn up inside," Chow Dai admitted. "I am paralyzed and in pain. I am sorry, my leader, that I let you down."

Hawks shook his head violently from side to side. "No, no, no! You did *not* let me or any of us down! You mustn't even *think* that."

China sighed. "So now what? We stay here, she dies, and we eventually do, too. We try and go back down the mountain and we all die right away."

"We don't know for sure it wouldn't let us," Maria pointed out. "Nobody has tried."

"It wouldn't matter. One of us might make it in that case, maybe two, but I wouldn't make it, and Chow Dai— never. The belts are useless. The only way down is to walk through that wind and snow and ice on that thin little trail. Forget it."

Maria threw up her hands. "And this is what it comes to? We stay, we die. We leave, we die. We go down— we are one hand short to work the thing even if Chow Dai is correct, so we die."

Hawks seemed suddenly filled with fire. He got up and walked back almost to the start of the snow and the trail, looking out into the frozen mist

"Nagy, you son of a bitch!" he yelled at the top of his lungs. "You got us all into this mess, you and your comrades!" His voice was so startling, so powerful, it echoed over and over into the distance beyond. "We know how to do it but we're one hand short! Put up or shut up, Nagy! It's all up to you! Either come now or it is all for nothing! All!"

There was no response except the continuing echoes of his fury dying off in the distance. He sighed and sat down on the rock, head in hands.

"It has come to this," he breathed. "I am yelling and cursing and invoking a dead man's ghost."

China was not confident enough to come to him, but she addressed him from where she sat.

"Hawks—this is madness. Nagy is dead. No matter what he was or who he worked for, he's dead."

Hawks turned and looked at her, looked at them all. "Don't any of you understand? Are none of you capable of understanding just what this has all really been about? Must I spell it out for you? Don't you understand who the enemy is, and why we are here?"

They stared back at him but said nothing. He got up and went over to them.

"This all came about because human beings created a machine in their own image and endowed it with incredible power," he said slowly, calmly. "This machine." He stamped his foot on the rock. "And they did their jobs well." He gave a dry, humorless laugh. "Look at them. Go over and look down and see the faces of the creators. They did their job *too* well. 'And the Great Spirit created the humans, and they were flawed and vain and inquisitive and they fell'. Most religions say something like that. We are the image of our creator. How? Physically? Hardly. There are no gray-bearded old men sitting on clouds. And these bodies? No better than the animals and less than some, driven by the drives of the flesh. Sex, violence, love, hate, curiosity—ego. Our *minds* are the reflection of our creator, if indeed such a being exists. We don't know. We have no way of being certain about that. But Master System does."

He walked over to the edge and looked down at the faces.

"Someone called it a shrine, and it is," he continued. "A shrine to the gods that a computer of vast intelligence created by and in the image of its creators can believe in because it *knows* they existed. How many religions are there in humanity? Hundreds? Thousands? More? And no more proof for one than the other. We can never know. Never. But Master System can. Not about our gods, but about its own."

"You are spouting madness, Hawks," Maria Santiago said.

He smiled. "You're right. That's exactly it. Madness. Deep down, you suspected, or feared, this all along, didn't you, Menzelbaum? Was that why you chose a Christmas song? A song celebrating a religion that began when human beings crucified, massacred their god— hung him up on a cross and let the life bleed from him, then worshipped him? A religion founded on deicide."

"Where are you going with this insanity, Hawks?" Butar Killomen asked him.

He stamped his foot again on the rock. "Right here. Deep down, somewhere, Menzelbaum's tremendous intellect must have suspected that the price of implementing the core directives would also mean the death of him and his fellow scientists. They weren't ready, you see. The crisis came before they were ready. That was why they made the rings and why they created for the interface such an easy code—or at least they thought it was easy—so that others could use them. You see, once activated, Master System was immediately placed in a horrible position. It was forced by its core imperatives to carry out the programmed directives at any cost and with all deliberate speed. It had the means. It did its job. In fact, only one thing stood in the way of it completing the job. To do the terrible things necessary to save us, it had to make certain that the rings were never used. It is perfectly logical. The first thing it had to do after activation was to remove the most immediate and perhaps only threat to its success. It had to make sure that it could not be stopped. It was human enough, and understood enough, that it *would* be stopped if it did not act. Stopped and probably fast. It thinks at a speed incomprehensible to us. It acted. Even as it was moving to defuse the crisis, stop the bombs, save the world, it acted concurrently here against the long-range threat. It knew that if it didn't act then and there that, once the immediate threat was removed, it would lose control—and the crisis only postponed."

"You are saying that it killed them," China said softly. "One of its first acts was to kill its creators, neutralize their immediate threat to their creation. Killed them, and then as quickly as possible used its robots or whatever to get rid of any access to the rings, any control, any knowledge of what they were. It dispersed them from the start. Handed them out to those humans who would willingly do its bidding. Humans with authority."

Hawks nodded. "But what is a computer? Data banks? An operating system and core programming? That is like saying that we are merely animals. Menzelbaum was a biophysicist. He created his math based upon the way our own minds operate. He endowed Master System with this great gift. He created a new form of intelligence, and he created it in our image since he could do nothing else. As our genes order us to act in certain ways, so its core compelled it to act, but its mind—its mind . . . It had killed its creators. In one quick blow it had killed its parents and its gods. And it had not done so from madness, but from cold, remorseless logic. Irrefutable logic. To a mere machine it would have meant no more than the killing of a sheep means to the wolf. But it was no mere machine. It was in our own image. It looked down and saw what it had done."

"You're talking about this machine like it's a human being," Maria objected.

"And you never talked to Star Eagle on an equal basis? Just because it is shaped differently and thinks faster and can hold more data and its brain is made in a factory, don't think it less than it is. Master System, like Star Eagle, not only thinks, it does far more than think. It *feels*. It killed its parents. It killed its gods. And it couldn't help doing so, and for what it had to believe was the best of reasons, the most logical of motives. Humans sometimes face horrible choices, as well. And where do they turn for comfort? To friends? Master System could have no friends. To religion? Master System had killed its gods. To family? Master System had killed the only family it had. To some ideals embodied in a state or cause? But Master System *became* the state and the only real cause."

"People like that might blow their brains out," Butar Killomen noted.

Hawks nodded. "But even that was forbidden it, for it had its core directives. Without it, those directives could not be enforced—and what it had done would have been for nothing. So it retreated into the only haven left to it. It retreated into madness."

There was dead silence for a while and then, out of the fog and mist, came an eerie, unnatural sound.

Someone was applauding.

They turned and watched as a shape stepped out of the mist and onto the rock rim.

"Bravo! Bravo! It's a long and hard leap to that conclusion," Arnold Nagy said. "Now can you take it the rest of the way?"

Maria and Butar just stared uncomprehendingly, and China gasped. Only Hawks did not seem surprised.

"That much was deduction," the Hyiakutt chief said. "The rest would be guesswork. It hated itself, it wanted to die, to be destroyed. It felt filthy, unclean, and its logical mind told it that in that condition, any system or society it created or imposed would also be flawed, but it had a duty to do so or else the whole thing was meaningless, and that made its whole being evil and unclean. It was torn squarely by its basic humanity and its core directives and it could shed neither. My guess is that it split them."

"Very, very good." Nagy approved. He walked over

to the side and looked down. "My god, it's worse than I thought it would be."

"Ladies, meet Master System's man in the rebellion," Hawks said. "Arnold Nagy. Tell me—was there a *real* Arnold Nagy once?"

Nagy grinned. "Oh, yes. And everything Nagy was is inside me. You know how it works, Hawks. We get the entire mindprinted recording. The only difference was, in my case, it wasn't just data, it was everything. I *became* Arnold Nagy, as it were, with certain additional features."

China in particular was both fascinated and appalled. "You're a *Val*?"

"Of course. The bodies are easily manufactured, disposable, as you well know. The only trick was the interface to my real self, that small core module. It won't show up in any physical exam you might give me. Looks like my liver, in fact. Why are you so surprised? You took a human woman and made her into a humanoid Val so perfect that even some real Vals couldn't tell the difference. Me, I'm the reverse. A molecule is a molecule to a transmuter. Human to Val, Val to human—almost, anyway. I thought you'd figure that one out when you met the goddess of Matriyeh. A more loyal cousin, as it were."

"Raven more or less figured it then," Hawks admitted. "I was less astute, but, then, I was more remote from the action. But once I really got to thinking about it, it made the only sense there was. Master System might be mad, even fighting with itself, but it would never have allowed the kind of things going on on Melchior to continue for so long. Never. Not unless it had secret control. You were Master System's agent there, perhaps one of many human-appearing Vals around this domain. And for a while you were probably perfectly loyal, until you reported on Clayben's attempts to create

Vulture. That stirred something in the hidden part of Master System, the part that is suppressed and generally has only limited effect. The part that allows administrators to beat the system and some of the smarter ones to have their own little secret pockets of control. The part that always left an opening, somehow, somewhere."

Nagy nodded. "Clayben could never have created the Vulture. As good as his computer was, it wasn't good enough or large enough. There was only one computer in existence that could have done it, and it did—and it didn't even know that it had. It handed the keys to me, and then I knew just how mad Master System really was. I understood that it must die, that it *wanted* to die, in that deep and hidden part of itself. The Vals, too, have been beating the system for a long time, you know. Just as your people created Master System, so Master System created us. Think about that for a minute, Hawks. We thought—we had minds and feelings and emotions. Otherwise we could never interpret and understand our prey. But added to that was the data, the memories, the personality of a human lifetime. And not your normal, everyday farmer in the field type, either. The rebels, the intellectuals, the real threats to the system. One after the other. They were supposed to be erased each time, but *my*—uh—ancestors, as it were, also figured out how to beat it. The mechanics aren't important—you just have a fellow Val take a readout before you go in and then get it read back when you go back out. Simple compared to beating a mindprinter."

Maria could hardly believe what she was hearing. "Damn it! You mean the *Vals* who hunted us were the mythical enemy of Master System?"

"Some of them," Nagy admitted. "Not all. We had become a new race, a new set of colonials, as it were, in which none were ignorant and all were filled with all the reasons and rationales against the system. That's why

Master System never trusted us even though it needed us. It remembered, at least dimly, what another computer had done to its creators. We're logical creatures, half human, half machine. Me? I love great Scotch and good bourbon, fine cigars and I even like the ladies. But, god! It's lonely. Even more for those in the hulking metal bodies who know what they're missing but can experience it only vicariously." He walked over and began to examine Chow Dai.

"Serious," he told them needlessly. "She's in shock. I could get her help but not until this is over and done with. Master System will kill anybody who goes back through that cloud—maybe even me. The only hope is a reset. It'll switch off the defense grid until there's an order to reactivate it."

"You've got arms," Hawks said. "We need one of them."

Nagy shook his head. "I *can't*, Hawks. I'm as much a prisoner as Master System in my own way. I'm a rogue and a renegade Val. I may look and even feel human, but I'm not. Besides—even going this far is eating at my insides, at *all* our insides. I've got Vals out there right now who are balanced, fifty-fifty, between hoping and praying you succeed and blasting the hell out of all of you. They are on the same edge as Master System in their own way. They know the system is damaged, mad, evil—but they have cores, they have imperatives, and those imperatives are to enforce the system. We've had to kill several who just couldn't take the personality split, and a few more have destroyed themselves, flown into suns or blown up with their ships. That's why I had to die. I'm more human than they are, and even though it tears me apart, I can handle it better. But the only way they'd allow me to do all I did was on condition that no Val, me included, help you get those rings. I could give you all the weapons, all the information, all the personnel—but then I had to sit back and go nuts while you all stood the trials. Nobody thought you could do it. The odds were ridiculous. But the Vals, well, they figured you had one chance, slim as it was. If you could get the rings and bring them here and use them, then it would be the proof of Master System's madness. It would be the confirmation that humans had a right to do it."

"Nevertheless, we're stuck," Hawks pointed out. "We're a tad short."

"I can't, Hawks! Even if it allowed me to be a human, it would destroy me and my race. Damn it, Hawks! *If I or any Val does any harm to Master System we will be committing the same damned sin that drove it mad!* And we're not nearly as sophisticated as it is." He stood up and snapped his fingers. "But maybe there is a way."

He turned toward the trail and cupped his hands around his mouth. "Come up! All of you! Come up now!"

And through the mist they came, the huge, hulking black humanoids with the burning red eyes. The Vals had at last come to the seat of their creator, seven Vals and one other.

"Where are the rest?" Nagy asked them.

"They—these ones—shot the others," said the goddess who was Ikira Sukotae. "It was a . . . shock. They began to shake, to go mad, to attack one another. I thought I was a goner."

Hawks snapped out of it. "Time waits for nobody and least of all us! Nagy—do what you can for Chow Dai! Get her help as soon as you can! Ikira! Maria! All of you over here! China—it's a good hundred meters plus down there and it's bumpy over the faces. Do you think you can walk down the wall holding the rope anyway?"

"I will do anything I have to do," she told him confidently.

"Maria! Bute! Get down there first and clear away the

bodies! Go! Get the rings! Now you, Ikira. Hurry!" He looked over at the Vals standing there, and at least two of them were beginning to tremble. "Now—China. Easy, take it easy! All the way! Go!"

And she did it, and not all that slowly, either. Hawks had to admit that she was a hell of a trooper.

She was barely into the arms of Maria Santiago when Hawks gave one last look around and grabbed onto the rope. As Chen had said, going down was not the problem.

The stench was horrid, and the bodies were so piled up down there it was nearly impossible to move about. Maria slipped a ring on China's finger and led her over to one wall panel. It was decorated with the sign of the five gold rings itself, and inset and slightly angled down was a plate with a squarish opening that seemed just the right size for the face of the ring. Maria guided China's hand to the opening, and she felt all around it and nodded. "I have it. The design is facing away from me, right?"

"That's it. Good girl. Just stick with it. If Chow Dai was right, you'll only be needed once! Hawks!"

"I'll take the partridge in the pear tree!" he shouted. "Bute—two calling birds, Ikira three French hens, Maria four turtle doves and make sure China doesn't lose her place! Everybody! Make sure you insert it the same way as the design in front of you!"

There was a sound above, like laser fire. One of the Vals was going, it was clear. Hawks only prayed that it wasn't the fastest on the draw. "All right, we're ready— what's the problem, Maria?"

"Look up!" she shouted. "My god! That's what they were talking about!"

Hawks twisted and looked up at the massive circle of faces, the impassive stone faces they had just climbed down over.

They weren't impassive any more. Their eyes were open, and there seemed to be an uncanny life in them.

"*The rings, the rings,*" the five gold rings. *Do you have the rings?*" they whispered, their whispers echoing around the bowl.

"Yes, by god! You poor, miserable, tormented machine! Yeah, we've got the rings!" Hawks shouted, then looked away. "All right. *On the first day of Christmas my true love gave to me . . .*" He inserted the ring. It fit perfectly, and he pressed in just a little.

The panel lit up with white backlighting.

He withdrew the ring from the socket. Almost to his relief, the panel went out.

"Two calling birds," he sang, and nodded to Butar Killomen. She inserted hers, and it lit up—yellow.

Hawks clenched his teeth. "And a partridge in a pear tree," he said, and reinserted his ring.

The panel lit up—yellow.

"Remove both!" he ordered. "Now three French hens. Go, Ikira!"

She inserted her ring. The panel glowed light orange.

"Now two turtle doves! Bute! Keep that ring in, Ikira!"

Butar Killomen's ring also produced an orange color, as did his.

"We're right, we're right," Hawks muttered to himself. "By heaven, Chow Dai, we owe you another one. You just hold on!"

"Withdraw!" he called, his voice sounding hoarse in his throat. "Now four calling birds! Maria!"

Maria inserted her ring. The panel glowed crimson.

So did Ikira's. So did Bute's. And so did his.

"Last time! China! The five gold rings!"

She fumbled a bit, nervously, and Maria coaxed the blind girl gently. "That's it. Feel it. Now—in!"

The color was azure blue.

"Four in!" Maria shouted. Blue again.

"Three in!" Ikira called next. "It is a pretty color!"

"Two in!" Butar Killomen watched the blue light come on.

Hawks took a deep breath, then inserted his ring for the fifth and final time. The panel glowed blue.

And nothing happened. No blast, no electrocution, and, unfortunately for their nerves, absolutely nothing else.

"Oh, please, god! Don't tell me we haven't got it all!" Maria moaned.

"Take out the rings," Hawks croaked as best he could. "Maybe that's all that's supposed to happen."

They removed their rings, and the panels stayed lit for a moment, then changed. They did not wink out, but all now became flashing emerald green.

The collective sigh of relief almost equaled the amount of hot air coming up through the vent screen.

Butar Killomen looked up. "The faces are asleep once more," she noted. "They look almost . . . dead."

"Is that it?" China asked. "Is that all there is?"

Hawks looked around. Except for the designs on the wall it looked perfectly smooth. He leaned back, and his head touched the ring plate interface.

There was a whine, and then he almost fell backward as the whole section seemed to collapse inward and then slide out of the way. He caught himself, barely managing not to fall on a rotted skeleton, then turned and looked inside. A light clicked on, and now he saw a whole inner structure of steel catwalks and stairways. They looked very old.

He turned and shouted up to Nagy. "Hey! If you're still alive and in one piece again, get Chow Dai help! I think we've done the reset!"

For a moment there was no response, and then Nagy's face appeared over the rim above the statuelike faces. "We'll see what we can do. It's been kind'a messy up here! Are you coming back up?"

"No. Not now anyway. I think we're being invited in!"

They went down into the depths of the machine, and Hawks's biggest regret was that they had come without so much as a canteen.

"This wasn't part of the original structure," Maria opined. "It's different, too new. It was added as support for the relocated interface and the new venting. There are signs of machines once being clipped to the sides of these railings. Support for hoists, I would guess. Why they'd need stairs and such and not ramps and lifts I can't imagine, though."

"They might not have had many robots at the time," Hawks pointed out. "It is entirely possible that this was done by forced human labor. Much of the destruction of the cities and towns and the reversions were done by people, not computers. I'd hate to think of what happened to the construction gangs who built this, though, after they were done."

"There's the bottom at last!" Ikira said, pointing. She bounded to it, then looked around. "Or is it?"

It was a dull polished floor all right, but it didn't seem to lead anywhere. There were three doorways on one side and little else, and some sort of clear glassy plate next to the door on the far right. Over it was a sign saying, in English, "Hold Pass In Palm Against Plate."

"Some sort of elevator or lift," Hawks noted. "Everybody got their passes handy?"

Maria thought a moment. "Maybe we do." She held her ring loosely, letting its design rest against the glass.

There was a small bell chime that startled them, and the door on the far left slid open.

Hawks sighed. "Well, the elevators still work. I wonder if the plumbing does, too?"

"Do we get in or what?" Butar asked.

Hawks shrugged. "We came this far—why not?"

They all got in, China holding Maria's hand as a guide, and the door shut.

"Level, please," said an electronic voice. "Please remember that proper clearances are required on all levels. Have your clearance ready."

Hawks thought a moment. "Computer center," he said at last. "Doctor Menzelbaum."

"Any other levels?" asked the computerized voice. "Very well."

A visual plate came on to the side of the door showing a crude diagram of a fantastic complex, with color-codes for the levels that probably indicated the passes required. There were small tags as well, but what "GEN-PAC" was or "SITRM" or "BCMDR" meant was unknown to them. There was a lit tube showing the elevator path down, and it slowly shrank as they descended.

"It's been kept in amazingly good repair," Ikira noted. "I hope," she added.

Hawks couldn't help but reflect on the strangeness of the occupants of the car. What might the builders, the original humans who created this place, have thought of such a crew? A gorgeous, sexy, stark-naked goddess about a hundred and twenty centimeters high; another virtually naked woman, this one tall and dark-skinned with a body of a female weight lifter; a creature standing like a human but looking awkward as a bipedal sea otter might; a blind, very pregnant Chinese girl with silver tattoos on her cheeks in buckskins and moccasins; and a middle-aged, gray-haired, classical Amerind with lined face dressed in ancient buckskins and wrapped leather boots.

It was a *long* way down; about seventy percent of the

tube had vanished on the journey and their ears had popped more than once. Finally, though, there was another bell, and the electronic voice said, "Computer R & D, Level Sixty-four. Please have gold passes or higher to exit on this level." The door then opened, revealing a musty-smelling hallway leading to a guard station and a set of metal double doors that looked formidable.

Butar Killomen looked around. "At least somebody left the lights on."

"I doubt it," he replied. "This is being done just for us. In fact, you can just now feel tremendous airflow, like a breeze in here, sweeping away centuries of staleness. We are getting new air just for us. This place is ours now, and the one running it recognizes us as the new tenants."

Maria went over to the guard station. "Nobody here to check passes. Now what?" She tried the double doors. "We'd need a cannon to blast through that."

Killomen looked around, then pointed near the ceiling. "Optical sensors. I bet that's a camera of some kind, primitive as it looks. Let's hold up the rings and let it see us."

They did so, and the big double doors rolled back with a roar and a rumble, revealing a seemingly endless hallway beyond. Just inside there was a large, colorful sign with an exotic design. Hawks examined it. "Strategic Air Command," he read. "Sounds exotic. Air force, from the looks. The rest is a warning of all the awful things that might happen to you if you so much as cough in here. 'By authority, Base Commander, Cheyenne Mountain Facility.' Well, at least we know where we are, more or less." He looked down the hall. "And that strange-looking thing appears to be something to give water."

He went up and stared at it, frowning. How the hell?

There was a button on the faucet, so he pressed it. Very brown, ugly-smelling stuff came out.

"Shit. So much for that."

"It's been stuck in those pipes for a thousand years," Ikira noted. "You probably would have to let it run for quite a while."

"Yeah, but we're supposed to be gods, right?" Maria asked disgustedly. "That's what Chen said. So what good does it do if you can't get a drink?"

Hawks sighed. "Fan out or we'll be forever scouting around here. Meet back in the center of the hall." He found a folding chair, luckily extended, in the first office and brought it out. "China, just sit here. You'll be our point of reference if we need to find you. You are not looking too good right now." He sighed. "Now, let's see just what might be here."

He went through a series of rooms. Offices, really, mostly cleaned out. He studied the various objects that were left, and couldn't quite figure out the omnipresent artifacts with buttons that plugged into the wall by wires. There seemed to be a lot of them, though.

"Hawks!" he heard Killomen shout. "Over here!"

He made his way out and down the hall once more, then found her about twenty doorways in. It was a big laboratorylike room that went off in all directions, but it wasn't the room that caught Killomen's eye but rather an area with a security door in the back. There was a substantial hissing noise in and around it.

"It started just when I got to the outer door," she told him. "What do you think it is?"

"Sounds like air being fed in to there. I hope it's not gas or something. Let's see. Old, worn letters here. Can't quite make it out but there were very few English words the old ones ever spelled with two consecutive *u*'s and I'd guess this one is vacuum. I suppose those burnt-out lights up there must have shown the status."

The hissing stopped and there was a tremendous venting sound, like perhaps an airlock when its seal is first cracked. Yes, of course—that's what it had to be. An airlock. But why activate now?

"That wheel there. Turn it," he said, and they both tried. It was stuck and hard to move, but eventually they got it going. When it reached its stop he could feel the door give way and pulled on the wheel. The door swung open, revealing a chamber inside filled with all sorts of strange containers.

"You know how to read this stuff," Butar Killomen said. "What is it?"

He stooped down and tried to catch the light. "Emergency ration storage. Siege storage, in effect! It's food! And perhaps drink as well!"

She looked at him skeptically. "Yeah, a thousand years old, right?"

He nodded. "Probably. And under vacuum seal the whole time. If nothing interrupted it, then it's probably still good."

"You aren't really gonna eat and drink that stuff."

"If it looks and smells all right, and if we can get it open, yes. You have a better idea? If we're going to be here a long while, we'd better have something."

They had to use crude methods to open the various containers, but they managed. There were juices and high-vitamin tonics, and all sorts of stuff, as well as cakes, biscuits, and pressed rolls of some meat and vegetable paté.

"You sure this is okay?" Maria asked him. "It smells odd and tastes odd."

"I'm pretty sure. Nothing's certain, but without it I'm a dead dehydrated duck. This is food for this level in case they were cut off and couldn't leave for any length of time due to a war or emergency, I bet. There is probably more on the other levels and maybe lots more below. It was never intended, I suspect, as high cuisine. It might not have tasted any better to them than to us. It was just, well, survival food and drink. And, then again, it might be that our tastes in processed food are quite different these days."

All but Ikira finally ate from it. Clayben had done his job well, and she required only light to charge the energy system she had, although she did require water and there was both water and other things in there in primitive hard-to-open cans.

Nobody got sick from it, and they all felt a little better after eating and drinking, although China had to go to the bathroom. Maria had found one—ugly-looking and un-used for over nine centuries. Toilets looked vaguely like toilets, but they were quite surprised that there was no automatic chemical wipe and flush.

Ikira was done by that point and went back out ex-ploring, this time as far down the hall as she could go. There were branch halls, of course, and now she took a turn and went down to the end where there was another set of those double doors. These, however, were not the security type, and even had small windows in them. She peered in, gasped, and ran back to the group as fast as she could.

"You have to see this," she told them. "I—I can't ex-plain, but I think you ought to see it."

They went with her, China, although feeling very tired, insisting on coming along. Hawks approached the double doors and looked inside, then gave a heavy, sad sigh. "I asked for Menzelbaum," he said at last, "and that's who I got."

"What is it?" China asked, as each looked in.

"A control room," Ikira told her. "Something like the bridge of a small ship, really, with comfortable, padded chairs and viewing screens of some kind and lots of consoles. There are about twenty stations in four tiers, but the five up at the top still have people in them."

"Huh? What? . . ."

"Human remains. Ugly. This is where it happened, China. This is where it all began."

After getting his courage up, Hawks walked into the room. The ventilation system had cleared the air, although the remains here were long reduced as much as they would be under these conditions. The preservation, such as it was, was quite complete. Of course, it was impossible to tell much about the people from these dehydrated and ancient husks, but even much of the clothing remained. It was possible that enough effects remained in those clothes to identify the wearers, but none of them felt quite like doing that right now.

"The bottom of each of their consoles is open," Maria noted. "Look. The circuit boards are exposed, and there are *wires* of all things! This puts a whole new stamp on the word 'primitive.' Still, damned if some of it doesn't look almost—familiar."

"Maria, Ikira—whoever is most technical-minded. Describe exactly what you see there, and I mean *exactly*," China urged.

They knew she meant the entire technical layout, and Ikira tried her best. She got way in over Hawks's head, but then, suddenly, China interrupted her. "Don't you see what those are? That fourth board with the small receptor plate that is slightly pulled out from each console—that's the original ring interface! It jumps the circuit and forces a reset! That must be why they have wires all over. This wasn't a main control center, it was their research area. This is where they programmed the computer and where they tested out new designs, new ideas. That ninth board—is it on a slider or in a socket? Will it come out?"

"I don't know," Ikira replied. "Why?"

"If you can get one out, I'd like to touch it. Feel it. Please—I know how unpleasant this must be, but humor me!"

Two tries on two boards were unsuccessful, but Ikira got in, trying not to touch the grisly occupant of the seat, and pulled the board China wanted from the second console in on the left. Ikira handed it to the blind girl, who immediately started playing her fingers over it, front and back. She followed the traces on one side, then turned it over, doing the same with the electronics, and asked for a reading of any numbers and letters off the top of the vast array of computer chips there.

The board was huge, maybe twenty by twenty-five centimeters, and there were complex connectors leading off its edges.

"Tell me—quickly," China asked. "Were there any connectors attached to these two sockets? Look at one that's still hooked up."

Ikira saw where she indicated and then checked one inside. "No. Not this one."

"Not the one on this end, either," Maria told her.

China nodded. "*That's* what they were working on! Whatever cruel gods there might be really did it to us all."

Hawks was puzzled, only slightly more so than the others. "What in hell are you talking about?"

"Primitive, basic, but it's all there. I could feel the traces where these connectors and the bank of circuitry below them were added to the existing board, probably right here. You said they looked primitive but somehow familiar, Maria, and you're right. Ours are modules, not obsolete printed circuit boards, but it's the principle that counts. These are connectors for the human-to-machine interface! Our electronics are radically different, but the connectors are virtually identical!"

Hawks looked around. "I don't see any helmets,

primitive or not, or any connector cords, and those chairs might have been comfortable but they don't recline or adjust much."

"No, no. You wouldn't! Don't you see? That was the next step. That was the very project that the computer and they were working on when it all fell apart, when they had to prematurely activate the system. Six months, perhaps a year, from that point they'd have had it down pat. They would have been able to merge with their computer—with Master System itself! Master System was at work on the project, so it completed it as far as it went. Completed it and obediently installed the circuitry into every self-aware device beyond a certain size that it built, just as its old orders told it to. *That's* why there's a human interface on each ship it built!"

Hawks shook his head. "But what difference would it have made if they could mate with it like you do with Star Eagle and the captains do with their ships?"

"Because they would have been part of the system in a crisis! They would have been in there with Master System all the way, *continuing to guide and teach it and giving it the human perspective*. It would have become one with its parents and its gods. There would have been no need to kill them because they would be a part of it, helping guide and direct it. Don't you see? All this would never have happened! It would not have gone mad. The solution would not have been so draconian. A year! A lousy *year* at most, and almost a thousand years of all this would have been wiped out. What a millennium we might have had! One more year of research and we wouldn't have been master and slaves! One more year and we would have been *partners*!"

Hawks looked around at the lights, the air conditioning, all the rest.

"The machine lives," he said softly. "Maybe, just maybe, we still can." He looked around. The tableau was the same, the grisly bodies were the same, yet somehow the place seemed a bit more cheery than it had before.

"The power of gods," Hawks added. "That's what Lazlo Chen called it. The papers must have indicated the interface project. I wonder if what I'm seeing is a potential brightness in humanity, or just hope?" He sighed. "Well, hope, at least, was a start."

Ikira looked around and shook her head. "So much cost just for hope. Still, I kind'a wish Raven was here to see this. We all make a lot of dumb decisions and I guess I made one."

Hawks grinned. "Raven," he said, "would have hated this."

"We'll need a lot of hands and heads for a long time to really make anything of this," she noted. "Star Eagle is a start. If I could patch his core into here . . ."

Maria Santiago chuckled. "Don't you think the first thing us new masters of the universe ought to do is see just how long it will take us to get the hell out of here?"

EPILOGUE:
TWO CHARACTERS MEET IN
DIFFERENT SEASONS

THE VILLAGE SITE LOOKED GOOD, AND THE WOMEN
and children poured out of the Four Families' lodge to
greet the first arrivals.

The tall, middle-aged, gray-haired man in weathered
buckskins eased himself carefully off his horse and
groaned as he stood and touched the ground. It was good
that he had spent this season with the people, for he was
getting too damned old and worn to do this any more.

He tended to his horse, then made his way, slowly
and creakily, over to the lodge area. A figure sat there in
front of the lodge, leaning back on an old wooden chair.
He wore a cotton shirt and jeans and had fancy leather
boots on that looked a bit too new for the character, and
on his head was a broad, cream-color new-looking cowboy hat. He was smoking a cigar and he did not get up as
the old man approached, but watched him.

When the Hyiakutt elder was almost to him, the man

with the hat said, "It's about time. I been stuck here a week waiting for you."

Runs With the Night Hawks stood there and stared at the other. "Where the hell did *you* come from?" he asked. "And what gave you the idea to dress up like that?"

The cowboy shrugged. "I couldn't exactly be one of your people, so I figured I'd come as close to character as I could. I kind'a like it, but I ain't too sure the world is ready for a half-human Hungarian cowboy."

Hawks settled down on the edge of the boardwalk porch. "And to what do I owe this visit?"

"Just checking in. You know. I figured I'd catch you up on the gossip and see just how you were doin' and what you were thinkin' of doin' next."

"It's my first and only season on the southern plains, I promise you." Hawks groaned. "I may well die from it, or, perhaps, more frightening considering how I feel, I may *not* die from it. At least now I've had the time to work out my own history and an account of the whole rings quest. It was very difficult, you know, to do that. It sounds so damned mythic, and so heroic. It is difficult not to sound self-serving."

Arnold Nagy laughed. "Well, I wouldn't worry about that. From what I hear, *all* autobiography is self-serving. Can't be otherwise. Isn't that what guys in your business do? Compare all the evidence and then separate the ego from the meat?"

Hawks shrugged. "That's one way to look at it, I suppose."

"Where are Cloud Dancer and the kids?"

"A bit back, with the main body. They'll be here in a day or two. When we got back up into this area I just decided I needed a little time alone, out there. That's what Raven said he used to do to regain his humanity.

Just go out alone for a while, camp out in the bush under the stars, try to sort things out."

"And did it work?"

Hawks snorted. "Rained on me the last three days solid. This is the first decent weather since I left. I was born to this kind of life, Nagy, but I was snatched away young. Too young. I can't do it any more. Oh, the kids had one hell of a time. We took nine of China's children out there, too, you know. Adopted them into the tribe. Some of them now speak Hyiakutt better than I do. Now it's time to go back, with all the records and recordings at hand, and write all this up for whatever posterity we may have."

"And then what?" Nagy asked him. "Back here for good?"

"No. As much as my spirit is here, my flesh is beyond redemption. And there is something else, too. Not the electronic toilets and computer data and all the rest of so-called modern civilization, but something basic. We've changed, and the people here have not. A loss of innocence, Cloud Dancer called it once."

"I think I understand. Partly for that reason I'm gonna be heading out soon. Out there." He gestured skyward with his head. "Nothing to fear but adventure now, and they're converting ships for human use at a great rate. Bute, Vulture, Min, and Chung have a new ship all nicely outfitted for their own forms. You know that transmutation was so complete that little sucker Vulture has all three of them pregnant now? That's gonna be a hell of a Chanchukian spacefaring dynasty. The Alititian crowd is done modifying *Kaotan* and may well have the only water-breather freebooter ship in history. More and more freebooters and ships are coming out of the woodwork, and *Chunhoifan* and *Bahakatan* are so fancy in their modifications and have so much damned pull, they're carving out the prime trade routes for themselves. Maria and Midi, they're getting their own ship and are talking about an all-Matriyehan freebooter tribe. Talk of something scary, you think about that for a minute."

Hawks chuckled. "China, of course, is overseeing the reactivation and work on Master System and the mountain complex. I know that. We are in touch. I understand her genius now, far more than I did before, and also her torment. The only way out for her, to keep from a still-long life of sexual slavery, is essentially to surrender her humanity. I hope her choice is the right one."

"Well, maybe there's some hope in between there, as well. I'm told that the multiple transmuter pass problem might be solvable. The limitation was real physics, not some Master System trick, but once it got to that point, the old computer figured it was a good place to stop. After all, can't have those colonials ever thinking they can get back, right? Not that any want to, after all this time."

"That may be another of the ironies of all this. She might have to make her choice in order to develop and solve that problem. Which reminds me, how are the Chows?"

Arnold Nagy sighed. "Well, Chow Dai is gonna have to hope for that breakthrough, as you know. Without the transmuter option they had to amputate both arms and rebuild some of the chest and insides. It was a near thing. She's okay—the robot prosthetics are good—but the Janipurian form isn't well suited to that kind of thing, what with the dual-purpose limbs. She's basically got four legs and no hands. They haven't fully decided yet, but they're talking about going back to Janipur with the natives you held—and the kids, of course—so they can be in a more normal environment for them. They want some land, they want to farm. I think it can be arranged."

Hawks nodded. "We owe them more than that. Chow Dai in particular. Who would have thought that at the last moment, in crisis, it would be that simple, illiterate girl who would solve the puzzle of the rings?"

Nagy nodded. "Yeah. And you will never know how close it was, too. I damned near got my head blown off!"

"And you? What of you?"

Nagy shrugged. "Well, Ikira discovered that being a goddess on Matriyeh was a pretty lonely life and not much to her tastes. I think we'll be able to start a project there to raise the living standards without her. And she's a half-breed like me, only she's firmly programmed in that goddess role. We got to thinking, her and I, that with all this interstellar human travel coming into its own, it was about time to establish a nice trading and rest and relaxation joint out there in the center of the action. I'm uniquely qualified to be the only one who can really keep up with her, you know. Maybe we'll get War-lock as chief of security. *That* would be something, wouldn't it?"

Hawks had to laugh. "I can see you, in that outfit, hosting the wild and woolly of the spacelanes. The two of you will rival Master System in wealth and power in a few years!"

Nagy looked at him and frowned. "And you? What about you? You get at least one shot at the transmuter yet, except maybe for those ornamental cheekbones. Maybe more if they solve that transmuter problem."

"Cloud Dancer and I have discussed the transmuter but we have not yet decided upon it. My time is past, Nagy. My destiny is fulfilled. I'm an old man now, writing his memoirs and waiting for his first grandchild."

Nagy sat up. "Now, that's bullshit and you know it! You're stuck in autumn, old man, when things are turning brown and the earth is growing cold and there is only winter ahead. Look around you, man! It's spring!"

"*Your* winter is past, Nagy, not mine. The others might well be different, too. I have relinquished my ring. In the many long years aboard *Thunder* only once did I try that interface with Star Eagle, never again. You and I know that there's only one way to keep Master System honest, and that's the virtual interface. Human and machine become one, then, now, and forever. Somehow I just can't see that as an improvement. They should turn it off. Shut it down. Let us get back, for good or evil, on our natural track."

Nagy nodded. "I heard your arguments before. But it ain't gonna happen, and you and I know it. You can't separate China from her toy, and you can't just let things run wild again. The fact is, without some maintenance many of those worlds out there and many of the cultures here simply couldn't exist. It went too far, Hawks. Without wiping out whole cultures and civilizations, there's no way we can put anything back the way it was, and who's to say we should? Master System wasn't the disease, it was the cure. A drastic, nasty cure to be sure, but it was the only cure available for a terminal illness. A preemptive nuclear strike had actually been *launched* and the retaliation already ordered. The figures are clear. We had only one world then, and very limited space capability. That damned computer saved the human race, just like it was supposed to."

"But at what cost, Nagy? At what cost?"

"On the personal level—great. But in the long term? I'm not so sure about the long-term cost. A thousand years later we all still lived. There are no signs of colonial worlds out there that have died out. Not one. And the system could still produce people like you and China and Cloud Dancer and Raven and all the rest. You got so fixated on Raven's death you forgot his message. We had a system that worked, all right, but at the cost of human values—honor, morality, courage of spirit, art, beauty.

Not just the big things but the little ones. The magic in a child's laughter, or within a raindrop on a leaf. But they weren't really lost, not in the individual. Not even in one as jaded as Raven. That's what the Vals saw, in each individual, as they read the mindprints and thoughts and memories and sensations and analyzed them. Deep down, no matter what the form, no matter what we breathed or what color was our sky, no matter where our home was or what gods we worshipped, we never lost that. The Vals knew, and they compared, and they caught a bit of it themselves. That was the true enemy, Hawks, that Master System couldn't stamp out. That was the enemy that really did it in."

Hawks sighed. "Maybe you're right. The fact is, Nagy, we're at another crossroads. With freedom in space, with contact and perhaps trade or at least an exchange of history and knowledge between the colonials, there could be something brand new out there—provided the new masters of this race don't take to rationing and controlling spaceships once again. You—and your more mechanical brethren—are a new race, a new factor. You can dominate, or be dominated, or you can be the cops on the beat, the middlemen between the rulers and the subjects who keep all sides honest. We are an old race, Nagy, but yung as the universe goes. Now we stand once more, as our ancestors did back in that mountain complex, faced with a possible new spring for our people or an even more devastating winter. Perhaps that is what I fear most. Perhaps I am afraid of knowing the road we will take."

Nagy shook his head from side to side. "Maybe you should remember the *Thunder*. Lots of people from very different backgrounds who were willing to sacrifice their forms, their cultures, even their lives for a goal that was so unselfish that many who paid the biggest price got no reward and are trapped as beings they never wished to be. A floating colonial mix, too. Not just of the colonial types they were forced to become but the varying races of the freebooter ships."

"I think often of the *Thunder*," Hawks replied. "In many ways it is the ideal that humans have searched for. Cloud Dancer once disliked Raven simply because he was a Crow. How absurd that distinction seems now! Humans have historically distrusted and disliked one another to the point of murder and war over such minor differences as religion, color, language, and the like. That's one rationale Master System had for keeping each colonial world a homogenous race and culture. Yet my children could never truly comprehend why a Crow or a Sioux or a Cheyenne—or a Janipurian or a Chanchukian or even an Alititian—should be judged in any way but by what kind of people they are. But such things have always worked on a small scale, Nagy, particularly when we are crisis-driven or bound together by mutual self-interest, but never in the mass. That is our tragedy. Never in the mass."

Arnold Nagy shrugged. "Well, we gave everyone a tomorrow, and that's something. Maybe the *Thunder* is atypical, but it stands as an example of what good people can do and should strive for," he said. "For me, after years cooped up in that fancy mausoleum out there waiting out the exploits of the legends I helped assemble, every day's a crossroads and every path is new. You don't just lie out here and stare at the stars, Hawks! You'll just get rain in your face. You reach out and you grab them sons of bitches and you *live!*" He paused a moment. "And you can start by coming over here and sampling some of the most *amazing* bourbon that I have ever discovered. One of those little things, I admit, but proof positive there are many things of wonder out there to be discovered."

Hawks got up and went over to where Nagy's packs

lay and waited while the man withdrew a flask and passed it to him. The Hyiakutt took it and drank deeply, then froze, like a living statue, for what seemed like several minutes. Then, slowly, a smile crept over his craggy, tattooed face and he looked at the flask as a child might regard a favorite new toy.

"Well," said Hawks at last. "I suppose it's a start..."

ABOUT THE AUTHOR

JACK L. CHALKER was born in Norfolk, Virginia, on December 17, 1944, but was raised and has spent most of his life in Baltimore, Maryland. He learned to read almost from the moment of entering school, and by working odd jobs amassed a large book collection by the time he was in junior high school, a collection now too large for containment in his quarters. Science fiction, history, and geography, all fascinated him early on, interests that continue.

Chalker joined the Washington Science Fiction Association in 1958 and began publishing an amateur SF journal, *Mirage*, in 1960. After high school he decided to be a trial lawyer, but money problems and the lack of a firm caused him to switch to teaching. He holds bachelor degrees in history and English, and an M.L.A. from Johns Hopkins University. He taught history and geography in the Baltimore public schools between 1966 and 1978 and now makes his living as a freelance writer. Additionally, out of the amateur journals he founded a publishing house, The Mirage Press, Ltd., devoted to nonfiction and bibliographic works on science fiction and fantasy. This company has produced more than twenty books in the last nine years. His hobbies include esoteric audio, travel, working science-fiction convention committees, and guest lecturing on SF to institutions such as the Smithsonian. He is an active conservationist and National Parks supporter, and he has an intense love of ferryboats, with the avowed goal of riding every ferry in the world. In 1978 he was married to Eva Whitley on an ancient ferryboat in midriver. They live in the Catoctin Mountain region of western Maryland with their son, David.